RAIDERS OF THE NILE

RAIDERS OF THE NILE

A Novel of the Ancient World

STEVEN SAYLOR

MINOTAUR BOOKS

NEW YORK

RAIDERS OF THE NILE. Copyright © 2014 by Steven Saylor. All rights reserved. Printed in the United States of America. For information, address St. Martin's Press, 175 Fifth Avenue, New York, N.Y. 10010.

www.minotaurbooks.com

The Library of Congress Cataloging-in-Publication Data is available upon request.

ISBN 978-1-250-01597-6 (hardcover)
ISBN 978-1-250-02606-4 (e-book)

Minotaur books may be purchased for educational, business, or promotional use. For information on bulk purchases, please contact Macmillan Corporate and Premium Sales Department at 1-800-221-7945, extension 5442, or write specialmarkets@macmillan.com.

First Edition: February 2014

10 9 8 7 6 5 4 3 2 1

It irks me that Eurypyle, so glamorous,
For boorish Artemon has cravings amorous.
He used to go out shabby and threadbare
With wooden earrings poking from his hair.
Wrapped in a smelly oxhide cloak
Repurposed from a shield, he was a joke,
A good-for-nothing crook and a bore,
Seen now with cook, now with whore,
Making a criminal living.
Often I saw him in the stocks, giving
A yelp as he was slapped about
And had his hair and beard plucked out.
But *now* the son of Kyke appears
In a chariot, with gold rings in his ears,
Carrying an ivory sunshade—
Worthy of a pretty maid?

—ANACREON, c. 500 B.C.
POETAE MELICI GRAECI 43

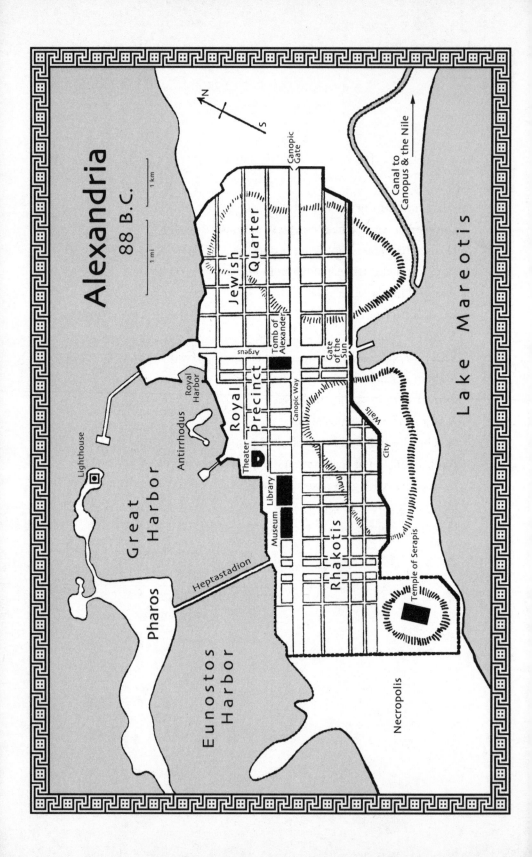

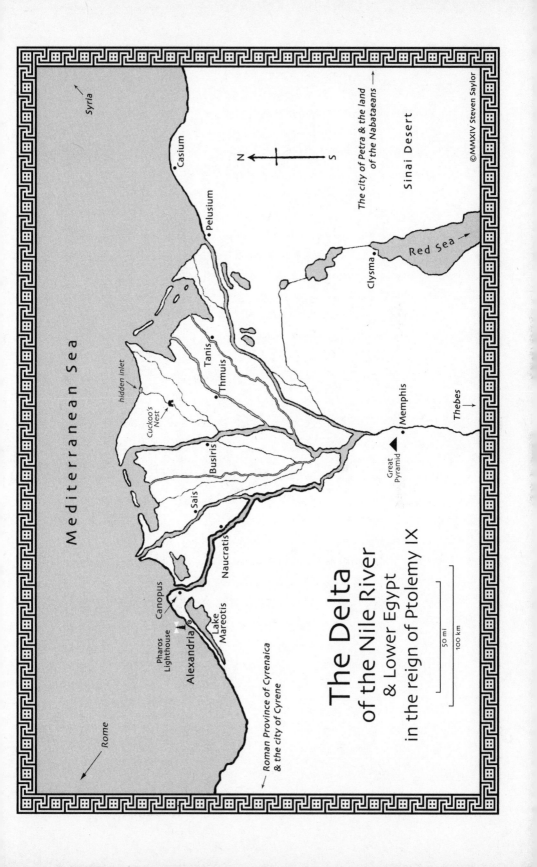

I

Like any young Roman who found himself living in the most exciting city on earth—Alexandria, capital of Egypt—I had a long list of things I wanted to do, but taking part in a raid to steal the golden sarcophagus of Alexander the Great had never been among them.

And yet, there I found myself, on a morning in the month we Romans call Maius, doing just that.

The tomb of the city's founder is located in a massive, ornate building in the heart of the city. A towering frieze along one side depicts the exploits of the world conqueror. The moment of inspiration that gave birth to the city itself, some 240 years ago, is vividly depicted on the frieze: Alexander stands atop a sand dune, staring at the shore and the sea beyond while his architects, surveyors, and engineers gaze up at him in wonder, clutching their various instruments.

So realistically sculpted and painted was this massive frieze that I almost expected the giant image of the conqueror to suddenly turn his head and peer down at us as we scurried below him, heading toward the building's entrance. I would not have been surprised to see him raise an eyebrow and inquire in a booming, godlike voice, "Where in Hades do you fellows think you're going? Why are some of you

brandishing swords? And what is that the rest of you carry—a battering ram?"

But Alexander remained immobile and mute as my companions
and I rushed past him and surged into the colonnaded entranceway.

On this day the tomb was closed to visitors. An iron gate barred
entry to the vestibule. I was among those who carried the battering ram.
We pivoted into formation, perpendicular to the gate. As Artemon, our
leader, counted to three, we heaved the ram forward, then back, then
forward again with all our might. The gate shuddered and buckled at
the impact.

"Again!" shouted Artemon. "On my count! One—two—*three*!"

Each time the ram butted against it, the gate moaned and shrieked,
as if it were a living thing. On our fourth heave, the gate flew open.
Those of us carrying the battering ram retreated back into the street
and tossed it aside while the vanguard of our party, led by Artemon,
rushed through the sundered gate. I drew my sword and followed
them into the vestibule. Dazzling mosaics celebrating the life of Alexander decorated every surface from the floor to the domed ceiling high
above, where an opening admitted sunlight to shimmer across the mil-
lions of pieces of colored glass and stone.

Ahead of me, I saw that only a handful of armed men offered resistance. These guardians of the tomb looked surprised, frightened, and
ready to run—and who could blame them? We greatly outnumbered
them. They also looked rather old to be bearing arms, with weathered, wrinkled faces and gray eyebrows.

Why were there so few guards, and why were they of such a low
grade? Artemon had told us that the city was in chaos, wracked by daily
riots. All the most able-bodied soldiers had been summoned by King
Ptolemy to protect the royal palace, leaving only this feeble handful to
defend the Tomb of Alexander. Perhaps the king thought that even the
most violent mob would never dare to violate such a sacred place, especially in broad daylight. But Artemon had out-foxed him. "Our greatest advantage will be the element of surprise," he had told us, and it
appeared that he was correct.

I heard a clash of swords, followed by screams. I had deliberately volunteered to man the battering ram, so as to avoid being on the front line of whatever battle might take place. I wanted no blood on my hands, if I could possibly avoid it. But was I really less guilty than my comrades ahead of me, who were gleefully hacking away with their swords?

You may wonder why I was taking part in such a criminal act. I had been compelled to join these bandits against my will. Still, might I not have slipped away at some point and escaped? Why did I stay with them? Why did I continue to follow Artemon's orders? Did I do so out of fear, or misplaced loyalty, or simple greed for the share of gold we had all been promised?

No. I did what I did for *her*—for the sake of that crazy slave girl who had somehow got herself kidnapped by these bandits.

What sort of Roman would stoop to such criminal behavior for the sake of a girl, and a mere slave at that? The blinding Egyptian sun must have driven me mad, that I should find myself in such a spot!

As I rushed through the vestibule, toward the wide corridor that led to the sarcophagus, I realized I was whispering her name: "Bethesda!" Was she still well, and unharmed? Would I ever see her again?

I slipped on a pool of blood. As I spun my arms to balance myself, I looked down and saw the pale face of a fallen guard. His lifeless eyes were wide open and his mouth was set in a grimace. The poor old fellow might have been someone's grandfather!

One of my companions helped to steady me. *Careless fool!* I thought. *You might have broken your neck! You might have fallen on your own sword! What would have become of Bethesda then?*

I heard the sounds of another battle ahead of us, but its duration was brief. By the time I stepped into the chamber, only one guard remained standing, and even as I watched, Artemon stabbed him in the belly. The poor fellow crumpled lifeless to the hard granite floor. His sword fell beside him with a clatter, and then a hush fell over the crowded room.

Lamps set in niches in the walls provided the only illumination.

Though it was bright daylight outside, here all was dim light and shadow. Before us, raised upon a low dais, was a massive sarcophagus. In form and style it was partly Egyptian, like the angular mummy cases of the ancient pharaohs, and partly Greek, with carvings along the sides that depicted the exploits of Alexander—the taming of the steed Bucephalus, the triumphal entry into the Gates of Babylon, the terrifying battle with the elephant cavalry of the Indus. The gleaming sarcophagus, made of solid gold, was encrusted with precious stones, including the dazzling green gem called the emerald mined from the mountains of southernmost Egypt. The sarcophagus glittered in the flickering light of the lamps, an object of breathtaking splendor and of value beyond calculation.

"Well, what do you make of that?"

I shivered, as if startled from a dream. Artemon stood beside me. His bright eyes sparkled and his handsome features seemed to glow in the ruddy light.

"It's magnificent," I whispered. "More magnificent than I ever imagined."

He grinned, flashing perfect white teeth, then raised his voice. "Did you hear that, men? Even our Roman comrade is impressed! And Pecunius"—that was the name by which he knew me—"is not easily impressed, for has he not seen the Seven Wonders of the World, as he never tires of telling us? What do you say, Pecunius—is this sarcophagus the equal of those Wonders?"

"Can it really be made of solid gold?" I whispered. "The weight must be enormous!"

"Yet we have the means to move it."

Even as Artemon spoke, some of the men brought forth winches, pulleys, lengths of rope, and wooden shims. Another group appeared from the vestibule wheeling a sturdy wagon down the wide corridor. The wagon was loaded with a lidded wooden crate made especially for our cargo. Artemon had thought of everything. Suddenly he looked to me like the young Alexander as depicted on the frieze of the building, a visionary surrounded by adoring architects and engineers. Artemon knew what he wanted and had a plan to achieve it. He inspired fear in his enemies and confidence in his followers. He knew how to bend others to his will. Certainly he had succeeded at making me do as he wanted, against all my better judgment.

The wagon was wheeled into place alongside the dais. The top of the crate was lifted off. The inside was padded with blankets and straw.

A hoisting mechanism was deployed to remove the lid of the sarcophagus.

"Should we be opening the sarcophagus?" I said, feeling a prickle of superstitious dread.

"The lid and the sarcophagus are both very heavy," said Artemon. "They'll be easier to manipulate if we separate them and lift them one at a time."

As the lid began to rise above the sarcophagus, a thought occurred to me.

"What will become of the body?" I asked.

Artemon looked at me sidelong but did not speak.

"You're not going to hold it for ransom, are you?"

He laughed at the look on my face. "Of course not. The remains of Alexander will be handled with utmost respect, and will be left here where they belong, in his tomb."

Robbing a mummified corpse of its sarcophagus hardly constituted respect, I thought. Artemon seemed to be amused by my misgivings.

"Here, Pecunius, let's have a look at the mummy before we remove it from the sarcophagus. They say the state of preservation is quite remarkable."

He took my arm and together we stepped onto the dais. As the lid was hoisted onto the wagon, the two of us peered over the edge of the sarcophagus.

So it came to pass that I, Gordianus of Rome, at the age of twenty-two, in the city of Alexandria and in the company of cutthroats and bandits, found myself face to face with the most famous mortal who ever lived.

For a man who had been dead over two hundred years, the conqueror's features were remarkably well preserved. His eyes were closed, as if he slept, but his eyelashes were perfectly intact. I could almost imagine that he might suddenly blink and gaze back at me.

"Look out!" someone shouted.

I turned around to see that we had company—not royal soldiers, but a handful of regular citizens, no doubt outraged at the desecration of their city's most sacred monument. A few had daggers. The rest were armed only with clubs and stones.

As Artemon's men fell on the newcomers, cutting them down and driving them back, one of the angry citizens raised his arm and took aim at me. I saw the jagged rock hurtle toward me.

Artemon grabbed my arm and pulled me sharply to one side, but too late. I felt a sharp blow against my head. The world turned upside down as I fell from the dais onto the wagon, striking my head against one corner of the crate. Groggily, I drew back and saw blood—my blood—on the wood. Then everything went black.

How had I come to such a sorry pass?

Let me tell you the story.

II

It all started the day I turned twenty-two.

That was on the twenty-third day of the month we Romans call Martius; in Egypt it was the month of Phamenoth. Back in Rome, the weather was probably bitter and damp, or at best chilly and brisk, but in Alexandria my birthday dawned without a cloud in the sky. The warm breath of the desert filled the city, relieved by an occasional breeze from the sea.

I lived on the topmost floor of a five-story tenement in the Rhakotis district. My little room had a window that faced north, toward the sea, but any view I might have had of the harbor and the water beyond was blocked by the fronds of a tall palm tree outside the window. The breeze caused the foliage to perform a listless dance; the motions of the fronds as they slowly slid against one another produced a languorous, repetitious music. The shiny foliage reflected the rays of the rising sun, causing points of light to dance across my closed eyelids.

I woke, as I had fallen asleep, with Bethesda in my arms.

You may wonder why my slave was in bed with me. I might point out that the shabby little apartment in which I was living was so small there was hardly room for one person to turn around, let alone two.

The bed, narrow as it was, took up most of the space. Yes, I could have made Bethesda sleep on the floor, but what if I rose in the night? I would likely have tripped over her, fallen, and cracked my skull.

Of course, it was not for considerations such as these that I had invited Bethesda to share my bed. Bethesda was more than merely my slave.

When I was a boy, and my father taught me the facts of life, he made clear what he thought about masters sharing their beds with slaves. "A bad idea, all around," I could remember him saying. My mother had died when I was small, and the only slave in our household was an old fellow called Damon, so I was not sure if he spoke from experience.

"Why is that, father? Is it against the law for a master to sleep with a slave?"

I can remember my father smiling at such a naive question. "If a man were to sleep with another man's slave, without permission—that would be against the law. But with his own property, a Roman citizen may do whatever he wishes. He may even kill a slave, just as he may kill a dog or a goat or any other animal he owns."

"Is it adultery, then, if a married man has relations with a slave?"

"No, because for adultery to occur there must be the chance of free-born offspring—such a birth might threaten the wife's status and the status of her children, you see. But since a slave has no legal existence, and any child born to a slave is also a slave, no union with a slave can pose a threat to the marriage or to the heirs. That is why many wives make no objection if their husband cavorts as much as he wishes with his slaves, male or female. Better he should do so in the home, at no expense, and not with a freeborn woman or someone else's wife."

I frowned. "Then why do you say it's a bad idea?"

My father sighed. "Because, in my experience, the act of sexual union invariably produces not just a physical reaction, but an emotional one as well—whether good or bad—and in both master and slave. And that leads to trouble."

"What sort of trouble?"

"Oh, a Pandora's box full of woe! Jealousy, blackmail, betrayal, trickery, deceit—even murder." My father's experience of the world was wider than that of most men. He called himself Finder, and he made his living by uncovering other people's secrets, often of a scandalous or criminal nature. "Digging up the dirt," he called it. He had seen the full range of human behavior, from the best to the worst— but mostly the worst. If his experience had led him to believe that carnal knowledge between a master and a slave was a bad thing, he probably knew what he was talking about.

"I can see that it might be unwise, but is it *wrong* for a master to sleep with a slave?" I asked.

"Certainly the law does not object. Nor does religion; such an act does not offend the gods. Nor do philosophers have much to say about how a man uses his slaves."

"But what do *you* think, father?"

He gave me a penetrating look and lowered his voice, so that I knew he spoke from the heart. "I think that when any two people have carnal relations, the greater the difference in their status, the more likely it is that one of them is being forced to act against his or her will. When that occurs, the act is demeaning to both parties. Or the tables can be turned. I've seen so-called philosophers behave like fools, wealthy men bankrupted, powerful men humiliated—and all for the love of a slave. To be sure, not every union can be of equals. Not every pairing can be like the one that existed between me . . . and your mother."

He fell silent and turned his face away.

That was the end of the conversation, but the words my father had spoken remained in my memory.

On my journey from Rome to Alexandria, I had done a number of things of which my father would be proud, or so I hoped. I had also done a few things of which my father would probably disapprove. Sleeping with Bethesda fell into the latter category.

Vague thoughts of my father must have been in my mind as I woke that morning—perhaps I had been dreaming about him—but what he might or might not think quickly became the furthest thing from my mind. My father was a long way off, in Rome, but Bethesda was very close. With her body pressed against mine and our limbs entwined, it was hard to think of anything else.

From those places where we touched emanated the most exquisite sensation imaginable—warm flesh against flesh. Those few areas of my body that were not touching hers experienced a kind of jealousy, and cried out to rectify the situation at once. Every part of me wanted to be pressed against every part of her, all at once. From the way she responded, I had no doubt she felt the same. Is it possible for two mortal bodies to meld into one? Bethesda and I frequently made every effort to do so, sometimes several times a day.

Our bodies became sheened with sweat. As we turned this way and that, the faint breeze from the window gently wafted the sweat from our skin. Our sighs and moans joined the music of the rustling palm fronds, then rose above it in pitch and volume until surely the vendors in the street below and the laborers on their way to work could hear us cry out.

At last—our union consummated, uttermost pleasure attained—we drew apart.

"Was that a good beginning to your birthday, Master?" said Bethesda.

The question was so unnecessary, I laughed out loud. Neither of us spoke for a long time. We lay side by side, barely touching. The morning sun reflected more brightly off the swaying palm fronds, scattering the room with bits of light. I heard the cry of seagulls, and the blaring of navigation horns from the distant Pharos Lighthouse. I closed my eyes and dozed for a while, then slowly woke again.

Bethesda walked her fingertips over my knee and up my thigh, then reached for a more intimate part of me.

"Perhaps we could make the day's beginning twice as good," she said.

And so we did, very slowly, taking our time. Her body was a landscape in which I became hopelessly lost—the forest of her long black hair, the maze of her smooth brown limbs, the ever-changing topography of her shoulders. Her hips and breasts became undulating sand dunes as she stretched, twisted, and turned. Her mouth was an oasis, the place between her thighs a delta.

When we were done, I felt wide awake. "I don't think I could ever grow tired of that," I said, mostly to myself, since I spoke the words in Latin. Though Bethesda knew Hebrew, Greek, and Egyptian, I had so far managed to teach her only a smattering of Latin. She raised an eyebrow, clearly not comprehending, so I repeated my comment in Greek, the language we had in common. "I don't think I could ever grow tired of that."

"Nor I," said Bethesda.

"But sometimes . . ."

"We have to eat."

So it was hunger that finally forced us out of bed. I dressed in my blue tunic—my best, despite a few stains and the fact that the threadbare linen fit me a bit tightly across the shoulders; just the night before Bethesda had stitched up a tear in the sleeve and repaired the frayed hem. I allowed her to dress in my second-best tunic, which was green, a color that suited her. On her much smaller frame the simple tunic made for a rather modest garment; it covered her elbows and knees and, cinched with a hemp belt, fitted snugly around breasts that had filled out considerably since the day I purchased her.

Bethesda stood by the window and ran an ebony comb through her hair, which had become tangled during our lovemaking. She grimaced and muttered a curse when the comb encountered a particularly stubborn tangle. I laughed.

"You could always shave your head, like the rich women do. They say it's more comfortable in this climate. Keeps lice away."

"Rich women have wigs to wear when they go out," she said. "Very fancy wigs. A different one for every occasion."

"True. But no wig could be as lovely as this." I circled behind her and with my fingertips I gently smoothed the knot from her hair. I took the comb from her and ran it slowly through her long tresses. Her

hair was thick and heavy and perfectly black, shimmering with rain-
bow highlights, like the wings of a dragonfly. Every part of her was
beautiful, but her hair held a special fascination for me. Sated as I was,
I felt a fresh stirring of desire.

I stepped away from her, put down the comb, and took a deep
breath. I willed my excitement to subside—something my father had
told me a man could and should be able to do. It was time to venture
out to the world beyond my little room.

The Rhakotis district is said to be the oldest part of Alexandria, built
over the little fishing settlement that existed even before Alexander
founded his city. Most of Alexandria is laid out in an elegant grid of
broad avenues and grand porticoes, but the Rhakotis retains its maze
of winding alleys, as if the chaotic spirit of the old village could not be
tamed and made to submit to the modern metropolis that grew around
it. Rhakotis reminds me of the Subura in Rome, with its tall tenements,
taverns, and gaming houses. Lines for drying laundry crisscross the
space above one's head, while ragged children run zigzags up and down
the street. Around a corner, half-naked women solicit customers from
upper-story windows; keep walking while you look up and you're
likely to trip over a cat napping in the middle of the street. Cats do
whatever they wish in Alexandria. Despite the merging of Greek and
Egyptian gods that began with Alexander's conquest, the locals still
worship animals and insects and strange divinities that are part man,
part beast.

As was fitting for master and slave, I walked ahead and Bethesda
followed a little distance behind. Had we walked side by side, what
would people have thought? My first stop was a small tavern where the
owner's wife prepared my favorite breakfast—hot farina cooked with
a little goat's milk and mashed dates, served in a clay bowl. I ate a bit
more than half the contents, scooping out mouthfuls with a bit of
bread, then handed what remained of the bread to Bethesda and let
her finish the bowl. She devoured it so quickly that I asked if she
wanted more.

She smiled and shook her head. "Now that you've eaten, what else do you desire to do on your special day, Master?"

"Oh, I don't know. I suppose I could find a good book in the great Library, and read it aloud to you. Or perhaps we could examine the collection of fabulous jewels in the Museum. Or climb to the top of the Pharos Lighthouse to take in the view." I was joking, of course. The Library and Museum were open only to royal scholars and visitors with suitable credentials, not to a lowly Roman who made a living by his wits, and the island of Pharos was off-limits to all but lighthouse workers and the soldiers who guarded it.

I shrugged. "On such a fine day, before it gets too hot, I propose that we take a long walk and see where it leads us. Surely some grand adventure awaits me on my birthday." I smiled, having no idea what lay in store for us.

To be sure, there was always the chance of encountering some sort of violence when one was out and about in Alexandria. It had not always been so. When I first arrived in the city, I was able to go anywhere, at any time of the day or night, without concern for my safety. But in the two years and eight months since my arrival, Alexandria had become increasingly dangerous and disorderly. The people were unhappy, and they blamed their discontent on King Ptolemy. Every so often, there would be a riot. The riot would lead to a bit of looting and perhaps a fire or two, then the appearance of royal soldiers, and then, inevitably, bloodshed. You might think the Alexandrians would dread these outbreaks of chaos, and flee from them. Instead they seemed to relish them. Whenever a riot broke out, hundreds or even thousands would converge on the scene, like moths to a flame.

Why did the people hate their king so bitterly? Some years ago he had risen to power by driving his older brother from the throne; as far as I could tell, he had done so with the support of the Alexandrian mob. Then, as if to patch things up, he married his deposed brother's daughter. (These Egyptian rulers were always marrying family members, even siblings.) Then he killed his mother, who apparently thought that she should be the true power behind the throne. Now the people were restless, and to show their desire for a change, they rioted. This was what passed for politics in Egypt!

To a Roman who had grown up with yearly elections and magistrates and written laws, trying to make sense of Egyptian politics and history could induce a terrible headache. All the kings and queens seemed to have been brothers and sisters, or mothers and sons, or uncles and nieces, and they were forever marrying each other, then killing each other, then sending the survivors into exile, whereupon the ones in exile plotted a way to return and kill those who exiled them, perpetuating the cycle.

The first King Ptolemy, the founder of the dynasty, had been one of Alexander's generals. When the Great One died, Ptolemy made himself king of Egypt, and his descendants had ruled the country ever since, becoming the longest reigning dynasty in the world. To those who loved royal romance and intrigue (which seemed to be everyone in Egypt), the Ptolemies provided a source of endless fascination, like characters on a stage. The personal and public drama of their lives amused, enthralled, and enraged the populace. In taverns and shops, outside temples and courts—anywhere you went in Alexandria—people talked of little else.

Like a typical Alexandrian, Bethesda could name every one of the Ptolemies in chronological order, the good and the bad, the dead and the living, going all the way back to Ptolemy I. Listening to her, I would become hopelessly confused, since the same names recurred in every generation: Berenice, Arsinoë, Cleopatra (the name of the king's late mother), and of course, Ptolemy—sometimes several of them living at once, and in every branch of the family. With all the enthusiasm of a Roman recounting famous battles, or a Greek swooning over Olympic athletes, Bethesda had tried to explain to me who had done what to whom and when and where, and why it mattered so much, but I could never keep the players straight. One Ptolemy was the same as any other to me.

I only knew that every so often, if one dared to venture out, there was likely to be a bit of screaming and trampling, and perhaps some smoke and cinders, and probably a bit of slaughter. And all because the people hated King Ptolemy.

But on such a splendid day, even the threat of a riot was not going to keep me indoors. At the age of twenty-two, one feels invulnerable. I was quick-witted and fleet of foot. What had I to fear? If anything, the increasing disorder in the city had been a boon to me. When public order fails, private misconduct increases; and when people no longer trust the authorities, to uncover the truth they turn to people like me. Finder my father called himself, and the skills he taught me had proved quite useful. I could pick any lock, I could follow a man without being seen, I could tell by a woman's eyebrows if she was lying to me, and I knew when to speak and when to keep my mouth shut. The fact that I was an outsider only enhanced my usefulness; I was a free agent, with no ties to any particular family or faction. I was not getting rich by plying my father's trade on foreign soil, but I was managing to make ends meet.

I happened to have a few extra coins on my person that morning, with which I planned to buy something special.

"Shall we play tourist today?" I suggested. "I've been so busy lately, grubbing about in lowly taverns and disreputable gaming houses, I've forgotten how beautiful the city can be. Let's take in the sights."

So we set out. We made our way out of the Rhakotis district and headed up a broad boulevard lined with palm trees, fountains, obelisks, and statues. Our route took us to the sacred tomb precinct in the center of the city, where magnificent buildings set in lush gardens housed the mummified remains of the Ptolemies.

At a very broad intersection, we came upon a towering structure that dominated the skyline—the Tomb of Alexander. Its walls were decorated with extraordinary relief sculptures that depicted the career of the conqueror. Though not quite as grand, the structure reminded me of the Mausoleum at Halicarnassus, one of the Seven Wonders of the World. But whereas the burial chamber of King Mausolus was sealed, the room that held the remains of the mummified Alexander was open for paying visitors. On this morning, even though the tomb was not yet open, the line to enter wound all the way around the building and out of sight. From their costumes, the visitors appeared to come from all over the world—Persian astrologers wearing ziggurat hats and pointed shoes, Ethiopians the color of ebony, Nabataeans in flowing robes, and even a few Romans in togas. All had come to file past the famous golden sarcophagus of Alexander and pay their respects—something I myself, in all the months I had lived in the city, had not yet done.

Bethesda made bold to draw alongside me. "Perhaps, Master, on your special day, you would like to visit the tomb of the Great One."

"And stand in that line under the hot sun all morning? I think not. No matter how large and elaborately decorated, a mere golden sarcophagus is unlikely to impress a traveler who has seen the Seven Wonders of the World."

"You would prefer to go on one of the days when visitors can gaze upon the face of Alexander himself?"

"Now that might be more interesting," I admitted. The sarcophagus was opened and the mummy displayed to the public on only two days each year, Alexander's birthday and the anniversary of the founding of the city. On those occasions, the admission price would be doubled and the lines would be ten times as long.

Taking my eyes from the line of tourists waiting for the tomb to open, I was struck by the great number of royal guards around us, even more than was usual in the precinct of the royal tombs. Holding their spears aloft, a contingent of soldiers made a show of marching up and down the broad boulevard. More soldiers formed a virtual cordon along the line of visitors queuing to see Alexander's sarcophagus. Looking up, I saw yet more soldiers stationed on balconies and along parapets and on the rooftops of the tombs of the Ptolemies. Soldiers almost outnumbered the ordinary people thronging the street. No doubt they were there to protect the tourists and keep order in one of the city's most prominent public areas, but the sight of so many royal guards made me uneasy. Knowing the Alexandrians, I thought such a show of strength would as likely spark a riot as prevent one.

We moved on, into a neighborhood of grand houses and elegant apartment buildings. Here lived many of the minor officials and bureaucrats who served in the huge royal palace complex, including the Library and the Museum, but who were not important enough to have quarters within the palace itself. Some of Alexandria's best and most expensive shops were in this area. On previous walks I had noticed Bethesda's fascination with the luxury items displayed outside the shops, as she stole glances at a necklace strung with lapis and ebony, or at a silver bracelet set with tiny rubies. Such items were far beyond my means, as anyone could tell by looking at me; the brawny servants posted as guards outside each shop gave me nasty looks if I so much as slowed my pace.

Nevertheless, in front of one of the shops, I dared to come to a complete halt.

"Why are we stopping here, Master?" said Bethesda.

"Because it's my birthday, and I intend to spend a bit of money." I hefted the coin purse I carried in a fold of my tunic.

"Here, Master?" Bethesda wrinkled her brow, for we stood before a shop that sold nothing but women's garments. Hung on pegs outside the storefront, linen gowns fluttered in the breeze. Some were so simple and sheer they looked hardly more substantial than bits of gossamer. Others were cut in a variety of styles, dyed in brilliant shades, and decorated with embroidery along the hems and necklines. Several days ago, as we passed this shop, I had noticed Bethesda slow her stride and steal a lingering glance at a particular gown. It was dark green with yellow embroidery, and longer than most, with pleated, fan-shaped sleeves.

I studied the garments hung on display, then smiled when I spotted what I was looking for. As I stepped toward the shop, a brawny servant crossed his arms and glowered at me, then relented when I hefted my moneybag and made the coins jingle.

The shop owner appeared. She was a stooped old woman who gazed up at me from a wizened face. "Do you see something you like, young man?"

"Perhaps." I dared to touch the green gown with my fingertips. The linen was of a much higher quality than I was used to. Even on the hottest day, such a fabric would feel soft and cool against the wearer's skin.

Bethesda whispered in my ear. "Master, what are you thinking of?"

I turned to her and smiled. "I'm thinking it's my birthday, and I should buy something that pleases me."

"But—"

"And what could please me more than the sight of you wearing this gown?"

A little later, I stepped out of the shop with a coin purse that was considerably lighter.

Bethesda followed me. The green linen shimmered in the sunlight. The yellow embroidery had an almost metallic sheen, like the luster of gold. The dress transformed her, elegantly clinging to the supple lines of her arms and legs and accentuating rather than hiding the fullness of her hips and breasts. When she raised a hand to shield her eyes from the bright sun, the long, pleated sleeve opened like a fan and undulated in the breeze. With her face obscured, I might not have recognized her. She could have been the privileged daughter of a fine Alexandrian household, the sort of young woman who shopped in such a place on a regular basis, buying whatever she desired.

Even the wizened old shopkeeper had been impressed. When Bethesda withdrew to the dressing room, I tried to wrangle a lower price, but the woman had refused to budge—until Bethesda emerged. At the sight of her, the old woman softened. Her eyes glimmered. She clapped her hands and sighed, and named a price that was half of what she might have demanded.

Even Bethesda's posture was transformed. She seemed to stand taller than before, with her shoulders back. Staring at her, I decided that the green gown was the best purchase I had made in a long time.

A flash of movement caught my eye. Someone was running toward us, shouting and laughing.

As the figure drew closer, I noticed several things in quick succession.

It was a young woman.

She was not exactly running, but rather skipping, whirling, and dancing as she hurtled forward, giggling and crying out.

Also, she appeared to be completely naked.

And, if Bethesda had not been standing next to me, I would have sworn that the naked, laughing woman was—Bethesda!

III

"Follow me! Follow me!" shouted the girl.

As she passed the dress shop, she looked me in the eye and gave me a playful tap on the chin, then performed a somersault right in front of me, never breaking stride, and continued on her way, waving her hands in the air. Had she truly been naked, the somersault would have given me quite an eyeful, but instead I perceived that she was wrapped in some sort of close-fitting, very sheer garment that matched the shade of her tawny skin. Exactly where the girl ended and the garment began was a mystery, which could be solved only by taking a closer look.

I began to follow her up the street.

"Master!"

I turned to see that Bethesda remained where she was. She gave me a blank, catlike stare.

"Come on," I said. "You heard the girl. She wants us to follow her!"

"She wants *everyone* to follow her," muttered Bethesda—and to be sure, a considerable crowd was coming up the street. "She must be rounding up a crowd to watch a mime show."

"A mime show? Wonderful! A mime show would be just the thing."

I laughed and waved to Bethesda to follow. When she continued to hesitate, I hurried back, took her by the hand, and pulled her after me.

"Besides," I said, "did you not notice her face?"

"Was it her *face* you were looking at, Master?" Bethesda sounded skeptical.

"Among other things! But seriously, did you not notice whom she looked like?"

"I'm sure I don't know what you mean."

"She looks like *you*, Bethesda. The resemblance is uncanny."

"I hardly think so."

"Nonsense. You're alike enough to be sisters. Twins, even."

"I do not have a sister," she said, rather firmly. Though she had been born a slave, and though both her parents died young—her father first and then her mother—Bethesda had known them both, or so she had told me. She would have known if she had any siblings.

"I don't mean to suggest that she's literally your sister," I said, then shrugged and gave up the argument. Nothing made me feel more absurd than to realize I was struggling to explain myself to Bethesda, who was, after all, my possession, and by every law and custom was supposed to accept everything I said without question.

Not far from the street of luxury shops, but closer to the harbor, we came to a small public square decorated with splashing fountains, flowering shrubs, and towering palm trees. In the center of the square a mime troupe had set up a small tent and was getting ready to put on a performance. A considerable crowd had already gathered. A muscular juggler wearing a *nemes* headdress and not much else was cracking jokes and warming up the spectators, who seemed to be in a boisterous mood.

"A rather elegant part of town for a mime show," I commented. "You can even see a bit of the royal palace from here, above those rooftops. Most of the mime shows I've seen are in shabbier neighborhoods, where the officials don't seem to care what goes on."

Bethesda made no reply, but I could see that she had relaxed and was getting into the spirit of things. I think she was enjoying the chance to show off her new gown. A number of spectators, especially the men, gave her second glances. Who could blame them?

Mime shows were peculiar to Alexandria; in my travels, I had seen nothing like them elsewhere. Plays are different; plays are put on everywhere in the Greek and Roman world, because scripted dramas and comedies are part of religious and civic festivals, paid for by the authorities and featuring professional actors, all of whom are men. Alexandrian mime shows are very different. Women as well as men perform—what a scandal that would cause in Rome!—and the performances can hardly be called plays. A typical mime show is a ragbag of topical skits, naughty songs, and indecent dances, with jokes, strongman acts, and acrobatics to fill the intervals. No civics authority controls or regulates the mimes, and while the targets of their satirical skits are often stock types—the nosy housewife next door, the sadistic tutor, the fast-talking lawyer, the lying businessman—the mimes are also known to make targets of those in power, though the names and circumstances are changed to sidestep charges of slander or sedition.

We Romans like to think we are freer than other people, since we elect our leaders, but it would be hard to imagine the authorities permitting anything like a mime show in the streets of Rome. People would object to the indecency, for one thing, and powerful Romans do not like to be made fun of, especially in public. If a Roman magistrate did not ban such a performance, the gang of some riled politician would surely break it up, and crack a few heads in the process. So, while they may be ruled by a king, it seems to me that the Alexandrians are freer than the Romans at least in this regard, because virtually anything can be said about anyone, even including the king, so long as the ridicule takes place in a mime show and no one is identified by his real name.

This mime show was not only being staged in a nicer part of town than usual, but it seemed to be attracting a more rarified audience. As I watched, a magnificent litter arrived. The occupant was hidden inside a box screened by yellow linen curtains. The box was fitted atop long wooden poles that were elaborately carved and brightly painted, like two lotus columns from an Egyptian temple laid on their sides. The poles rested upon the shoulders of bearers who were veritable giants, half again as tall as me, twice as broad, and midnight black; such giants are said to come from the land where the Nile begins. Making way for the litter, a vanguard of bodyguards, also giants, bullied their way through the crowd, so that the litter was able to claim a spot at the very front. Some of the spectators who were forcibly displaced grumbled and shook their fists, but the bodyguards stared them down. The curtains of the litter were opened a finger's width on all sides, allowing the occupant to see out without being seen.

Two young boys circulated through the crowd, holding out cups to solicit offerings for the troupe. One of the boys stopped in front of me and rattled his cup.

"Shouldn't I see a bit of the show before I decide what I wish to pay?" I said.

"Better to pay now." The boy grinned. "You never know what might happen."

I wasn't sure I liked the sound of that, but begrudgingly I pulled the thinnest copper coin from my depleted purse and dropped it into the cup. The rattle it made seemed to satisfy the urchin, who moved on to badger the people next to me.

Some moments later the two boys disappeared from view, slipping around to the far side of the tent. With its entrance hidden from view and its rear side facing the crowd, the tent would serve as both changing room and backdrop for the presentation. The two boys soon reappeared, both clutching Pan pipes, and stood to either side of the tent, using their bodies to mark the boundaries of an imaginary stage. As they played a shrill fanfare, the crowd settled down, and the show commenced.

It began innocently enough with a skit about a befuddled brothel keeper, who was all leering eyebrows and salacious grins, and his oldest "girl," an actress with wrinkles drawn on her face with kohl and a huge pair of drooping stage-breasts. She was not merely her employer's oldest whore, but was also the first well ever drilled in Alexandria—or something like that. The Greek dialogue contained a great many puns that seemed to play off the local dialect. Bethesda got more of the jokes than I did, laughing at bits of dialogue that were merely Greek to me.

When not reciting her lines, the actress turned this way and that, knocking over small props (chairs, table, standing lamp) with her massive breasts. To accompany this buffoonery, the two boys played rude notes on their pipes. Some of the men and women around me laughed so hard they wept and had to blow their noses. A mime show cannot be too bawdy for Alexandrian tastes.

Suddenly, despite her makeup and costume, I recognized the actress.

"Bethesda, look! It's her. Your double."

Bethesda gave me a sour look.

"No, seriously. It's that girl who was running through the streets naked—well, practically naked. You can hardly recognize her, but that's the girl. I'm sure of it. Amazing, how these mimes can transform themselves!"

Bethesda rolled her eyes and shook her head, still unconvinced of the resemblance.

The skit came to a climax with yet another pun that was completely unintelligible to me but that set off howls of laughter in the audience and earned a sustained round of applause. As the two performers took a bow, it seemed to me that the actress made a special flourish toward the unseen occupant of the elegant litter.

A musical interlude followed, then an acrobatic act in which three men balanced themselves atop the shoulders of a fourth. Then a trained monkey appeared and tried to snatch away the loincloth of the man on the bottom, which caused the human monolith to stagger and sway and finally come tumbling down. The crowd roared with laughter.

More skits followed. The subject matter grew more topical as the program progressed, leading up to a skit about a grotesquely fat merchant throwing back cups of wine and getting very drunk while dictating letters to a scribe. When the fat merchant felt the need to relieve himself, and had to summon two servants merely to rise from his chair, even I knew whom he was meant to represent: King Ptolemy. Everyone in Alexandria knew the story—the king had become so enormously fat, he could no longer relieve himself either fore or aft without assistance.

While the audience hooted with laughter, the actor in the fat-suit waddled across the stage area toward an imaginary latrina (represented by a chair with a hole in it). Assisting him were the two young pipe players, each clutching an elbow and struggling to support his massive weight. When the three of them arrived at the latrina, one of the boys made a great show of searching amid the voluminous robes hanging from the merchant's vast belly. At last, with a squeal of triumph, the boy revealed a small phallus that looked to be made of leather and brass and was evidently attached to a hidden wineskin or some such container, for a moment later the merchant threw back his head and gave a loud sigh of relief as golden liquid streamed forth from the spout. At first the boy carefully aimed the stream into the latrina, but then, mugging shamelessly to the audience, he began to direct the stream this way and that, deliberately making a terrible mess. The merchant, with his head thrown back and his eyes shut, remained oblivious.

At last, with his bladder finally empty and his phallus tucked away, the merchant began to waddle back toward his chair—then suddenly raised his eyebrows in alarm and shouted for his servants to reverse course. With a great deal of awkward confusion, the three of them turned around and headed back to the latrina.

What followed was an incredibly vulgar display, with the merchant repeatedly attempting to settle his enormous posterior on the latrina, and his two assistants frantically striving to pull apart his huge, unseen buttocks (which remained hidden by the folds of his garment). When at last the merchant was seated, with a great deal of grunting and heaving and a cacophony of gassy squeals (produced offstage, from within the tent, I think), he began to eject a peculiar array of debris from his rear end, which the assistants stooped down to retrieve, one by one. These included various pieces of pottery and bronze ware—lamps and bowls and serving implements—which the servants first displayed to the audience, then offered to the merchant, who wrinkled his nose and waved them away, as anyone would at something that came out of his backside. The laughter of the audience was thick with derision.

At first I took this display to be mere nonsense humor, until a nearby spectator suddenly got the point and muttered aloud, "Ah! They all come from Cyrene!"

Observing the pottery more closely, even I recognized the blue and yellow pattern distinctive to the workshops of Cyrene, a city some five hundred miles to the west of Alexandria—and then I understood the joke. Since the time of Alexander, Cyrene and its surrounding territory, called Cyrenaica, had been a part of Egypt's kingdom, a western frontier traditionally administered by a younger brother or cousin of the king. Until eight years ago, the regent of Cyrene had been King Ptolemy's bastard brother, called Apion; but when Apion died, childless, he left a will that bequeathed Cyrenaica to the Roman people. King Ptolemy, deeply in debt to Roman bankers and fearful of Roman arms, did not dare dispute the will—and so the kingdom had lost one of its principal cities, and the Romans had been allowed to establish a province bordering directly on Egypt, only a few days' march from the capital.

The people of Alexandria had reacted violently to this turn of events. Armed force had been necessary to quell the riots. Though eight years had passed, their resentment still simmered, and their conviction that King Ptolemy had betrayed his birthright had only deepened. In their view, Cyrene had mattered no more to the king than his own feces mattered to the merchant.

Emptied at both ends, and assisted at every step by the two boys, the merchant gave a sigh of relief and waddled back to his chair. He began a conversation with his scribe having to do with two rivals who were engaged in a fierce competition. One was from Rome and the other was a distant relative from Pontus, and the merchant was in a quandary because he couldn't decide which side to take.

If the mime in the fat-suit was meant to be King Ptolemy, then the rival merchants clearly represented Rome and King Mithridates of

Pontus, who (by some genealogical twist I had never untangled) was a cousin of King Ptolemy's. In the last year, Mithridates had overrun all of Asia, driving out Rome's provincial magistrates and Roman businessmen. The impacts of this war were being felt all over the Mediterranean world, but Egypt had managed to remain neutral.

"If only I didn't owe so much money to that filthy Roman," the merchant whined, "I'd stab him in the back this minute!"

"Why don't you simply pay him off, and be free of him?" asked the scribe.

"Pay him with what? My cousin from Pontus took the rest of my money. And took my little boy, to boot!"

This was a reference to King Mithridates' recent seizure of the island of Cos, where Egypt kept a treasury and where King Ptolemy's son, still a teenager, had been residing, presumably at a safe distance from the palace intrigues of Alexandria. (This was a son from the king's first marriage, not his current marriage to his niece.) Mithridates had seized not just the island, but the Egyptian treasury and the Egyptian prince as well, ostensibly treating the boy as an honored guest but in fact holding him hostage.

"And don't forget the cloak he took!" said the scribe.

"Piddle! What's a moth-eaten old cloak to one who wears silk?" At this the crowd loudly booed the fat merchant. The reference was to one of the treasures seized by Mithridates, a cloak that had belonged to none other than Alexander the Great.

"They say your cousin goes about wearing it and putting on airs," said the scribe. "Don't you want it back?"

"I hardly think it would fit me!" said the merchant, shaking his bulbous arms and getting a laugh from the audience. "Oh, if only my mother were still here, to tell me what to do!"

"But she's not," said the scribe. "Don't you remember?" He made a hacking sound and mimed the universal gesture of a finger drawn across the throat.

"What about my big brother? Where is he? He'd know what to do!"

The scribe rolled his eyes. "You and the old lady ran him off! Have you forgotten that, as well?" This was a reference to the king's older brother, who had his own turn at the throne before being driven into exile some years ago.

"If only big brother could come home!"

"Really? Most husbands dread a visit from their father-in-law!"

"He was my brother before he was my father-in-law."

"And master of the house before you kicked him out!"

"If only big brother would come, I'm sure he could sort things out."

"Be careful what you wish for." The scribe shook his head. "Two of your sort are two too many. And yet, I wish there were three of you."

"Three?"

"Three hatchlings from your mother's nest, so I could have another choice for a master. Are you sure you haven't got a bastard brother hidden away somewhere?"

"A bastard?"

"You know, a cuckoo's child, slipped into the nest when no one was looking?" The scribe mugged at the audience.

"Of course not. There's only the two of us."

"Ah well, then, I suppose your older brother will have to do. I've heard a rumor that he's on his way here right now."

"Right now?"

"Right now!" The scribe looked straight at the audience and enunciated in a slow, dramatic voice. "And he may . . . arrive . . . *any* . . . *minute!*"

The merchant clapped his hands to his cheeks with an expression of horror. The two boys took up their pipes and played shrill notes to mimic his alarm. Then the discordant music suddenly changed to a giddy tune, so infectious that the fat merchant forgot his worries and leaped to his feet. With various parts of his body jiggling in different directions at once, he performed an absurd dance, spinning, jumping, kicking his legs, and waving his arms. This was another jab at King Ptolemy. Despite his drunken laziness and his inability even to take a piss on his own, he was still known to break into wild dances in the midst of his orgies.

Beating drums and shaking rattles, other members of the mime troupe emerged from behind the tent to join the merchant in the dance. Among them I spotted Bethesda's double, no longer made up to appear old but looking quite lovely in a green linen gown; the wooden bangles adorning her tawny arms made a clacking sound as she cavorted. Encouraged by the players, members of the audience joined in the dance. The music became louder and shriller, and the atmosphere grew raucous. Even the Nubian bearers of the elegant litter joined in, clapping their hands and stamping their feet.

Then, in the blink of an eye, the mood changed. I heard shouts and screams. A thrill of panic shot through the audience. Standing on tiptoes and looking over the crowd, I saw the flash of drawn swords at the far side of the square. A sea of terrified faces abruptly turned toward me.

Riot!

IV

"Time to get out of here!" I said, taking Bethesda by the hand.

Everyone else seemed to have the same thought at the same moment, for suddenly we were all rushing in the same direction, away from the armed troops. Even amid the panic, I saw a few men stoop down and pick up whatever stones or other debris happened to be lying about, as if arming themselves for a skirmish.

From the corner of my eye I saw the tent collapse. While the trained monkey screamed and hopped madly about, the mime troupe rolled up the tent and gathered their props. They moved so quickly and efficiently it was evident they had done this before.

With Bethesda and me leading the way, the crowd fled down a narrow street that led to the harbor. With a quiver of dread I wondered if this was what the king's men intended—to drive the spectators to the waterfront, where we would be trapped and easy to slaughter—but looking back I saw they made no effort to follow us. It seemed that their intent was merely to break up the mime show and to clear the public square.

The crowd reached the waterfront. As people realized they were no longer pursued, the panic subsided. Some began to laugh and joke.

Others debated whether to turn back and join the handful who had chosen to fight the soldiers. Their enthusiasm was dampened by the arrival of stragglers with broken heads and bleeding wounds. I drew to one side and kept my mouth shut. The squabbling between the Egyptian king and his people had nothing to do with me.

Little by little the crowd dispersed.

The day was warm and clear, with only a few thin clouds in the sky. The waterfront had an air of quiet calm, broken only by the rustling of palm trees in the breeze, the cries of seagulls, and the occasional blaring of a horn from the Pharos Lighthouse.

I sat at the top of a flight of steps leading down to the water and gazed across the harbor at the lighthouse, a magnificent sight that always seemed slightly unreal, no matter how many times I saw it. Bethesda sat beside me, ignoring the protocols of status, and I did not correct her. What man would object to being seen in the company of such a beautiful girl wearing such a lovely new dress?

"That was exciting!" I said.

"You said you wanted an adventure on your birthday, Master."

"Yes, well, let's hope that was it."

I gazed at the islands in the harbor, which belonged to King Ptolemy and were covered with temples, gardens, and palaces. But where were the ships? At this time of year, as the sailing season resumed, the harbor should have been crowded with merchant ships from distant lands carrying all sorts of goods in and out of the port of Alexandria. I counted only a handful of vessels, and most of those were local fishing boats and pleasure craft. The war between Rome and Mithridates had caused uncertainty and chaos and made the sea a dangerous place. Now, whenever a seafaring vessel entered the harbor, it was likely not to be a merchant ship loaded with goods but a boat full of refugees in search of a safe haven, bringing whatever treasures they possessed in hopes of purchasing the favor of King Ptolemy and his ministers.

"What did you think of the mime show, Master?"

I laughed as an image of the merchant on the latrina popped into

my mind. "Very funny. And shocking! I can't imagine how those players thought they could get away with it, putting on a show like that
practically in the shadow of the royal palace. In some alley in Rhakotis,
perhaps, but not in a better part of town, with soldiers patrolling every
street. I suppose it shows just how far things have gone. That last
skit . . . it seemed to hint that the king's brother might be heading to
Alexandria—with an army at his back, no doubt. Is there going to be a
war here in Egypt, I wonder? War here, and there, and everywhere. . . ."

It seemed that the whole world had been plunged into war in the
last few years. First there was war in Italy, between Rome and her Ital-
ian confederates. Then, seeing Rome's weakness, King Mithridates
had swept across Asia and the Greek islands, driving out the Romans.
Now it seemed that Egypt, too, might become a battleground, between the king and his brother. I thought it strange that the audience
had appeared sympathetic to the idea of a return by the king's older
brother; perhaps they took seriously the title he had given himself
when he was on the throne, Soter, which meant something like "Savior." But had they not already driven him off the throne and out of the
city once before? Now they wanted to drive out the younger brother,
and welcome the elder brother back. How fickle the Alexandrian mob
was, and what short memories they had!

If war came to the city, what would it mean for Bethesda and me?

A burst of boyish laughter interrupted my brooding. Two figures
ran down the steps next to us. I recognized them as the young pipe
players from the mime show. At the last step, the boys slipped off their
thin sandals and stepped into the water.

After cooling their feet, they came running up the steps again. I
watched them head toward a nearby stone bench beneath a large
palm tree, where others from the mime troupe had gathered.

"Well, it's good to know those two survived the skirmish, and seem
no worse for wear," I said. "The rest of the players are smiling and laughing, too. I wonder if that's the whole group? I count only eight, including those boys. What do you think, Bethesda? Shall we go say hello to
them?"

"*Them?*"

"Yes, we can tell them what we thought of their show, and see if they all escaped unharmed."

"*They?*" She looked at me askance.

"The mime troupe." I tried to make my face a blank, but there was no fooling Bethesda. Among the players under the palm tree, I had spotted Bethesda's double. It was her, and her alone, I was curious to meet.

I stood, took Bethesda's hand, and pulled her up beside me. "Come. It's my birthday, and I shall indulge my every whim."

Begrudgingly, Bethesda followed me.

I tried to think of a way to break in on their conversation, but I need not have bothered. One of the young flute players saw us approaching, then did a double take and nudged his partner, who did likewise.

"Look, Axiothea!" cried one of the boys. "It's *you!*"

The actress, who was seated on the bench, glanced in our direction, then looked at the boy. "What do mean?"

"That girl—she looks like you, Axiothea. She's even wearing a green dress, like you are."

The actress rose from the bench and stepped toward us, gazing steadily at Bethesda, until the two of them were face to face.

To be sure, they were not mirror images. Bethesda was slightly shorter and had longer hair and a somewhat shapelier figure. Their faces were by no means identical—Bethesda was clearly the younger of the two—but only a blind man could fail to see the similarity. The green color of their clothing was so close that the garments might have been cut from the same cloth, although—even excluding my prejudice in the matter—Bethesda's dress was the more elegant, with finer embroidery.

Axiothea took a step back. She shook her head. "I don't see it."

"Nor do I," said Bethesda.

A handsome, broad-shouldered man was seated on the bench, dressed in a thin linen robe that covered him from head to foot. He slapped his knee and laughed, which caused the monkey perched on his shoulders to chatter loudly and scurry back and forth.

"Isn't that just like a woman?" The man grinned. "Can't see what's right in front of her—even when she looks in a mirror!" The others laughed, and the monkey bared its teeth and clapped its long, bony hands. From the way the others deferred to him, I took this fellow to be the leader of the mime troupe.

"Seriously, Melmak," said Axiothea with a sigh, "I don't see any resemblance." Even her manner and the inflection of her voice reminded me of Bethesda.

"Nor do I," Bethesda repeated.

The two of them locked eyes again and seemed to hold a staring contest, like two Egyptian cats. Then, in the same instant, they both smiled.

"But you are very pretty," said Axiothea.

"And so are you," said Bethesda.

"Vanity, vanity!" cried Melmak. "You're merely flattering yourselves, if you could but see it."

"Who are *you*, then?" said Axiothea, addressing me.

"My name is Gordianus. I come from—"

"Rome," said Axiothea. "With such a name and such an accent, you couldn't be from anywhere else. But I will say your Greek is better than that of most Romans I've met."

I nodded at the compliment. "And this is Bethesda, my slave."

"Ah, the girl is your property, then?" Melmak stood up and approached us. I saw just how tall and broad-shouldered he was. The monkey came along for the ride, clinging to the locks of his thick black hair. "Does she have any acting experience?"

"Why do you ask?"

"Given the fact that she and Axiothea look so alike . . . we might be able to do something with that. Pull a switch on the audience."

"A switch?"

"Make one disappear, and the other appear. You know—a bit of magic. How can one woman be in two places? The audience loves that sort of thing."

"That's my Melmak, always thinking," said Axiothea.

"Even without any sleight of hand, the sight of twins—and beautiful twins, at that—is inherently exciting to the men in the audience," said Melmak. "Don't you think so, Gordianus?"

I looked at Bethesda and Axiothea, felt a prickling of my imagination, and then cleared my throat as the two of them stared back at me.

"What do you think, Gordianus?" said Melmak. "I'm not proposing to buy the girl from you, but I'd pay for the loan of her services, as part of the troupe."

I shook my head. "From what I've seen, your work is far too dangerous."

"Dangerous?" said Melmak.

"I was there today, in the audience. I could have been killed—and you lot might have been arrested and thrown in a dungeon, for ridiculing the king. For all I know, some of you *were* arrested."

"No, we're all here," said Melmak.

"Only eight, in the whole troupe? Surely there must be more. How could only eight of you perform so many parts?"

"Makeup, costumes, props, and padding."

I looked from face to face. Besides Melmak and Axiothea and the two boys, there were four men, all of average size and a bit older than I. "But which of you played the fat merchant?"

"That was me, of course." Melmak beamed.

"Not possible! I realize the merchant's costume was padded, but he had a fat face. And his voice was completely different from yours."

"It's called acting, my good fellow. I know that Rome is a backwater when it comes to the theater, but—"

"And there was an acrobat who's not here. The muscular man in a *nemes* headdress who juggled before the show."

"Me again!" said Melmak. He made a fist and drew it to his forehead, then pulled back the long, loose sleeve of his tunic to show off his biceps. "As you can see, the muscles are real, and not a costume. We all take on many parts. At present, Axiothea is the only female in the troupe, so some of us men play the occasional matron."

"The old whore in the first skit—that was Axiothea?"

"Yes. We've tried it with a man, but it's not as funny."

"Very impressive," I said, amazed that so few could play so many.

"Ha! Acting, he calls it!" One of the men stepped forward. In some ways he was the most striking member of the company, for although his physique was ordinary and his features nondescript, his dark, longish hair and neatly trimmed beard were bisected from front to back by a stripe of white. Such a marking would have seemed more likely on a furry animal than on a man, but the curious coloration appeared to be natural. "My name is Lykos, and I am *not* an actor. And no matter how fervently Melmak and the others may think that their thespian talents create the illusions of the mime show, it's *I* who do most of the work in that department."

Melmak begrudged the man a smile. "Lykos is our artificer, and I suppose he does deserve some credit."

"*Some* credit? Well, that's more than I usually get."

"Artificer?" I said.

"Lykos makes the costumes and wigs," said Axiothea.

"Costumes and wigs? Is that all I am, a glorified seamstress and wigmaster?" Lykos snorted. "I design and create the props. I oversee the makeup. It's I who make Melmak as fat as the king, I who can make even Axiothea old and ugly. The artificer, not the actors, is the true master of theatrical illusion, the miracle worker of the mimes!"

I cleared my throat. "Well, it's certainly a miracle that you all got away from those soldiers."

"No gods or magic were involved," said Melmak. "Just careful planning and quick reflexes. We've worked out a system for making fast getaways. Emergency change of scene, I call it. It hasn't failed us yet."

"But one of these days, if you keep putting on shows like that, you're bound to get into trouble. You're tempting the Fates."

"We are a mime troupe, Gordianus. We must give the people what they want. And we do! We draw the largest crowds and collect the fattest purse of any troupe in the city. Oh dear, I shouldn't have admitted that. Now you'll want even more money for the use of your lovely slave."

"As I already told you, she's not available." I had a sudden vision of Bethesda at the mercy of a troop of royal guards, and shuddered. "Not at any price."

"Ah, well." Melmak sighed and cast a wistful gaze at Bethesda. "Your master is denying you a marvelous career as an actress, my dear."

Axiothea laughed. "Give it a rest, Melmak! The young Roman has spoken. But I find his company congenial, don't you? Would you like to share our midday meal, Gordianus? We have only simple fare—some pickled tilapia from the Nile, olives, hearts of palm, dates, flatbread. No wine, but there's some Egyptian beer. Will you join us?"

And so I ate my birthday meal with an unexpected circle of new-found friends, sitting in the shade of a palm tree in the most exciting city in the world, gazing at one of the world's most spectacular sights, the harbor of Alexandria and the Pharos Lighthouse. The food was delicious and the company delightful. The actors had all traveled widely and had many stories to tell. Having traveled myself, I had a few stories of my own. I felt quite happy, thinking this was how a birthday should be celebrated, until the subject turned to Rome.

"Have you been away for long?" asked Axiothea.

"I left Rome exactly four years ago today, on my eighteenth birthday. I haven't been back."

"Do you miss it?"

"Sometimes."

"One hears such terrible things about the war in Italy, between Rome and the rebel cities. Do you get much news from home?" asked Melmak.

"Letters from my father. It's been a while since I received one." In fact, it had been several months since his last letter arrived. I was beginning to worry about him.

Axiothea read my expression. "So many letters and messages go astray these days, or take forever to arrive. The war in Italy, the war in Asia, the war on the sea—it's a wonder any ship ever arrives in port. Everything is scarce. Everything costs more. It's the times we live in."

"And thank goodness we all have someone to blame!" said Melmak with a laugh.

"Who?" I said.

Melmak shook his head. "Obviously, you are not an Alexandrian, or you wouldn't need to ask. Whom do we blame for everything that goes wrong? Must I put on my fat-suit and waddle up and down the waterfront to remind you?"

"Is King Ptolemy really to blame for high prices?" asked Bethesda. I felt a bit uneasy, seeing my slave join freely in the conversation, but to the actors, who were all freeborn, her slave status seemed to make no difference. My father had told me that actors were not like other people, that they tended to live outside the constraints and expectations of normal society.

"Is the king to blame? Probably not," said Melmak. "But we blame him nonetheless. And if things get worse, we shall blame him all the more."

"What if things get better?" I said.

"Then we shall credit the gods and offer prayers of thanksgiving!"

"It seems the king can do nothing right."

"And thank the gods for that, or else we actors would be out of work!"

"Is it true, what you hinted at in the show—about the king's brother coming to Alexandria?"

Melmak shrugged. "Who knows? That's the rumor. We'll know for sure, if and when he gets here."

"But if that happens, there's likely to be chaos, isn't there?" I had never been in a city under siege. The idea was unsettling, but the actors seemed unfazed.

"Chaos?" said Melmak. "Most certainly, there will be chaos. Chaos before, chaos during, and chaos after. Chaos at all times and everywhere—that is the natural state of Egypt. But the mime shows will continue, no matter what. The troupe of Melmak never misses a performance, come rain or shine."

"At the rate things are going, it may not take an invading army to bring down the king," said Axiothea.

"What do you mean?" asked Bethesda.

"Did you not notice the marked lack of enthusiasm on the part of those soldiers who broke up the show today? Listless, I would call them."

"Practically somnambulant!" said Melmak. "Two months ago, with a company of royal guards breathing down our necks like that, we'd have had to scramble for our lives. Today, we simply packed up our things and trotted off—and they didn't even come after us!"

"Yes, that surprised me," I said. "I was afraid there might be a bloodbath."

Melmak shook his head. "A bloodbath takes a lot of work—all that hacking, and cleaning up the mess afterward. It simply wasn't worth the soldiers' time. I suspect their commander ordered them to stop the scandalous show and break up the crowd, and that's exactly what they did—no more and no less."

"But why?"

"Because the king isn't paying them! He's not paying anyone any longer—not the workers in the Library or the clerks in the Museum, or the stokers at the Pharos Lighthouse, not even the zookeepers in the royal gardens. He's run out of money, and everyone knows it. Instead of gold or silver or even copper, people on the royal payroll are being issued promissory notes drawn on the royal treasury. A royal decree has ordered all merchants to extend credit based on those notes, but more and more merchants are now openly refusing to do so. So everyone in royal service is doing as little as possible—including the soldiers. Alexandria is grinding to a standstill."

"I hadn't realized things had gotten so bad," I said.

Axiothea nodded. "Bad, and likely to get worse. So says . . ." Her voice trailed off.

I raised an eyebrow. "You were about to quote someone?"

Melmak flashed a knowing smile. "Axiothea was about to quote her mysterious patron."

"Patron?" I said.

"Perhaps you noticed that fancy litter at the front of the audience?"

"Yes. I saw it arrive."

"It seems the fellow inside has taken quite a fancy to our Axiothea."

"I never got a glimpse of him."

"Neither have we! Nobody knows who he is—except Axiothea. Every now and again, she goes missing for a day or two, and then comes back smelling of some expensive new perfume, and we all know she's been visiting her rich friend. But will she invite us along? Or even tell us the fellow's name, or where she's going, or how long she'll be gone? No!"

"Believe it or not, Melmak, some things are none of your business." Axiothea smiled, but it seemed to me she was straining to keep an even tone.

"Melmak is just jealous," said Lykos. "He wishes some wealthy lady would choose him to be her favorite, and shower him with gifts, the way Axiothea's patron showers her."

One of the actors nodded. "That's why Melmak insists on doing his juggling routine before the show, prancing about practically naked and showing off those muscles—hoping some rich filly will take notice and invite him home with her. Get himself a nice, comfy spot doing stud service, and then—goodbye to acting!"

They all shared a laugh at this, even Melmak. Axiothea visibly relaxed.

The sun was hot but the shade was pleasant. Our stomachs were full. Everyone had consumed a generous share of the beer, drinking from the same cup—including the monkey. Because it was my birthday, they had insisted that I drink a double share, and I had not refused.

While the two women stood to one side, talking, we men sat in a circle around the big palm tree, facing outward, leaning back against the trunk with our legs outstretched. I began to doze. When Bethesda crouched down beside me and touched my hand, I had to struggle to open my eyes.

"Master, Axiothea wishes to go to the little open-air market off the waterfront. You can see a bit of it, just over there."

"Yes, and I was wondering if Bethesda could go with me," said Axiothea. She stood over me with her hands on her hips, wearing an expression that said she wouldn't take no for an answer. If Bethesda were a free woman, would she be as brash and willful as her double?

I hummed and nodded, half-asleep. "I don't see why not." Then I smiled, for I happened to know that Bethesda had recently stored up a few coins by sometimes keeping the change when I sent her to make a purchase. She must have brought those coins with her, I thought, and now she intended to spend her meager treasure to buy me a birthday present. I closed my eyes again, and thought how sweet she was . . . how very, very sweet. . . .

My dream was sweet as well, doubly sweet, for I was back in my little room in Rhakotis, which was filled with dappled sunlight, and naked in the bed with me I beheld not one but *two* Bethesdas, equally beautiful, equally loving, equally delightful. The dream went on for quite some time, with each development more exciting than the last, until there was a knock at my door. Though the two Bethesdas both laughed and playfully tried to hold me back, I insisted on seeing who it was. I got out of bed and opened the door, but the hallway was empty. Or was it? The passage was dimly lit, but at the far end, almost lost in shadows, I thought I saw a figure. His face was hidden, but I could see that he wore a Roman toga. Something about his posture alarmed me. He held himself in an unnatural way, clutching himself as if he were in pain. I heard him moan. My heart began to race.

"Father?" I whispered. "It that you?"

I woke in a cold sweat, chilled by the breeze from the harbor. For a long moment I stared at the distant Pharos Lighthouse, my mind unable to comprehend it. This happened to me from time to time in Alexandria; I would wake with no sense of where I was, and feel confused, as if I had never left Rome and suddenly found myself in a place completely strange to me.

But of course, the place was not strange. I had come to know the waterfront of Alexandria better than I knew many parts of Rome. My acute disorientation faded. I had a slight headache—from the beer, no doubt. The chill quickly passed as the breeze blew the sweat from my body. The sunlight felt warm on my skin. I was in Alexandria on a beautiful afternoon, and all was well. I yawned and stretched and looked around.

I was alone.

The members of the mime troupe had vanished.

So had Bethesda.

V

"Bethesda!" I called, thinking she must be nearby. I got to my feet, feeling a bit stiff. My head was pounding. I peered up and down the waterfront.

"Bethesda!" I called again, louder.

There was no response. Above my head, a seagull squawked. To my befuddled senses, the noise sounded suspiciously like laughter.

How long had I been asleep? Judging by the position of the sun, it could not have been more than an hour. Could she still be at the nearby market, shopping?

And where had the actors gone? I looked around and saw no trace of them except scattered date pits and other detritus from our midday feast.

I scanned the area again, making sure there was no sign of Bethesda, then headed toward the market.

The place was a maze of small tents and partitioned stalls, deliberately meant to slow one's progress and baffle the eye. If a person wished to hide, such a crowded, jumbled market would be an ideal place. Was Bethesda teasing me, playing a game of hide-and-seek? That did not seem like her.

I made my way through the market, trying not to be distracted by all the hanging baubles and trinkets and pots and pans. Almost every vendor offered a selection of souvenirs for tourists, including little images of the Pharos Lighthouse for every budget, rendered in cheap pottery or glass or ivory. At the stall of a garment vendor I spotted a green dress that looked almost exactly like the one I had bought for Bethesda, for a much cheaper price, but when I took a closer look, I could see that it was of inferior linen and shoddily made.

I reached the end of the market without seeing Bethesda. I turned around and made my way through the stalls again, and still did not see her. I went back to the palm tree, thinking she might have returned in my absence, but she wasn't there.

I began to feel uneasy.

I went from stall to stall in the market, questioning the vendors. A few were so unfriendly they wouldn't talk to me, probably because of my Roman accent—a prejudice I encountered from time to time in Alexandria—but a few of them remembered seeing the two pretty girls dressed in green.

"Like twins!" said a mustachioed rug-seller, with a lecherous gleam in his eye. "I certainly wouldn't forget those two. Giggling and whispering to each other and acting silly, the way girls do." This did not sound like the Bethesda I knew, who carried herself at all times with a quiet, catlike grace. Away from me, in the company of another female, did she behave with less restraint?

"Oh, but that must have been an hour ago," said the rug-seller. "They took a quick look at my wares, said something rude about my mustache—silly girls!—and then moved on. I haven't seen them since."

Nor had any of the other vendors, it seemed. Bethesda and Axiothea had certainly visited the market, and had been noticed by several of the vendors, but this had happened an hour ago, when I first began to doze under the palm tree. No one knew when they left or in what direction they headed.

Bethesda and Axiothea seemed to have spent the most time in the garment stall, comparing their own dresses to the inferior version on sale there, to the displeasure of the old woman in charge of the stall, who thus had reason to remember them. She gave curt answers to all my questions, but then, as I was leaving, she lowered her voice. "But now that you've reminded me, I did notice something a bit odd. . . ."

"Yes?"

"I'm trying to think. Yes, it was at the same time that those girls came in to look at my garments. I noticed a couple of fellows hanging about, peering this way and that. I didn't like the look of them."

"What did these men look like? How were they dressed?"

She shrugged. "Common tunics, nothing special. It wasn't their clothes I noticed. It was the expression on their faces. They were up to no good."

"What does that mean?"

"When you work in a market like this, you learn to tell who's a customer and who's not. You also learn to spot the ones who are here to steal something. These fellows weren't here to shop. They weren't locals from the neighborhood. Nor were they tourists, passing through. And they didn't have the look of petty thieves or pickpockets, if I'm any judge. So why were they here, hanging about, and what were they up to? Nothing good, that's for sure."

"Were they following the girls?" I heard my voice break.

"That's what I'm asking myself. I was just about to shoo the girls from the stall when I noticed those two men. Then the girls left, giggling—richly amused by the dirty looks I was giving them, I suppose."

"And the two men?"

She shook her head. "I don't remember seeing them again, after that. They must have moved on, but I don't know which way they went. Perhaps they followed the girls. Or perhaps they didn't." She shrugged.

At last I returned to the waterfront, feeling completely stumped.

Should I return to my room in Rhakotis? The chance that Bethesda would have gone there, without me, seemed remote. Nevertheless, if she had gone back, she would have been able to let herself in, for the door had no lock and key. (The only lock was a simple block of wood that swiveled to bar the door from the inside, to insure our privacy when we slept or were otherwise engaged; security was provided by the landlord and his wife, who lived on the ground floor and kept an eye on people coming and going.)

There was another possibility: that Melmak had forcibly taken her. He had mentioned wanting to use her in his troupe and had offered to pay me. I had refused, and that seemed to end the discussion. Melmak had seemed like a nice enough fellow, but what did I really know about him, or about Axiothea?

What if Melmak had put some sort of drug in my beer, causing me to fall asleep even as Axiothea lured Bethesda from my side? That would have allowed the whole troupe to scurry off, absconding with my slave and leaving me to wake up an hour later, alone.

Then I recalled that we had all drunk the beer from the same cup; it seemed unlikely that Melmak could have drugged my share. Nonetheless, he had encouraged me to drink more than the others, and beer alone could be counted on to put a man to sleep on a warm day.

I was suddenly certain of it: Melmak had taken Bethesda from me. The scoundrel! Well, I thought, soon enough he would realize his mistake. I had been able to afford Bethesda only because she had been a highly problematic slave, causing nothing but trouble for all her previous masters. Many had owned her for less than a day before returning her to the market. She was the exact opposite of the compliant, obedient slave most men desired. Bethesda could be counted on to put up quite a fight—

Or could she? If Melmak and the troupe had forcibly taken her, against her will, why had the abduction gone unnoticed by the vendors in the marketplace?

Because they had befuddled her with beer, I thought, for she too had drunk a small portion. And because they had lied to her, saying that I had gone somewhere and they were taking her to meet me, or spinning some other tale to lure her away quietly. Or because . . .

Had she gone with them *willingly*?

This thought disturbed me more than any other. Had Bethesda left me to go with the mime troupe of her own volition? If so, why? Was the lure of the acting life so appealing to her? Or . . . had she grown weary of me? Or—most chilling thought of all—had she never cared for me in the first place? Had all her sighing and moaning during all the hours of our lovemaking been a pretense, a show to please a master whom she secretly despised as much as she had despised all her previous masters? Was that the emotion that lurked behind her unreadable, catlike facade—derision for the feckless young master she had played for a fool?

No, that was not possible.

Or was it?

The fears and doubts that assailed me were most unseemly for a Roman to experience in regard to his slave, no matter how beautiful and alluring and special that slave might be. I experienced many conflicting, confusing emotions at once, but most of all I felt anxious.

Where was Bethesda?

I decided that my next course of action would be to seek out the mime troupe. Actors were notorious for keeping no fixed abode, moving from place to place to stay ahead of the disapproving authorities, but surely someone would be able to put me on to their scent. I had spent the last two years in Alexandria practicing my father's livelihood, making contacts and digging up dirt for others. Now I would put those skills to use for myself.

So I spent the rest of my birthday crisscrossing Alexandria and inquiring after the mime troupe of Melmak. People knew at once whom I was talking about. "Ah, the troupe with the trained monkey," some would say, or "the one with those two adorable pipe players," or (most frequently) "the one with that ravishing young actress who runs through the streets naked!" Many people would also nod if I described a man with a white stripe bisecting his hair and beard, though few knew the artificer Lykos by name.

Everyone knew Melmak's troupe, but no one knew where they lived or how to contact them. It was a curious thing, in such a teeming city, that seven males, one female, and a monkey, all so conspicuous when they wished to be, could be so invisible offstage.

While asking questions about the mime troupe, I also made sure to mention, as if by chance, the waterfront market, just to see if anyone had been there that day. As it turned out, a few of my contacts had indeed gone shopping or at least passed through the market. Unfortunately, I encountered no one who had seen two girls fitting my description of Bethesda and Axiothea—until, toward the end of the day, I dropped in on a pair of elderly eunuchs who were retired from royal service and lived together in a beautifully furnished apartment not far from the palace.

Their names were Kettel and Berynus. They had never asked me to pay for information, but instead always seemed glad to see me, steering me to a comfortable couch, lighting a bit of incense, and doting over me like aunts with a favorite nephew. The two eunuchs were a font of information about the private lives of just about anyone connected with the palace, but experience had taught me that they were not entirely reliable; they tended to let their imaginations run away with them. Since palace gossip was their specialty, I had no reason to think they would know anything about Melmak, and indeed they did not. But when I mentioned the waterfront market, their eyebrows shot up.

"Oh, they have the most lovely jewelry there!" Kettel, who was enormously fat, held up one arm. A great mass of flesh hung from the limb like a chicken's wattle. He shook his plump hand, rattling the bangles at his wrist. "I bought this lovely bronze bracelet there earlier today."

"And paid too much!" said Berynus, who was as slender as his companion was fat. He touched a bit of lapis that hung from a chain around his bony neck. "I got this pretty necklace for half the price of that hideous bracelet."

"Both pieces are very nice," I said.

Kettel tittered at the compliment. Berynus fluttered his eyelashes and reached up to adjust his wig. I took it for granted that both eunuchs shaved their heads, but even in the privacy of their home I had never seen either without an elaborate and expensive-looking hairpiece.

"What time were you there, at the market?" I asked, trying to sound casual.

"Oh, a little before midday," said Kettel. "Any earlier and the prices are too high. Any later and all the good stuff is gone."

"I see. Did you happen to notice a beautiful young woman, wearing green, with black hair—?"

"Why, yes, we did," said Berynus.

"That's right, we did," said Kettel.

My heart skipped a beat. "You both seem very certain."

Berynus raised an eyebrow. "That's because we had an argument."

"An argument? Did you speak to her?"

"No, no, no. Not an argument *with* her; an argument *about* her. Neither of us spoke to her. We only saw her. Except we didn't see the same thing," said Kettel.

"What do you mean?"

They looked at each other, as if deciding who should speak first. Kettel began. "I had to leave the market for a moment, to attend to the call of nature. Up the street, a block past the market and around a corner, there's a public latrina. When I finished and stepped outside, a little farther up the street I saw the very girl you've just described. She was being dragged off by a couple of rather rough-looking fellows, and putting up quite a fight."

My heart pounded in my chest. "Did no one stop them?"

"This was some distance from the market. Not a lot of people were around. I did call out, but the fellows told me to shut up and mind my own business. They said the girl was a runaway slave, and they were returning her to her master."

"And you believed them?"

"Why not? Even if things were not quite as they appeared—well, these days, when one sees any sort of scuffle in the street, one never knows what to think. You never know who might be on the royal payroll, never mind how brutish they look, or who might be a common criminal, or who might even be a spy! Everything is so out of control. Not like the good old days, when old Queen Cleopatra was firmly in charge. These days it's best to mind one's business and not get involved."

"So no one helped the girl?" I tried to keep my voice steady. "The two men just took her off?"

Kettel shrugged. "I suppose so. I didn't really think much about it, until I rejoined Berynus at the market and happened to mention what I had seen—and he told me I must be imagining things!"

"Why did you say that, Berynus?"

The eunuch folded his long, slender hands. "Because I had just seen the *same* girl—and with no ruffians about. The girl in green was heading off in the *opposite* direction, toward the waterfront, and she was in no distress whatsoever. A little boy was leading her by the hand."

"A little boy?"

"A messenger, I presume. Well-dressed, so from a wealthy household, but on his own, so not freeborn but a slave. The dark-haired beauty in green was following along behind the boy and looking rather pleased with herself."

"What made you think it was the same girl that Kettel saw?"

Berynus pursed his thin lips. "The more closely Kettel described the girl he had seen, the more exactly she matched my girl—and really, what are the chances of *two* ravishing young brunettes in green dresses both being in the market at the same time? I'm sure Kettel saw *something*, but he probably misunderstood what was going on. This happens all the time. It's sad, at his age, how his mind has begun to play tricks on him."

"Oh, you son of a crocodile!" snapped Kettel. "You're the one who imagines things! You probably never even saw such a girl. It was only after I described her that you suddenly 'remembered' seeing her. It's *your* mind that plays tricks!"

"Or perhaps you *both* saw just what you thought you saw," I said, my heart sinking.

"How could that be?" Berynus raised an eyebrow. "Why are you asking about such a girl, Gordianus? Who is she, and what is she to you?"

I shook my head and made no answer, and quickly took my leave.

Escaping the clouds of incense that perfumed the eunuchs' apartment, I was desperate for fresh air, but it gave me no relief. My chest was so tight I could hardly breathe.

The sun was beginning to sink and cast long shadows. Dinnertime sounds and smells of cooking wafted on the air, but I had no appetite.

As I finally headed home, I tried to make sense of what the eunuchs had told me. If their stories were to be trusted, one had seen Axiothea and the other had seen Bethesda, at precisely the same time. One of the girls had been abducted, while the other was led off by a slave boy—but which was which?

I arrived at the tenement more uncertain and anxious than ever. I entered the building, walked past the landlord's apartment, and trudged up the stairway. In my heart of hearts, I was hoping that when I reached the top floor, and pushed open the door to my room, Bethesda would be there, waiting for me.

What possible explanation could she have for her disappearance? It didn't matter. I only wanted her to be there.

I opened the door. I stepped inside.

The room was empty.

I closed the door and barred it with the little block of wood, then fell onto the bed, thinking I would never fall asleep. But the long day had worn me out. I closed my eyes and fell into a dreamless slumber.

VI

When I woke the next day, the room seemed emptier than ever.

Where was Bethesda? What had become of her?

I began my search for Melmak and his troupe all over again. I had exhausted my regular sources, so I started from scratch, brazenly approaching complete strangers. I regretted that I had spent so much money on the new dress for Bethesda. Coins can loosen tongues, but my moneybag was almost empty.

At the end of that long, miserable day, I knew no more than when I woke.

Another day passed, and still I learned nothing new. Waves of anger and despair surged through me, alternating with a numb sensation. Each time I returned to my room, a part of me expected Bethesda to be there, waiting for me. But the room was always empty.

It was quite by chance that I entered a tavern in Rhakotis one afternoon, only a few steps from the building where I lived, thinking I would spend my last few coins on a cup of decent Greek wine—and at the back of the dim room I saw Melmak.

Shadows hid his face, but it had to be him. The monkey was sitting on his shoulder.

I stepped back into a dark corner and for a while I simply watched him, making sure he was alone. Then I carefully scanned the room, spotting all the possible exits. Now that I had finally found him, I didn't want him to slip from my grasp. It occurred to me that I had no weapon except a small knife, more suitable for intimidating a monkey than a man. Also, Melmak was probably stronger than I was. He was certainly bigger. But I would have the advantage of surprise, not to mention righteous anger.

At last, drawing a deep breath, I stepped from the shadows, strode across the room, and stood before him, clenching my fists and bracing myself to block his way should he try to bolt.

But when Melmak looked up and saw me, he did nothing of the sort. He flashed a broad grin, then released a loud belch. His breath stank of beer. I waved it away and wrinkled my nose.

"Gordianus!" he said. "My young Roman friend! Sit down and join me. The monkey and I were just talking about you."

He stared up at me. Receiving no response, and seeing the stern look on my face, he frowned.

"Well, we weren't actually talking about *you*," he said. "We were talking about Axiothea, and the last time we were all together—the monkey, Axiothea, and me. But you happened to be there, too—it was your birthday, wasn't it? So in a way, we *were* talking about you. In a roundabout way, I mean. Very roundabout. If you see what I mean."

"How much beer have you had to drink?" I said.

"I don't know. The serving girl keeps bringing it, and I keep drinking it. The monkey insists on a share. Don't look at me that way! He's drunker than I am. Aren't you?" He held up a finger to the monkey, who grabbed it and let out a tiny belch.

"Where is Bethesda?" I said.

"Who?"

"Bethesda. My—"

"Oh, yes, the slave girl who looks like Axiothea. I remember. Of course I do. Well, I don't know. Where is she?" He looked about blearily, turning his head this way and that. "Is she supposed to be here? Is she meeting us?"

His obliviousness seemed genuine. But I reminded myself that he was an actor. "I think you know exactly where she is, Melmak. I think you took her from me."

His eyebrows shot up. "Took her? Took her where? Where would I put her if I took her?" At that moment, he looked as guileless as the monkey, and not much smarter.

Could it be possible that Melmak was *not* lying? If that were the case, the alternatives were even more alarming. Either Bethesda had run off of her own volition, or two unknown men had abducted her, for an unknown purpose.

My legs felt weak. All the pent-up indignation drained out of me, like wine from a cracked amphora. I felt hollow inside. I sank down on the bench next to Melmak and buried my face in my hands.

"There, there!" He patted my shoulder. "Is it as bad as that?"

"She's gone," I said. "Missing."

"The slave girl? What of it? You'll get another."

I shook my head.

Melmak sighed. "I know how you feel. Axiothea is gone, too."

"What?" I looked at him, suddenly alert. If both of them were missing, what might that mean? Was it a good thing or a bad thing? "Axiothea is missing?"

"Well, not *missing,* exactly. I mean, I know where she must be. Which is not with me. Which is the problem."

"What do you mean? Where is she?"

"With that wealthy patron of hers, of course. I should have known this would happen, after he saw fit to attend our last performance in that fancy litter of his. The fellow snaps his fingers, and Axiothea goes running to him, giving the rest of us not a word of notice. She's like a cat, thinking she can disappear for days at a time and then come back and act as if she never left. It's infuriating."

"Axiothea is safe, then? You're not worried about her?"

"Worried? Of course not. When she decides to come back, she'll be all sleek from the delicacies he feeds her, and sporting a few new pieces of jewelry, I expect. And acting like a princess, all spoiled and thinking she can boss the rest of us around. Which of course she can, because I let her, the wicked girl! Can I buy you a drink, Gordianus?"

I looked at him sidelong. "I'm not sure I should accept a drink from the man who deserted me on the waterfront that day. You and the others left me to fend for myself."

"Deserted you? You weren't exactly in dire straits when I last saw you. You were napping quite peacefully, with a full stomach and a bellyful of beer, all of which I generously provided."

"I was unconscious. Any thief who happened by might have robbed me blind."

"*If* you had anything worth robbing. But to be honest, your well-being was not my primary concern at that moment. The fact is, the rest of us all left in a bit of a hurry."

"Why?"

"Because you were snoring so loudly!"

He laughed at his own joke, then saw the forlorn look on my face.

"All right, Gordianus, here's what really happened. I sent one of the young flute players to scout the perimeter, as I do on a regular basis, and just as I was nodding off, the boy came running back, all flushed and alarmed. 'A troop of royal guards is heading this way!' he said. 'And what of it?' I said, because most of those fellows in royal uniforms are so stupid, they never have a clue who we are as long as we keep the monkey quiet. But the boy recognized the leader of this contingent, a commander who has a grudge against us."

"A grudge?"

"I've been known to do an impersonation of the fellow—uncanny, if I say so myself—and for some reason he finds it insulting. So we gathered up our things and were out of there in the blink of an eye. And yes, we left you just as you were, snoring as loudly as those navigation horns on the lighthouse."

"What about Axiothea? And Bethesda?"

"Axiothea is perfectly capable of fending for herself. I assumed that sooner or later she and your slave would return from the market and wake you up, probably long after the soldiers passed by."

"And what would I have told Axiothea, when she asked where you were? I had no idea where you'd gone, or why."

He shrugged. "Sometimes the troupe has to disperse and disappear on short notice, as well she knows."

"But Axiothea never came back," I said. "Or if she did, she didn't wake me. And I never . . ." My throat constricted. "I never saw Bethesda again."

"Oh, I see. That's when the slave girl went missing?"

I nodded.

Melmak looked thoughtful. "I haven't seen Axiothea since that day, either. You haven't seen Axiothea, have you?"

"No. But I spoke to someone who may have seen her leave the market that day."

"Alone?"

"Not exactly. She may have been following a little boy."

Melmak smiled. "Ah, well, there you have it. You've just confirmed my suspicion, that Axiothea received a summons from her patron. There's a boy he sends to deliver messages, who knows Axiothea by sight. No doubt that was the boy, and he was taking her to his master."

I felt a chill. "But that must mean . . ."

"Yes?"

That the woman abducted by the two ruffians was indeed Bethesda, and not Axiothea, I thought. "So, after you left me at the waterfront, you saw neither Axiothea nor Bethesda again?"

"That's correct."

"Then Axiothea was the last of us to see Bethesda. I need to speak to her. Where is she, Melmak?"

"I have no idea."

"You say she must be with her patron."

"Yes, but I don't know where he lives. I don't even know his name."

"How can that be? Aren't you curious?"

"Indeed I am. But whenever the question comes up, Axiothea makes it quite clear that whatever relationship she has with this man, she intends to keep it private. I bite my tongue and mind my own business. Not an easy thing for me to do, I'll admit."

"But I *must* talk to Axiothea. I've got to find her."

He shrugged. "You managed to find me."

"After days of looking—and then purely by chance!"

Melmak nodded blearily, then brightened. "And look who else you've just found—Lykos!"

I turned to see the artificer with the distinctive white stripe in his hair.

"Lykos, you remember our friend Gordianus."

The man gave me a blank look, then recognized me and nodded. He turned to Melmak. "What news of Axiothea? I don't suppose she's turned up?"

Melmak pouted his lips. "No. Still missing."

Lykos shook his head. "Sooner or later, Melmak, we're going to have to replace her. She's left us no choice. After all the work I put into her makeup and costumes! The costumes can be reused, of course . . . if we find a girl the same size." He looked at me and raised an eyebrow. "You have that lovely slave girl—what's her name?"

"Bethesda," I whispered.

"Only she's gone missing, too," said Melmak.

"Has she?" Lykos frowned. "Too bad."

Hopelessness engulfed me. And yet, chance and sheer persistence had led me this far. Might they lead me to Axiothea, as well?

I stared into the shadows. "There must be a way," I whispered, thinking aloud.

Then I thought of the two eunuchs.

I turned and left the tavern without another word.

An hour later I was in their apartment, seated between the two of them. Kettel took up more than half the couch, with Berynus and I wedged into the remaining space. They refused to let me state my business until they had plied me with almond-stuffed dates and flatbread smeared with pomegranate jam, washed down with a very good wine from Cos. ("The last of the vintage to escape the island before that monster Mithridates invaded!" said Berynus.)

At last they allowed me to describe the litter I had seen at the mime troupe's performance, with its lotus-column poles and midnight-black bearers.

"Tafhapy," said Kettel.

"Without a doubt," agreed Berynus.

"That's the owner of the litter?" I said. "You're sure?"

"Oh, yes," said Kettel, dabbing a bit of jam from the corner of his mouth. "Tafhapy bought both the litter and the bearers at the same time, a few months ago, from a business rival he drove to bankruptcy. What a ruthless fellow! What is it you want to know about him, Gordianus?"

"Where he lives, for a start."

"On the Street of the Seven Baboons, in a big saffron-colored house with a balcony overlooking the street. You can't miss it. But please, tell us you have no business with this fellow."

"Why?"

"Because he's a scoundrel! Completely unscrupulous. Highly dangerous."

"A criminal?"

Berynus sniffed and drummed his long, bony fingers on his knee. "Tafhapy has never been arrested, if that's what you mean, but that doesn't mean he hasn't cracked a few heads and made a few business rivals disappear in his time. Men like Tafhapy don't submit to royal judges, they bribe them. No one can call you a criminal if you're above the law. Now he's one of the wealthiest men in Alexandria, so rich and powerful, they say he has the ear of the king himself."

"Where does his money come from?"

"He inherited a shipping business from his father. Owns a fleet that traffics all sorts of goods up and down the Nile and across the sea. For all I know, it was one of his ships that delivered this very fine wine from Cos. More, Gordianus?"

"No, thank you."

"What *is* your interest in Tafhapy?" asked Kettel.

I saw no reason not to tell them. "You may remember, when I last called on you, I was looking to find the members of a certain mime troupe. Among them there's a young actress called Axiothea. Tafhapy seems to have taken a liking to her."

"Taken a liking, you say?" Kettel looked past me, to Berynus, who returned his skeptical gaze.

"Why not? Axiothea is very attractive. Beautiful, really. She looks like . . ." I swallowed hard.

Berynus nodded. "She should be beautiful, considering her name."

"How so?"

He laughed. "Gordianus, I know your Greek is charmingly rudimentary, but surely even you can work it out. Axiothea: 'worth looking at.' Probably a stage name."

"I hadn't thought of that." For a beautiful performer who ran through the streets practically naked, attracting as much attention as possible, the name Axiothea certainly fit. "But the two of you exchanged a look a moment ago, when I mentioned Tafhapy's attraction to her."

Berynus cleared his throat. "Well, from what I know of Tafhapy, it seems more likely that he would take a liking to *you*, Gordianus, than to this young actress, no matter how 'worth looking at' she may be. Tafhapy has never taken a wife. Nor has he any children, as far as I know."

Kettel pursed his lips and nodded in agreement. I squirmed a bit, feeling trapped between Kettle's rolls of fat and Berynus's bony elbows.

"Nonetheless, the leader of the mime troupe seems quite certain that Axiothea is staying with this Tafhapy right now. And I need to talk to her—urgently."

"Good luck getting in to see her, if she's at the house on the Street of the Seven Baboons," said Berynus. "That place is like a fortress."

"Perhaps I can talk my way in, if I can think of some pretext. . . ." I frowned.

"Yes, you're a clever boy," said Kettel, squeezing my thigh with one of his big, sweaty hands. "You'll think of something. Would you care for another date?" He plucked one of the delicacies from the tray on a nearby table and, keeping his little finger extended, held it to my lips.

I waved it away and sprang up from the couch. "I have to be off now."

"But where are you going?" Berynus made a long face. Kettel looked at me, then at the date he was holding in mid-air, which he popped into his mouth. He appeared to expand, filling the vacant space I left behind on the couch, so that it was hard to see how I could ever have fit between them.

"I'm off to the Street of the Seven Baboons," I said. "There must be some way I can speak to Axiothea."

Berynus unfolded like a stick insect and followed me to the door. With considerable difficulty, Kettel rose from the couch, grabbed another date, and waddled after him.

As I was stepping out the door, Berynus grabbed my elbow. "Gordianus, whatever you do, take care! Don't do something to offend Tafhapy. As I told you—he's a dangerous man."

VII

The Street of the Seven Baboons was only a few blocks long. Its name came from a circular fountain situated at one end. Seven baboons sculpted from red marble stood at the center, all facing out, with jets of water pouring from their gaping mouths.

The house of Tafhapy was the largest on the street, with saffron-colored walls that towered above the surrounding houses. It was indeed a veritable fortress, as Berynus had said. Before I even dared to approach the entrance—two high wooden doors with a heavy iron lock clasping them shut—I surveyed the structure from all the angles and vantage points available to me. I saw at least two guards patrolling the rooftop, and no easy means of ingress, only high walls and inaccessible windows. No neighboring building offered a means of leaping onto the roof. No adjacent palm tree could be scaled to gain access to a balcony. I would have to enter by the door.

How might I get inside, or get Axiothea to come outside to see me? Should I pretend to be a relative, desperate to see her? She might resent such a ruse, or worse, her patron might resent it. "Unless it's unavoidable," my father had taught me, "one should not lie outright to powerful people. They don't like it."

Might I simply bang on the door, wait for the peephole to open, and then tell whoever answered the plain truth—that I was Gordianus of Rome and that I wanted to speak to the actress Axiothea, whom I thought to be residing inside the house? "Sometimes the most straightforward approach is the best," my father had taught me. But the impregnability of the house made me wary, and the warnings of the two eunuchs raised my guard. To simply ask for what I wanted seemed too easy.

Eventually I screwed up my courage, approached the door, and knocked, using a large iron ring that also served as a handle. A moment later the peephole slid open and a dark face peered out at me. It was one of the litter bearers I had seen in the square.

"Who are you and what do you want?" he asked, speaking Greek with a heavy, unfamiliar accent.

"My name is Gordianus—"

"A Roman?" The name always gave me away.

"Yes. I want to see Axiothea."

"Who?"

"The mime troupe actress called Axiothea. I think she's in this house, and—"

"Do you have business with the master?"

"No. I only want to see—"

"Does the master know you?"

I took a breath. "No. But—"

"Then go away!"

The peephole slammed shut.

"Can you at least tell me if Axiothea is here?" I shouted. "Do you know the woman I'm talking about?" I lifted the iron ring and banged it against the door.

"Move on!" said a stern voice above me.

I looked up to see a guard on the rooftop peering down at me.

"Move on, before I make you move on." He brandished a spear.

I moved on.

. . .

From a safe distance, I kept watch on the house. Perhaps I would see Axiothea coming or going, and have a chance to speak to her, away from the house and the watchful, wary eyes of her patron's servants.

For hours I watched. People came and went—slaves delivering packages, wealthy-looking Egyptian merchants, even a few Roman businessmen in togas—but I did not see Axiothea.

At last, one of the doors opened and a little boy stepped out, no older than seven or eight. Could it be the messenger boy I had heard about, the one who fetched Axiothea at the market? He certainly had the look of a slave on a mission as he headed across the street with a quick, steady gait, his shoulders back and his head held high, exhibiting a confidence that belied his years and lowly station.

I followed him.

Once we were a few blocks from the house, and I was sure that no one was following, I overtook him and stepped in front of him, blocking his way.

He put his hands on his hips and stared up at me. "Who are you?"

In no mood to have yet another Egyptian identify me as a Roman before I could even finish introducing myself, I kept my mouth shut and stared down at him.

"Two can play at that game," he said, crossing his arms and staring back at me. If I had thought he would be easily intimidated, I was to be disappointed. "Perhaps you don't know who *I* am," he said. "I am Djet, the slave of—"

"I know who your owner is. A man called Tafhapy."

"That's right. And you, stranger, are blocking my way. Do you really want to interfere with the business of a slave who's carrying a message for Tafhapy? Think carefully, Roman." (I'd hardly said a word, and still he detected my accent!)

"Precocious little bastard, isn't he?" I muttered. Djet wrinkled his brow and frowned, unable to follow the Latin I spoke to myself. I resumed speaking in Greek. "Listen, little man, I'll let you pass if you'll tell me something."

"You'll let me pass, period."

This was not going to be easy. I considered my options. I was certainly capable of overpowering him, but did I really want to harm or even threaten a possession of a man like Tafhapy? Probably not. Perhaps the little fellow could be bribed.

"Listen," I said, "I'll bet you have a sweet tooth. What do you say we go to that baker's shop down the street and—"

"Are you trying to bribe me, Roman?"

"Well . . ."

"The last messenger boy from the house of Tafhapy who accepted a bribe was soundly lashed, hung upside down for three days, and then fed to a crocodile. If you think you can bribe me, Roman, you're wasting your time. Now get out of my way."

I sighed. "Djet, I just want to ask you a simple question. Is there a woman in your master's house called—"

"The last messenger boy from the house of Tafhapy who answered questions posed by a stranger was also soundly lashed, hung upside down—"

"Yes, I understand." I took a deep breath. I leaned over him and lowered my face to his, until we were eye to eye. "What if I simply say the name . . . Axiothea?"

He blinked. A faint, almost indiscernible tremor of recognition disturbed his rigid demeanor.

"Aha! Then you *do* know her," I said.

"I never said that! You're trying to trick me!" In the blink of an eye, he was no longer the immovable servant of his master, but merely a little boy.

"Is Axiothea in the house right now?"

Djet tried to make his face a blank, but his cheeks grew red and his lips twitched.

"Aha! The answer is yes—Axiothea *is* in the house."

"I never said that!" he cried. "You're trying to get me into trouble, and I won't have it!"

"You may speak like a man, Djet, but you have the will of a boy. You can control your words, but you can't control your thoughts, which are plain to read upon your face. You have years to go before you can maintain a blank expression. Some men never learn to do it."

"This isn't fair! I'm doing everything I can to be true to my master, and still you're finding out the things you want to know. If the master discovers—"

"But he never will, Djet. I promise you that. Now tell me how I might get Axiothea to come out of the house to talk to me—or, if she can't leave the house, how a lowly Roman like myself might get inside."

"Call yourself Gordianus and live on the top floor of a tenement in Rhakotis!" he blurted out, then clapped his hands over his mouth.

I was nearly as taken aback as he was. "What did you say?"

He kept his hands over his mouth and shook his head.

"How do you know the name Gordianus? How do you know where Gordianus lives?"

He made no answer.

I felt a chill. What sort of coincidence was this? What could it mean?

"Let me guess, Djet. You've been sent by your master to fetch this Gordianus. Am I right?"

He shook his head, but his eyes betrayed him.

"Well, you needn't go all the way to Rhakotis to find him. Here I am."

Djet slowly uncovered his mouth and stared up at me, wariness replacing his chagrin. "You? You're the Roman called Gordianus? I don't believe you."

"Take me to your master and let him be the judge."

"If you're not Gordianus . . . if you're just some other Roman, trying to get me into trouble . . . or looking to get this Gordianus into trouble . . . or thinking you can fool my master . . . I warn you—"

"Let me guess: I will be soundly lashed, hung upside down for three days, and fed to the crocodiles."

"At the very least!"

I stood upright, pulled my shoulders back, and took a deep breath. "I don't suppose you know *why* your master wants to see me?"

He narrowed his eyes. I could see that he was no longer quite sure what to make of me. "I have no idea." His face and voice betrayed no signs of lying.

"How were you to convince me to come with you? A little boy shows up at my door and says I must come to see his master, a man I might never have heard of—why would I do that? Were you to offer me money?"

"No."

"Deliver a threat?"

"No."

"How, then?"

"I was to say a name. An odd name, neither Egyptian nor Greek, nor Roman, I think. A woman's name. . . ."

I drew a sharp breath. "Bethesda?"

"Yes, that's it." He scrutinized me for a long moment, perceiving that all my defenses were down. "You really are Gordianus, aren't you?"

"Yes, I am."

He nodded, accepting my word.

"Lead me to Tafhapy," I said.

VIII

As we stepped through the doorway and into the courtyard beyond, I knew this was the house of the man who had come to watch the mime show in the elegant litter, for the conveyance in question rested on large wooden blocks against one wall of the courtyard.

There might be two such litters in Alexandria, with lotus-column poles and a yellow canopy, but surely there were not two such sets of bearers. The Nubian giants sat beside the litter in a patch of sunshine, playing a game with dice. A couple of them looked up as we passed, giving me a curious glance before they smiled and waved to Djet.

I had never been in such a large and lavishly decorated house. Even the finest houses I had visited on my journey to see the Seven Wonders, such as that of Posidonius in Rhodes, seemed modest in comparison. I followed Djet through one room after another, all filled with sumptuous rugs, fine furniture, beautiful paintings, and marvelous pieces of sculpture. At last we arrived in another courtyard, this one planted with a lush garden of flowers and citrus trees. A pathway paved with colorful mosaics led to a shady spot where a man of middle years sat in a chair made of ebony inlaid with bits of ivory and turquoise.

The man's head was shaved, but his barber had neglected to trim his bushy black eyebrows, which bristled like the legs of a tarantula. Despite this striking feature, he was not a bad-looking man; nor was he as old as I had expected, though he still looked old enough to be Axiothea's father. He was dressed in an elaborately embroidered linen gown and elegant leather sandals, wearing a bejeweled ring on every finger and many necklaces of silver and gold. In all my travels I had never met a man as ostentatious as Tafhapy.

A scribe with writing tools sat cross-legged on the mosaic floor beside him—a beautiful young man wearing nothing but a loincloth, I noticed. At least two bodyguards watched us from the shaded recesses of the garden. Facing Tafhapy were two vacant ebony chairs, not quite as grand as the one in which he sat.

My host gave me an appraising look, then turned his gaze to Djet. "That was quick," he said. "Too quick. You can't possibly have gone all the way to Rhakotis and back in the time since I dispatched you."

"It was a sign from the gods, Master," said Djet. "I ran into the very man you wanted, only a few blocks from the house."

"Did you indeed?" Tafhapy raised a bristling eyebrow, then looked at me sidelong. "My doorkeeper tells me a Roman came calling earlier today. I suppose that was you, Gordianus—if you *are* Gordianus?"

"Yes, Tafhapy. That was me who called on you. And I am Gordianus."

"How curious. You desire to see me, and I to see you. Perhaps the gods indeed intend for us to meet."

"The will of the gods is manifest in all that transpires," I said, having learned in my travels that this sort of comment was appropriate for almost any occasion, and usually appreciated by those to whom the gods had shown special favor.

Tafhapy merely nodded. He told Djet to go sit in the shade of a lemon tree at the far side of the garden, and indicated with a gesture that I should sit in one of the vacant chairs. Though the afternoon was warm, he offered me no refreshment. For a long time he merely looked at me. Unlike Djet, he was skilled at banishing all expression from his face. I had no idea what he was thinking.

At last, without taking his gaze from me, he extended one hand toward the scribe. The young man placed a rolled-up piece of papyrus in his hand.

"Do you read Greek?" said Tafhapy.

"Even better than I speak it."

Tafhapy snorted derisively but held out the papyrus, indicating that I should take it.

"Read it aloud," he said.

I cleared my throat. "'To the esteemed Tafhapy, blessed many times over by Serapis, greetings. We have taken into our care the girl called . . .'" I drew a sharp breath but strove to keep all emotion from my voice. "'. . . called Axiothea. She will not be harmed. But you will not see her again until we receive from you a gift commensurate with the greatness of your affection for her. Leave a black pebble in the fountain of the seven baboons to show that you have received this message. Then we shall send further instructions.'"

I looked up. "The message is unsigned."

"What do you make of it?" said Tafhapy.

What indeed? If it was Axiothea who had been kidnapped, was it Bethesda who had been seen going off with the little boy? And was the boy who had been seen in fact Djet, and if so—was Bethesda here in the house of Tafhapy? My heart pounded in my chest.

Until I knew more, I was not yet ready to reveal to Tafhapy my reason for coming, or my acquaintance with Axiothea. To play for time, I held up the letter and examined it more closely. I took a deep breath. "The papyrus and the ink are of low quality. The Greek letters are competently made, but not elegant; this wasn't written by a scribe, taking dictation. But the writer is an educated man, as can be deduced by the fact that the message contains no grammatical errors or misspellings, or at least none that I can see. Indeed, the style of address is rather elevated."

Tafhapy smiled faintly. "You are an observant young man. Observe this as well." He took a second piece of papyrus from the scribe and handed it to me.

This specimen was smaller, and the message shorter. I read aloud: "'No black stone in the fountain. Did you not receive our previous message? Axiothea misses you. Place a black stone in the fountain if you wish to see her again.'"

Tafhapy nodded. "What do you make of these two messages, Gordianus?"

"The girl Axiothea was kidnapped. She's being held for ransom. And yet . . ."

"Go on."

"They asked for a sign, which you haven't given them. Do you intend to pay them, or not?"

"Why should I pay them?"

I shrugged. "It's not my place, Tafhapy, to say what this woman is worth to you—"

"You misunderstand, Gordianus. Why should I pay ransom for a woman who . . ."

Tafhapy's voice trailed away. From his resting place beneath the lemon tree at the far corner of the garden, Djet had risen to his feet to greet someone—a woman, to judge by her general outline. So deep was the shade in that part of the garden that I could not see her face at all, only her silhouette. The woman turned away from Djet and walked toward us, keeping to the shade of a leafy bower. As she drew near, a bit of sunlight penetrated the leaves to strike her face, and I saw that it was—

"Bethesda!" I whispered, my heart skipping a beat. I dropped the papyrus and rose from my chair.

But as the woman moved from the shadows into the light, I saw that I was mistaken. My heart turned to lead.

"As I was saying," Tafhapy continued, "why should I pay ransom for a woman who was never kidnapped?"

Rising from his chair, he took Axiothea's hands in his and gave her a kiss on the forehead. They smiled at each other for a long moment, then Axiothea sat in the chair next to mine.

"Sit, Gordianus," said Tafhapy.

I did so, gripping the armrests to steady myself.

"Did you not come to my house earlier today, asking to see Axiothea? Here she is."

I glanced at her, but had to look away. Her resemblance to Bethesda had amused me when I first met her, and delighted me in my dreams. Now it brought me pain to look at her. Yet my eyes were drawn to look at her again, and then I could not look away.

By what magic of the gods does a certain human face, that face and no other, become so important to us, the focus of our deepest longings, the answer to all questions? To gaze upon that face, and no other, is to find stillness in the midst of chaos, contentment in the midst of despair, pleasure in the midst of whatever pain and confusion life may throw at us. Axiothea's face was very nearly that face—almost, but not quite. Looking at her, I felt many things at once, and my thoughts became a jumble.

Axiothea leaned toward me and put her hand on my arm. I looked at Tafhapy, thinking he might be displeased by her show of affection, however mild, but his demeanor remained aloof. If anything, he seemed to approve of Axiothea's compassionate gesture.

"Why did you send Djet to fetch me?" I whispered.

"Answer my question first. Why did you want to see Axiothea? Did you have a question for her?"

"Yes."

"Ask it now."

I looked into her eyes. Curiously, they were the part of her that least resembled Bethesda; never could I have mistaken the eyes of one for the other. Looking into Axiothea's eyes, I was able to maintain my composure.

"When did you last see Bethesda? How did you come to be parted? Do you know what's become of her?"

"I last saw Bethesda in the market on the waterfront. She said she needed to relieve herself. She knew where to find the public latrina. I offered to go with her, but she insisted there was no need. While she was gone, Djet appeared, sent by his master to find me. Tafhapy had watched our performance, sitting in his litter. When the king's soldiers arrived, his own bodyguards formed a cordon around him, so that he didn't see the escape of the mime troupe, and had no idea what had happened to us. He was terribly worried about me. I couldn't leave him in suspense. I had to go to him."

"So you left Bethesda behind?"

"Not at once. I waited for her—for a while—but at last I went off with Djet. You and Melmak and the rest were only a short distance away, and the market was full of people. I never imagined that any harm would come to her. I certainly never imagined that . . ."

She reached down to retrieve the scrap of papyrus I had dropped and handed it back to me.

"They say they captured me, Gordianus, yet here I sit. When the first message was left on the doorstep a few days ago, Tafhapy didn't tell me about it. But he did insist that I stay here at the house, thinking to protect me from these deluded kidnappers while he tried to figure out who they were and what they were up to. To keep me from leaving, the sweetheart plied me with every indulgence. I thought he was merely doting on me! But today, when this second ransom note arrived, he showed it to me, along with the first. I found the messages as baffling as he did—until I realized what must have happened. The kidnappers must have had some idea of what I look like and where they might find me; perhaps they even knew I was dressed in green. But the woman they came upon was Bethesda. Thinking she was me, they ran off with her. They sent the first message to Tafhapy, believing they had me in their power. The second message indicates that, as of today, they're still holding Bethesda, thinking she's me."

"Unless . . ." My tongue turned to stone and refused to utter the thought.

Axiothea lowered her eyes. "Yes, I thought of that. What if . . . what if they killed the girl they thought to be me, and they lie when they say their captive is still alive. Yes, that's possible, but—"

"But not likely," said Tafhapy. "Kidnapping is quite common these days. People of property must deal with such unpleasantness on a regular basis. But almost always, certain rules apply."

"Rules?" I said.

"Yes. First and foremost is that the hostage is kept alive and well—indeed, often pampered, as if he or she were a sacred cat in a temple—and returned unharmed after the money is paid. It's the way this sort of thing is done. Only a very stupid or very careless kidnapper would kill his hostage—especially if the man he dared to extort was me."

Axiothea smiled. "Tafhapy the Terrible, they call him."

"Who calls him that?" I asked.

"Anyone who dares to cross me!" said Tafhapy. "I suspect this girl called Bethesda is being kept alive and well by her captors, who thought she was Axiothea when they abducted her, and continue to think so."

"Bethesda is deliberately passing for Axiothea?" I said.

"Why not? This girl looks like Axiothea, does she not? And if she's even half as clever as Axiothea, she will have figured out what's happened and realized it's to her advantage to go along with her captors' mistake. Quite likely she's being held in some degree of comfort, given the high value they attach to their prize. Perhaps the girl is living in better circumstances than she's used to. She may even be enjoying herself. If she's being coddled enough, she may even prefer the company of these brigands, as opposed to being your captive."

"*My* captive?"

"Isn't every slave a captive, strictly speaking, no matter how mild her master?"

I was torn by powerful emotions—distress at the likelihood that Bethesda had been kidnapped in Axiothea's stead, relief that Tafhapy believed she was safe, then more distress at his suggestion that she might actually be enjoying the separation that was causing me such misery.

"What am I to do?" I muttered.

"Go after her, of course," said Tafhapy.

"What?"

"Go after her and get her back. That is, if you're as smitten with the girl as you appear to be."

"Smitten? Of course, I'm upset. Bethesda is my property. She's been stolen from me. They had no right—"

"Ah, so this is a matter of honor and justice," Tafhapy said. "Whatever your motivations, if you want the girl, you must find some way to get her back. Can you pay the sort of ransom these bandits are likely to demand?"

I shook my head. "I don't suppose . . . that you . . ."

"That *I* might pay the ransom?" Tafhapy threw back his head and laughed.

"Perhaps . . . perhaps you could communicate with the kidnappers, and let them know that they've taken the wrong person. Once they know Bethesda is merely a poor man's slave, they'll understand what she's worth, and I might be able to buy her back."

"And how would that be to my advantage? As long as these men think they're holding Axiothea, they'll leave the real Axiothea alone. Against my better judgment—because Axiothea insisted I do so—I've done you the favor of telling you what's become of your slave, Gordianus. I didn't owe you even that much."

"But how am I to find her?"

"Ah, with that I may be able to help you. When I was trying to make sense of that first, nonsensical ransom demand, I did some asking around, and I think I know which culprits are involved. No others, at this particular time, would dare to engage in such a risky enterprise, aimed at a person as powerful as myself. All signs indicate that we are dealing with the gang of the Cuckoo's Child."

"The Cuckoo's Child?"

"That is what they call their leader. They are a particularly brazen gang of cutthroats who operate from a base somewhere in the Nile Delta. No ship travels up or down any of the river's many branches, and no party traverses the land routes across the Delta, without fear of encountering these raiders. Until recently, their operations have been confined to the Delta, and here in Alexandria we had nothing to fear from them. But as King Ptolemy's hold on the city has weakened, bandits and rebels everywhere in Egypt have been emboldened. The Delta has become a lawless place." He shook his head. "Now even Tafhapy, minding his own business in his house in Alexandria, is targeted to pay ransom for a kidnapping. This can only be the work of the Cuckoo's Child and his gang."

Where had I recently heard the phrase "cuckoo's child"? It had been in the mime show, in reference to a fictitious bastard brother of the king, but that seemed to have no relevance at the moment. "Who is this Cuckoo's Child you speak of? Why do they call him that, and what's his real name? And how did he become the head of such a gang?"

"Ah, those are very good questions, Gordianus, to which King Ptolemy and his agents would very much like the answers. As far as I know, no one outside the gang knows the real name of the Cuckoo's Child. These bandits take an oath, upon pain of death, never to reveal the true name of their leader, or that of any other member." He smiled. "Perhaps you can find the answers to your questions from the Cuckoo's Child himself, when you track him down and ask for the return of your slave."

"Are you making fun of me, Tafhapy?"

His smile faded. "No, I am not. Though I may appear aloof to your misery, Gordianus, I, too, know the power of the heart's desire, even over the strongest of men." He glanced at Axiothea. "True, it was Axiothea who insisted that I bring you here, from a desire to help her new friends, you and this girl Bethesda. But I, too, wish you the blessings of Fortuna, if that Roman goddess will deign to influence the outcome of such a peculiar enterprise—the retrieval of a slave kidnapped by mistake."

I shook my head. "The Delta is enormous, or so I've been told."

"It is indeed," said Tafhapy.

"Is it not a settled region, with villages and farms and roads?"

"Many areas are settled, yes. And there are roads that cross the Delta, with ferries to carry travelers and their camels across the many waterways, from one stretch of road to the next. But many parts of the Delta are wild and uncharted, and have been so since the time of the pharaohs. As it nears the sea, the Nile splits into countless channels, creating countless islands, large and small. Maps of the Delta are meaningless, because overnight a storm or a flood can change water to land, or land to water. There are marshes that no horse or camel can pass, tracts of quicksand that have swallowed whole armies without a trace, swamps and lagoons thick with man-eating crocodiles. Vast expanses are totally flat, covered with thick, scrubby vegetation, and devoid of landmarks, so that even the most experienced guides become hopelessly lost. These inhospitable regions of the Delta have long been a haven for all sorts of miscreants and misfits—criminal gangs, escaped slaves, deserters from the army and ex-soldiers fallen on hard times, outcast courtiers and even exiled members of the royal family. The most desperate men in all Egypt live in the Delta. They do as they please with impunity, beyond the reach of any law."

"Surely no man in his right mind would venture into such a place," I said.

"Surely not," agreed Tafhapy.

I thought about this. Could I be described as a man in his right mind? Not since Bethesda's disappearance. "If some fool were to go there, how would he find this gang of the Cuckoo's Child?"

"The easternmost branch of the Nile is called the Pelusian. The westernmost, nearest to Alexandria, is called the Canopic. Between them, along with countless smaller waterways, are the five other major branches of the Delta. My informants believe they know on which of these branches, and approximately how close to the sea, the Cuckoo's Child has established his latest stronghold—the Cuckoo's Nest, it's called. Should some fool decide to make the journey, I can provide more detailed directions."

I swallowed hard. "But . . . what if Bethesda is being held not in the Delta, but here in Alexandria? For all we know, she may be only a stone's throw from this house."

"Unlikely," said Tafhapy. "That's not how these kidnappers operate. They will have taken her to the place where they feel most secure and where she will have the least chance of escape: the Cuckoo's Nest."

I considered everything he had told me. "If I should try to find this place, I'll need to stall for time. These kidnappers must be made to think there's still a chance they'll receive a ransom. If you could lead them on, Tafhapy . . . if you could reply to their latest message, and to any others that may come . . . make them believe you're willing to pay—"

"No, Gordianus. I thought I made myself clear: there will be no communication whatsoever between me and these brigands. Even so, I don't think they'll dispose of this girl too quickly. In kidnappings of this sort, it's quite common for negotiations to drag on for months. The kidnappers will be patient. But from me, they will receive no response. This concerns your property. I've turned the matter over to you. I leave it entirely in your hands."

"But I can't take on a gang of brigands single-handed!"

"Hire bodyguards."

"With what? I have no money."

"Then *get* some money, Gordianus!" Tafhapy grunted, growing impatient. "Or simply get yourself a new slave girl."

"But don't you want to take revenge on these villains yourself, Tafhapy? Don't you want to punish them for showing disrespect to you? Help me get the better of them. Lend me some of your bodyguards. Let me take a couple of those ebony giants sitting in your courtyard. You'd hardly miss them—"

"Alas, Gordianus, I have no bodyguards to spare. I shall need all the protection I can get, soon enough."

"What do you mean?"

"Foreigner you may be, and too young to have much sense, but surely even you have some idea of what lies ahead. Do you not realize that Egypt is on the verge of civil war? The Delta has descended into utter lawlessness, a full-scale revolt has broken out upriver in Thebes, and the king may lose his hold on the army any day now. Anything may happen. Anything! I'm a man of property, Gordianus, facing an uncertain future. I would flee, but no port anywhere offers safe haven; the war between Mithridates and the Romans has seen to that. Whatever may befall Alexandria, here I shall stay. My home is my fortress, my bodyguards are my soldiers—and I have none to spare. And I have no money to spare, either, not even so much as a copper coin to give you. You're on your own."

I took this in, and felt thoroughly downhearted.

"But consider your advantages, young Roman," said Tafhapy. "Quick wits, quick reflexes, a strong body, and the fearlessness of youth, born though it may be from ignorance and inexperience. I wish you well, Gordianus."

Axiothea placed a hand on my shoulder and gave me a consoling look, then rose from her chair, drew close to Tafhapy, and whispered in his ear.

He considered what she had to say, then nodded. He called to Djet. The boy came running.

"I can't spare any bodyguards, Gordianus, but I can grant you the loan of this boy."

"What! He's just a child." And a rude one at that, I thought. "He'd only be a burden to me. A mouth to feed."

"I myself have found Djet to be reasonably intelligent, mostly reliable, and adequately loyal. You may find him more useful than you think. If not, and he proves to be an encumbrance, feel free to feed him to the crocodiles—as long as you buy a replacement for me. This is my offer: for as long as it takes to track down your missing slave and bring her back to Alexandria, I grant you the use of this slave, free of charge. Take it or leave it."

I shook my head. "It wouldn't be fair to the boy. There's certain to be danger—great danger. To take him from the safety of this house, on a trip into the wilds of the Delta, where bandits and raiders hold sway—"

"The Delta!" cried Djet, with a glimmer in his eyes. "I've always heard of it. A wild place, full of monsters and outlaws!"

Tafhapy laughed. "The boy's enthusiasm alone must be worth something to you, Gordianus."

I sighed. The idea of a feckless Roman and an even more feckless child heading to a hinterland full of cutthroats and crocodiles filled me with dread. But the alternative was to stay in Alexandria and watch the world fall apart—without Bethesda.

"Thank you, Tafhapy. I accept your offer. Well, then—where is this so-called Cuckoo's Nest?"

IX

After collecting every debt owed to me, and accepting a surprisingly generous loan from Berynus and Kettel, I set out the next day with Djet for the southern gate of Alexandria.

To the north, Alexandria faces the sea, but to the south it faces a large body of water called Lake Mareotis. A canal connects this lake with the distant Nile, allowing river barges to travel directly to the capital without venturing out to sea. Much of the grain grown along the floodplain of the Nile arrives on the southern wharves of Alexandria via the canal and Lake Mareotis.

Travelers also use the canal, which can be faster and cheaper than taking a camel or horse, especially since the roads in Egypt are notoriously bad. To be sure, the barges can be crowded—so crowded that sometimes they overturn. I found myself thinking about this as Djet and I were ushered, along with many others, from a pier on Lake Mareotis onto a long, narrow vessel manned not by rowers but by four men with long poles, two standing fore and two aft. The few places to sit were given to the oldest and most infirm among us, and the rest had to stand.

When the barge could hold no more passengers, the boatmen raised their poles and pushed against the mud on the lake bottom. The vessel left the dock, rocking from side to side so abruptly that Djet grabbed hold of my leg to steady himself, and more than a few of our fellow travelers uttered what I took to be prayers, some in Greek but most in the language of the native Egyptians.

I gazed back at the crowded shipyards and docks of the city, then I slowly turned, taking in the many-colored sails of the fishing vessels that dotted the lake. Towering palm trees ringed the shoreline. We headed steadily toward a break in the trees to the east; this was the mouth of the canal, marked by ornamental pylons on either side. The canal was wider than I expected. Even as I watched, two barges passed one another going in opposite directions, one entering the canal and the other leaving. As this second barge, heading for the pier, passed us, I saw that the deck was as crowded as ours, and the passengers looked even more miserable. Some of them had probably been standing all the way from Canopus.

Canopus! What stories I had heard about the place. As if opportunities for amusement were not great enough in Alexandria, the wealthy of the city (and those who could gather enough money to pretend they were wealthy, if only for a day) regularly flocked to the town of Canopus, only a day's journey away, where their every whim could be indulged. Rich foods and fine wines, shops offering exquisite merchandise, venues for gambling, entertainments staged by exotic dancers and acrobats, and every imaginable pleasure of the flesh—all could be had in Canopus, for a price. The town had become a watchword not just for diversion and debauchery, but also for discretion. Thus the saying: things that happen in Canopus never leave Canopus.

In all my months in Alexandria, I had never ventured to Canopus, seeing no point; to enjoy Canopus, a man needed money, and for me that was always in short supply. Now I finally had a reason to take the trip, but I might as well have been venturing to some sleepy village in the middle of nowhere, for all that I would be able to enjoy the sights and sounds. True, my purse was not empty; in fact, it was fatter than it had been in quite some time, thanks to the loan from the two eunuchs. But I intended to hold fast to every coin in my possession, giving them up only under dire necessity. Who could say what expenses I might incur on my journey, or how much I might have to pay to buy back Bethesda from the kidnappers?

Once we entered the canal, mules on the road alongside were harnessed to the boat and were made to pull us forward. The boatmen continued to use their poles to avoid the banks and oncoming boats. For a while I took some interest in watching them work, and in looking at the barges passing by. But the work of the boatmen was repetitious, and so were the boats; over and over we passed a mirror image of our own craft, loaded with nondescript passengers or with nondescript cargoes—stacks of brown amphorae likely to be packed with dates or dried figs, or bundled sheaves of papyrus, or mats made of woven reeds.

Occasionally, an ornately decorated pleasure barge sailed by. Elegantly dressed passengers sat in chairs with awnings to shade them and slaves to provide an artificial breeze by wafting fans of peacock feathers. The men and women on these vessels looked either bored or sleepy, and paid no attention whatsoever to our barge as we passed them. In their wake, breathing the warm air stirred by those peacock-feather fans, I caught whiffs of various perfumes—jasmine and spikenard, myrrh and frankincense. These indolent, perfumed Egyptians were the jaded rich of Alexandria, returning to the city after spending a few days and nights sating themselves with the pleasures of Canopus.

Meanwhile, Djet and I stood exposed to the bright sunlight. I had forgotten to bring a hat, but at some point a vendor appeared on the canal bank, walking alongside the mules. To any passenger who tossed him a coin he would toss a broad-brimmed hat made of woven reeds. I took him up on the offer. When Djet complained that he had no hat, I advised him to stand in my shadow.

The hat shaded my eyes and provided some relief from the merciless sun, but the smell of mule dung from the shore was inescapable, as was the smell of my fellow passengers. After a couple of hours in the hot sun, we could all have used some of that perfume that wafted from the pleasure barges. Flies and gnats harassed my eyelids and tickled my lips; as soon as one was brushed away, another appeared to resume the torment.

I had thought the barge might make a stop to allow the passengers to eat, but this was not the case. Instead, food was offered by vendors on the bank, just as the hats had been offered; it paid to be a good catch, unless one had no objection to eating food that had landed on the deck. In this way I bought a bit of flatbread stuffed with goat cheese. After I gobbled it up, Djet complained that he was hungry, too. I bought another flatbread, and watched begrudgingly as he ate the whole thing. I was still not convinced that his services would compensate for the bother of taking him along.

Nor were there stops for the passengers to relieve themselves. This necessity could be tended to behind a small screen at the back of the barge, using a hole in the deck. When I grumbled about the awkwardness of this arrangement, a fellow passenger told me that it was a great improvement over the last barge he had taken, which had no such hole; men and women alike had to do their business over the side, holding fast to the railing while at the same time hitching up their garments and hoping not to fall off.

The journey seemed interminable, but at last, as the day began to wane, the canal opened into the small harbor of Canopus situated on the northern bank of the canal.

No sooner had we disembarked than a group of boys swarmed around us, each extolling the virtues of a particular tavern or gambling den and insisting that we follow. Though I told them I had no money to spend, the boys were as persistent as the gnats that had tormented me on the barge. It was Djet who at last got rid of them. He was only a little older and bigger than most of the boys, but he seemed to know just what pose to strike or what threat to utter to dissuade them. At last they dispersed and moved on to badger some other poor passenger. I decided Djet might be worth the cost of his passage after all.

Though I had done nothing but stand all day, I felt exhausted and was ready to find lodgings for the night, the cheaper the better. The least expensive accommodations, so Tafhapy had told me, would be the farthest from the center of town, out on the road that led to the westernmost branch of the Nile. To get there, we would have to walk through the very heart of Canopus, with its crowded streets, tightly packed shops, and pleasure establishments.

I set out, feeling a bit intoxicated by the sheer vibrancy of the place. Beautiful dancing girls beckoned from doorways. In other doorways, men wearing more jewelry than was seemly rattled dice in their fists and promised that a fortune was waiting to be made inside. I passed perfume shops and purveyors of exquisite bronze ware, bakeries and wine merchants, sellers of fine furniture and plush fabrics, and even a small and very expensive-looking slave market where the man in charge announced that any sort of slave could be rented for an hour or a day, from a humble body slave to a highly trained scribe, "in case you left yours at home in Alexandria and can't do without." Curio shops sold amulets to ward off the Evil Eye, along with souvenir images of the Great Pyramid and the Pharos Lighthouse.

Simply getting through Canopus proved to be a challenge. Instead of running straight, the crowded streets meandered and doubled back on themselves, mazelike. Again and again we passed the same curio shop, the same dancing girls in doorways, the same slave market. So many lamps were lit that twilight seemed to linger indefinitely, forestalling the coming of night. Thus the saying: Canopus never sleeps. As my stomach growled, and my weariness increased, and my feet grew tired, this endless circular progress took on the character of a nightmare. I seemed to be trapped in a place where everything imaginable was for sale, yet I had no money to spend; where the sun never set, yet I longed only for a bed where I might sleep.

At last I came to a standstill, not knowing whether to go forward or back, since either direction led to the same place. It was Djet who took the matter in hand.

"Give me three copper coins," he said.

"What?"

"Do you want to get out of this place or not? Give me the coins."

After a bit of hesitation, I did so, and Djet vanished into the milling throng.

He was gone for a long time. I began to think he had abandoned me, but how far could he go with three copper coins? At last he came back, and with him was one of the boys who had pestered us at the dock.

"Who's this?" I said.

"The most honest of the bunch, if I'm any judge."

"What is he good for?"

"Leading us out of here!"

The newcomer put his hands on his hips and looked up at me. I had the uneasy feeling that I was outnumbered by precocious and willful boys, but I nodded and made a gesture that he should show the way.

Just past the curio shop, the boy took a turn that I had repeatedly missed. What I had assumed to be a recessed doorway was in fact a narrow passage between two buildings. As the way twisted and turned, we left the glow of the lamps behind. The sudden darkness made me uneasy, but I was relieved to be away from the crowds and the endless, maddening circuit of Canopus.

The way grew less narrow. On either side, taller buildings gave way to shorter ones. The space between buildings grew larger. We passed sheds and goat pens. Vague moonlight showed the outskirts of what could have been any quiet little village anywhere in Egypt.

We set out on a road that ran eastward, toward the Nile. The village ended. The open land around us was sandy and dry, peaceful and quiet, with only a scattered palm tree here and there. Then we came to a stretch of road with large estates on either side, most of them surrounded by high walls, from behind which I could hear the faint sounds of conversation and laughter, and occasionally the splashing of water. These must have been vacation estates where the Alexandrian upper classes took refuge from the hurly-burly of Canopus. The estates grew farther apart, and at last we seemed to leave civilization altogether.

I was exhausted, barely able to keep my eyes open, but Djet looked wide awake, as did our guide.

"This is all very lovely," I said. "But I'm not sure why you've led us here. Unless I'm to sleep on the ground. Or . . ."

Unless you intend to hand us over to bandits who'll take my purse, cut our throats, and leave our bodies for the vultures, I thought. So much for Djet's abilities as a judge of character!

"It's just ahead," said the boy.

"What?"

"The inn."

"I don't see any inn." I squinted at the darkness before us.

"It's just up there, where you see those palm trees."

The outline of the palm trees I was barely able to discern, but I saw no lights or any sign of a structure.

"Are you sure?"

"The inn that's farthest from the town—that's what your boy told me you wanted."

"The *cheapest* inn, more to the point."

"Oh? I see." The boy sounded slightly chagrinned. He turned to Djet. "But you said—"

"Never mind what I said. You're the local guide!"

"And you're the customer, you little fool!"

"Stop squabbling," I said. "Now, young man, if I were to tell you I wanted the cheapest possible accommodations—"

"I understand. Well, that would be the Inn of the Red Sunset, all the way back through town, on the side toward Alexandria—"

"No, no, no. After hiking all this way, I'm not going back through town. What is this place up ahead? What sort of establishment is it?"

"Oh, I'm sure you'll love it!"

"That doesn't answer my question."

"Well . . . it's not the cheapest inn outside Canopus, that's for sure. But it is the farthest east, and you're heading for the Nile, aren't you? When you wake up in the morning, the river will practically be right outside your door! Come on. Follow me. Come and see!"

Reluctantly, I trudged after him.

The palm trees loomed larger. There were so many of them, with such masses of foliage clustered beneath, that I took the location to be a small oasis. At last I glimpsed two points of light, which turned out to be lamps set on either side of the door of an inn, just where the boy had said it would be.

"This is it," said the boy.

The place seemed to have no windows. Above our heads, the fronds of a palm tree rustled in the faint evening breeze. "I'm not sure I like the look of this place. What is it called?"

"The Inn of the Hungry Crocodile."

I frowned. "I don't care for the name. But I suppose, having come all this way . . ."

As we approached the door, I reached for the knocker, then pulled my hand back with a start. The bronze knocker appeared to be a crocodile's head, though a small one, with the snout pointing down, so lifelike that it might have been cast from an actual crocodile. It was in two parts connected by a hinge, with the bottom of the jaw fixed to the door and the top serving as the knocker. The nostrils provided finger holds. When I raised the knocker, rows of sharp bronze teeth glinted in the lamplight.

I let the knocker drop. The noise reverberated in the stillness. There was no response. I raised the knocker again, but before I could let it drop, from within I heard the sound of a bolt thrown back.

The door opened, and I stood face to face with the strangest mortal I had ever seen.

X

For a long moment the man who had opened the door stood there, staring at us. He looked first at me, then lowered his eyes to Djet, and then to Djet's companion, whereupon I saw a flash of recognition in his heavy-lidded eyes, and the man's face cracked open—I can think of no better way to say it—to display a wide grin.

The man's skin was quite dark. That in itself was not unusual, for many Egyptians come from a region close to the place where the sun rises, and in consequence acquire a slightly scorched look. It was not the color of his flesh but the texture that seemed so odd, for it had a dry, scaly appearance, almost reptilian. Where it reflected the luster of the lamplight, this flesh appeared to be the darkest possible shade of green. His face protruded in what could only be described as a snout, with a small nose and a very large, very wide mouth. His grin stretched from ear to ear, showing two rows of unusually sharp teeth.

Since he seemed disinclined to speak, I finally did so. "My name is Gordianus."

He continued to study me for a moment. "A Roman?"

"Yes, but living in Alexandria. That's where I've come from. The boy traveling with me is named Djet. The other boy—"

"Yes, this one I know. One of our local lads."

"He brought us here, in search of lodgings for the night."

"Did he? Did he, indeed? Welcome, then, to the Inn of the Hungry Crocodile. I am your host." He took a bow.

"And are you the Hungry Crocodile?" I said, thinking to make a joke.

"Why, yessss!" he hissed. I half expected to see a reptilian tongue come flickering from between his thin lips, but he kept his tongue inside his mouth, hidden behind those rows of pointed teeth. "Can you imagine how I came by such a name?"

Nonplussed, I opened my mouth and stammered.

"Because I am notoriously hungry! Always hungry I am. And do you know what I'm hungry for?"

His grin was unnerving. Before I could answer, he produced a pair of copper coins, one between each forefinger and thumb, and held them in the lamplight for a moment before making a great show of biting them, one at a time, as if they were made not of copper but gold and he wished to test them. "Hungry for such as these, I always am! Ever and always hungry for more. You must give me such as these if you wish to spend the night." He pressed his grinning snout toward me.

"I can do that," I said, trying not to flinch.

"But these particular coins must be for the boy who brought you here. Here, boy, take them from me."

The boy held out his right hand and unclenched his fist to reveal two coins already nestled in his tiny palm. The Crocodile added his two, plunking them down one at a time.

"A consideration, young man, for bringing me custom."

The boy grinned. "Thank you! And now I have four!"

"Yessss! Two and two make four. Ah, the beauty of it!"

I frowned. "Djet! Did I not give you three coins, when I sent you to find the boy?"

He looked up at me and crossed his arms. "You did. And two of them I gave to him."

"And the other?"

"Don't I deserve a . . . what's that you called it, innkeeper? A consideration!"

"Yessss, for all we do, such as these must constitute our consideration. It's only right and proper." He patted Djet on the head with a dark, scaly hand. His fingernails were dark and dull and as pointed as his teeth. "This little one is like his host, a hungry one, hungry for such as those." He pointed to the coins, which the local boy now held tightly in his fist. "Run along, then, you, and let me make my new guests welcome."

The boy turned and ran. I watched him leave the glow cast by the lamps and vanish into the darkness.

"Don't stand here on the doorstep. Come inside!"

We stepped into a dimly lit vestibule. The Crocodile closed the door behind us.

The place was very quiet. "Is the inn empty?" I said.

"Not at all, not at all!"

"The other guests are all abed, then?"

"Not at all! They're in the common room, enjoying each other's company."

I looked around. The vestibule opened onto a hallway, but the passage led only to shadows on either side. "I see no common room," I said.

"Downstairs it is. Cooler down there, especially in the heat of summer."

"It's not summer yet."

"Always cool down there, whatever the time of year. Nice and cool in the common room under the ground. Come, I'll show you." He gestured to a doorway that opened onto a descending stairway.

"I only want a room for the night, for me and the boy. We can share with others, if that's cheaper—"

"No cheap rooms here. All rooms the same."

"Fair enough. How much for the night? And which way to the room? I'm very tired—"

"But surely you need food and drink at the end of the day, before you sleep. Included in the price!"

"Yes, well, then . . ." I heard Djet's stomach growl. "If it's included. But what is the price? If you said, I didn't hear—"

Even as I spoke, he ushered us down the stairs. Djet traipsed ahead of me, reached a landing, and disappeared around a corner. When I reached the turning, I saw a faint light from below and heard soft music and the sound of voices. The air was cool and dank and smelled of Egyptian beer.

"Down, down we go," said the Crocodile, following me. "Just follow the boy."

I rounded another corner and found myself in a subterranean chamber. The size of the room was impossible to discern, since the edges disappeared into darkness. In the zone between shadow and light, a girl sat cross-legged on the floor, strumming some sort of stringed instrument. Even by the uncertain light, I could see she was not pretty. In fact, she looked so like my host that I took her to be his young daughter.

In the middle of the room, with a lamp hung above them, five men and a boy sat on rugs in a circle. The boy was no older than Djet. He wore a bright red tunic and had curly black hair, so long that it might never have been cut. One of the men was a big fellow whom I took to be a bodyguard. While he and the boy looked on, the other four men appeared to be playing some sort of game.

As I watched, one of the players, with a cry in some barbaric language, let fly a handful of dice. The throw must have been good, for his craggy features, starkly lit by the lamp, broke into a smile of triumph as he reached forward to remove a colored wooden peg from a perforated playing board and replace it in another hole.

Framing the man's clean-shaven face was an elaborate headdress made of cloth and knotted rope, such as the desert-dwelling Nabataeans wear. Though I couldn't see his hair, I suspected there would be some gray in it. He wore a loose white robe belted at the waist, with long sleeves decorated with colorful embroidery at the cuffs. On several of his fingers were rings, each set with a jewel. From a necklace of thick silver links, sparkling in the lamplight, hung the largest ruby I had ever seen.

"Can you believe that fellow traveled all the way across the Delta like that?" whispered the Crocodile in my ear.

"In Nabataean garments? Is he not a Nabataean?"

"Indeed he is. He calls himself Obodas and he's a dealer in frankincense, scouting overland routes to Alexandria—or so he says. When foreigners go traveling in Egypt, who can say what they're up to?"

Did he include me in that question? His heavy-lidded eyes and grinning snout gave no indication.

"But when I say 'like that,' I mean not his Nabataean garments, but his rings and necklace—that Obodas should wear them so openly. How many coins might those be worth?" The Crocodile clicked his teeth.

"Does he not travel with bodyguards?"

"Two, and two only! One is that burly, bearded fellow who sits behind him. The other bodyguard keeps watch over their camels outside."

"What about the boy in the red tunic who sits beside him? Is that his son?"

The Crocodile snorted. "I hardly think so! With only two bodyguards and such a pretty boy for his bedmate, all the way from Petra to my inn Obodas traveled dressed like that, flashing those jewels and making himself a target for who knows how many bandits? Some Nabataean god must be watching over this Obodas, for such a fool to cross the Delta without falling prey to the Cuckoo's Child."

I swung about to face my host. "What do you know about—?"

"The other three guests are Egyptians from the Delta," he went on, "city fathers from the town of Sais." The men he referred to were less ostentatiously dressed than the Nabataean. They had the look of farmers wearing their best clothes, in which they were not quite comfortable. "Their leader, the one with the long gray beard, is called Harkhebi, and they're returning home from a mission to Alexandria. They tried to gain an audience with King Ptolemy, to petition for repairs to the road that crosses the Delta; last summer's inundation of the Nile washed out a great many sections. How many coins would it take to fix that road, I wonder? But the king refused to meet them, and they return to Sais with nothing. So don't ask them about their trip unless you want to hear an earful about the king! But look, the Nabataean gestures to you. He's inviting you to join the game."

I turned to see that all four players were looking up at me from their places on the rug-strewn floor.

I shook my head. "Thank you, gentlemen, but I never gamble."

This was the truth. From earliest childhood I had been taught by my father that gambling was a ruinous pastime, a vice to be strictly avoided. In his career as Finder, he had seen many men (and even a few women) of every rank in society, from humble shopkeepers to haughty senators, destroyed by gambling. "Every man takes risks and calls upon Fortuna from time to time," he had told me. "But the gambler taxes the goddess's patience, until he practically begs Fortuna to withdraw her favor."

My father lived what he taught, and so far I had followed his example.

"We play only for tiny stakes," said the Nabataean. "A friendly game to pass the time."

"I'd do better to pass the time by sleeping," I said.

"Sleep!" The Crocodile clicked his tongue and shook his head. "No man sleeps at night in Canopus. Here we sleep in the day, and amuse ourselves at night. You must at least have something to eat and drink. Here, sit on the floor with your boy. Join the circle and watch while the others play."

While Djet and I settled ourselves on the floor, our host clapped his hands. A couple of young men appeared. By their dark, scaly appearance, I took them to be the Crocodile's sons. One brought me a small plate of food—bread, dates, and olives—while the other brought a large cup of beer. The food I felt obliged to share with Djet, but he had no business drinking beer, so I kept that to myself. The cup contained more than I wanted, but the frothy liquid helped to assuage my hunger, and soon I found that I was staring into an empty cup.

"Could I have some more?" I said, meaning more to eat. One of the sons brought another minuscule portion of food while the other insisted on refilling my cup.

Meanwhile, I watched the others play. The game was called Pharaoh's Beard, because the playing board was carved to resemble one of the long ornamental beards that one sees on old statues of the pharaohs. Each player let fly a pair of dice—not the Roman sort made from sheep bones, but cubes carved from wood, with markings on each of the six sides—and then moved his peg up or down the playing board a certain number of spaces; odd throws moved the peg up, while even throws moved it down. The rules allowed a player to disregard a certain number of throws and either pass or recast the dice. One could also displace an opponent's peg by landing in the same hole; this was sometimes desirable and sometimes not.

The game did not appear to be particularly complicated—at first. Gradually I began to perceive that there was indeed some strategy involved, and that some of the participants were better players than others, not because of anything to do with Fortuna, but because of their own skill.

The longer I watched—and the more beer I drank—the more fascinated I became by watching the others play. Certain moves were so clever and unexpected that everyone clapped and jabbered with excitement. Other moves were so boneheaded that we all groaned and shook our heads. At critical moments we watched with bated breath, or laughed with nervous excitement.

Each time a new round began, I was invited to join, and each time I declined, until there came a round when I said yes. To play I had to place a wager, but the bag of coins tucked inside my tunic felt reassuringly heavy.

I looked down at the full cup of beer beside me. When had it been refilled? Was it my fourth cup? Or my fifth?

I shook my head to clear it of all extraneous thoughts, for the game—my very first game of Pharaoh's Beard—was commencing.

XI

I won the first game. The victory gave me a heady feeling. From each of the other four players I took a gleaming Alexandrian drachma. It was no great amount, but the coins made a nice addition to my purse.

I won the next game as well, and tucked away another four coins. I silently congratulated myself for wisely sitting out so many rounds while I watched the game and mastered its strategy. If my first two games were any indication, I was simply a better, smarter player than the others—and why not? Was I not the son of the Finder, one of the cleverest men in Rome? And were not Romans the master strategists of the world?

As the players took a break before the next round, Djet whispered in my ear: "Raise the stakes!"

"Don't be silly. And don't snatch any more olives off that plate. Those are for me."

"But tonight Fortuna smiles on you. You should take advantage of her favor."

"What do you know of Fortuna?"

"Isn't that the goddess who looks after Romans like you?"

"Sometimes she looks after us. Other times not."

"But tonight is one of those times. Can't you sense it?"

Djet was right. Listening to the twanging music played by our host's daughter, nibbling the scarce delicacies and drinking the never-ending beer provided by his sons, I savored my small victories at Pharaoh's Beard and felt a sense of well-being such as I had not felt in quite some time. After all, what did my father know about gambling, since he never did it? If a man kept a cool head, and more importantly, if he had Fortuna on his side, where was the danger? And if a small win could bring such pleasure, would not a larger win bring even more?

For the next round of play, I proposed that we double the stakes. Obodas and Harkhebi and the others agreed. And again I won.

Then, on the next round of doubled stakes, I lost. Ah well, I told myself, I was still ahead of where I started, and not even the best player could win every round. It also occurred to me that if we tripled the original stakes, in a single round I could make back the money I had lost and more. And so I did.

Little by little the stakes grew higher. Sometimes I lost. More often, or so it seemed to me, I won. I basked in each victory, and discounted my losses as mere accidents. Even a lamp brimming with oil may flicker from time to time; so it is when the glow of Fortuna lights a man's way, I told myself, as occasionally my luck faltered.

At every turn I felt myself to be in control, not only of my own actions but of the overall course of the game, as we progressed from round to round, wagering ever greater numbers of coins. Why did I become so greedy? It was for Bethesda, I told myself. The fatter my purse, the greater the chance that I could ransom her, no matter the cost.

Then I began to lose.

I lost one wager, then another, and then another. As each new round began I thought that surely my luck would correct its course and return to me the winnings that had been mine only moments before. Like a leaf on the tide, I could not stop. It seemed for a while that I had controlled the game; now the game took control of me.

Suddenly, almost all my money was gone.

I held up my bag of coins and saw that it was sadly deflated, almost weightless, so empty that when I shook it I heard only a thin, pathetic tinkling, not the rich metallic music of the bulging coin purse that had been mine when I left Alexandria.

When I left Alexandria . . . how long ago was that? It seemed a lifetime ago. In that windowless room underground, time had lost all meaning. And I had lost almost all my money.

My face flushed hotly. My heart pounded in my chest. I suddenly felt wide awake. Had I been asleep before? I blinked and looked around. Clearly now I saw the dimensions of the room, which was smaller and shabbier than I had imagined. The discordant twanging of the so-called music was suddenly intolerable. The beer I had drunk turned sour in my belly.

The city fathers from Sais looked as dazed as myself. They too had lost a great deal. Their leader, Harkhebi, fussed with his long beard as they whispered among themselves, then he waved his hands dismissively to show that the three of them wished to play no more.

The Nabataean had a thin smile on his face, as did the bearded bodyguard sitting behind him. In front of Obodas was a great pile of coins—many of which, only moments before, had been mine. Pressed close beside Obodas, looking sleepy, was his young traveling companion. With one hand the Nabataean idly fingered a stack of coins, while with the other he fondled the boy's thick locks of jet-black hair.

I had lost virtually all my money, and I had no way to win it back, for I had nothing left to wager. The few coins I had left probably would not even pay for my night's lodging. I groaned and hid my face in my hands.

Djet leaned toward me, as if to whisper something. I recoiled, then reached for one of his ears and twisted it sharply.

"Don't dare speak to me, you little whelp!" I whispered. "This is all your fault! Curse you, Djet, and curse your master for sending you with me!"

My face flushed hotter still, for even as I blamed him and cursed him, I knew that what had happened was no one's fault but my own. Yet Djet surprised me by agreeing that he was to blame.

"You're right," he whispered. "It *is* my fault. I've watched my master gamble, and I've seen how he wins, and I thought it would be the same for you. But you are not Tafhapy! I should never have told you to wager more. Who knew your Roman goddess would be so fickle?"

"It's not Fortuna's fault, either," I said, shaking my head and feeling impossibly stupid. I released his ear.

"But we still have a chance to make it right," whispered Djet, rubbing his red, swollen ear.

"How?"

"Wager *me*."

"You?" I snorted. "Don't be ridiculous. A tiny slave like you is hardly worth a fraction of that pile of coins. You're little and weak and unskilled—"

"But the Nabataean desires me."

I made a dubious face.

"Have you not noticed, Roman? He's been watching me all night, like a hawk watches a sparrow. I thought that must be why he was losing for a while, because he was paying so much attention to me and so little to the game."

I stole a glance at Obodas. Even as he fondled the hair of the boy beside him, his heavy-lidded gaze was fixed on Djet—who fluttered his eyelashes and smiled demurely back at him, then abruptly drew his eyebrows together, as if wincing at the pain of his swollen ear. The Nabataean pouted back at him in sympathy.

I frowned. "I think you might be right," I whispered.

"Of course I am. Do you think a messenger like myself, who goes everywhere in Alexandria, doesn't learn to notice who watches him, and how long, and why? Little and young I may be, but not stupid, or blind."

His tone clearly imputed the latter two qualities to me, but I ignored the insult. "Very well, I see that you may be right. But of what use is this to me?"

"I told you. Use me for a wager."

I sighed. "In the first place, you are not my property, Djet—"

"The Nabataean doesn't know that."

"And in the second place, what if he wins?"

While he considered this question, Djet made his face a blank and stared at the Nabataean. Obodas stared back at him. Like a hawk watching a sparrow, Djet had said, and truly, so concentrated was the man's gaze that I think I could have scooped up half the coins and made off with them before he noticed. But there was the bodyguard to contend with.

Djet at last turned back and whispered in my ear. "He won't win."

"How do you know?"

"I can see it in his eyes. He cares nothing about the money, and so he was able to play without effort, and win. But he will want to win me, very badly. And so he will lose."

"That makes no sense."

"What do you know, Roman? You're not a gambler."

That was true. And if I wanted to get my money back—without which I could hardly hope to reach the heart of the Delta, and Bethesda—I would have to do something bold.

The Egyptians from Sais had withdrawn from the circle, but were still in the room, eating and drinking and watching to see what would happen next. The girl continued to play, and the serving boys moved about the room. The Crocodile stood in the shadows, his strange, un-smiling visage impossible to read. Obodas made a signal to his body-guard, who stood and then reached down to help his master to his feet.

"This boy," I said, gesturing to Djet.

Obodas was halfway to his feet. "What did you say?"

"I'll wager this boy."

Obodas peered at me sidelong, then waved back his bodyguard and slowly resettled himself on the rug.

"His name is Djet. He's my slave," I said, trying not to choke on the lie. "And a very talented slave he is. Very talented and clever, and . . . pleasing . . . if you know what I mean. He's yours if you win the next round."

The man looked at me shrewdly.

"And if I don't win?"

"I get the entire pile of coins . . . and . . ." I watched his face carefully. "And . . . the ruby necklace you're wearing."

The three Egyptians laughed. The Crocodile made a hissing sound. The girl's strumming fingers went astray, assaulting our ears with sour notes. Even Djet must have thought I had misjudged the moment, for I heard him draw a sharp breath. But the Nabataean's bodyguard, who knew his master best, shot me a curious look, raised an eyebrow, and pursed his lips.

Obodas glanced at Djet and then at me, then at Djet again, then at the pile of coins. He pulled his fingers from the curly locks of the boy beside him and touched the ruby at his breast.

"What are coins?" he finally said, and shrugged. "And what is a ruby?" Everyone in the room drew a sharp breath. He had accepted the wager. "But you must send the boy from the room while we play."

"Why, Obodas?"

"Because he distracts me. Send him from the room."

"No."

Obodas frowned. He was not used to being challenged. "What did you say, young Roman?"

"The boy stays. Would you send the coins from the room, or the ruby? When men gamble, their wagers remain before them, clearly in sight. Is that not the rule? So Djet remains. Besides, it would be unfair to change the course of his life in an instant, and prevent him from seeing how such a thing occurred."

"Unfair?" Obodas glowered at me. "The boy is your slave. How can you speak of treating a piece of property *fairly*?"

For a moment I thought he had realized that I was deceiving him, and that Djet was not my slave to wager. But he was only scowling at my inscrutable, foreign way of thinking. At last he nodded curtly to show that he agreed. He spoke to the long-haired boy, who reached under Obodas's headdress to unclasp the silver chain. Obodas himself removed the necklace and placed it beside the stacks of coins. The ruby glittered brightly beneath the hanging lamp.

"Very well, Roman. The boy for the coins and the ruby necklace. Shall we begin?"

While the others looked on—even the Crocodile's daughter stopped her strumming to watch—we began the game.

At first, it seemed that Fortuna smiled on me. My throws were good and my progress on the game board steady, while the Nabataean had a slow start. Beside me, Djet squirmed with excitement. The Crocodile hissed and nervously clapped his dark, scaly hands. The three Egyptian travelers, safely out of the game, drank more beer and cheered me on, glad to see the Nabataean bested.

Then everything changed. I threw the dice, and the worst possible sum came up. My progress on the board was reversed, while Obodas swiftly passed me. Each time I threw the dice, Djet moved his lips, muttering a silent prayer or incantation, but to no avail. I suffered one terrible throw after another, as the Nabataean sped toward the finish.

One throw remained. I cast the dice. Disaster! Obodas took his final turn and won the game.

With a lascivious smile, he crooked a finger and summoned Djet toward him.

"No!" I cried. But as I began to rise from the floor, the two sons of the Crocodile restrained me. They were stronger than they looked, and probably used to dealing with troublesome guests.

Obodas stood up, yawned, and stretched his arms while the bodyguard and the long-haired boy collected his takings. "Come, boy," he said, for Djet, frowning and shaking his head, had not budged.

"Djet!" I whispered. He gave me a stricken look. "Forgive me," I said.

Obodas, growing impatient, dispatched the bodyguard to fetch his new acquisition. The hulking brute stepped across the now-empty playing area, took Djet by the hand, and pulled the boy after him, yanking harder than was necessary.

"Careful!" said Obodas. He waved the bodyguard back, then put his arm around Djet. The gesture looked gentle at first, but I noticed that his hand was clamped firmly on Djet's shoulder. "Come, boy.

Your new master is weary, and my host has promised me the softest bed in all Canopus, stuffed with goose down."

Again I tried to stand. Again the sons of the Crocodile restrained me.

Obodas and his little retinue made their way up the stairs. The Egyptian travelers, embarrassed for me, quickly vacated the room. The girl put away her instrument and vanished. The two sons let go of my shoulders, stepped back, and followed their sister.

No one remained in the room but the Crocodile and me.

"Time now to blow out the lamp," he said.

"But . . ."

"Are you not weary and longing for rest?"

I shook my head. "I'll never be able to sleep tonight."

"No worry," said the Crocodile. "I shall give you a sleeping draft, made from herbs that grow in the marshes of the Nile. You will sleep like a child, I promise."

I finally got to my feet. My legs were stiff. My head ached. I touched my nearly empty coin purse. "I'm not sure I have enough money to—"

"Oh, never mind that! Always hungry for coins I may be, but I can be generous, as well. You shall have a fine room tonight, and a fine bed, at no charge."

I sighed, confused by his kindness. Or perhaps it was not so confusing, after all. For keeping a wealthy customer amused all evening, my room and board were a small concession. The Nabataean would go to bed happy and probably leave his host a generous tip when he departed.

I was unsteady on my feet. The Crocodile helped me up the stairs, across the dim vestibule, and down a short hallway, where he showed me to my room. He helped me into my bed, and then produced the sleeping draft he had promised, uncorking a small glass vial to reveal a strange-smelling green concoction within.

After a moment's hesitation, I drank it down, hoping it would bring forgetfulness, for a few hours at least, of the sorry mess I had made of things.

I sank into oblivion.

At some point in the night, I heard a shrill cry. Was it some noctur-nal bird—or was it a boy, crying out in terror, or pain? Was it Djet?

Or did I only dream it? Agitated as I was by the scream, the draft had so stupefied me that I never fully woke, but seemed to hover in the darkness of my little room, semi-conscious, unable to move, with that boyish shriek echoing around me, growing quieter and quieter, until Somnus pulled me back into oblivion.

XII

"Wake up! Wake up!"

Someone was whispering loudly in my ear, and shaking my shoulder.

"Wake up, you half-witted Roman!"

My eyelids seemed to be pasted shut. With a great effort I managed to open them, then saw, by the faint light of a flickering lamp, the face that had been haunting my uneasy dreams. Did I still dream, or was I awake? Was it an apparition I saw, or the boy himself?

"Djet?" I said.

"Shhh! Lower your voice!"

"Is it really you?"

He narrowed his eyes and glowered at me, as if vexed by the sheer stupidity of such a question.

"But . . . what are you doing here?" I said.

"Waking you up, so that we can get away as quickly as possible. Out of bed, now, if you want to save your neck!"

Despite my growing alarm, I could not seem to fully waken. It was the sleeping draft, I thought, stuffing my head with cobwebs and filling my limbs with lead. I managed to roll from the bed, practically falling on the floor, then staggered to my feet.

Djet did his best to steady me. "You're as heavy as a hippopotamus," he complained, "but not nearly as graceful! Now, come!"

"Come where?"

"Anywhere, as long as it's far from here. Pick up that sack and bring it with you. It's too heavy for me. I've carried it as far as I can."

He referred to a cloth sack roughly the size of his head, tied at the top with a bit of hempen rope. I picked it up. The weight was substantial, but not too heavy for a grown man to carry, slung over his shoulder. From within the bulging bag I heard the slithering, clanking sounds of metal sliding against metal. "What's inside?"

"What do you think?"

"Coins?"

"Yes. All that you lost, and more. Now, come!"

I dropped the sack onto the bed. I blinked and rubbed my eyes. Slowly, fitfully, my senses were returning to me. "Djet! It's one thing to abscond with you in the middle of the night. I should never have used you for a wager. I should never have allowed that man to take you from the room! What was I thinking? If you've managed to escape him, good for you! I'll do whatever I can to get you away from here. But if you've robbed him—"

"The coins are yours!"

"No, Djet. I lost them in the game. Fool that I was—"

"Are you coming, or not?"

I stared at the sack. "Perhaps . . . if I take only some of the coins, and leave the rest. We must have money to feed ourselves. . . ."

"Whatever you do, do it quickly!"

I tried to undo the knot and open the sack, but the rope was tightly tied. My head was still groggy from the sleeping draft, and my clumsy fingers refused to obey me. I grunted with frustration and gave up trying to untie the knot.

"What hour is it, Djet?"

"Nearly dawn, I think."

I sighed. "If I'm to run off like a thief, taking you and the money, it would have been better to do so in the middle of the night, to give ourselves a head start. What if the Nabataean rises with the sun? He'll see that you and the money are gone, and send his bodyguards after us."

"No he won't."

"Why not?"

"Because they're all dead."

For a long moment I simply stared at him. "Who is dead?"

"The Nabataean and his bodyguards. And the boy, as well."

My blood ran cold. "Djet! What in the name of all the gods have you done?"

Again he gave me a look to show his vexation at such a stupid question. "It wasn't *I* who killed them, you half-wit! Look at me. Do you think a little fellow like me could overpower two bodyguards and a grown man? The long-haired boy I could have taken in a fight, perhaps—"

"Then, who . . . ?" I left the question unfinished, for the answer was obvious.

"The Crocodile and his sons," said Djet. "Don't ask me how they killed the bodyguards. I didn't see. I was in the room with Obodas and the boy, and the bodyguards were outside somewhere. But I knew they must be dead when the two sons crept into the room, followed by the Crocodile, because I could see they all carried daggers, and there was already blood on those daggers."

"You saw the Crocodile and his sons enter the room?" I whispered.

"Because I was the only one awake."

"Obodas?"

"Fast asleep. So was the boy. Obodas didn't even wake up when they slit his throat. It must have been that green stuff the Crocodile gave him before we went to bed."

"Green stuff?"

"The Crocodile said it was a love tonic. When he heard that, Obodas couldn't drink it fast enough, but instead of making him randy, it put him right to sleep. He never even took off his headdress."

"The sleeping draft," I said. "The Crocodile gave me a dose of the same concoction."

"But the boy did wake up. He was awake when they . . ." Djet shivered. "Did you not hear him cry out?"

I drew a sharp breath. "The scream in the night! Yes, I heard it. But I thought it must be . . . you. How is it that you're still alive, Djet?"

"They were about to kill me, but the Crocodile said they should question me first, to find out more about *you*—where you came from, what you're up to, and so on. While the Crocodile stripped the jewels off Obodas and tucked away the valuables, the two sons gagged me and tied me up. Then they left me there, lying on the floor, while they dragged the bodies out of the room. And that's the last I saw of them."

"But how did you get away?"

"They did a poor job of tying me up. I managed to wriggle free."

"And you brought that sack with you . . ."

"Exactly. And the Crocodile and his sons are likely to come back at any moment. They'll see that I'm gone, and that the sack is gone, and they'll come for you. Do you finally understand, you half-wit Roman? We need to go, at once!"

At last I was fully awake. My heart pounded in my chest. I picked up the sack and slung it over my shoulder.

"Show me the way, Djet."

Holding the lamp before him, he led me from the room and down the hallway. In the vestibule, he blew out the lamp. I quietly opened the door. The world outside was dimly lit by the first faint promise of dawn.

The air was fresh and cool. A maze of leafy silhouettes surrounded us, revealing no clear way out of the little oasis. We had approached the inn in darkness, with the local boy to guide us. I could not remember the route.

"This way," whispered Djet.

"Are you sure?"

"Yes. This will lead us back to the main road."

I was dubious, but since I had no better idea, I followed him—and a moment later I tripped over something large and fleshy lying in our path. As I stumbled, the metallic clanging of the sack slung over my shoulder seemed loud in the stillness.

I recovered my balance and looked down. The thing I had tripped over was a body lying on its back. The corpse's face was hidden by deep shadows, but by his beard I took him to be the bodyguard who had sat behind Obodas while we played. The gore of his slashed throat glittered darkly.

Startled into silence, Djet took my hand and urgently pulled me onward.

The way was closely hemmed by fronds and leaves that barely made a sound as we brushed past. The sand beneath our feet was well trodden and firmly packed. Still, I held my breath at the faintest noise, and kept the sack as steady as I could.

We emerged from a densely shaded patch and suddenly confronted the soft glow of a lamp, the same lamp that had hung over the game of Pharaoh's Beard, now held aloft by the Crocodile to illuminate the digging of a shallow grave.

Practically at our feet, heaped together, were the corpses of Obodas and the boy. The boy was still dressed in his bright red tunic, which was covered with stains of a darker red, especially at the neck, but Obodas had been stripped of his Nabataean robes and headdress. One of the Crocodile's sons had put them on—strange garments to wear while standing in a hole and shoveling dirt.

The other son was using his bare hands to scrape dirt from the hole, while the Crocodile stood over them with the lamp. By its lurid glow, I saw the faces of all three, and barely suppressed a gasp. Their features were no longer even remotely human. They were animal-headed nightmares.

"Deeper than that!" said the Crocodile. He made a sound between a giggle and a hiss. "It has to be big enough for all four of them. Deeper, boys! Faster! As soon as we're done here, we'll go back to the inn and take care of that sleepyhead Roman and his squirmy little slave. Come daylight, we'll send those three simpletons from Sais on their way. And then—"

"Then we'll count the coins, eh, papa?" said the son with the shovel.

"And put the rings on our fingers, and take turns wearing the pretty ruby necklace?" said the other.

"The ruby is for your sister, boys. With a dowry like that, she can marry into the richest family in Canopus. But for now, keep digging. Deeper! Faster!"

Djet tugged at my hand, trying to lead me back the way we had come. Slowly, silently, my heart pounding in my chest, I drew back from the area illuminated by the glowing lamp.

Djet and I retraced our steps until we found another path, which branched to one side. As we stepped into a small clearing, I tripped over another body—the corpse of the second bodyguard. Tied to a nearby palm tree were the Nabataean's camels, stripped for the night of their riding accouterments, which were neatly bundled and stacked nearby. There were also some leather skins filled with water and a bit of food, ready to be loaded onto the camels.

I had never yet met a camel I liked, or one that liked me. But I had learned how to ride one. I quickly outfitted the strongest-looking beast, and amid the trappings I found a place to store the bag of coins. Speaking the words I had been taught, I convinced the beast to kneel. I mounted it, and then reached for Djet, who stepped back, out of reach.

"What's wrong?" I said.

"I've never been on one of those."

"This will be your first camel ride, then. Lucky boy."

"Don't they bite?"

"Never. Nor do they spit. The camel is the kindest and most docile of all creatures."

"You're lying!"

"Had you rather stay here and end up like that?" I gestured to the corpse of the bodyguard. The growing light now revealed the full horror of the gaping wound at his throat.

Djet scrambled onto the camel and seated himself behind me.

"Hut! Hut!" I grunted, and snapped the reins. The camel gave a snort and rose to its full height. Djet squealed and clutched me, holding fast. "Hut! Hut!" I repeated, and off we went at a steady trot, leaving the oasis and the Inn of the Hungry Crocodile behind.

The last of the stars had vanished. The road before us and the scrubby vegetation on either side grew lighter by the moment. With the sun poised to rise in our faces, we headed toward the Nile.

XIII

That day I strove to put as much distance as I could between us and the Hungry Crocodile.

I smelled the river long before we reached it—the rich, fecund, moist, reedy, fishy scent of the Nile and the alluvial soil of its widespread mouth, so powerful and pervasive that for as long as we remained in the Delta, the smell was around me everywhere and at every moment, day and night. Every part of me—my clothes, my hair, even my skin—would become steeped in this odor.

Following the route dictated by Tafhapy, I turned south when we reached the first branch of the Nile and took the road toward Sais.

There was little traffic on the road. When we stopped to eat at a roadside inn, we were the only customers. When we were obliged to cross the water, we were the only passengers on the ferry. This was not the harvest season, nor the trading season, but the quietest time of year. The growing fear of bandits also discouraged travelers. I felt rather conspicuous clopping along on camelback with Djet behind me—but conspicuous to whom? For long stretches, there was not another person in sight.

Not far from Sais, during a break to stretch our legs and relieve ourselves at the river's edge, I decided to broach a delicate subject.

"You know, Djet, that I regret having wagered you."

He shrugged. "It was my idea."

"Yes, Djet, but you are a child, and a slave, while I am a free man. It was my decision, and it was a bad one."

"Yet it turned out all right in the end."

"Did it?"

"Of course. Are we not here, away from that awful place, standing in the pleasant shade of this sycamore tree, adding water to the Nile? I am still a slave, yes. And you are still a Roman and a half-wit, yes. But are we not both alive? And do you not have a bag full of treasure?"

I nodded slowly. "Yes, all that is true—"

"Even the part about you being a half-wit?" He giggled.

I bit my tongue. "But I have to wonder . . ."

"You want to know if the Nabataean took advantage of me."

I sighed. "Yes."

"Because if he did so, it was without my master's knowledge or permission, and Tafhapy will be very angry with you."

"No, Djet. It's not Tafhapy I'm concerned about."

"Oh, is it me that you're worried about? Me, the piece of property you wagered to get your hands on that ruby?"

Again I bit my tongue. "Yes, Djet."

"I already told you what happened. Obodas drank the sleeping draft, thinking it was a love potion, and that was that."

"He fell asleep at once?"

"He drank the draft one moment, and was snoring the next, lying there fully dressed with drool spilling from the corner of his mouth."

"He did nothing to abuse you, then? When I heard that scream in the middle of the night—"

"That was the other boy, having his throat cut."

"I know that now. But at the time—"

"You thought it was me." He raised an eyebrow. "Yet you didn't come running to rescue me."

"I was drugged, Djet, just as Obodas was."

He smirked. "I suppose I should spin a long, hair-raising story about the tortures to which he subjected me, and all the terrible things I was made to do, just to watch your face. But it would be a lie." He threw back his head and laughed. "How great this goddess Fortuna must be, and how she must love you!"

After my foolish behavior at the inn, and with Bethesda still gone, I judged myself the most wretched of men, not the most fortunate. "Why do you say such a thing, Djet?"

"Think about it. If you *had* won that final round, and with it all the coins and the ruby necklace, then the Crocodile and his sons would have come to kill *you* in the night—and me as well, since I would have been in the room with you. Instead, the Nabataean is dead, and you're alive, and here we are, happily on our way, with more treasure than you could dream of. Had you won, you'd have lost everything. By losing, you won."

I nodded, then gave a start.

"What did you just say about the treasure?"

"More than you could dream of!"

I peered across the river, scanning the distant bank. I walked up to the road and looked in all directions. There was no one in sight. I retrieved the sack from the camel's trappings, then hurried back to our secluded spot by the water's edge. I untied the rope and looked inside the sack.

I drew a sharp breath, then groaned with dismay.

In my addled state, and in our desperate rush to escape from the inn, I had failed to understand exactly what the sack contained. For some reason, I had thought there were only coins inside. Indeed, there were a great many coins—but that was not all.

With trembling fingers, I reached inside and pulled out the ruby necklace. It had been dazzling by lamplight; it was even more so by daylight. The crimson stone glittered in the dappled sunlight, so brightly that it seemed to contain a dancing flame within.

I peered inside the sack and saw more jewels—lapis and turquoise, carnelian and sapphire—mounted in the rings that the Crocodile and his sons had pulled from the dead man's fingers.

I sat down on the riverbank, shaking my head. "Disaster!" I whispered. "Doom and disaster!"

"What's wrong?" said Djet. "Why are you not happy? You're a rich man!"

"A dead man, more likely."

Djet frowned.

"Don't you see, Djet? If I had taken only the coins, that would be one thing. Any man might have a bag full of coins, even me. But a ruby? And all these rings? They mark me as a thief, as surely as if I had a brand on my forehead. Men have their hands cut off, or worse, for stealing nothing more than bread. What will become of me if an agent of the king or of some local magistrate should stop us and find the jewels?"

"You didn't worry about that when you wagered me for the ruby."

"Because I wasn't thinking straight. These treasures are a curse, not a blessing!"

I drew back my hand to cast the ruby necklace into the river, but Djet grabbed my forearm with both of his small hands.

"Give it to me, then, if you don't want it!" he cried.

"And pass the curse to a child?"

"Why do you say that it brings bad fortune?"

"What sort of luck did it bring the Nabataean?"

Djet slowly released my arm and stepped back. From the look on his face I knew he was thinking of Obodas as we had last seen him, lying naked with his throat cut beside the grave being dug for him.

"But why should any agent of the king stop and question you?"

"The Crocodile may set them on our trail. With the money and jewels gone, what's to stop him from reporting the theft to the authorities, showing them the dead bodies and blaming me for the murders?"

"But . . . he doesn't know where you're headed."

"Yes, that's true. But . . ." I felt a prickle of dread. "He knows my name! Don't you remember? I introduced myself to him at the front door."

Djet frowned. "Yes, I wondered about that at the time."

"What do you mean?"

"Well, in all the legends and fables, a traveler at an inn always gives a made-up name and a false account of himself. Even a child and a slave such as I knows that. Don't ask me why, since I myself have never told an untruth, but that's how it always goes in the stories. So when I heard you say, 'My name is Gordianus, and I come from Alexandria,' I thought: *That is very strange. I wonder if this Roman has any idea what he's doing?* But of course, I didn't say anything. Who am I? Only Djet, a child and a slave, as you keep reminding me."

Not for the first time on our journey, I felt an impulse to strangle him.

For a long moment I sat on the riverbank and stared at the ruby, fascinated by the dancing of the red fire inside as I turned the stone this way and that to capture the glittering sunlight on the water.

I narrowed my eyes until I saw only the fiery scintillation of the ruby, and suddenly I had a vision of Bethesda wearing the necklace, a fantasy so beautiful that it brought tears to my eyes, and so compelling that I wondered if it might be a premonition of the future.

I made up my mind. I would bring the ruby to Bethesda—or let the ruby bring me to her.

I put the necklace in the sack, tied the rope, and returned the treasure to its hiding place amid the camel's trappings.

Thus did we arrive, a short while later, in the sleepy town of Sais. Did we look like two desperate outlaws in flight, carrying jewels stolen from a dead man? Or simply like two weary travelers, a slightly bemused young Roman and an even younger slave boy? I had nothing to feel guilty about, I kept telling myself, and I tried to compose my features accordingly while we shopped for food and provisions in the market.

When it came time to find lodgings for the night, I chose the most unfrequented-looking inn I could find, at the far end of town. It was a modest structure made of clay bricks daubed with mud. To my relief, the woman who answered the door more closely resembled a friendly hippopotamus than a hungry crocodile. The widow Teti was a woman of middle years with a toothy smile. Since the day was drawing to a close, and it appeared we would be her only guests for the night, she invited us to make ourselves at home. The only other person in the inn was a young serving girl as slender and silent as her mistress was plump and talkative.

Mindful of Djet's observation, I introduced myself not as Gordianus but as Marcus Pecunius, youngest son of a Roman businessman in Alexandria, and I told her I was on a pleasure trip, traveling upriver to see the pyramids. If you must pass yourself off as something you are not, my father once told me, make your story simple, plausible, and easy to remember.

"Why 'Pecunius'?" whispered Djet, as we led the camel to its sleeping place for the night amid the pens for sheep and goats and a small chicken coop behind the inn. Flies were everywhere.

"It's a name I just invented, from a Latin word for wealthy."

"You made it up?"

"If you must give a false name, my father once told me, make sure it doesn't already belong to someone who might be in even more trouble than yourself. What could be safer than a name that doesn't exist? No Egyptian will know the difference, I should think. And Pecunius makes a good name for the bearer of that ruby. Which raises a question: what should I do with this sack tonight? It might look suspicious if I carry it with me at all times. I suppose it can stay in our room while the widow feeds us, and when I go to bed I'll use it for a pillow, though I usually prefer something softer."

"I should think such a pillow will give you beautiful dreams of the goddess Fortuna," said Djet. "You must tell me more about her, and how I should go about worshiping her."

"You, Djet?"

"Did she not save us both from the Crocodile, and me from the clutches of—"

I raised my finger to shush him, for the widow was coming toward us. Her ample breasts swayed in one direction while her hips swayed in the other. Dangling from one of her fists was a dead chicken. Teti came to a halt in front of us and proudly displayed the carcass. Flies swarmed around her.

"This one's stopped laying, so it was time to put her to rest," she said.

"Did you wring its neck yourself?" said Djet.

"I did. I'd have let you watch, little boy, if I'd known you were interested. Which do you prefer, Marcus Pecunius, the succulent thigh or the plump breast? I promise they will be equally moist and delicious." Teti gave me a coy look and began plucking feathers from the chicken.

"Whatever you prepare, I will gratefully receive."

"Oh, what a way you have with words! I've heard about you Romans and your slippery tongues."

"We *are* known for giving speeches," I admitted.

"Well, let me go see what I can conjure up for you and the boy." Feathers flew this way and that. "My late husband always bragged that I was the best cook in Sais. A young fellow like you must work up quite an appetite, seated high atop that camel all day, gripping its hump with your strong thighs."

"Yes, I'm quite hungry," I said.

"A good meal will give you back your strength. You just might need it."

"For what?"

She threw back her head and laughed, then waddled away amid a flurry of feathers and swarming flies.

Djet gave me a sidelong look.

"What?" I said.

"I escaped from Obodas, thanks to Fortuna. But I'm not sure that even Fortuna can protect you from Teti."

I frowned. "What are you suggesting? The widow is old enough to be my mother."

"Have you never known the touch of an older woman?"

"As a matter of fact . . ." I recalled my visit to Halicarnassus, and the time I spent with another widow; but in no way did Teti resemble the beautiful and alluring Bitto. "What would you know about such things, anyway?" I smacked his head. "Now keep quiet and help me tend to the camel. An awful lot of flies around here, aren't there?" No sooner did I wave one away than another took its place.

"Yes, when you return me to my master and he asks for my report, I shall call this the Inn of a Thousand and One Flies."

I laughed and lowered my voice. "I was thinking we might call it the Inn of the Friendly Hippopotamus."

Later, Teti joined us in the small common room of the inn while the silent girl served us the chicken, which had been cut into small pieces and smothered in a delicious sauce of ground dates and almond paste. Teti asked me a great many questions. The more personal of these I deflected as best I could, keeping in mind my guise as Marcus Pecunius. Having never stepped foot outside Sais, she appeared to know little of the world, and it seemed that virtually anything I said about myself, true or made up, was likely to satisfy her.

She did, however, know a great deal about the royal family, and was eager for any news or gossip I could give her. Was the king really as fat as everyone said? Had the people lost all love for him? Was it true that his son on the island of Cos had been kidnapped by their cousin Mithridates? Had I heard the rumor that there existed a member of the royal family brought up in secret who might any day now present himself to the people and stake a claim to the throne? I finally confessed that she must know far more about the Ptolemies and their doings than did I, an inattentive and not particularly observant foreigner.

After the meal, Teti offered to have the serving girl sing for us—apparently she was not always silent—but I pleaded weariness, and with Djet headed straight for our room.

I threw off all my clothes and reclined naked on the narrow bed, covering myself with the linen sheet and using the treasure sack for a pillow. Djet took the real pillow and slept on the floor, directly in front of the door. So it often happened in stories, he told me, that a slave would serve to block the doorway. This simple precaution struck me as quite sensible.

And yet, somehow, at some dark hour of the night, another person joined us in the room. I woke from a troubled dream, my forehead beaded with sweat, to see a hulking silhouette looming over me.

XIV

"Teti!" I whispered. "What are you doing here? How did you get in? Where is Djet?" I tried to sit up, but felt strangely lightheaded.

"I don't know where the boy has gone," she said. "But I saw him leave the room a few moments ago—and I took that to be my cue."

"Your cue?"

"To join you, Marcus Pecunius. Or should I just call you Marcus? Is that not the Roman custom, to use the first name when two people become . . . close friends?"

As far as I was concerned, she had already come close enough. Again I tried to sit up, and again I was thwarted by an odd sensation in my head and a weakness in my limbs. Had I been drugged again, this time by Teti? Was it a standard practice for Egyptian innkeepers to sedate their guests so as to take advantage of them?

"Teti, I'm not feeling well."

"Ah, you're tired, that's all. Some fresh air will revive you." She walked to the small window, unlatched the shutters, and pulled them open. By the moonlight I saw her more clearly.

She was completely naked.

I swallowed. My throat felt dry and scratchy. "I closed that window to keep out the flies," I said.

"Flies?" She laughed. "The flies are all asleep, silly man."

"You'll let in the damp night air." I was used to sleeping in a city by the sea, refreshed by salubrious sea breezes. The air of the Delta was sultry and humid, especially at night, when oppressive vapors rose from the riverbanks and marshes. Was that why I felt so sluggish and out of sorts?

Despite my objections, Teti left the shutters open. She stepped away from the window and drew relentlessly closer.

To be honest, and to be fair, I was not entirely put off by her advances. The sight of her naked figure by moonlight had in fact stirred something in me—if not exactly lust, then at least a quiver of curiosity. Teti was no Venus, at least not as Greeks and Romans like to picture the goddess of love, with a slender waist and elegant breasts. She more closely resembled those archaic images I had seen in certain temples in my travels, goddesses of fertility who were all voluptuous hips and breasts and buttocks. Seeing Teti unclothed, no one could say she was not a robust specimen of womanhood. And if one liked that sort of thing, there was a great deal of her to like.

But what she had in mind was simply not possible. There were two reasons for this.

The first reason was Bethesda.

Like an actor in a play, I had an impulse to clutch the thin coverlet to my chin and cry out, "No, Teti! I cannot do it! My heart belongs to another!" While I did cover myself with the sheet, I kept my mouth shut. Staid Roman that I was, all my instincts cried out against making a public declaration of my feelings for a slave, even if the only person present to hear it was Teti.

From whence came this impulse to be faithful to Bethesda? To be chaste is hardly a Roman virtue, at least not for a man; to be faithful might be, if the woman is one's wife, but Bethesda was not and surely never could be that. I was a man—a freeborn, unmarried citizen of Rome—so what was there to prevent me from indulging in a bit of harmless sport with an available female, if I desired to do so?

There was the problem: I did not desire it, and would not have done so even if Teti had looked like Helen of Troy. Indeed, the more beautiful the temptress, the more I would have shrunk from her. Such was the state of my manhood. Whatever stirrings I felt at the sight of a desirable female—I had seen quite a few in Canopus—became transmuted at once into thoughts of Bethesda, and those thoughts brought not pleasure but pain.

Was she remaining faithful to me during our separation? Even if that were her desire, had some brute forced himself on her? Had more than one brute done so? Had Bethesda forsaken me? Had she forgotten me? Was she making any effort to return to me? Would I ever see her again? Was she even still alive?

One tortured thought led to another—all beginning with the sight of an attractive woman. Thus did the faintest quiver of desire lead me not to lust but to misery. I could no longer even please myself. My natural instincts had become perverted, and all because of something the poets call "love." Love had made me a eunuch.

There was no way I could explain all this to Teti as she stood there naked and grinning at me. So I simply said nothing.

There was a second reason why the union Teti desired could not possibly be consummated. At any moment, I was going to be violently sick.

More beads of sweat erupted across my forehead. The veins at my temples pounded, and a million flies buzzed inside my head. My hands felt clammy. My belly stiffened with cramps. My chest heaved. My throat began to spasm.

As waves of nausea surged through me, I knew that I must have been poisoned. Had Teti put a love potion in my food and mistaken the dose? Was she a cold-blooded murderer and a thief, like the Crocodile?

More likely, I thought, the chicken was to blame.

Never eat chicken from a stranger's kitchen: so my father had told me. It seemed that the longer I was away from him, the less I heeded his wise counsel, and the more trouble I got myself into.

I threw back the linen sheet. Seeing me naked and covered with sweat, Teti mistook the gesture for an invitation. As she attempted to climb onto the bed, I struggled to slip past her, and our limbs became entangled. Any god who happened to be looking down at us must have had a good laugh at such a grotesque parody of the act of love, all flailing flesh and desperate grunts.

At last I extricated myself and ran to the window. I stuck my head outside just in time. My whole body heaved and convulsed.

From directly below me, I heard a wail of distress. It was Djet. He scampered out of the way on all fours. When he was clear, he looked up at me with a miserable expression. "You, too?" he said. And then, as if to mock me, he likewise began to vomit.

So that was why he had abandoned his post at the door—the malady must have struck him only moments before it struck me.

For quite some time the two of us were gripped by nausea. Djet stayed where he was, on all fours, while I leaned out the window. Gradually, the paroxysms subsided, then returned, then subsided again.

Wiping his mouth, Djet spoke in a weak voice. "Do you think it was . . . ?"

"The chicken," I said.

He nodded, then proceeded to convulse yet again. It seemed remarkable that such a small fellow could have so much inside him that needed to come out.

At last my nausea subsided, leaving me faint and exhausted. I turned around to see that Teti had vanished from the room. Had she been repulsed by my sickness, or had she too been afflicted?

Whatever the case, I was glad to be left in peace as I staggered across the room and fell back into bed. I grimaced as my head struck not a soft pillow, but the hard, bulging treasure sack. At least the problem of the ruby gave me something to think about other than my physical misery, and I found myself clutching the sack as I gradually, fitfully, returned to a realm of uneasy dreams.

I was up at dawn. Djet had returned to the room and had taken his place on the floor in front of the door. I nudged him awake and told him to go and prepare the camel so that we could set out at once.

"But I don't know how to dress a camel," he complained.

"You saw me put on the trappings yesterday, and you helped me take them off. You can at least fill the water skins."

"What if the beast bites me?"

"I told you, camels never bite. Now run along."

I headed for the kitchen, where a great many flies were already buzzing about. The serving girl was up, and asked if I wanted some dates or a bowl of farina with goat's milk. My empty stomach was growling to be fed, but I dared to eat only a few crusts of stale bread and to sip some cool water.

Teti appeared, wearing a loose sleeping gown made of linen so sheer that I could see every voluptuous curve and recess of her body. To judge by her cheerful demeanor, she had not been sick after all. Nor did the serving girl appear to have been ill.

"Marcus Pecunius," she said, opening her arms to give me a commiserating hug. "Are you feeling better this morning?"

"Weak, but well."

"And will you be staying another night, so that I may have the chance to send you from Sais with a better estimation of my house?" The words were formal, but her fluttering eyes spoke a different language.

"Alas, Teti, I must leave at once. The pyramids call to me."

"And how can I compare with those?" she sighed, placing a hand upon her heaving breasts.

"Don't worry about last night," I said. "I couldn't have asked for a warmer welcome."

"Ah, you silver-tongued Roman! Perhaps, on your way back . . . ?"

"Perhaps."

"You will always be welcome here, Marcus Pecunius. Now, you and the boy will need food for your journey. There might be a bit of last night's chicken still in the clay jar—"

My stomach gave a lurch. "No, no, Teti, I bought some simple provisions yesterday, and I'm sure we'll find plenty to eat along the way."

"As you wish, Marcus Pecunius."

I settled my account with her, then went out back to help Djet. To my surprise, he had already fitted the camel with its trappings. I checked all the straps and other pieces of tack and saw that he had done an excellent job. He had also filled the water skins. I had only to tuck the treasure sack safely away, and we could be off.

From the place where we stood, behind the inn, I had a narrow view of the street that ran in front of the establishment. As we made ready, I saw a figure approaching the inn, but he did not see me. I had only a fleeting glimpse of the man, but there was something familiar about his long gray beard. I heard him knock on the front door.

"Teti!" he called. "Teti, are you up?"

I recognized his voice at once. It was Harkhebi, the leader of the city fathers of Sais with whom I had played Pharaoh's Beard at the Inn of the Hungry Crocodile.

I turned to Djet. "Keep very quiet and stay where you are," I whispered.

"What's happening?"

"Never mind. Just stay here until I come back."

I crept along the side of the inn and got as close to the entrance as I could, staying out of sight. Teti had stepped outside to greet her visitor. From the way they spoke, I realized that Harkhebi and Teti were neighbors and knew each other well.

"How was your trip to Alexandria?" said Teti.

Harkhebi made a rude noise. "The king gave us nothing! He's useless—and if you believe the gossip, not long for the throne."

"Ah, speaking of Alexandria—"

I drew a sharp breath, thinking she was about to mention me. But Harkhebi interrupted her.

"We returned to Sais late last night, after traveling all day."

"But here you are, up bright and early."

"Because there's something I need to tell everyone, and I'll start with you, Teti. On the trip back from the city, we stopped at a place called Canopus. What a disgusting sinkhole of vice that town is! Full of prostitutes and drinking establishments and gambling dens."

What a hypocrite! When it came to guzzling beer and placing wagers, Harkhebi had matched me round for round. Now that he was back in Sais, he played the upright city father.

"It must be a terrible place," said Teti, in a tone that indicated she would gladly hear more.

"More terrible than you can imagine—for when we woke, after spending the night in one of those places, what should we discover but that one of the other guests had been murdered."

"Murdered? Holy Isis! Tell me more."

"The victim was a wealthy trader from Nabataea. A boy traveling with him and two bodyguards also had their throats cut."

Teti gasped. "But who would do such a thing? And why?"

"The killer was one of the other guests. He raced off on a stolen camel at dawn, taking with him all the money the Nabataean had been carrying, as well as the poor man's rings. He also took a ruby necklace."

"A ruby?"

"A fabulous gem, worth a fortune. The crime was so audacious that the city fathers of Canopus have put a bounty on this killer and promised a reward for the return of the ruby."

"'This killer,' you say—was it only one man? How did one man overcome four victims?"

"He isn't just any man. He's a Roman! Truly, they must be the most bloodthirsty people on earth. I shall never stay under the same roof with a Roman again."

"A Roman, you say?" Teti's tone was suddenly flat.

"Yes, a young Roman who'd come from Alexandria, traveling with a boy."

"With . . . a boy, you say? The two of them, traveling on a camel?"

"Yes. No one is sure which way they went, but there's a chance they were headed here to Sais. I'm warning everyone in town, especially the innkeepers, to be on the lookout for this monster."

"And if he should appear?"

"My advice would be to kill him on the spot, as you would a

dangerous snake! Then send his head to Canopus and claim the bounty. There's a very generous reward for the recovery of the ruby, as well."

"Is that so?"

"Yes. Of course, he may never come to Sais; I don't want to alarm you unduly, Teti. Even if he does come here, what are the chances he would stay at your inn?"

There was a long silence, during which I held my breath.

At last I heard Teti sigh. "Well, there's been no such person here at my inn."

"For your sake, I'm glad to hear it. But be on the lookout, Teti. This Roman has killed once and may kill again."

"He sounds like quite a man."

"A dangerous man, Teti!"

"Yes, indeed."

"Well, I must be off, to warn everyone else in town. Farewell, Teti."

"Farewell, Harkhebi."

I quickly crept to the back of the building. I pulled the treasure sack from the camel's trappings, reached inside, then put it back.

"What's going on?" said Djet.

"I'll tell you later. Now keep your mouth shut!"

Teti appeared at the back door.

"Marcus Pecunius . . . ," she began, a stricken look on her face.

"Say nothing, Teti!" I raced to her and pressed a finger to her lips. "There are no words for such a parting. Alas, what might have occurred last night did not occur—the gods looked down and were jealous of us, Teti! But I promise I shall not forget you. And so that you don't forget me, I want to give you something."

"A gift . . . for me?"

"Yes, Teti. Do you like it?" I produced the ring I had pulled from the sack. The band was of silver and the setting of lapis lazuli.

"Oh, Marcus, it's beautiful!"

"Think of me when you wear it, Teti."

"Oh, Marcus, I shall." Her face glowed, and tears came to her eyes.

She hid her face and turned back toward the door. "You mustn't see me cry, Marcus. And you must be off—at once! Soon everyone in Sais will be looking for you. Go, Marcus!" She ran inside.

Djet gave me a look as if to say: what in Hades was that about?

I induced the camel to kneel, mounted the beast, and helped Djet climb behind me. "Hut! Hut!" I cried.

Djet, who could keep his mouth shut no longer, squealed with laughter as the camel rose up. "Fortuna shows how she loves you again!" he cried.

"What are you talking about?"

"Last night, I thought: how terrible, that the Roman should be so sick. What a disgusting sight you were! But that was Fortuna's way of saving you."

"From what?"

"From that hippopotamus! Isn't that what you called her yesterday? A friendly hippopotamus? How terrible, if Teti the hippopotamus had had her way with you. But Fortuna struck you ill, and so you escaped such an awful fate. Still, I don't see why you spoke all that gibberish to her and gave her that ring—"

"By Hercules, Djet, keep your voice down! What if she were to hear you?"

As we rode away from the inn, I glanced back to see Teti standing on the front doorstep. Her arms were tightly crossed and there was a scowl on her tear-stained face. Had she overheard the insult? Perhaps not, I told myself. Perhaps she was simply upset to see me go.

But as we rounded a corner and rode out of sight, I saw her pull the lapis lazuli ring from her finger and throw it onto the ground.

"Harkhebi!" she shouted. "Harkhebi, come back!"

"Hut! Hut!" I cried, and snapped the reins, urging the camel to go faster.

XV

Thus did I become a wanted man and an outlaw, racing across the Delta with a bounty on my head.

Harkhebi must have been slow to mount a pursuit, or perhaps he sent the men of Sais in the wrong direction, thinking I was heading upriver, as I had told Teti. In any event, driving the camel at a swift pace, we made our escape from Sais without incident.

As soon as I could, I left the main road, and from that point onward I kept as much as possible to side roads. I skirted the towns, thinking it safer to ask for directions and buy provisions at isolated trading posts. I feared to seek shelter at any inn, so we slept in whatever secluded spot I could find. Fortunately, the nights were dry and mild, but each morning I woke in despair. Necessity had driven me to stray from the directions I had been given by Tafhapy, and as a result I was often lost and unsure which way to go next. Finding the Cuckoo's Nest had always been a tricky proposition; now I feared I might never do so.

What a mess I had made of everything!

And yet, day by day, we made steady progress, penetrating farther and farther into the heart of the Delta. The languid mood of the place began to calm me. Low, desolate hills alternated with marshes and mudflats. Sluggish streams and stagnant pools teemed with insects. Hippopotami became a regular sight, as did crocodiles. Because the Nile was near its low point, crossings that at other times of year would have required a ferry ride were easily crossed on camelback, as long as one avoided becoming mired in mud.

The drabness of the Delta alternated with unexpected splendor. One morning, in the middle of nowhere, we came upon a vast, shallow lake inhabited by thousands of long-legged birds with magnificent beaks and wings of a delicate pink color, like the inner surface of a seashell. As we watched, a large group of them took to the air, wheeled above our heads, and then returned to the water, whereupon another group took off. The lake became an arena of constant motion, with some of the birds performing their aerial dance while others flocked together on the water.

"Flamingos!" cried Djet.

"You've seen these creatures before?"

"Only in pictures in the temples of Ra. I never thought to see a real one. I wonder if we shall see a phoenix, as well?"

"But surely the phoenix exists only in legends."

"Not so! They live in the Delta. Everyone says so."

Who was I to contradict him? Until that morning I had not known that such a bird as the flamingo existed. "Beautiful!" I whispered, and for as long as I watched the pink birds I felt at peace in that strange, secluded place.

As our progress continued, and no one we met seemed to be unduly alarmed by a young Roman and a boy traveling on camelback, I began to let down my guard. It seemed that I had outrun the warnings about me. Perhaps, if my pursuers thought I had traveled south, news of the murders in Canopus would never reach the inner Delta.

My despair also began to recede, for I began to think that we might indeed be drawing nearer to the Cuckoo's Nest. Whenever I spoke to the locals, I tried to bring up the subject of bandits in a casual way, expressing the natural curiosity of a stranger passing through. Many of the people I met refused to talk about bandits, as if they feared reprisals for doing so, but others conversed freely about the raiders, pirates, thieves, and kidnappers who inhabited the Delta. Many spoke of these villains in tones of admiration or even awe, as if they were some sort of heroes.

One day I found myself at a drowsy little trading post located on the branch of the Nile along which, according to Tafhapy, the Cuckoo's Nest might be found. The day was warm, but an awning along one side of the ramshackle building offered shade, and a few simple benches provided places to sit. As is typical of such trading posts, along with the proprietor there were several locals hanging about, regulars who probably spent the better part of each day sitting idly in the shade, sipping beer, happy to chat with any traveler who happened by. Among them was a toothless, white-haired Egyptian so weathered by the sun that he looked to have been carved from a block of ebony, and so wrinkled I could hardly make out the eyes in his face. His name was Hepu, and he had a lot to say on the subject of bandits.

"Ever since I was young, roaming gangs of outlaws have lived in the Delta," Hepu told me. He turned his gaze to Djet. "When I was a boy—no older than you, little man—I dreamed of joining them, and living the bandit's life. But soon enough my father whipped that idea out of me!" He cackled at the memory.

"But why would any man wish to become an outlaw?" I said. It was not an idle question, considering the situation in which I found myself.

"Better to ask, why should a man wish for the law-abiding life of a farmer or tradesman, with hungry children to feed, a wife to scold him, and the king's tax collectors to make his life a misery? The bandits live as free men, without those cares."

The owner of the trading post laughed. Menkhep was a squat, thick-limbed man with big shoulders. The top of his head was perfectly bald, but the fringe of hair above his ears was iron gray and as curly as lamb's wool. "Old Hepu is always spouting nonsense about what a wonderful life the bandits lead. Yet here he sits, day after day. I don't see you running off to join the Cuckoo's Gang, Hepu."

I pricked up my ears.

"That's because I'm too old," said Hepu. "They wouldn't have me. The Cuckoo's Gang recruits only the young and able-bodied, or men who have some useful skill. Ah, but a fellow like you, Menkhep—you might be of interest to them."

"Me? What use would a bandit gang have for a shopkeeper?"

"You know how to count money!" Hepu laughed. "And since your wife died, you have no woman to hold you back. You're still young and strong."

"So it might seem to an old man like you." Menkhep sighed. "To my eyes, the Roman here looks young and strong." He gave me a friendly punch to the shoulder.

Hepu nodded. "And he must speak Latin. That's a skill the bandits could use."

"How so?" I said.

"Imagine that a ship founders on the coast—shipwrecks happen more often than you might think—and the bandits raid the cargo and carry off the survivors. Among their captives are some wealthy Romans. The kidnappers would need someone to translate the ransom demands."

Another of the chin-waggers, who was almost as old as Hepu, gave me a leer. "And if some of those Roman prisoners were women, the bandits would need someone to sweet-talk them out of their clothes—in Latin!"

Hepu turned up his nose. "To the contrary, as a rule the bandits are very respectful of any female they capture."

"Really?" I said, thinking of Bethesda.

"If the woman is poor, the bandits are likely to simply let her go, out of mercy. If she's a slave, she's treated as booty, and sold at the first opportunity—or she might even be set free. If she appears to be wealthy and might fetch a ransom, the bandits keep her captive but treat her with great care. There's a code of conduct among such men, and that code decrees that no woman, slave or free, rich or poor, is to be mistreated. Any bandit who breaks that code soon finds himself cast out."

Did Hepu know what he was talking about? I wanted to believe him.

"What *do* the bandits do for female companionship?" I asked.

"They do without it—lucky fellows!" Hepu chortled. "No women live with the bandits, or travel alongside them. Only men are allowed—and what a paradise that must be! Oh, I daresay some of them have sweethearts in villages here and there, or visit brothels when they venture into town to spend their money. But no women are allowed to live among them—nor any young boys, either." He cast a glance at Djet. "Women and pretty boys lead to nothing but trouble."

"I should think there would always be trouble among such men," I said. "With no rule of law to guide them, they must fight constantly—arguing over booty, bullying each other—the stronger dominating the weak."

Hepu shook his head. "If they wanted that sort of life, they would stay in the regular world! Were you not listening when I said the bandits follow a strict code of conduct? There's no fighting over spoils. They divide everything that comes to them, equally—that's the rule."

"Every man takes the same share?" said Djet.

"Just so."

"Even the leader?" Djet seemed fascinated by such an idea.

"Especially the leader! How do you think a man becomes the leader of a bandit gang? The others choose him, by a vote. If the leader should ever cheat them, or abuse them, or claim special privileges, soon enough he finds himself without a head, and the bandits pick a new man to lead them. It's not like in the regular world, where a man who's above you is above you all your life, because that's how you both were born and you have no say in the matter. Ah, the bandits live a freer life than most of us can dream of."

"But they pay a price," I said. "They're outcasts. They have no families. If they're captured, they're hanged or crucified. And what about the terrible things they do? They kill and rob innocent people, and they . . . they kidnap people, too."

"I never said they weren't lawbreakers," said Hepu. "Why do you think my father beat the idea out of me, when I spoke of joining them?"

I nodded thoughtfully. "You make it sound as if the ideal life would be one that allowed a man to move back and forth between the ordinary world and that of the bandits. To have the best of both worlds."

"In fact, there are such men," said Hepu. "Spies, scouts, go-betweens. Men who live among us, with wives and families and regular work, but who also lead a double life, consorting with the bandits. And such men live not just in the Delta. They say the Cuckoo's Gang is so widespread it has informers and affiliates as far as Pelusium to the east and Alexandria to the west—and even farther, all the way to Cyrene."

"But Cyrene is Roman now," I said, without thinking. Coming from a Roman, the statement drew cool looks from the men around me. "I mean, ever since old Apion died . . . King Ptolemy's bastard brother . . . and left Cyrene to the Romans . . . in his will . . ." By continuing to talk I was only digging a deeper hole for myself.

"Be that as it may," said Hepu, "they say the reach of the Cuckoo's Gang extends even to Cyrene."

I cleared my throat. "You make it sound as if this Cuckoo's Gang is a veritable state within a state. King Ptolemy has one government, and the bandits have another, invisible but operating right alongside the legitimate authorities."

"Just so," said Hepu.

"So this Cuckoo's Gang is everywhere—and nowhere," I said. "But surely they have some sort of home base."

"It's called the Cuckoo's Nest," said Hepu.

"Is it? And where is this Cuckoo's Nest?"

Hepu laughed, as did the others. "That, young Roman, is a very good question, to which many would like the answer—including the agents of King Ptolemy."

"Do *you* know where it is, Hepu?" I asked.

"Indeed I do not. Nor does any man here, I daresay, or else they'd have lost their heads."

"Is it close?"

"Less than a day's journey from here, or so they say."

"Yes, but where?" I tried not to sound too eager.

"All I know is this: if you turn south on that path over there, and follow it along this little branch of the Nile, you don't have far to go before you begin to see warning signs."

"Warnings?"

"Clear indications that you should go no farther. A crocodile's skull on a stick . . . a rusty length of chain across the path . . . spikes sticking up from the roadbed. And then, if you dare to venture farther still, there are actual snares and traps—pits full of stakes, tripwires, loaded slingshots, falling objects. So they say. No man finds his way to the Cuckoo's Nest by accident."

"No man finds his way there alive, I should think!" said Djet.

Hepu cackled. "Smart boy!"

I considered all the old man had told me, and felt a mingling of hope and dread. Bethesda might yet be alive and well, and very close, but how was I to reach her with such frightful obstacles before me?

The conversation drifted to other matters—weather, crops, local gossip. I asked Menkhep if he might recommend a place where Djet and the camel and I could sleep for the night. He told me there was a village a mile or so to the east where I might find lodgings, but for a very small price he offered to share his dinner and let us sleep in a small lean-to behind the trading post. Since I intended to travel south the next day, and the village would be out of my way, I took him up on his offer.

To thank everyone for their hospitality, including my host, I bought a round of beer for everyone. Menkhep's beer seemed rather thin and slightly sour to me, but the locals seemed to enjoy it, especially old Hepu. When everyone's thirst had been slaked, I excused myself and headed off with Djet to tend to the camel and arrange a comfortable sleeping place for us on the packed-earth floor of the lean-to.

Menkhep served me more beer with our frugal dinner. It must have been the beer that allowed me to sleep that night, despite the excitement I felt. In the morning I would head south, watching for the signs that Hepu had spoken of. By day's end, I might arrive at the Cuckoo's Nest—or be floating lifeless down the Nile, having failed in the attempt.

XVI

The hour was not yet dawn when I woke to the familiar but unexpected voice of old Hepu, urgently saying the same thing over and over.

"Wake up, Roman! Wake up!"

I opened my eyes but saw nothing but a dark shape looming over me. Hepu, himself the color of night, was practically invisible in the darkness. He gave me a swift kick. The old man was not as feeble as he looked.

I sat upright. Next to me, Djet rolled to one side but continued to snore.

"Hepu!" I whispered. "What are you doing here? What do you want?"

"All the way from my house outside the village I've walked, in the darkness, stepping over who knows how many scorpions and snakes—and this is how you thank me?"

"For what should I be thanking you? Waking me up in the middle of the night?"

"It's not the middle of the night. It's almost dawn. And that means they're likely to come for you any time now."

I felt a prickle of dread. "What are you talking about, Hepu?"

"You *are* the thief, aren't you? The young Roman who killed that man in Canopus and ran off with his ruby?"

"I—"

"Don't deny it! How many young Romans are traveling through the Delta on camelback, with no companion but a boy? It must be you."

"And what if it is? What are you trying to tell me?"

Djet mumbled, then loudly shushed us. I gave him a firm nudge, but he hugged himself and clung to sleep.

"They'll be coming for you, very soon, young Roman. Coming for you, and for the ruby, so they can claim the reward."

"*Who* will be coming? And how do you know about this ruby?"

"Yesterday, after I left the trading post, I walked home. After dark, a neighbor paid me a visit. He said some men from Sais had arrived in the village while I was here at Menkhep's."

"Men . . . from Sais?"

"Yes. They were led by a man with a long beard, called Harkhebi."

I rose to my feet and gave Djet a kick. He blinked and rubbed his eyes. "Go on, Hepu."

"The men from Sais called everyone to a meeting, where this fellow Harkhebi told a curious tale about a terrible murder in Canopus, and a Roman outlaw thought to be somewhere in the Delta, traveling on a camel with a boy. This man Harkhebi said there's a generous reward for the Roman's head and for the return of the treasure he ran off with."

Djet at last scrambled to his feet, his eyes wide open.

"All this my neighbor told me," said Hepu, "just because he likes to gossip. Neither he nor any other villager at the meeting knew anything about you; only those of us here at Menkhep's trading post yesterday met you, and none of us were at the meeting. My neighbor's news so surprised me that I almost blurted out, 'The Roman is spending the night with Menkhep!' But before the words came out, I thought better of it, and shut my mouth. Who was I to betray a bandit like you, after all the things I said to you yesterday? I only wish I had known who and what you really are. What tales you might have told me, about you and your bandit friends!"

I shook my head. "I'm not actually a bandit, Hepu."

"Ah, well, of course you have to say that, don't you? Bandit's oath of honor?" He gave me a toothless smile. "After my neighbor left, I went to bed. But sleep would not come. I tossed and turned. Surely, I thought, one of the men who was here yesterday will betray you. Old Rabi will do it, if no one else does."

"Rabi?"

"It was he who made that rude joke about Roman women, and gave you such a sour look when you spoke of Cyrene. Rabi doesn't like foreigners, and he's a greedy bastard. If he didn't hear about the meeting when he got home last night, he'll surely hear about it first thing this morning, and then he'll hurry at once to find this Harkhebi and set him on your trail. I couldn't sleep, thinking of the terrible things they'll do if they capture you. The hours of torture, the terrible pain, the slow, agonizing death—"

"Yes, yes, I understand!"

"So at last I gave up on sleeping, and I rose from my bed and walked all the way here to warn you. How my old feet ache! But why are we still talking? You must go at once, young Roman. I suppose you were heading for the Cuckoo's Nest, anyway, eh? What other reason could you have to pass through this miserable backwater?" By the first faint light of dawn, I saw a twinkle of admiration in his rheumy eyes.

"Yes, I . . . I *am* heading for the Cuckoo's Nest." I only spoke the truth.

"Then you must be off at once, if you want to keep ahead of them. Ha! And there I was yesterday, telling *you* about the deadly traps and snares that keep outsiders from ever reaching the Cuckoo's Nest! You must know all about those perils, and how to pass them safely."

"If only I did!" I muttered under my breath.

Djet, who had apprehended the situation, needed no order from me to begin gathering up our things. He ran to the camel, which was tethered to a nearby palm tree, and began to rouse the beast, which shook its sleepy head and spat at him.

I rushed to help Djet put on the camel's riding tack, but the beast, irritated at being awakened so early, made the job twice as difficult as it should have been. As the dawn grew brighter, and still the camel was not yet ready to be mounted, I felt a rising panic.

At last we were ready to set off. I checked the bag of treasure a final time, then reached inside and pulled out a silver ring set with a blood-red carnelian.

I turned to Hepu and pressed the ring into the weathered palm of his hand.

"Thank you, Hepu."

His rheumy eyes lit up. "Never have I seen something so lovely! Never have I held so much wealth in my hand!"

I pressed his fingers shut. "Whatever you do, don't let them find this on you. Hide it somewhere and come back for it later."

He nodded, and then, to my surprise, he put the ring in his mouth and swallowed it.

"An old bandit trick," he said. "But of course, you know that."

As I turned to mount the camel, he touched my arm.

"Young Roman, one last favor!"

"What is it, Hepu?"

At the same moment, Djet grabbed my other arm. He pricked one ear, as if his keener hearing had detected a sound too faint for me to notice. His eyebrows shot up in alarm.

"The ruby," said Hepu. "I've never seen a ruby. Will you show it to me? Just one look . . ."

"That noise," whispered Djet. "Can't you hear it? A twig breaking . . . and something rustling . . . over that way . . ."

As quickly as I could, I pulled the ruby necklace from the sack and held it before Hepu. He let out a gasp. With trembling fingers he touched the crimson stone.

A thought struck me: why not give the ruby to Hepu, and be rid of it? Such a bold gesture might please Fortuna, whose favor I needed now more than ever. But if it were truly cursed, why should I pass my misfortune to a man who was trying to save me? And what if the ruby was the price required to ransom Bethesda?

The debate in my head abruptly ended when a voice cried out: "Look! The ruby!"

I wheeled about and saw, framed by a patch of underbrush some thirty feet away, the face of Harkhebi. More men appeared to be bunched in a crowd behind him, largely hidden by the greenery.

Harkhebi simply stood there and stared, as if transfixed by the ruby. I had been caught red-handed.

In a single motion I stuffed the necklace back into the sack, mounted the camel, pulled Djet in front of me, and snapped the reins. The beast sprang upright with a sudden flailing of limbs that sent Hepu staggering backward.

"Hut! Hut!" I cried, and off we went, with Harkhebi and his party scrambling to follow.

XVII

Galloping as fast as I could, we headed south on the riverside trail. Trees and shrubs hemmed the way, so that I seemed to fly through a leafy tunnel, dazzled by flashes of slanting sunlight as morning broke across the Delta.

Why had I not left at once when Hepu delivered his warning? Whatever head start I might have had was gone. Behind me I heard men shouting, and the bleat of their camels. Could their camels outrun mine?

They drew closer and closer, until I could hear what they were shouting.

"Is he making for the Cuckoo's Nest?"

"He must be one of the gang!"

"The danger—"

"Think of the reward!"

"Perhaps we should turn back—"

"Think of the ruby!"

So swiftly did I ride by the crocodile skull mounted on a pole that the strange image registered in my mind only after I had passed it. According to Hepu, it was the first notice that we were entering the territory of the

Cuckoo's Gang. Every part of me was already in a state of high alert—my heart pounding, my hands sweaty, my thoughts a blur—yet above all else I felt a quiver of dread.

The crocodile skull had an even more chilling effect on my pursuers, for the pounding of hooves behind me abruptly faded. I glanced back and saw that Harkhebi's men had come to a halt and were frantically conferring, shaking their heads and gesturing wildly. The locals among them had recognized the warning sign, and refused to go on.

I seized the chance to lengthen my lead, and snapped the reins. "Hut! Hut!" I cried.

The wind raced in my ears. The dappled sunlight became a blur. Then, in the blink of an eye, I found myself desperately clutching Djet and whatever else I could grab hold of. Rounding a bend, we had come upon the trunk of a palm tree lying across the path. The camel cleared it with an awkward leap, then staggered forward, nearly throwing us as it struggled to regain its balance.

Hepu had spoken of such hazards. This was only the first. How soon would we encounter the next? What would happen if there were spikes in the roadbed, or a rope pulled taut across the way? I pulled on the reins, bringing the camel to a sudden halt. From this point onward, we had no choice but to proceed more slowly, I thought—then gave a start, as a nearby voice spoke my thoughts aloud.

"If you want to stay alive, slow down!"

To my left, a side path converged with the trail. There, on a camel, sat Menkhep. The burly shopkeeper and his mount were both breathing hard, as if they had raced to this spot to head me off, and had only just arrived. I made ready to snap the reins and race off, but Menkhep raised his hand.

"Calm yourself, Roman. Take a deep breath. Think! You're going to need all your wits if you want to come out of this alive. And you're going to have to trust me."

"Trust you? To do what?"

"To get you to the Cuckoo's Nest, you fool! It's either that, or face that bloodthirsty mob."

I looked behind me. There was no sign yet of my pursuers.

"But . . . *you*, Menkhep?" said Djet, staring at him wide-eyed and stealing the words from my mouth. Hepu had spoken of go-betweens and informers who lived in the workaday world but who were also part of the Cuckoo's Gang. I would never have suspected genial, easygoing Menkhep.

"Ever since my wife died. My trading post sits on the outskirts of the gang's territory. I'm their eyes and ears. I take a good look at everyone who passes through. Most travelers are harmless. Some are dangerous. A few are worth robbing. And a very, very few are worth recruiting."

"And me?"

"Worth recruiting, for sure—*and* worth robbing!" Menkhep laughed. "I'm thinking the Cuckoo's Child will be quite pleased when I bring him the notorious cutthroat thief of Canopus."

I shook my head. "But I'm not—"

"I must admit, I'd never have guessed you were so dangerous. When that mob from the village arrived at dawn, and the fellow from Sais told me who you were, I could scarcely believe it. They invited me to join them and share in the reward. Instead, I took this shortcut—and here we are. Are you really carrying a ruby as large as a hen's egg?"

I sighed. "It's smaller than that."

"Still, the Cuckoo's Child will be very pleased to see both you *and* your treasure. You're quite a catch, young Roman."

I bristled. "Am I to be your guest, Menkhep, or your prisoner?"

He grinned. "Maybe both."

I shook my head, desperately wishing I had some other choice—then gave a start. From up the trail I heard a rallying cry, followed by cheers.

"They've made up their minds to come after you, despite the danger," said Menkhep. "Greed triumphs over common sense, as usual. Now listen! Follow me, and do exactly as I do. Go at the speed I go, no faster and no slower. When you see me keep to one side of the trail, do likewise. Otherwise, you'll end up with your head cut off or an arrow in your guts. Do you understand?"

"Yes." I heard clattering hooves, and cast a nervous glance behind us. The first of the pursuers came into sight.

Menkhep wheeled his camel about and set off without another word.

"Hold tight, Djet," I whispered, and followed.

Menkhep kept to a steady pace, neither fast nor slow. I gnashed my teeth with impatience as our pursuers drew closer. Did Menkhep not realize how quickly they were gaining on us? Then I heard a cry of terror, and looked back. The man leading the pack went flying off his camel as the beast tripped over the palm trunk lying across the path.

Menkhep glanced back. "One down!" he shouted.

So it went. My skills as a camel rider were pressed to their limit as I followed Menkhep, veering this way and that, mimicking his movements as precisely as I could, trusting that he knew the snares and traps along the way and how to avoid them. Behind us, our reckless pursuers were less fortunate as they encountered one hazard after another. Some of these hazards were merely inconvenient. Others were deadly.

That long, jostling, breathless ride took on the quality of a comical nightmare. Again and again one of our pursuers gained on us and drew close, so that I could hear the man shouting behind me and could see his face clearly if I dared to look over my shoulder. Again and again some terrible fate befell these pursuers.

We came to a place where the path split in two around a clump of foliage that grew like an island in the middle. We veered to the left. Our nearest pursuer veered to the right—and went plunging, camel and all, into a shallow pit concealed by palm branches. The camel bellowed in pain. The rider went flying through the air.

The path widened. We kept to the right side. The pursuer breathing down my neck rode straight down the middle, and struck a trigger that caused a barrier on a hinge to spring across the path, knocking camel and rider both to the ground. The next pursuer, following too closely to stop, collided with the fallen rider.

With this obstacle effectively blocking the path, the pursuit ended, at least for a while. Menkhep took the opportunity to slacken our pace, which was a good thing, for the hazards grew ever more frequent and more dangerous, and it required all my strength and attention to keep up and follow his movements exactly.

Eventually, the path behind us must have been cleared, for more pursuers came thundering after us. One by one they dropped by the wayside, felled by a variety of ingenious traps—arrows released by hidden triggers, slingshots set off by tripwires—until only one dogged pursuer remained. As the path twisted and turned, I tried to get a look at the man, and at last I caught a glimpse of his long beard flapping like a pennant in the dappled sunlight. It was Harkhebi.

The oldest of the pursuers he might have been, but perhaps he was also the most experienced on camelback, and the most cautious, which accounted for his survival thus far. But if Harkhebi was that cautious, why did he not give up the pursuit? Having tracked me—and the ruby—all the way from Canopus, and having come so close to catching me, the old man must have found it impossible to abandon the hunt. Even wise men lose all common sense when caught up in the thrill of the chase.

If Harkhebi had had his way, my head would have been cut off and sent back to Canopus as a trophy. My body would have been defiled and my memory blackened, and who knows what might have become of Bethesda, or of Djet, for that matter? I had no reason to shed a tear for Harkhebi. Still, his fate sent a shudder through me.

The trail widened. The leafy tunnel opened, and I saw blue sky above. The road rose before me, heading slightly uphill. Behind me, I heard Harkhebi shout encouragement to his camel. His hoarse voice sounded very close.

Ahead of me, Menkhep veered suddenly to the left, off the trail entirely. His beast knew the way, and made the small leap onto a low shelf of rock without breaking stride. Could my mount do likewise, at such a speed and at such short notice? It seemed madness to follow Menkhep, but I pulled hard on the reins to steer the camel sharply to the left.

I felt the beast resist. I had no time to think. I pulled the reins harder. At the last possible instant, the camel made the leap and went clattering along behind Menkhep.

Harkhebi may have attempted the same maneuver—I heard him shout something—but if so, his camel could not or would not respond in time, and instead went hurtling forward.

Just beyond the crest of the low hill, a deep, narrow trench ran all the way across the road. Had the camel been traveling at a slower pace it might have seen the trench in time, and simply stepped across it. But the ingenious placement rendered the trench invisible to anyone traveling at a gallop until it was too late. The camel's forelegs landed in the narrow trench, causing it to stumble and pitch violently forward.

Harkhebi was thrown from the beast and went flying through the air. He did not land on the road, for this was where the road ended. Where the road should have been there was a long, wide pit as deep as a man is tall, filled with wooden stakes set close together and sharpened to a fine point.

I didn't see him land in the pit, but I heard his cry as he hurtled through the air, and then his scream as he landed on the spikes, accompanied by sounds of his body being punctured in many places—ripping, gasping, liquid sounds quite unlike anything I had ever heard before, and would never want to hear again.

Menkhep drew his camel to a halt, then circled back to take a look. I followed. At the edge of the pit, the camels turned their heads away and nervously stamped their forelegs. It was a curious thing, I thought, that two dumb animals should be more squeamish than the creatures who rode them.

Djet cried out at the terrible sight. Too late, I covered his eyes with my hand.

Since Harkhebi had landed front-down, we were at least spared the sight of his face. The stakes impaling him glistened with blood and gore. He continued to live for a short while—unless, as sometimes happens, the rattling of breath and the convulsing of limbs were the spasms of a man already dead. Then his arms and legs contracted, his chest deflated, his hands curled into claws, and Harkhebi moved no more.

I saw that many of the stakes were darkened by older bloodstains. Harkhebi was not the first victim of the pit.

I felt compelled to call his name. "Harkhebi?"

He made no answer. I swallowed the bile rising in my throat and spoke more loudly. "Harkhebi?"

The silence was broken by a plaintive sound from his camel, which lay on its side before the pit, thrashing its limbs and unable to stand. The poor beast had broken both forelegs.

Menkhep snorted. "A city father from Sais, he called himself. A wise old man, supposedly. He should have known better than to follow us all this way, the crazy fool! What a mess will have to be cleaned up—not just here, but all up and down the trail."

"Cleaned up?" I said.

"Corpses must be stripped of their valuables and disposed of. Traps must be reloaded and reset. Camels must be rescued, or put out of their misery. I shall take care of this beast now." He pulled the dagger from the scabbard at his waist. "What a lot of work for the Cuckoo's Gang! I hope you're worth the bother, Roman."

Menkhep stared at me with a stiff jaw and eyes like flint. Where was the easygoing shopkeeper with whom I had dined the previous night? What sort of man had I followed into this place of merciless death, from which there could be no turning back?

XVIII

We had come to the end of the road. When I turned my back on the pit with its deadly stakes, and rose as high as I could on my camel, I saw before us what appeared to be an impenetrable thicket.

Menkhep tied his own mount to a tree some distance away, and indicated that I should dismount and do likewise. "Gather your things and carry them with you," he said. "And don't forget that ruby!" He flashed a crooked smile. "From here we proceed on foot."

"How much farther?" I peered into the thicket and listened to the silence. It seemed impossible that any sort of camp or settlement could be nearby.

Menkhep ignored my question. "Have you got everything?"

I nodded.

"Then follow me."

He seemed to disappear into the thickest part of the foliage, but when I arrived at the same spot, I saw an opening amid the leaves. The winding path, such as it was, grew so narrow in places that I had to step sideways. Djet had an easier time, though at one point he tripped and fell over a tangle of roots.

We headed gradually downhill, until the pathway ended on the banks of a small, heavily shaded lagoon. Our arrival startled a pair of long-beaked ibises. The birds flapped their broad white wings and took flight.

Pulled up on the muddy bank and tied to posts were several boats. Menkhep pulled one of these long, slender vessels into the shallow water and held it in place while Djet and I climbed aboard. The boat was so narrow that we had to sit in single file. I was in the middle, with Djet in front and Menkhep behind.

"Know how to row?" he asked.

"Well enough," I said.

Menkhep laughed. "A shopkeeper learns to tell when people are lying. You've never held an oar in your life, have you?"

"Well . . ."

"Dip your paddle in one side, then the other, like this." He demonstrated while I craned my neck to observe. "I'll steer. The stronger and faster you stroke, the sooner we'll get there and have something to eat. I don't know about you, but I'm starving."

With Menkhep observing my strokes and giving me pointers, we traveled from one lagoon to another, threading our way through floating lotus gardens and tall stands of reeds that swayed in the breeze, shaded now and again by miniature forests of papyrus along the marshy banks. Dragonflies flitted around us. Gnats and midges and multitudes of other winged insects danced in swarms above the water. Everywhere I looked, the world seemed to buzz and sigh and throb with life. I fell into the rhythm of rowing and beheld the teeming spectacle with detached bemusement—until the gnats began to buzz in my ears and the midges landed on my lips and eyelashes and flew up my nose. I blinked and snorted and batted at them helplessly, almost losing my paddle.

Laughing at my torment, Menkhep instructed Djet to turn around and dispatch the insects by blowing at them and waving them away.

I resumed rowing, and eventually fell into a steady rhythm, feeling the pull of the sparkling green water against my oar, matching my strength against the river. The routine at length gave way to monotony, and the monotony to boredom, and then to fatigue, and at some point it seemed to me that we must be going in circles, passing through the same lagoon over and over, traversing a watery vista with no discernible landmarks. Perhaps Menkhep actually did trick me into crossing the same stretch of waterway more than once, so as to confuse me and make it harder for me to find my way in or out.

At last we turned up a narrow inlet with grassy marshes on either side. Menkhep told me to stop rowing. The boat came to a stop, and for a few moments we floated in place, watching sparkles of sunlight on the water and listening to the buzzing of insects. Then, from the tall grass to our right, I heard a series of whistles that did not sound like any bird I had heard in the Delta. Putting his fingers in his mouth, Menkhep replied with a similar series of whistles. After a pause, we heard yet more whistling.

"That's the go-ahead signal," said Menkhep. "Start rowing again, while I steer us around that little bend. Then you'll see it."

"See what?" I started to say, but a moment later my question was answered. At the far end of the narrow lagoon I saw a little village of huts. The huts were made of dried mud and wattle, with thatched roofs. They looked like the Hut of Romulus on the Palatine Hill, which my father had shown me when I was little. Rome itself had begun as a settlement of huts such as this.

Projecting into the lagoon was a long, low pier, to which were tied a great many boats. These vessels were twice as wide as the one in which I sat and much longer, large enough to accommodate perhaps twenty men or more. From the direction we had come, a young man went running along the bank of the lagoon ahead of us, holding a whistle to his mouth and blowing a series of notes. This was the lookout who had given us the go-ahead, who was now alerting his comrades to our arrival.

Men began to emerge from the huts and the surrounding greenery. What had I expected the members of the Cuckoo's Gang to look like? Wild-eyed savages, I suppose. In fact, they were a motley group. Most were in their late twenties or thirties, but some were my age or even younger. There were no old men among them, and the few who had gray in their beards looked exceptionally fit.

Some were unshaven and shaggy-headed, but others were well groomed. Some wore ragged tunics or loincloths, but others were well dressed, and all were adorned with jewelry—flaunting the finery they had robbed from their victims, no doubt. A few, except for their jewelry, were completely naked. This startled me, for where I came from, outside the baths, only slaves and children were ever seen naked in public. Of course, this was not a public place, but quite the opposite; we had arrived in one of the most secluded and secret spots on earth. The members of the gang were all male—with one curious and surprising exception, as I was soon to discover—and whether a man went dressed or undressed mattered not at all to them. Those who preferred to walk about naked did so.

A few scowled at the sight of us, but others regarded us with blank expressions or even smiled. Several of the men gave a friendly wave to Menkhep.

More and more men gathered. From where I sat it was hard to estimate their numbers, but there must have been well over a hundred, perhaps as many as two hundred.

As we approached the pier, Menkhep called for me to stop rowing. He steered us into place, turning the boat so that we came to a stop perpendicular to the end of the pier. My legs were stiff from sitting, and my arms ached from rowing. I was eager to step out of the boat. So, apparently, was Djet, who sprang up at once.

"Sit down!" snapped Menkhep.

Djet gave him a puzzled look.

"Do as he says," I whispered. "Wait until we're invited."

Red-faced, Djet settled back into the prow of the boat.

From the crowd at the far end of the pier, I heard shouts and murmurs. One name was repeated over and over.

"Where is Artemon?"

"Go and tell Artemon!"

"Artemon needs to come!"

I turned my head and looked at Menkhep. "Who is this Artemon?"

"The Cuckoo's Child, of course. Our leader. That must be him, coming now."

The crowd parted. The shouts and murmurs died down. The little lagoon was suddenly so quiet that I heard only the croaking of a frog from the reeds nearby—and then another sound, which seemed to come from much farther away, the roar of some giant beast. It reminded me of sounds I had heard in Alexandria, coming from behind the high wall of the zoological garden attached to the royal palace, where King Ptolemy kept a private menagerie of exotic creatures. What sort of fearsome animal made such a deep, menacing roar? And why did no one in the crowd appear to be startled by it?

I had no more time to think about the strange sound, for at that moment a figure emerged from the crowd and stepped onto the pier. Like most of the men, he was dressed in dull colors, greens and browns that blended with the landscape, but unlike the others he wore a bright red scarf tied around his head. I remembered something my father had told me, that Roman generals were known to wear red capes so as to set themselves apart and make themselves conspicuous to their troops.

Gesturing for Djet and me to stay in the boat, Menkhep deftly stepped past us and onto the pier. He walked to the figure at the far end. The two conversed for a while in voices too low for me to hear. Then the man with the red headscarf began to walk toward us, with Menkhep following behind.

Artemon was tall and broad-shouldered. His footsteps on the pier sounded heavy and solid. Everything about his bearing conveyed confidence and an aura of command, but when he came close enough for me to see his face clearly, I was taken aback.

I had expected the leader of the bandits to be a scarred, grizzled veteran, a craggy-featured brute who could inspire terror with a look. Instead I saw a handsome youth with high cheekbones, a smooth forehead, bright blue eyes, and lips so red he might have colored them, as women do. The wispy shadow across his square jaw was more the suggestion of a beard than a beard itself. He had to be even younger than I, perhaps still a teenager.

Keeping his gaze fixed on me, he reached the end of the pier. "My name is Artemon. And who are you?"

Staying seated in the boat, I had to tilt my head up at a sharp angle. "My name is Marcus Pecunius," I said, deciding to stay with the false name I had been using ever since our stay in Sais.

"Are you a Roman?" he asked—speaking, to my surprise, in Latin.

I answered in Latin. "I live in Alexandria now. But yes, I come from Rome."

Artemon nodded. Menkhep stepped beside him, and he reverted to Greek. "My comrade here tells me that you have quite a reputation. He says the whole village came after you, led by some old coot from Sais. But he says you managed to outrun them all. Left them choking in the dust—if any survived the traps along the way."

"We had an exciting morning," I said.

Artemon smiled. "Menkhep says the city father from Sais made a rather shocking accusation against you—claimed that you murdered a band of travelers in Canopus single-handed, then ran off with a bag full of jewels." He raised an eyebrow and peered down his nose at me. "You don't look like a cold-blooded killer to me, Marcus Pecunius."

"And you don't look like the leader of a bandit gang."

He threw back his head and laughed. "And how many leaders of bandit gangs have you met?"

I made no answer.

"As I thought," he said. "Whereas I see cold-blooded killers every day." He waved to indicate the crowd at the far end of the pier. "So in this instance, who's the better judge of the other's character, Pecunius, you or I?"

His unblinking stare caused me to shiver. Young he might be, and also pretty, but I could see that Artemon was not to be trifled with. I was also puzzled. A young Egyptian who spoke Latin, and who could frame his arguments in such elegant terms, must surely have received a formal education. How had such a youth come to be the leader of the Delta's most notorious gang of bandits?

Artemon saw the consternation on my face and seemed to be amused. "Don't worry, Pecunius, I'm not going to stand here and press you with awkward questions. If Menkhep vouches for you, that's good enough—for now, at least. In this place, you'll find that we don't ask too many questions. Here, it's what a man does that matters, and how he gets along with his comrades—not where he comes from, or what language he speaks, or who his parents were . . . or whether he did or did not kill some people. But I will want to have a look inside that bag you've brought. If it's full of loot, as Menkhep seems to think, you'll be allowed to keep a portion of it—by Isis, you've earned it, if you've run all the way here from Canopus with a mob breathing down your neck! But you'll be expected to share. That's the rule here: share and share alike. If you want to step foot on this pier, you must accept this."

I shrugged. "I understand. If it weren't for Menkhep, I'd be a dead man now. I'm grateful for your hospitality."

Artemon nodded, then looked at Djet. "What about the boy? Is he your son?"

"No."

"Your slave?"

"No."

"What is he to you, then?"

"That's . . . a bit complicated."

Artemon pursed his lips and shrugged. "About that sort of thing, also, we don't ask prying questions. Still, it's not a good idea, bringing a boy into a place like this. For one thing, a boy can't do the work of a man."

"What he lacks in size and strength, the boy makes up in cleverness," I said.

Djet nodded and grinned, but Artemon looked dubious. "Also, some of the men might be distracted by such a pretty face."

No prettier than your face, I thought. "His name is Djet. I'll take full responsibility for him."

"See that you do. Well, then, Pecunius—and Djet—welcome to the

Cuckoo's Nest. Step out of that boat. We're about to eat. You're welcome to join us, as my personal guests."

Djet nimbly leaped onto the pier. As I rose to my feet, the boat rocked, and I swayed unsteadily. Artemon took hold of my arm and pulled me onto the pier beside him. He had a powerful grip and stood a full head taller than I.

As we approached the crowd at the end of the pier, I took a closer look at the faces staring back at me. Most of the men looked normal enough, but were these not the most dangerous criminals on earth, the scum of society, the lowest of the low? I felt a sudden thrill of panic. *What have you gotten yourself into?* I thought. *What in Hades are you doing in such a godsforsaken place?*

Then I caught a glimpse of a figure who stood a little beyond the crowd, alone and apart. I couldn't see her clearly, but from her hair and clothing and the way she carried herself I knew it must be a woman.

Could it be Bethesda?

My heart turned upside down in my chest. I wanted to push Artemon aside and run ahead of him, elbow my way through the crowd and stand before her. Instead, I caught my breath, clenched my fists, and walked as steadily as I could. Gazing beyond the crowd, I tried to get a better look.

The woman had vanished.

XIX

I followed Artemon—and my nose—to the roasting pit and clay ovens located in a clearing some distance from the huts, where the crowd lined up to be fed.

I had thought that Artemon would be served first, but there seemed to be no rule about this, except that the first to arrive were the first to be served. Fallen tree trunks provided places to sit. Since these were gathered in a circle around the periphery of the clearing, there was no place of honor, and everyone seemed to sit wherever he wanted. The spot Artemon chose did have the advantage of being upwind from the roasting pit, away from the smoke.

The meal was far better than I expected. There was freshly caught tilapia from the river cut into pieces and roasted on skewers, a porridge made from a bean unfamiliar to me, generous pieces of flatbread, and even a relish for the fish made from pickled hearts of palm, all served on smoothed sections of bark from a palm tree.

All the food was delicious, but I had little appetite. I was too excited at the possibility that Bethesda might be nearby. How and when was I to reveal my purpose in coming, without putting us both in even greater danger? For the moment, it seemed wise to keep my mouth shut.

"He eats like a grown man, I must say," said Artemon, taking note of Djet's hearty appetite.

"I don't think either of us has enjoyed a meal this good since we left Alexandria," I admitted.

"We happen to have some very good cooks among us."

"Nor do I think I've ever eaten off a plate such as this. Rather ingenious."

"We also have some very skilled craftsmen."

"If these men are so skilled, then why . . . ?"

"Why are they here, instead of living a normal, law-abiding life, plying their trade in a normal village? Is that what you're wondering?"

I nodded.

"But you caught yourself before you finished the question, so I hope you understand: this is not the sort of thing you should ask any particular man. But I see you have an inquisitive mind, Pecunius, and curiosity, in moderation, is a virtue." He paused to eat a bit of fish, then resumed. "You and I are young, Pecunius—younger than most of the men here. They've seen more of life than we have. Whether free or slave, the life of every man is full of perils—sickness, the death of loved ones, hardship, hunger. When a man falls on bad times, his best choice may be to leave his old life behind and see what a different sort of life might offer."

This was as neat an excuse as I had ever heard for falling into a life of banditry. I was skeptical, but kept my mouth shut. Djet, on the other hand, suddenly squirmed with excitement.

"But what man *wouldn't* be curious about the bandit life?" he blurted. I noticed the awestruck way he looked at Artemon.

"The boy's head is full of stories," I said.

"As is the head of every boy, eh?" Artemon tousled Djet's hair. "But the boy is right. Not every man joins us because he's run away from heartbreak or hardship. Some join us simply because they want to. They've had enough of the law-abiding life and thrown it off, the way you might discard a pair of shoes that pinch your feet. The life we lead wouldn't suit every man, but for those it does suit, no other life will do."

He was silent for a while, sitting upright on the trunk next to me and eating his food, taking small bites and chewing thoroughly before he swallowed. I looked around the clearing and saw that many of the men had manners no better than swine, but those of Artemon were quite elegant—almost ludicrously so, I thought, considering the circumstances.

"What about you, Pecunius? From what Menkhep told me, you didn't exactly choose to come here, did you?"

I was reluctant to lie to him outright. "I arrived here by an odd chain of circumstances, to be sure. I think perhaps the goddess Fortuna guided me here."

"Really? Most of the time the gods have nothing to do with us, or we with them—an arrangement suitable to all concerned."

"You speak like a philosopher, Artemon."

"And what do you know of philosophers, Pecunius?"

More than I do about bandit chiefs, I thought. "A wise man tutored me from time to time when I was growing up in Rome. That's how I came to know Greek. He was more a poet than a philosopher, if there's a difference. What about you, Artemon? How is it that you speak Latin? Or is that a forbidden question?"

He made no answer. Instead, he put down his empty plate, rose to his feet, and looked north.

"That's a storm," he said.

The sky above our heads was blue, but dark clouds were heaped along the northern horizon.

"Those clouds weren't there a moment ago," I said.

"No. They're over the open sea, beyond the mouths of the Delta. Storms can come up very suddenly at this time of year."

I shrugged. "Your huts look sturdy enough to me. The wind and rain may not even reach this far."

Artemon smiled. "I'm not *worried* about the storm, Pecunius. Quite the opposite."

I noticed that several of the men had joined Artemon in gazing toward the north. Some nodded gravely. Some nudged their comrades, pointed at the sky, and grinned.

I shook my head, not understanding. "Is it an omen?"

"What do you think, Pecunius? Aren't you Romans always reading the sky for signs and portents?"

"The men who do that are called augurs. They train for years."

"So you have no skills at augury?"

I shook my head.

"Ah, well. Fortunately, we already have a reliable soothsayer among us."

I looked around, dubious that any member of this motley band might possess even a sliver of divine insight. Hadn't Artemon just admitted that his gang had nothing to do with the gods?

"You've eaten hardly anything, Pecunius. I thought you liked the food."

I shrugged. "The excitement of the day . . ."

"Well, if you're finished, don't waste the food. Menkhep is over there, eating with friends. Give your portion to him. Djet, come with me. We'll rinse our plates in the river and return them to the stack. Then I suggest we withdraw to my hut."

From the outside, the hut of Artemon was indistinguishable from the rest. Inside, on a dirt floor, a raised pallet held a straw mattress. Next to this was a trunk with a lock on it, which for all I knew was crammed with stolen treasures.

The rest of the hut *was* different from the others, I suspected, for every bit of available space was crowded with what we Romans call *capsae,* portable leather drums for storing scrolls. On every flat surface I saw a scroll, unrolled and held open by little lead weights. Most of these scrolls were covered with Greek writing, but some appeared to be maps.

I stepped closer to one of the maps, which lay open on a low table beside the bed, and saw that it depicted Alexandria. I gazed at the symbols for familiar landmarks—the Moon Gate and the Sun Gate, the Temple of Serapis, the Tomb of Alexander—and felt a stab of homesickness.

Even Djet, who could not read, recognized the map. He put his finger on the image of the Pharos Lighthouse and said, rather astutely I thought, "I wonder if that storm will reach as far as Alexandria?"

"Probably not," said Artemon, following us inside and tying back the piece of cloth that covered the doorway so as to let in more light. "The wind appears to be blowing more east than west, and mostly south."

I looked down at the map again. Someone had drawn a red circle around the Street of the Seven Baboons, and a red dot marked the exact location of the house of Tafhapy. My breath quickened and my heart pounded in my chest. Surely this meant that Tafhapy's supposition had been correct—this was indeed the gang that had attempted to kidnap his beloved Axiothea, but had taken Bethesda instead. Was she here among them or not?

"Are you a reader of books, Pecunius?"

"When I can get my hands on one."

"You sound quite breathless! It's good to meet another man who gets excited at the mere sight of scrolls. It must be frustrating for you, living in Alexandria. No city on earth has more books, but only those permitted by the royal librarians are allowed to see them. Still, there's quite a trade in bootleg copies turned out by royal scribes eager to earn a bit of extra money. A man can find just about anything in Alexandria, if he looks hard enough."

I nodded dumbly.

"Most of these scrolls are just boring old documents—administrative letters, tax records, travel permissions . . . the kinds of things you find when you raid a caravan or scavenge a shipwreck. Still, I never throw any scroll away, at least not until I've had a good look at it. You can learn some interesting things from those boring old documents. And sometimes you find a real treasure. The complete poems of Moschus are in that capsa at your feet. But speaking of treasure . . . let's have a look inside that sack you carry."

He removed the map from the low table, rolled it up and put it away, then held out his hand and took the sack from me.

He sat on the bed and opened the sack, then peered inside and let out a low whistle. First he removed the coins and sorted through them, dividing them into neat piles. Then he removed the rings, one by one, and carefully examined each, like a jeweler assessing its value. All this he did without comment, but when he pulled the last item from the sack, the silver necklace with the ruby, he let out a gasp. He held the jewel in a slanting sunbeam from the doorway, causing the stone to glow with a smoldering red light, like a hot coal.

"So this is why the old coot from Sais followed you all the way here, and all the way to his death. Truly, it's magnificent."

For a long time, Artemon seemed unable to take his eyes off the ruby. At last he took my hand and pressed the jewel into my palm.

"I'm afraid you'll have to give up the rings, Pecunius, and half the coins. But the ruby necklace you can keep."

"What?"

"You object to giving up the rings?"

On the contrary, I was shocked that he was permitting me to keep the ruby.

He misunderstood. "Think, Pecunius! Next to the ruby, the rings are trivial, and so are the coins. Their greatest value is the goodwill they'll buy you when you share them with the others. No one is more beloved than a generous thief."

"Well . . . if you insist."

"I assure you, it's the right thing to do. But don't flaunt the ruby. All the men like to wear their booty, but no one here owns anything remotely like this. The mere sight of such a treasure might drive one of the men to do something we'd all regret."

I clutched the ruby in my fist. If Artemon considered it so rare and valuable, then surely I could use it to buy Bethesda's freedom—if indeed she was here. Had the time come to ask Artemon about her? Should I be circumspect, and begin by asking about the woman I had seen when we first arrived, or simply ask if any women at all resided in the Cuckoo's Nest? Or should I be more direct?

While I was mulling this over, and before I could reach a decision, Artemon stood and indicated that it was time to leave the hut. I scooped up my half of the coins and returned them, with the ruby, to the sack, then tied the sack securely around my waist. Artemon, I noticed, took one of the rings—the smallest, set with a sapphire, which Obodas had probably worn on his little finger—and tucked it inside his tunic, but the rest of the rings and coins he left in plain sight on the low table. He didn't even bother to cover the doorway with the cloth. His trust in his fellow bandits astounded me.

He showed us a nearby hut. "You and the boy can sleep here."

"It's empty?" I said.

He nodded. "The men who used to sleep here are no longer with us. Sometimes, as today, our numbers increase. Sometimes, we suffer a loss."

Any further explanation was interrupted by the appearance of Menkhep.

"You're needed, Artemon."

Artemon let out a sigh. He suddenly looked older than his years, a man with many demands for his attention. "What now? Another fight?"

"No. *She's* calling for you."

I drew a sharp breath. Artemon seemed not to notice. "What's it about, do you think? The storm? The newcomer?"

"I don't know. But she insists on seeing you."

Artemon nodded. He seemed to forget about me as he followed Menkhep.

"Artemon!" I called.

He paused and looked over his shoulder. "Make yourself comfortable in the hut, Pecunius, or feel free to explore. There's a bit of sunlight left."

"Can I come with you?"

Artemon thought this over. Finally he nodded. "If you wish. You'll have to meet her sooner or later."

My heart pounding, I hurried after him, with Djet at my heels.

XX

I followed Menkhep and Artemon through the little village of huts and across the clearing with the roasting pit. A narrow, winding trail led down to the water's edge and then through thick brush along the riverbank. At last, ahead of us, through the greenery I caught glimpses of a lone hut, situated far away from the others.

Menkhep had dropped a little ways behind Artemon. I touched his arm and spoke in his ear.

"This woman—who is she, Menkhep? What is she called?"

Despite the fact that I kept my voice low, Artemon overheard. He stopped and turned, allowing us to catch up with him.

"Her name is Metrodora," he said.

My heart sank. I had been hoping to hear him speak the name Axiothea, or perhaps even Bethesda. I tried to hide my disappointment. "Metrodora? A Greek name."

"Yes. She's not Egyptian. She comes from Delphi. When she was a girl, she trained to become the Pythia. Do you know who the Pythia is, Pecunius?"

"Of course. The priestess of Delphi, who utters the prophecies inspired by Apollo. Even in Rome, everyone has heard of the Oracle of Delphi."

"So I thought."

"Are you telling me a priestess of Delphi is living here, in the Delta?" The idea was absurd.

He smiled. "Stranger things have happened. But in fact, Metrodora never became a priestess. The journey of her life took a different course. She's lived in many places, done many things. But as with the men who come here, we don't press her with too many questions."

"I thought you allowed no women among you," I said.

"Metrodora is different. She possesses special gifts. I don't know what we'd do without her."

"When you said you had a soothsayer among you, you were speaking of Metrodora?"

"Yes."

"She sees the future?"

"Sometimes. And sometimes she sees far-off events, as they happen. She heals the sick. She casts spells for good luck, and puts curses on our enemies."

"She's a witch?"

He shook his head. "That's too simple a word to describe Metrodora. When we reach her hut, you'll wait outside. Enter only if I call for you." Artemon turned and walked on.

The secluded structure sat in a small clearing beside the water. It was twice the size of the other huts I had seen, and appeared to be made of two huts built back to back and joined by a connecting room or passageway. Artemon stood before the cloth that covered the nearest doorway and called the soothsayer's name.

When she called for him to come inside, I gave a start. The woman's voice stirred a distant memory, tantalizing but too faint to grasp. One thing was certain: it was not the voice of Bethesda.

Artemon stepped inside the hut. The rest of us waited. Menkhep sat on the stump of a tree nearby and closed his eyes. Djet amused himself by studying a frog at the water's edge. As the sun sank behind the trees, casting sidelong rays, the wind began to rise, carrying the scent of rain. The sky to the north grew darker. The dense greenery around us was suffused by a peculiar twilight.

At last Artemon emerged from the hut. He gave me a quizzical look. "She wants to speak to you, Gordianus."

I nodded and stepped to the doorway. It was only as I let the cloth hanging drop behind me that I realized he had called me by my real name.

The circular room was dimly lit by a single lamp hung from the ceiling. A woman sat cross-legged on a small rug. A hood obscured her face.

I looked at the clutter around me. By the faint light I saw the gleam of gold, silver, and jewels. Precious objects crowded the room. Were these the offering left by the bandits for her services? I also saw various implements of sorcery—lamps and incense burners, vials of liquids and powders, bits of bone, lead tablets for scrawling curses. Behind the woman I saw a curtained doorway that I presumed must lead to the adjoining hut.

The woman spoke. "You look perplexed, young Roman."

"How did Artemon know—"

"Your true name? Gordianus *is* your name, isn't it?"

"Yes." I saw no point in denying it. But how could she have known?

"Don't worry. Artemon won't hold it against you that you gave him a false name. Most of the men who come here do so. He'll continue to call you Pecunius, if that is your wish."

"And you?" I peered at her hooded face, but saw only shadows. "Is Metrodora your true name?"

She laughed. Like her voice, her laughter was naggingly familiar. "You've come through many dangers to arrive here, Gordianus."

"Yes."

"Did you think you were finally out of danger, now that you've reached the Cuckoo's Nest? Your greatest peril is just beginning!"

Despite the dank warmth of the room, I felt a chill. "How do you know my name? How could you know anything about me?"

"I know you came here seeking the thing dearest to you in all the world."

I gasped, for she seemed to have penetrated my deepest thoughts. Or had she? Might she simply be guessing, using the tricks known to every street-corner soothsayer in Alexandria? Didn't every man arrive in this place seeking his heart's desire, whether that desire was freedom, or adventure, or a new life?

"Will I find the thing I seek?"

"The thing you seek is very near."

"That's not an answer."

"Very near," she said again.

"How near?"

The woman gestured to the doorway behind her. "Just beyond this curtain. Only a few steps away—and yet, still very far from you."

What did she mean? Was Bethesda in the next room? My heart gave such a lurch that I thought my chest would burst. My head felt light. My breath grew short.

I stepped toward the curtain. The woman remained on the floor, but waved me back with a hiss.

"If you go to her now, Gordianus, you will surely die!"

I trembled with frustration. "Is Bethesda here or not?" I said through gritted teeth. "Why can't I see her?"

She held a finger to her lips. "Lower your voice, or else they might hear you."

"Who might hear?" I whispered. "Why are you tormenting me?"

She peered up at me, holding her head in such a way that for an instant the lamplight clearly illuminated her face.

"Ismene!"

There could be no doubt. The woman who sat before me was the witch of Corinth.

In my travels to see the Seven Wonders, I had taken several side trips. One of the most memorable had been a visit to the ruins of Corinth. When I first met Ismene, she seemed to be nothing more than a serving woman at a tavern, but subsequent events revealed her to be a practitioner of witchcraft. Many men died at that tavern during our stay, by the hand of a culprit other than Ismene; nonetheless, her sorcery seemed to have played a role in the murders, and when last I saw her, she was fleeing from Corinth, weighted down by a great deal of treasure scavenged from the ruins.

We had gone our separate ways, and I had whispered a prayer that I might never encounter the witch of Corinth again. By some strange twist of fate, our paths had converged in the Egyptian Delta.

"That was you I saw when I first arrived—the woman who stood behind the crowd," I said, keeping my voice low.

She nodded.

"You must have seen me too—and more clearly than I saw you, for it seems that you recognized me. How else could you have given my name to Artemon?"

She shrugged. "I'm not sure I would have known you, Roman, after all this time. But the arrival of the Roman named Gordianus was not entirely unexpected."

"You foresaw my arrival? How? By sorcery?"

"That's what Artemon thinks. He's quite impressed that I was able to tell him your true name."

I nodded, finally glimpsing the truth. "But in fact, you know who I am, and you expected me to come, because of . . ." I caught my breath, sudden unable to speak her name.

"Yes, because of *her*. Yes, Gordianus, Bethesda is here."

I felt such a flood of emotion that I couldn't speak. Ismene pulled the hood back from her face. She extended both hands, indicating that I should help her stand. She was a short, unremarkable-looking woman, no longer young but not yet old, neither ugly nor pretty, but her features were burned in my memory by the extraordinary events that surrounded our first encounter. Her manner was gruff, and her powers frightening—if they truly existed—but as far as I knew, she had never deceived me or done me any harm.

"On the day Bethesda arrived, Artemon put her under my care. He called her by another name: Axiothea. He told me that she was his prisoner, but that she was very precious, very valuable. He asked me to look after her, and to see that no harm came to her."

"And have you done so? Is she unharmed? Untouched?"

Ismene raised an eyebrow. "What do you think, Roman? The men in this place are all scared to death of me and my curses. Not one of them would dare to come into this hut uninvited. No one has so much as touched a hair on the girl's head. From the hour she arrived, your slave has been treated like a princess."

I felt another surge of emotion, this time of relief. "Bethesda!" I whispered.

"You must never call her by that name, not if others might overhear. The men who brought her here thought she was a woman called Axiothea, and that's who Artemon believes her to be. That is the name she called herself when she arrived, and she maintained her pretense even with me, until she saw there was no point in trying to hide anything from Metrodora the Soothsayer, and told me the truth. Eventually, she also confided to me that she was a slave, and her master was a man named Gordianus. The name was familiar. I questioned her further, and soon enough it was evident that the young Roman who purchased her in an Alexandrian slave market was the very same young Roman who passed through the Peloponnesus a few years ago, the traveler named Gordianus whom I last saw in the ruins of Corinth. Bethesda was certain that you would eventually come for her—and so you have. When I saw you step out of the boat and walk up the pier today, I thought I recognized you. When Artemon confirmed that the man who had joined us was a young Roman, I knew it must be you."

"And just now, you told him my true name as a sort of trick, to dazzle him with your skills as a soothsayer?"

She smiled. "Does it matter how a soothsayer comes by her knowledge, as long as she speaks the truth?"

I considered all she had told me. "You know that Axiothea is really Bethesda, but does she know that Metrodora is really Ismene?"

She laughed. "Of all the people in Egypt, only you know that I was ever called Ismene. And what makes you think that's my true name?

What do you actually know about me, Gordianus? Do you think I was always a serving woman at a tavern near Corinth?"

"But what are you doing here? What strange path brought the witch of Corinth to such a place?"

"Has my path been any stranger than yours, Gordianus? We have arrived at the same spot, in the same moment."

"Artemon says that once upon a time you trained to become the Pythia at the Temple of Apollo in Delphi."

"Do you find that hard to believe?"

"A bit."

Her face lost all trace of humor. "Where I came from, and how I came to be here, is none of your business. You know nothing for certain about me, Roman, and I suggest that you say nothing about me, if you know what's good for you. Here I am not Ismene, but Metrodora. Remember that."

I nodded. "Bethesda," I said. "Is she truly beyond that curtain? Why can I not see her?"

"Oh, you can *see* her, Roman. But you mustn't speak to her, not yet."

"Why not?"

"That will become evident when you see her."

Again I stepped toward the curtain, but Ismene gripped my arm to stop me.

"There is a price to pay."

"What do you want from me, witch?"

"Lower your voice!" she hissed. "Surely no price would be too great, to lay eyes on Bethesda again. Give me the most valuable thing you possess."

I looked at her blankly, then understood. I reached into the pouch at my waist and pulled out the ruby necklace.

"If I give this to you, what can I use to pay Artemon as a ransom?"

"I hear the jingling of coins in that pouch."

"They won't be enough."

"Nonetheless, if you want to see Bethesda, you must give me the ruby. Now!" She held out her hand.

I looked from Ismene's stern face to the curtained doorway and back again. I felt an impulse to return the ruby to the pouch, push her aside, open the curtain, and step through. But I remembered the deadly magic Ismene had wielded at Corinth, and also that she had never used it, thus far, to harm me. I would be a fool to make an enemy of her now. And was the sight of Bethesda, after all this time, not worth the cost?

I pressed the ruby necklace into Ismene's open palm. She held the jewel up to the hanging lamp. Red spangles of light played across her face.

"There's a curse on this jewel, just as Artemon suspected, but I'll find a way to remove it. Your payment is sufficient, Roman. You may step through the curtain. Tread softly and say nothing. I'll be right behind you."

XXI

The curtain doorway did not open directly into the adjoining hut, but into a passageway between the two. The dark little hallway was cluttered with trunks, boxes, and piles of clothing stacked all the way to the ceiling—yet more of Ismene's loot, I presumed. The clutter on either side created a passage within the passage, so that I had to turn this way and that to make my way forward. It also served to deaden the sound, so that a noise in one of the huts could hardly be heard in the other. The wind also covered any noise I made. It had begun to rise, whistling through the thatched roof above my head.

Even so, as I approached another curtained doorway—the twin of the one I had just passed through—I heard voices from the room beyond. First I heard a man's voice, so quiet that I could discern nothing more than the gender of the speaker, and then—my heart skipped a beat—a voice I would have known anywhere, even though she, too, spoke so quietly that I couldn't make out the words.

I reached for the curtain, intending to draw it aside, but Ismene drew beside me and stayed my hand. Keeping a finger pressed to her lips, she shook her head, then raised her palm, indicating that I should stay where I was and do nothing. Slowly and silently, she parted the curtain, but only to a finger's width, and indicated that I should put one eye to the narrow opening and take a look.

Even with her back to me, I instantly recognized Bethesda by her long black hair, and also by the way she stood, with her shoulders back and her head tilted up, looking at the much taller man who stood before her. I had no trouble recognizing Artemon, whose face was clearly lit by the lamp that hung above them.

Whenever I had thought of Bethesda in the days since she went missing, I had pictured her as I had seen her last, wearing the green dress that I had given her for my birthday. I was a bit disconcerted to see that she was wearing something altogether different—a robe of many colors, made of some rich fabric that glistened in the warm glow of the lamp, cinched at the waist with a leather belt ornamented with jewels and silver medallions. I had seldom seen silk, especially in such a quantity, but surely that was what this garment was made of. According to Ismene, Bethesda had been treated like a princess in her captivity. She had been dressed like one, too.

Artemon spoke again. Pressed to the narrow opening, I was just able to make out his words.

"When, Axiothea?" he said, his voice breaking with emotion. "When will you give up hope that the old man wants you back? If he intended to pay the ransom, he would have done so by now. He would at least have given some response to our messages."

Bethesda bowed her head. "Not yet, Artemon. The time has not come yet."

"But it *will* come—is that what you mean to say?"

Though I couldn't hear it, from the rise and fall of her shoulders I knew that Bethesda sighed.

"Give me a sign, Axiothea—some token to show me that what I long for is not beyond my reach. Do you share my feelings, or not?" His tone became strident.

From the look on his face, from the words he spoke, from the way he stood before her, like a suppliant rather than a captor, there could be no doubt. Artemon was in love with Bethesda.

On his face I saw a look of mingled hope and despair. I might have been looking into a mirror. His suffering was the same as mine. I had been deprived of the thing dearest to me, separated by miles of wilderness and water. Artemon, too, was being denied the thing he wanted most—even though she stood before him.

"If you won't give me a sign, then let me give you one," he whispered. He reached into his tunic, pulled out the little sapphire ring he had taken from me earlier, and held it before him, like an offering. "For you, Axiothea."

"Another?" Bethesda said. From the exasperation in her voice I gathered this was only the latest in a long line of gifts.

"Here, let me put it on your finger." He stepped closer to her. His eyes lit up and his face flushed. He looked so young and helpless that I found it harder than ever to imagine him as the leader of a dangerous band of brigands. He looked like a mere boy, and more than that, like a boy in love, breathless at the mere prospect of touching his beloved's hand.

"It fits your finger perfectly! That must be a sign, don't you think? Go on, hold it up to the light. See how it sparkles."

He raised her hand toward the lamp. The jewel caught the light and shone like a star in the space between them, but only for a moment. Bethesda pulled her hand from his.

"Perfect and beautiful, yes," she admitted. "Like this dress, and my shoes, and the necklace I'm wearing. Like all the lovely things you've given me. Even so, Artemon, I can't—"

"I don't imagine such gifts impress you, after all that Tafhapy must have given you. He's spoiled you, I suppose."

"No, Artemon, it isn't that—"

"A kiss!" he said. "That's all I ask. Only a kiss. Only one."

He drew closer still. Because he was taller than Bethesda, I was able to see his eyes until the moment he bowed his head, took her face in his hands, and turned it up to his. Bethesda dropped her hands to her sides. She clenched her fingers.

I gave a start. My body seemed to act on its own, without thought.

In another instant I would have been through the curtain, but Ismene dug her fingernails into my arm, so hard that I gasped at the pain. Had it not been for the rising wind and the rain that suddenly pelted the roof, Artemon and Bethesda would surely have heard me.

Or would they? Suddenly they seemed to be in a world utterly removed from me, totally absorbed in each other. Was he kissing her? Almost certainly he was, but all I could see was the back of her head, and a bit of his forehead just beyond. Was she kissing him in return? It was impossible to tell. Her body seemed tense, her shoulders stiff, but only her eyes could have revealed what she felt. Was Artemon looking into her eyes at that moment? What did he see there?

Time seemed to stop. The kiss seemed endless, suspended in time, like every kiss between true lovers. I felt the ground drop away below me. I seemed to hang in empty space, surrounded by darkness, seeing only the two of them through the narrow slit.

With a sudden, resounding crack, the moment ended. The crack was the sound of Bethesda slapping him across the face.

I stiffened, fearing that Artemon would strike her in return. Instead he staggered back, touching his flaming cheek. He gave her a stricken look and simply stood there, staring at her, for a long time. All expression drained from his face. At last he turned his back on her, squared his shoulders, and appeared to draw several deep breaths, as if composing himself. He pushed aside the cloth that covered the entrance and left the hut.

I reached for the curtain, eager to step into the room and join Bethesda, but again Ismene held me back.

"No!" she whispered, pressing her mouth close to my ear to be heard above the rising wind. "You can't go to her now. Artemon might yet come back. You've seen what you needed to see. Come back to my room. Come, Roman! Follow me!"

She clutched my arm, as a hawk clutches its prey, and pulled me back. Her strength was uncanny. Or was I weak, drained of my will by what I had seen? I allowed her to draw me through the cluttered passage and back into her room.

The lamp had burned low. The room was darker than before. The wind howled outside.

"Do you see now why I couldn't take you to her?" said Ismene. "Do you understand why you can't go to her, even now? If Artemon were to realize the truth—that you've come here to find Bethesda and take her back—there's no telling what he might do."

"Artemon is a boy!" I said. "A lovesick boy."

Ismene nodded. "Yes, that's true. But if you think that's all he is—if you think that makes him ridiculous, and harmless—then you're a greater fool than I imagined. There is much more to Artemon than you seem to think."

"But once he realizes that Bethesda isn't Axiothea, that she's merely another man's slave—"

"He'll lose interest in her? Do you really know so little of love? No, Roman, as far as everyone here is concerned, you must be Pecunius, and she must be Axiothea, and the two of you must never have met before."

"What about Bethesda? Does she know I'm here?"

"Not yet."

"Will you tell her?"

"I suppose I must, if only so she won't be startled and give you both away the first time she sees you."

"When will that be? When can I see her?"

Ismene shook her head. "I don't know. Not yet. For now, you must keep your distance."

This was not the answer I wanted. I began to object, but a rapping at the door interrupted me.

Artemon called out. "Metrodora, are you done with the Roman? We need to get back to our huts."

"Go," Ismene said, pushing me out the doorway.

Suddenly I faced the prospect of standing face to face with Artemon. Would I be able to hide what I felt? I braced myself, but before our eyes could meet, he turned away and headed back the way we had come, walking very quickly. Menkhep, Djet, and I followed.

Above our heads, glowering clouds were faintly lit with the last gray glimmer of twilight. Scattered raindrops pelted my face. The vegetation all around us shivered and thrashed like frenzied Bacchantes performing some ecstatic dance. Even the waters of the Nile were churned into a frenzy. Foaming waves splashed against the muddy shore, and when we reached the huts, I gazed between them to see little whitecaps dancing on the surface of the lagoon.

Artemon turned his face to the sky, narrowing his eyes against the wind and rain. "Metrodora predicted the storm would reach this far south. She knew there would be strong winds and rain."

"What else did she tell you?" said Menkhep. "Will there be an expedition?" His eyes lit up.

"We'll see about that tomorrow," said Artemon. "For now, take shelter. Get a good night's rest—if you can sleep amid this din."

As if to make his point, a blinding flash of lightning ripped across the sky, followed shortly by a crack of thunder that shook the ground.

Menkhep hurried off. For a brief instant, Artemon's eyes met mine, then he retreated into his hut.

Suddenly, above the sound of the rising storm, I heard again the animal's roar that had startled me when I first arrived. Or did I only imagine that sound amid so many noises? I thought I had already seen or at least been warned of all the dangerous creatures that resided in the Delta, but none that I knew of could produce such a blood-chilling sound.

"Did you hear that, Djet?"

"Hear what?"

"That roar. Some sort of animal—"

"It's only the storm. Come on! Hurry!" Djet took my hand and pulled me to our hut.

Fumbling in the darkness of the little room, we found our beds. I sat to take off my shoes. I pulled off my tunic, but left on my loincloth. I lay back, pulled the thin coverlet over me, and listened to the storm outside. Nearby, in his own bed, Djet began to snore softly; the boy could sleep anywhere. I remained wide awake, staring into the darkness, sensing the shivering and shaking of the hut as it was buffeted by the wind, seeing glimmers of lightning through tiny openings in the thatch, clutching the coverlet as thunder pounded the earth like a mallet. Though he mumbled in his sleep, nothing seemed to wake Djet.

Time passed. Minutes, hours—I had no way of knowing. The storm showed no sign of relenting.

At last I threw off the coverlet and rose from the bed. I put on my shoes, but not my tunic. I walked to the doorway and stepped outside.

Rain fell steadily, but it was lukewarm, not cold. I looked about and saw no sign that anyone else was awake. The huts were all shut up and dark. If the Cuckoo's Nest had sentries, surely even these had taken shelter. Except for the foliage that danced all around me, I was the only living thing that stirred.

What of the roar I had heard earlier? What sort of wild animal was lurking in the woods? Was it awake and watchful, ready to stalk and slay any man who dared to venture out? Or had that creature, too, taken shelter from the storm? Or did such a creature even exist? Djet thought I had merely imagined the sound of its roar, and perhaps he was right.

I took a deep breath, left the safety of the hut, and set out into the wild, wet darkness.

On the way back from the visit to Ismene, I had paid close attention to the twists and turns of the path. Even so, it was hard to find my way. A few times I took a wrong turn and found myself at the water's edge, or facing an impassible wall of vegetation. At last I came to the little clearing and saw the joined huts before me. Every part of me was soaked with rain. The loincloth around my hips was heavy and sodden.

I studied Ismene's doorway for a moment. I saw no glimmer of light or any other sign that she might be awake. Then I walked around the structure, to the entrance at the opposite side. That doorway, too, was dark.

The storm raged as wildly as ever, yet I heard nothing but the beating of my own heart and I saw nothing but the curtain that covered the doorway. After so many days of alarm, confusion, despair, searching, and hope—always hope—that curtain was the only thing still separating me from Bethesda.

I pulled it to one side and stepped into the hut.

The room was dark, but just before the curtain fell, lightning flickered behind me. I saw the room for only an instant—just long enough to glimpse a stark, dreamlike image of Bethesda sitting upright in her bed, facing me. She was awake, with wide-open eyes, no longer wearing the many-colored garment in which she had received Artemon, but a simple sleeping tunic.

What did she see? The figure of a man in silhouette, soaked with rain, wearing nothing but a loincloth. No wonder she gasped.

The flicker of lightning passed. The room became a hole of darkness. I stepped toward her.

"Stay back!" she said. Her words were echoed by a peal of thunder.

I tried to speak, but couldn't find my voice. The image of her on the bed remained imprinted on my eyes, unchanging as I moved forward in the darkness. My knees struck the bed. I groped the air. My fingertips touched warm flesh. I blindly reached out, captured her, and pulled her toward me.

Fists pounded my chest. "No, Artemon!" she whispered.

I opened my mouth, but something thick and heavy seemed to be lodged in my throat. I couldn't speak. Nor could I let go of her, no matter how she twisted and turned in my arms. The more she struggled, the more desperately I held her.

My lips found hers. I covered her mouth with a kiss. She resisted, but I held her fast. The taste of her mouth, so longed for and sweetly familiar, sent a quiver of delight through me. In the same moment, I felt a stab of pain and tasted blood from my broken lip.

My limbs acted of their own volition. I hardly knew how we came to be horizontal on the bed, her tunic torn, my wet loincloth cast aside. At every point she resisted me, and at every point I overcame her, until I found myself holding her down and poised on the verge of entering her.

It was then that my senses came to me—slowly, as if I emerged from a stupor. I remained as I was, motionless above her, gasping for breath. In that same moment, somehow—by taste, smell, touch, the sound of my breathing?—she realized who I was.

"No!" she whispered. "This can't be real. This is a dream."

"Not a dream," I said, finally able to speak.

Bethesda drew a sharp breath. Her hands, gripping my arms to hold me back, relaxed for a moment, then gripped me harder than before.

"Didn't Ismene tell you I was here?"

"Who is Ismene?"

I almost laughed. In a world where everyone seemed to have two names, no wonder there was so much confusion!

"Never mind," I said. Then I did laugh—a laugh of sheer joy as Bethesda suddenly took advantage of the lapse in my concentration and broke free, only to reverse our positions. Suddenly I was on my back and she was on top of me.

In the next instant, ecstasy swallowed me and held me in its grip, so firmly and completely that I thought it would never let me go.

We took a long, tumultuous ride into the vortex. At the end, who cried out the loudest, Bethesda or I? Outside, the wind continued to howl and the thunder to crash. Otherwise, Artemon and the others would have heard us all the way to the lagoon.

XXII

"Where have you been?" said Djet when I returned to our hut. The storm had relented a bit, but the world was still dark. "You've been gone half the night."

"Never mind." I fell onto my bed, utterly exhausted. I fell asleep at once.

"Wake up!" said Djet.

It seemed to me that only a moment had passed, but now bright sunlight entered around the curtained doorway.

"Wake up," Djet repeated, poking me in various places with his forefinger in a most irritating way. "Menkhep says you have to come at once."

My head was so muddled with sleep, for a moment I wondered if the events of the night before had been only a dream.

I sat up. No, it had not been a dream. No dream could have been so strange, so perfect—so dreamlike.

"What are you smiling at?" said Djet. "And where did you disappear to last night?"

"That is none of your business." I reached out and mussed his hair.

He drew back and frowned. "You're in a very strange mood."

"Am I? I'll tell you what I am: hungry. There'd better be some food out there."

"You'll have to hurry if you want any. The rest have already eaten. They're all busy getting ready."

"Ready for what?"

"How should I know? That's why Menkhep says you have to come, and quickly."

I wiped the sleep from my eyes and stood up. My arms and shoulders were stiff from rowing the previous day, and my back was stiff from certain other exertions, but no amount of physical discomfort could spoil my mood. I dressed myself and followed Djet into the bright sunshine. The cool, moist world around us seemed to have been scrubbed clean by the rain. The beads of water that clung to the tips of a nearby papyrus plant were turned into scintillating crescents by the slanting sunlight. Steam rose from the earth, and a veil of mist hovered above the lagoon.

"There you are!" Menkhep appeared and slapped me on the back. He was in high spirits. "Here, I saved you a bit of flatbread. Eat up! We'll take some food with us of course, but we won't break for a meal until—"

"Who are 'we' and where are we going?"

"Ah, you weren't awake to hear Artemon's announcement. As you know, Metrodora saw the storm coming yesterday . . ."

"Didn't we all?" I muttered under my breath.

". . . and last night, amid all the thunder and lightning, a vision came to her. It's what we hoped for. The wreck should be waiting for us when we get there."

"What wreck? And where?"

He shook his head and laughed. "It's a good thing you won't have to do much thinking today—just lots of rowing. Don't worry, you'll be in my boat. I'll look after you."

Some of the men had already boarded the long, slender boats tied at the pier. Others were pulling more boats from the foliage along the bank of the lagoon.

"Is everyone going?"

"Almost everyone. Artemon will leave sentries, of course, but those men will also be given a share of the booty."

"Is it a raid?" said Djet. "Will there be a lot of bloodshed? Do I need to carry a weapon?"

Menkhep smiled. "I'm afraid you won't be coming, young fellow. This is work for men."

Djet crossed his arms and stuck out his chin. "But I—"

"Quiet, Djet!" I frowned. "Will he be safe here, on his own?"

"Don't worry. Artemon has instructed everyone to leave the boy alone. No one disobeys Artemon. Now eat that flatbread and come along. Don't forget to bring a hat with you—and a knife. And a scarf."

"A scarf?"

"To cover your face, like this." He demonstrated by pulling the cloth tied loosely around his neck up to his nose. "So that no one will recognize you. It's for their own good. Otherwise, you'll have to kill them." He pulled the scarf down.

"I don't think I have one."

"Never mind, I have a spare I can give you. Now come along."

Moments later, I joined twenty other men in one of the boats on the lagoon, seated at the rear next to Menkhep, from whom the others took orders. Some of the men were to row while others rested, and for the moment I was among the latter. With Artemon's boat leading the way, one by one the vessels headed into the mist, leaving the Cuckoo's Nest behind. I turned my head and saw Djet standing at the end of the pier, looking forlorn, and then the mist swallowed him up.

"How can anyone see where we're headed in this mist?" I asked Menkhep.

"Don't worry, there are men in each boat who know the way. We could take this route in the dark, and sometimes we have. The mist is actually a good thing. It hides us from anyone on the shore. It's all right to talk, but keep your voice low."

"Are we going far?"

"We'll be traveling most of the day. Enjoy the rest while you can. Soon enough it'll be your turn to row."

"I'm already stiff from all that rowing yesterday."

"Lucky you! The best way to work that loose is more rowing."

We headed downriver. The boats glided almost silently through the water. The quiet splashing of frogs along the bank made more sound than we did. The mist was so thick, I could barely see the boat ahead of us, or the one behind. Occasionally instructions were conveyed from the front of the convoy to the rear, with the man in charge of each boat calling quietly to the boat behind.

A thought occurred to me. "Will you not be missed at the trading post, Menkhep?"

He shook his head. "My brother runs the place with me. We take turns."

"He's also a member of the gang?"

Menkhep nodded. "Happily for me, I get to go on the expedition today, while he stays behind and plays shopkeeper. He'll have to look stupid and keep his mouth shut while everyone jabbers about the terrible fate of that old coot from Sais and his mob."

The mist gradually cleared. The rays of the morning sun grew steadily warmer as it rose, but passing clouds provided shade. At times we passed through channels so narrow I could touch the foliage on either side. At other times we crossed open water, so far from land that the distant banks were mere smudges on the horizon.

We passed flocks of ibises and flamingos, small herds of hippopotami, dancing dragonflies and dozing crocodiles. When we weren't busy rowing, Menkhep was happy to converse.

"I'm thinking of something you said this morning, about Artemon," I said.

"Yes?"

" 'No one disobeys Artemon.' Why is that? Why do the men fear and respect him so much? He's so . . ."

"Young?"

"Yes. Even younger than I am."

"Alexander was young, wasn't he, when he led his men all the way to India and back?"

"Are you comparing Artemon to Alexander the Great?" I tried not to sound sarcastic.

"Some men have a certain quality. They were born to be leaders. Other men see that and respond to it. Age doesn't matter."

"But Alexander was born a prince and raised to be a king."

"Do you think only those of royal blood can be leaders of men? I thought you Romans got rid of your kings a long time ago. Don't you vote for the men who lead you? So do we bandits." Menkhep hummed and nodded. "But maybe you're right. Maybe that explains it. . . ."

"Explains what?"

"No one really knows where Artemon comes from. The same could be said of many of us, of course, but in Artemon's case . . ."

"Yes? Go on."

He shrugged. "As I say, none of us really knows the truth. Except perhaps Metrodora . . ."

"What are you talking about?"

"They call him the Cuckoo's Child. There must be a reason."

"You speak in riddles, Menkhep."

"What does the cuckoo do? It lays its egg into the nest of another bird, so that when the egg hatches, the unsuspecting mother bird is fooled into raising the chick as her own."

"Are you saying that Artemon was a bastard? Isn't that what's usually meant when a man is called a cuckoo's child?"

"Sometimes. When a child never seems to fit with the family, people think an outsider must have fathered it. But 'cuckoo's child' can mean something else. There's an old story told by the Jews, about one of their leaders here in Egypt, back in the long-ago days of the pharaohs. He was called Moses."

"I've heard of him," I said, and almost added, *from Bethesda*. Her Jewish mother had taught her many stories about the old Hebrews, just as my father had told me stories of old Rome.

"Then you'll know that Moses was born to a Hebrew mother, who set him adrift on the Nile when Pharaoh ordered that all Hebrew newborns should be killed. But Pharaoh's daughter discovered the baby and raised him as her own. Moses was a cuckoo's child—a slave raised to be a prince."

"So now you're comparing Artemon to Moses?"

"Except that Artemon's story would be the opposite. A prince raised among paupers."

"Are you saying that Artemon has royal blood?"

"Many of the men think so."

"Then how on earth did he end up here?"

"Have we not all arrived here by strange paths—even you, Pecunius?"

I thought about this. "What sort of royal blood? Are you saying Artemon comes from King Ptolemy's family?"

"Not his immediate family. Do you know the situation in Cyrene?"

I remembered the mime performed by Melmak and his troupe, in which the fat merchant meant to represent King Ptolemy had expelled one precious item after another from his backside, all of Cyrenaic manufacture. The point had been to remind people that during King Ptolemy's reign Egypt had lost the city of Cyrene to the Romans, thanks to a will left by the late regent.

"I know that Cyrene used to be administered by Apion, who was the king's bastard brother, and when Apion died he left all of Cyrenaica to Rome."

"And why did he do that?"

"Because he owed a lot of money to Roman bankers and a lot of favors to Roman senators." In recent years, Roman politicians had made an art of such bloodless conquests, inducing foreign rulers to bequeath their territory to the Roman people.

"Even so, most men favor their children in their wills."

"But Apion died childless."

"Ah, but did he?"

"What are you saying, Menkhep?"

"Apion himself was a bastard, sired by the father of King Ptolemy with one of his concubines. For a long time Apion had no place in the Ptolemy household, but by hook or by crook he got his hands on

Cyrenaica and ruled it as if it were his own. Then, on his deathbed, he gave it away so that no other Ptolemy could rule there."

"There's no love lost between members of your royal family," I said. "Mother and sons, brothers and bastards—all at each other's throats."

"And they say we bandits are the savages!" Menkhep laughed. "But what if the bastard Apion sired a bastard of his own—and refused to recognize him? And what if that son, of Ptolemy blood, was raised as a commoner? We might say such a son was a cuckoo's child twice over, in both meanings of the phrase—a bastard, yes, but also, like Moses, a man born to one status but raised by people of another."

"And this cuckoo's child would be Artemon?"

"If that were so, Artemon's birthright would be Cyrenaica—and perhaps more even than Cyrenaica, much more, given the chaos that's brewing in Alexandria."

I shook my head. "This is all rather fantastic, Menkhep."

"If King Ptolemy is forced to flee Alexandria, perhaps even a bastard nephew of the king might stand a chance at the throne."

"Not unless he has an army behind him! I think the hot Egyptian sun has made you delusional, my friend. Artemon as the bastard son of Apion—where did you get such an idea? From Artemon himself?"

"No. Artemon never speaks of his origins. We know he must be Egyptian, because he speaks the language perfectly, and we know he spent some time in Syria before he came to the Delta. But he never speaks of his family."

"Who says he's a bastard Ptolemy, then? How did such a rumor get started?"

Menkhep lowered his voice. "Some say that Metrodora had a vision and saw the truth about Artemon. She never revealed it directly, but from utterances here and there, some of us put together the story."

"These 'utterances' from Metrodora—are they always correct?"

"If you know how to interpret them."

"That's the problem with soothsayers and oracles, isn't it? Misinterpret a single word and you're likely to get the opposite of what you hoped for."

It was our turn to row again, and that put a stop to our conversation.

Menkhep had been right about one thing: the more I rowed, the more the stiffness in my shoulders and arms subsided. There was something exhilarating about being outside, on the water, in the company of other men, all of us bending our efforts toward a common purpose. Little by little I began to feel part of the group.

The snatches of conversation I overheard from the others were less serious than my exchange with Menkhep. These consisted of rude comments, good-natured ribbing, and some of the filthiest jokes I had ever heard. I thought I had grown quite jaded in my travels, and that nothing could shock me, but the coarse vulgarity of these men could have made Melmak and his mime troupe blush.

One of the men was even more vulgar than the rest, and louder. Even though he was seated at the very front of the boat, I could hear everything he said. He was a boaster, endlessly talking about all the men he had killed, all the women he had bedded, and the prodigious size of his member. Seeing me wince at the man's foul language, Menkhep whispered in my ear that his name was Osor and that he came from Memphis.

"A newcomer," said Menkhep. "Something of a show-off. Not especially popular with the others."

"They all seem to laugh at his jokes."

"But not as loudly as he does. Behind his back they call him Hairy Shoulders, for obvious reasons."

The man had stripped off his tunic, and though I saw only glimpses of his bearded face in profile, I could clearly see his bare shoulders, which were covered with the same thick, wiry growth that covered his jaw.

When it was our turn to rest again, I asked about something Menkhep had said. "Is it true that the men vote for their leader?"

"Yes."

"So the men selected Artemon to lead them?"

"That's right. It wasn't long after he joined us, about two years ago."

"He must have looked even younger then!"

"Even so, from his first day among us he proved himself with one act of daring after another. When our old leader was killed during a raid, the choice of Artemon to replace him was unanimous."

"You actually held a vote, as we hold votes for magistrates in Rome?"

"I suppose. Except the vote of each man here is equal, whereas in Rome, I'm told, the vote of a rich man counts for more than that of a poor man."

I did not dispute the point. "What if a man should wish to take Artemon's place?"

"Why do you ask? Do you have ambitions in that regard, Roman?" Menkhep seemed to find the idea amusing.

"Of course not. But what if it happened?"

"It did happen once. A Sidonian named Ephron challenged Artemon to single combat. Ephron was a hulking brute of a fellow, loud and mean-tempered, and even bigger than Artemon. The two fought hand to hand. That was something to watch! When it was over, nothing remained of Ephron but a mangled lump of flesh. The sight of him made my blood run cold. No one has challenged Artemon since."

"But it could happen?"

"Any man can challenge the leader any time he wishes. One would survive and one would die."

"But I thought you said you elected your leader?"

"If a challenger managed to kill Artemon, *then* we'd hold a vote to see if he should be the leader. But the men love Artemon so much, I think they'd vote to banish the challenger instead."

"Might the men vote to put him to death?"

"A man is never put to death by vote, only on orders of the leader, and only when he's broken a rule with such impunity that only his death can put things right."

"Who makes these rules?"

"The leader, with the men's consent."

I shook my head. "It all sounds a bit arbitrary."

"Does it? In the outside world, these men have no say at all about what laws they live by or what man rules over them. Here, every man is equal to every other, and any man can be the leader, if he has what it takes. Is the Roman way any better?"

I had no ready answer.

Had Artemon really killed a man using his bare hands? Artemon, the love-struck boy I had seen last night? No wonder Ismene had been so insistent that I mustn't assert my claim on Bethesda.

There was more to the so-called Cuckoo's Child than met the eye, that was clear. But could Menkhep's far-fetched ideas about Artemon's royal origins possibly be true?

Menkhep had compared his beloved leader to Alexander and to Moses, but another comparison struck me: Romulus, the first king of Rome. My first glimpse of the huts around the lagoon had reminded me of the Hut of Romulus, that venerated landmark in the heart of Rome, lovingly maintained through countless generations so that Romans would never forget their humble origins. Rome had begun as a village of such huts—indeed, as a village of bandits, for in the beginning the twin brothers Romulus and Remus were outlaws who gained ever greater wealth and power as they attracted more and more outlaws to their following, until there were so many men in Rome that they stole the Sabine women—a final act of banditry—then settled down to become respectable followers of a respectable king. Or perhaps not so respectable, since King Romulus's first act was to kill his twin. The murderous rivalries within the Egyptian royal family were appalling, but had it not been the same when Rome had kings?

The origins of Rome were steeped in fratricide and banditry. Was it so implausible, after all, that Artemon, the Cuckoo's Child, might be the descendant of kings, or that a future king of Egypt might come from a bandit's lair in the Delta?

The sun rose to its zenith, bore down upon us, and then began its descent. I fell into the rhythm of the day, rowing and resting, rowing and resting, bemused by the vulgar banter of the bandits and the wild ideas that Menkhep had put in my head.

At last, late in the afternoon, we drew near to our destination.

XXIII

To the ubiquitous smell of the Delta was added another: the tangy, salty odor of the sea.

"Are we drawing near to the coast?" I asked Menkhep. By imperceptible degrees, the landscape around us had changed. The vast mudflats with their scrubby vegetation and the inland lagoons with their floating lotus gardens were behind us. Now sandy banks rose on either side to form low, undulating dunes, pierced here and there by outcroppings of stone and scattered with gray, wind-swept grasses and bunches of flowering succulents.

"We won't actually reach the coast, but we'll see it in the distance," said Menkhep. "Our destination is an inlet where ships are known to take shelter when there's a storm. The inlet is safer than the open sea, but still dangerous, because of sharp rocks hidden just below the waterline at the southern shore. If the wind comes from the north, as it did last night, it can blow a ship right onto the rocks. Even captains who know the hazard can't always avoid it."

"And you think a ship was wrecked there during the storm last night?"

"It's not what I think. Metrodora saw it happen."

"What if we get there, and there's no wreck to be seen?"

"That's not impossible, I suppose. Metrodora could have misinterpreted her vision; perhaps she saw a shipwreck somewhere else. But we'll find out soon enough. Care to make a wager? My trading post against that ruby of yours?"

I stiffened, not caring to reveal to him where the ruby had gone.

"Look at your face!" Menkhep laughed. "Don't worry, Roman, I'm only joking. I'm not a gambling man."

Moments later, the boat leading the convoy rounded a bend and disappeared beyond the high, sandy bank to our right. The boat passed out of sight but not out of hearing, for a moment later I heard the sound of cheering. A ripple of excitement passed down the convoy. As each boat rounded the bend, the men aboard joined the cheering. In due course it was our turn, and I saw the reason for the celebration.

We had entered the inlet of which Menkhep had spoken. The vast circle of water was surrounded by low dunes on all sides except for the narrow channel through which we had entered and another, wider opening to the north, beyond which I could glimpse the sunlit expanse of the sea. On the southern shore of the inlet, immediately to our right, I saw the wrecked vessel. The ship lay on its side, half in the water and half on the beach, its broken mast trailing a tattered sail. The exposed hull was pierced by a gaping hole.

Debris from the ship was scattered up and down the beach, as were several bodies. The bodies showed no signs of life. It was all too easy to imagine how these doomed sailors had been swept overboard, sucked under the storm-churned waters, and cast onto the beach.

Artemon directed the lead boat to make landfall near the foundered ship. As the men jumped into the surf and pulled the long boat onto the beach, a figure emerged from the nearby wreck. At first, I took him to be a survivor, but his long, dark robes and cloth headdress were more suited for riding a camel than sailing a ship. The man gave a start, turned back toward the wreck, and cried out. Several more men, similarly dressed, emerged from the ruin of the ship. Seeing the approach of our little flotilla, they turned and ran toward a nearby sand dune, where a number of camels had been tethered. Stacked near the camels were various items that had been scavenged from the ship.

"It appears that someone's arrived ahead of us," I said to Menkhep.

"Fools! Everyone knows this inlet is the territory of the Cuckoo's Gang. Any ship that founders here is ours to plunder and no one else's."

"These fellows seem not to have gotten the message."

"They will, soon enough. Rowers, be quick! Double-time!"

The men from Artemon's boat were already in pursuit, knives drawn. The quickest of the scavengers managed to jump onto a camel and head off at a gallop, but his slower, less agile companions were not so lucky. They were still fumbling to mount their camels when Artemon's men fell upon them in a frenzy. Blades flashed. Crimson streamers of blood rose from the melee. For a few moments I heard screams and cries for mercy, then silence.

Menkhep steered our boat alongside the others that had already been drawn onto the beach. "Damn! We've missed the battle!"

"It was over before it started," I said. "But one of them got away. No one seems to be going after him."

"Artemon always lets one man escape, to tell others what happened. Worthless scavengers like him will think twice before they try to steal the plunder of the Cuckoo's Gang! As it is, these stupid fellows have simply done some of the work for us, sorting through the valuables and stacking them neatly on the beach."

Once all the men had beached their boats, we assembled in a group near the wreck. Artemon stood before us. His red scarf had been tied to conceal his face, and those of us who had not yet done so followed his example.

"It's just as the soothsayer told us," he said. "Last night's storm brought death and disaster to some, but their loss is our gain. For sending us here, we can thank Metrodora."

The men around me nodded. Some made superstitious signs with their hands, averting the jealous power of the Evil Eye that robs men of good fortune.

"We hide our faces because some survivor may yet be alive within that wreckage, or wandering the beach. It seems unlikely. Anyone who saw those scavengers, or us, will have fled into the dunes. And if anyone on the ship was still alive, I suspect those scavengers put an end to them. So I think it's unlikely that we'll encounter any survivors. But if we do . . ."

He paused to run his eyes over the men assembled before him, fixing his gaze on each of us in turn. With the lower half of his face hidden by the scarf, his eyes took on a peculiar intensity. When his gaze met mine, I shivered. What was this power Artemon projected over other men, and where did it come from?

"If we do encounter any survivors, they are not to be harmed. Nor is any woman to be molested. We are bandits—not assassins, not soldiers, not rapists. Does every man here understand? Does every man agree?"

I nodded, thinking this would suffice, but every man around me said the word "yes" out loud. Some noticed my silence and turned to look at me, until I, too, said it. This was apparently a ritual among them, in which all had to take part.

"If any man here does not agree, if he thinks he knows a better way, if he thinks he would make a better leader and make better rules, then let him step forward now and challenge me." Artemon strode from one end of the group to the other, looking from face to face. No one moved.

"Very well. I remind you of another rule. When a storm strikes at sea, some men aboard ship prepare for their fate by tying to their persons whatever valuables they possess. They do this as a signal to whoever should find their bodies: take these worldly goods in return for the favor of disposing of these remains in a decent fashion. This is a sacred bond between the dead and the living, between the victim of the storm and the scavenger. We honor and observe that bond. Using whatever dry wood we can collect from the beach and from the ship, we shall build a pyre. Any body we find, upon which the dead man's wealth has been attached as an offering, will be stripped of valuables and then laid upon the pyre and burned, so that neither fish nor vultures can devour it. Does every man here understand? Does every man agree?"

"Yes," I said, along with the others.

Artemon stared at us for a long moment. By the crinkling of his eyes, I could see that he smiled. "Then let's begin!"

Following Artemon's instructions, the men fell to various tasks. Some fetched the booty already collected by the scavengers and began loading it into the boats. Some ventured into the wrecked ship, carrying long axes to break through any obstacles; later they emerged carrying trunks and bundles of fabric and even a few amphorae of wine that had survived the wreck intact. Some began collecting wood and building the funeral pyre.

Others headed up and down the beach to comb through the debris and search the dead bodies. Among this last group I saw Hairy Shoulders, who apparently had left both his tunic and his loincloth in the boat, for he was going about the task completely naked. I had never seen a man with so much hair on his body.

I looked up and saw vultures circling overhead. Their wheeling flights converged above the little dune where the scavengers had been slain. While I watched, one vulture after another dared to land and pick at the corpses.

"Menkhep!" said Artemon, walking toward us. "You and Pecunius go and tend to those bodies."

"You don't expect us to drag them to the funeral pyre, do you?" said Menkhep.

"Of course not." Artemon drew closer and lowered his voice. "But someone needs to scare off those vultures and search the bodies, to retrieve any valuables. I can trust you to do that without defiling the remains. Some of the men—they're hardly better than animals, as you well know."

"Come on, Pecunius." Menkhep was clearly not pleased with our assignment.

The skittish vultures were easily dispersed. First we looked through the trappings of the camels, but found little of value. They had been hitched in a circle, their reins tied to a scrubby bush. Menkhep set about untying them, and indicated that I should do likewise.

"Are you sure we should let them go?" I said.

"We can hardly take them with us. Would you have them stand here in the hot sun and starve?"

Finally we turned to the task of searching the corpses.

I had as yet seen few dead men in my life, and touched even fewer with my own hands. The bodies were still warm and the wounds still wet with blood. From the similarity of their features and the range of ages—the eldest had a white beard, and the youngest was hardly bigger than Djet—I realized that the scavengers might all be members of a single family. If that were the case, the lone survivor would be returning to a household of women soon to be wracked with grief.

Some of the men wore rings and necklaces, none of any great value. Between them we retrieved only a handful of coins. Upon several of these the serene profile of King Ptolemy had been smeared with blood. Menkhep wiped the coins clean before dropping them in the bag tied at his waist.

Menkhep paused and tilted one ear upward. "Do you hear that?"

I listened. Above the quiet surf, the creaking of the wrecked ship, and the sound of the men shouting back and forth, I heard a noise like the whimper of an animal, very faint but from somewhere nearby. The noise faded, then I heard it again, louder and more plaintive than before.

"That's a woman," said Menkhep, lowering his voice.

"Are you sure?"

"Come!" He gestured for me to be silent and follow.

We trudged through the sand to the top of the dune. In the shallow depression below us, atop a bed of succulents, glistening with beads of sweat under the hot sun, I saw the heaving, hirsute backside of Hairy Shoulders. What he was doing was obvious, but the body beneath his was so much smaller that I could hardly see her. At last Hairy Shoulders pulled back, and I saw the bloodless face of a young girl framed by a nimbus of curly chestnut hair. Her eyes were shut and her mouth was frozen in a grimace. It was hard to tell whether she was conscious or not, but she was clearly in pain.

Beside me, Menkhep put two fingers in his mouth and produced a shrieking whistle.

A moment later, Artemon came running up the little hill, followed by several others. Interrupted by the whistle, Hairy Shoulders had withdrawn from his victim and rolled to one side. He looked up at us dumbly. His hairy chest was matted with blood, and for a moment I thought he must be wounded. Then I realized the blood had come from a deep gash across the girl's breasts. The tattered remains of her clothing were pasted with sweat and blood to her motionless body.

"It wasn't me who stabbed her!" shouted Hairy Shoulders. "It must have been the scavengers. They must have had their way with her before they started ransacking the boat, then they left her here to die." There was a note of panic in his voice. When I saw the look on Artemon's face, I understood the man's fear. Artemon's gaze was like that of a basilisk: furious, implacable, without mercy.

"Did you not hear what I said, before we began, Osor?" Artemon's low, chilling tone was more frightening than if he had shouted.

"Of course I heard. But it's not like I harmed the girl myself. I told you, this is how I found her. I ask you, what man wouldn't take advantage of such a situation, eh?" He managed a crooked grin. While he talked, his manhood, which appeared to be just as prodigious as he claimed, had withered until it almost vanished amid the forest of hair between his legs.

"You must see that you leave me no choice," said Artemon.

"What? Why do you say that?" Hairy Shoulders's voice broke. "It's not what you think, I tell you! She was enjoying it. Don't you see?" He turned to the girl, but when he touched her, he pulled back his hand and gave a stifled cry.

The girl was dead.

"Bring him to the beach, where everyone can see," said Artemon. The others descended on Hairy Shoulders and carried him, twisting and shouting, up and over the crest of the dune and toward the beach.

Artemon looked at Menkhep. "You and Pecunius, carry the girl to the funeral pyre."

It was a strange and loathsome duty, having to touch a body so recently alive. As we moved her, a warm breath issued from the girl's mouth so that she seemed almost to sigh, but the reedy, hollow sound was not like anything I had ever heard from the lips of a living mortal. Her body was limp and weighed very little. I could easily have carried her by myself, had I cared to pick her up in my arms, as occasionally I had picked up Bethesda for the simple joy of holding her and carrying her about. Instead, Menkhep and I shared the burden, carrying her like a sack or some other object, and our progress across the sand was slow and painfully awkward. Menkhep, who had searched the slain scavengers with no sign of squeamishness, appeared quite unnerved by this task. We both sighed with relief when at last, slowly and gently, we laid the girl's body atop the makeshift pyre of debris and driftwood.

In the meantime, Hairy Shoulders's ankles had been bound and his wrists tied behind his back. He had been lain over a crate taken from the wreckage, so that his head hung over the edge. He was quietly weeping.

From up and down the beach the men reassembled before the wreck. Their high spirits faded as they drew closer and realized what was happening.

Artemon stood before the prisoner. In one hand, like a chamberlain's staff or a military standard, he held an axe with a long handle. "You were caught in the act of raping one of the ship's survivors, Osor. Do you deny it?"

Hairy Shoulders strained to lift his head, and managed to look Artemon in the eye. "Any other man would have done the same! The girl was going to die, anyway, so what difference does it make?"

"I saw what you did. So did the men who carried you here. Does any man here wish to speak in defense of Osor?" Artemon ran his eyes over the crowd. No one spoke.

"Then I pronounce you guilty and declare that the punishment shall be carried out at once. Does any man here challenge my judgment?"

"This is madness!" shouted Hairy Shoulders. "Why does no one speak up? What a bunch of cowards you all are, taking orders from this high-born whelp!"

"The punishment is death," said Artemon. There followed a long moment of silence broken only by the quiet surf and the cries of the seagulls.

"By the laws of the outside world—the world ruled by King Ptolemy—you'd be made to suffer a terrible death, Osor. You might be crucified, or hanged, or stoned to death. But because you're one of us, you shall be given the death that the rest of the world reserves for men of rank and honor, the swiftest and most merciful means of execution. You shall be beheaded, Osor."

Hairy Shoulders averted his face and began to sob.

"Who will carry out the sentence? It should be done swiftly and surely, with a single blow. The task calls for an experienced killer of men." Artemon looked from face to face, until his eyes settled on me. "There's a newcomer among us, a man who's said to have done his share of killing. And because he's new, he can have no personal grudge against Osor." He stepped toward me and held forth the axe. "This is a chance to show us what you're made of, Roman."

I looked at Hairy Shoulders, bound and sobbing on the makeshift chopping block. I looked at the axe. The sharp blade gleamed in the sunlight. I looked at Artemon's face. He had the stern, determined look of a leader of men, but in his eyes I saw a strangely boyish glitter of excitement.

With trembling fingers, I reached for the axe.

XXIV

I had killed men before.

The first time had been in Ephesus, under very different circumstances. There, I had done what had to be done, but even so I had felt a tremor of doubt. Something similar had happened in Rhodes, though in that instance the man's death was the result of a struggle—more the choice of the gods than my own.

Artemon thought I was a cold-blooded killer, a man capable of murdering others in their sleep—or did he? Had he seen through my pretense? Was this a test, to see if I would falter and give myself away?

Hairy Shoulders was surely a despicable creature, but I was not at all certain he deserved to die. If I refused to carry out the sentence, would that refusal constitute a challenge to Artemon's authority? Would I be required to fight him, man to man?

For a crazy moment, I imagined what would happen if I actually won such a contest. Gordianus of Rome—leader of the most dangerous gang of bandits in the Delta! That would be one way of securing Bethesda's release.

But another outcome seemed far more likely: Artemon would kill me with his bare hands. I swallowed hard and felt light-headed. Whatever happened, at least Fortuna had allowed me to enjoy one final night of bliss with Bethesda!

To chop off Hairy Shoulders's head was easier than challenging Artemon, surely. Or was it? To kill a man I hardly knew, before a crowd of onlookers, in cold blood—the idea sent a wave of revulsion through me.

I reached for the axe, but my hand stopped short. My open fingers trembled, frozen in place. I felt the eyes of Artemon and all the others on me.

"Let me do it!" said Menkhep. He stepped forward and gripped the handle of the axe.

Artemon kept his grip on the axe and gave Menkhep a questioning look.

"Hairy Shoulders arrived in my boat. It should be my responsibility."

"You know it doesn't work that way among us," said Artemon. "We aren't King Ptolemy's army, with everyone sorted into ranks and some men lording it over others."

"Even so, I'm willing and ready to do it." He gave me a sidelong look. "Besides, the Roman isn't yet one of us, not fully. The men haven't yet voted to accept him. He hasn't undergone the ritual of initiation."

Several of the men muttered and nodded to show their agreement with Menkhep. Seeing my chance, I lowered my hand and stepped back. Artemon relinquished his hold on the axe and allowed Menkhep to take it.

"Menkhep speaks wisely," he said. "Do it quickly, then."

I had been spared the gruesome task, but to avert my eyes would show too much weakness. I forced myself to watch as Menkhep took a firm stance, secured his grip on the axe, raised it above his head, and brought it down.

There followed a series of sounds I would never forget: the whoosh of the axe, a sharp thud as it struck flesh, the crackling shriek of severed bone and flesh, the thump of the head striking the soft sand, the squish of spurting blood, the chorus of men groaning and gasping despite themselves.

Another man might have botched the job, failing to sever the neck or missing the target completely, but Menkhep's aim was true and his strength sufficient. The amount of blood that gushed onto the sand was ghastly, but the cut was cleanly made. The life of Hairy Shoulders ended as quickly as any man could wish. I decided then and there, if I should ever face a similar fate—and as long as I remained among the Cuckoo's Gang, that possibility would be ever-present—I would ask for Menkhep to carry out the task.

Once the flow of blood had subsided, some of the men carried the body to the funeral pyre and laid it beside that of the dead girl. Artemon himself picked up the head, gazed for a long moment at the lifeless features, then carried it to the pyre and positioned it above the body, reuniting the severed parts.

The men resumed the task of scavenging the ship and stripping the corpses scattered up and down the beach.

The sun was still up, with perhaps an hour of light remaining, when Artemon declared that our day's work was done. The boats were loaded and ready to embark. The funeral pyre was stacked with the bodies of Hairy Shoulders and the girl and several of the dead passengers and crew who had paid for the privilege by securing their valuables to their bodies before they died.

Artemon struck a fire. The men watched in silence as he set the pyre alight. No prayers for the dead or propitiations to the gods were offered. As Artemon had said, the men of the Cuckoo's Gang were not soldiers. There were no officers or priests among us to perform such rites.

The boats were so stuffed with valuables that the men could barely fit, and we rode so low in the water that great care was required of the rowers. We left the inlet just as the sun was sinking, and my last glimpse of the desolate beach was of the wrecked ship and the pyre, from which the flames now shot high into the air. Then we rounded the bend and headed back the way we had come.

Even as the twilight faded and the water turned black, we continued to row. The men in charge of each boat were so familiar with the route that they could navigate in the dark.

But the men were too weary to row for long. As the moon began to rise, we came to a secluded spot, pulled the boats ashore, and made camp for the night. The men ate cold rations while they talked and joked about the events of the day, then spread blankets in whatever spots they could find and fell asleep.

I dozed for a while, but only fitfully. I woke from a vague dream of fire and blood and found myself wide awake.

I stood and stretched, feeling stiffer in every limb than I had ever felt before. I followed the sound of croaking frogs to the water's edge, where I came upon Menkhep. He sat on the trunk of a fallen palm tree, gazing at the moon and stars reflected on the water.

"Do you mind if I join you?" I said.

He gestured to a spot beside him on the log.

"Can't sleep?" I said.

"Killing a man always has that effect on me." He looked at me side-long. In the uncertain moonlight, the two points of light that marked his eyes looked as distant as the stars.

"I can't sleep, either. I thought I might volunteer for sentry duty," I said.

He shook his head. "You won't be asked to do that until you're truly one of us."

"When will that be?"

"After Artemon puts it to a vote, and you've undergone the initiation."

This was the second time that day he had spoken of such a thing. I didn't like the sound of it. "What sort of initiation?"

"You'll find out, in due time." He stared at the water. "After what I did today, I think you owe me another favor, Roman."

"Do I?"

"I saw the squeamish look on your face when Artemon offered you the axe. You, the killer of all those men in Canopus! I asked myself: what sort of killer is this Pecunius, anyway?"

I shrugged. "Perhaps the cowardly kind, who prefers his victims to be asleep."

"Is that it, Roman? Or did something else make you hesitate? I thought I saw something like pity on your face—pity for that wretch Hairy Shoulders! For a moment there, I thought you were going to refuse to carry out Artemon's order. I thought you were about to challenge him. I believe he thought so, too. You weren't the only one who looked relieved when I took hold of the axe."

"Artemon was relieved?"

"I could see it on his face."

"Artemon, relieved, because he was afraid to fight *me*?" I felt flattered for a moment, until Menkhep let out a harsh laugh.

"No, stupid! Because he didn't want to have to kill you. Not yet, anyway. I think he likes you."

Menkhep had been tense and moody when I joined him. He now seemed more relaxed. I decided to venture a question.

"When we went to see Metrodora yesterday, I got the idea that there was another woman sharing the hut with her."

"What makes you think that?"

I shrugged. "Something Metrodora said."

He hesitated for a moment, then nodded. "Yes, there's a young woman there. Now some of the men call that hut 'the women's quarters'—as if such a thing could exist in the Cuckoo's Nest! I remember a time before Metrodora came, a time when no woman of any sort would have been allowed to reside among us, not even a witch."

"Metrodora has made a place for herself among you, but surely the young woman isn't here of her own free will."

"She's a captive, being held for ransom. Artemon says there's a rich man in Alexandria who'll pay a fortune to get the girl back, but so far, the rich man hasn't even bothered to reply to Artemon's messages."

"Is this girl the rich man's daughter?" I asked, making a show of my ignorance.

Menkhep shook his head. "His mistress, they say. An actress with a mime troupe."

"A rich man's mistress? She must be quite beautiful."

"She certainly is."

"You've seen her?"

"Only a couple of times, and then only for a moment. From the first day she arrived in the Cuckoo's Nest, Artemon has kept her hidden from the rest of us. He says it's better that the men don't see her at all, lest they be tempted."

"Tempted to do what?"

"What do you think? Hairy Shoulders wasn't the only randy goat among us, though I'd like to think he was stupider than most." Menkhep shook his head. "A girl that pretty could cause all sorts of trouble, even if no one lays a finger on her."

"How so?"

"Bat her eyelashes, flirt a bit, act all helpless—imagine the fights that might break out if she decided to play one man against another. Soon enough she'd talk some starry-eyed fool into helping her escape." He sighed, then lowered his voice. "I only wish that Artemon had followed his own rules, about not seeing the girl. I wish he'd never laid eyes on her!"

"Why do you say that?"

"Do you know the story of Alexander and the King of Persia's wife?"

"Refresh my memory."

"When Alexander killed King Darius and conquered Babylon, everyone expected him to call the wife of Darius before him, because her beauty was legendary. But the most important thing to Alexander was that the Persians should love him, and to ravish their queen would get him off to a shaky start. He also wanted to keep a clear head, and feared that her beauty would muddle his senses. So, even though the queen wished to meet him, Alexander refused to allow her into his presence, fearing that what he touched with his eyes he would be compelled to touch with his hands. He behaved like a king, not a conqueror, and he resisted temptation."

I nodded. "They tell a similar story about Scipio Africanus." Menkhep gave me a blank look. "You must have heard of him."

Menkhep shook his head. I sighed. Surely I was a stranger in a strange land, to find myself among men who had never heard of Scipio

Africanus. "He was merely the greatest Roman general who ever lived, the man who outfoxed and outfought Hannibal of Carthage."

"Hannibal—now *him* I've heard of."

I grunted. "That's all very well, but the story is about Scipio. When he was fighting in Spain, Scipio conquered the city of New Carthage. The daughter of his enemy was brought before him. Her beauty took his breath away. He could have taken her then and there, but instead he averted his eyes and returned the girl to her father. Poets have sung his praises ever since."

Menkhep nodded. "So far, Artemon has resisted this girl—but who knows how much longer he can do so? If only he had never fallen under her spell!"

"Are you saying this girl is a witch, like Metrodora?"

"Ha! It wouldn't surprise me if Metrodora has taught the girl a few spells since she's been in her care. But Metrodora's sorcery is child's play compared to the magic of Hathor." This was the name by which the Egyptians worshiped Venus.

"If Artemon wants her so badly, and she's his captive, at his mercy . . . what would happen, if he were to take this girl by force?"

"That would violate his most important rule, that captive women and boys must not be molested. Every one of us must obey that rule, on pain of banishment or death, and that includes Artemon himself. Otherwise he'd show himself to be a hypocrite, and the men would turn against him."

"What if it wasn't rape? What if he was to win the girl over, with sweet words?"

"Some of the men might be happy for him, but many more would be jealous. Why should our leader have a lover or a wife living with him in the Cuckoo's Nest, when we have none? And if he takes her for his own, that means the gang will have to forfeit the ransom, which the rich Alexandrian may yet be willing to cough up. Artemon knows all this, yet he can't seem to shake her spell. Yesterday, while you were with Metrodora, he was with that girl."

"Trying to seduce her?" I clenched my teeth, remembering the kiss.

"Probably. But without success. Just before Artemon left her, I heard a loud slap. And when he came out of her hut, one of his cheeks was as red as a hot coal."

"The girl struck him? And he let her get away with such a thing? Is her beauty so great?"

Menkhep smiled. "I'm not a rich Alexandrian, or a eunuch from the royal palace. I don't see beautiful women every day. But by any standard I can imagine, yes, the girl is exceptional. No wonder she's called Axiothea! But more than that . . ." He fell silent for a moment, searching for the right words. "There's a kind of fire in her. She's special. Anyone could see that at a glance. In fact . . ."

"Yes?"

"She reminds me a little of Artemon himself. She even looks a bit like him. She's much shorter, of course, but even so, when I first saw them side by side, I might have taken them for brother and sister—the same dark hair, the same fine features. They do make a lovely couple."

If only Artemon could love her like a sister! I thought.

Suddenly I yawned, and realized I was sleepy again. I left Menkhep and returned to my blanket.

I thought about all I had seen that day, and what I had witnessed of Artemon's abilities as a leader of men.

The journey to the inlet had taken place without incident. The interlopers at the shipwreck had been dispatched immediately and without any losses by the Cuckoo's Gang. The ship had been stripped of its valuables as quickly and thoroughly as anyone could wish. When one of the men violated the common law, Artemon ordered the culprit to be executed on the spot, without so much as a grumble from any man present. At the end of the day we made a clean escape, loaded with spoils. At every turn, Artemon had been in complete control of all that transpired.

His strengths as a leader were indisputable. He seemed to have only one weakness: his desire for Bethesda. As far as I was concerned, that made him the most dangerous man on earth.

XXV

The men who had stayed behind at the Cuckoo's Nest greeted our return the next day. They stood on the pier and along the shore, cheering as each boat sailed into the lagoon laden with booty. Djet stood at the very end of the pier and waved wildly when he saw me.

When all the boats were moored, the men who had stayed behind were tasked with unloading the booty and carrying it to the clearing next to the roasting pit, while those of us who had gone on the expedition stretched our limbs and rested.

This division of labor helped to spread the work among the men, but it had a purpose beyond that, for in this way everyone in the Cuckoo's Nest had a chance to see the booty and touch it with his own hands. Thus each man had an idea of what might constitute an equal share when the treasure was divided among us, as happened later that day.

First a meal was prepared and consumed, along with a considerable amount of wine. After everyone's appetite was sated, the men gathered in a circle.

Artemon gestured to the stacks of treasure in the middle of the clearing. "Look, men of the Cuckoo's Nest—see how much richer we are today than yesterday!"

The men clapped, hooted, and cheered.

"Every man here did his part," said Artemon. "Every man here deserves his share."

There was more raucous cheering.

"The task of disbursing the treasure falls to me. Does any man here doubt my judgment? Does any man doubt my fairness? Does any man challenge me?"

There was only silence, until Menkhep spoke up. "We trust you, Artemon. Now hurry up and get on with it!"

This was met with a round of laughter, and more cheering.

"Very well, then," said Artemon.

He began with several sacks full of coins. It struck me that the disbursal of these should be simple enough, but because the coins came from many different places and were of various qualities and weights, splitting them up in equal shares was not as simple as I had thought. Among the bandits there were a few men who had worked in counting houses or currency exchanges, and Artemon called upon them to assist him in evaluating and sorting the coins. This procedure took place in full view of anyone who cared to watch, and in the end each man was given as nearly as could be calculated the same share as every other, including Artemon, and myself, for that matter.

Goods that could be consumed, such as the amphorae of wine, were to be shared among the men over time; these were publicly displayed, so that everyone could look forward to the enjoyment in store for them. Goods that would have to be sold to realize their value, such as jewelry and silver vessels, were to be placed in the common treasury, to be dealt with later; these, too, were shown to everyone. As these precious objects were paraded through the clearing, I was reminded a little of the triumphal processions I had seen as a boy in Rome, in which the most fabulous spoils of war were shown off to the people of Rome by their conquering generals.

Artemon himself, to the objection of no one, claimed the few scrolls that had survived the wreckage; these mostly had to do with the ship's business, though there was also the soggy remnant of a play by

Menander. Other goods of a more personal nature, such as clothing, shoes, belts, satchels, coin purses, boxes, knives, lamps, unguents, brushes, and combs, were distributed to the men according to their need for such items, or to those who had been passed over in previous disbursements and were next in line. It appeared that Artemon maintained a ledger to keep track of which men were owed more or less, a wax tablet with markings in some code of his own invention. It seemed not to matter that only he could make sense of this ledger, since all the men appeared to trust his accounting, and the great majority of them were illiterate, anyway.

At the end of that day, every man in the Cuckoo's Nest had a full stomach and a coin purse fatter than the day before, and went to his hut with some new treasure, no matter how small. Djet was not included in the disbursement of coins, but made out especially well when goods were handed out, for the booty included a number of wooden toys and clothing suitable for a boy his age. Since these were of no use to anyone else, Djet was given the lot.

I myself received a pair of very finely made shoes, which fit me as if the leather had been tailored to my feet. Artemon chose them for me and insisted I take them, noting that my own shoes had grown quite worn and shabby in the course of my travels. I tried not to think of where the shoes had come from, or imagine the fate of the man who had worn them.

"Every man can use a good pair of shoes to protect his feet," said Artemon, as he handed them to me. "Especially a man about to face his initiation."

I swallowed a lump in my throat. "When might that be?"

"As soon as tomorrow, if all goes well."

"And what—" I began to say, for I wanted to know more about this so-called initiation. But I heard a grumble from the man behind me, who was impatient to receive his share of the booty, as were the men behind him. I took my new shoes and moved on.

For the rest of the day, talking to Menkhep and some of the others with whom I was becoming acquainted, I tried to learn more about the initiation. Everyone deflected my questions, some more clumsily than others. Not one of them would give me a clear answer. It became obvious that I was meant to know nothing more than I already knew—only that the ritual might take place the next day, and that it was better done wearing shoes than in bare feet.

That night in our hut, listening to Djet softly snoring, I lay staring at the darkness for a long time. It was not my worries about the initiation that kept me awake. It was an all-consuming desire to see Bethesda.

I had gone to her before. Did I dare to go to her again?

No, I told myself; a second visit would be too dangerous. The first night, the raging storm had allowed me to make the short trip to her hut unnoticed, but tonight the sky was clear and all was quiet. I would surely be seen. Artemon would be apprised of my movements. Disaster would be the result.

And yet, I could think of nothing else. I remembered my previous visit. I recalled every small detail, dwelling on moments of exquisite pleasure, recalling the sight, the sounds, the smell, taste, and touch of her. These recollections did nothing to calm me or quiet my longing. They only increased my agitation.

I did what I could to satisfy myself physically, more than once. Still, I could think of nothing else.

At last, weariness overcame me.

But even as I entered the world of dreams, I heard again that roar of some wild beast from the tangled woods beyond the Cuckoo's Nest. That sound did what nothing else could do—it drove Bethesda from my thoughts, and in her place instilled a cold, paralyzing premonition of dread.

The next morning, I rose before the sun was up.

I ate a bit of stale bread and a handful of dates, then found a se-cluded spot by the lagoon, in sight of the huts but some distance away, and watched as the world gradually woke to the new day. The surface of the water changed from dark green to pale blue as the daylight grew stronger. Birds began to call and sing. Some of the men emerged from their huts, but many slept late, taking a well-earned rest after the expedition. Those who noticed me across the water neither called nor waved to me, and no one came to join me, not even Menkhep, who almost certainly saw me across the water but quickly vanished from sight. I began to think this must be a part of the initiation ritual, that no one should speak to me or even look me in the eye.

Eventually, it seemed that all the men must have risen, and yet, except for myself, the perimeter of the lagoon was deserted. Suddenly, from the direction of the clearing with the roasting pit, I heard the sound of many voices shouting in unison. I realized that a meeting was taking place—to which I had not been invited.

The sound of the shouting finally awakened the latest sleeper of all. Across the lagoon, I saw Djet emerge from our hut. He yawned and stretched and rubbed his eyes, spotted me and made his way around the lagoon to join me. Occasional shouts still rang out from the clearing.

"What are they doing over there?" he said.

"Talking about me, I suspect."

His eyes grew wide. "Why? Have you done something wrong?"

I managed a weak smile. "Hopefully, I've done something right. We'll find out, soon enough."

Menkhep appeared across the lagoon, at the foot of the pier. He waved to me and gestured that I should come to join the others, then turned back. His face gave no indication as to what I should expect.

I made my way to the clearing. My heart began to race, though I told myself I had nothing to fear. Djet followed me. I glanced back at him only once and then avoided looking at him, for his eyes were wide with alarm.

The clearing was more crowded than I had seen it before. Every man in the Cuckoo's Nest had come to the assembly. Artemon stood above the crowd at one end of the clearing, standing on a dais fashioned from the sawed-off stump of a palm tree. He saw me and gestured that I should join him. Djet made his way to the front of the crowd.

Artemon's face was grave but his voice was friendly enough. "Are you ready for the initiation?"

Since I had no idea what the initiation entailed, how could I answer such a question? I nodded.

He raised an eyebrow. "A nod is good enough for me, Pecunius, but when I ask you the same question for the benefit of the men, I suggest you show a bit more enthusiasm." He turned to the crowd and addressed them in a loud, ringing voice. "Esteemed comrades, we have before us a newcomer. He calls himself Marcus Pecunius."

"A Roman name!" shouted one of the men, in a tone that was not very friendly.

"Pecunius is indeed a Roman," said Artemon. "But many of us came to the Cuckoo's Nest from lands beyond Egypt, and even those of us who are Egyptian come mostly from regions beyond the Delta. Having a Roman among us might be a good thing. He speaks Latin, for one thing. You never know when that might come in handy. And to get here from Rome, he must have done some traveling. A man who's seen the world could turn out to be useful."

Men nodded their heads and murmured agreement.

"Pecunius also arrived bearing gifts for us—a not inconsiderable amount of money, and jewelry, as well. He's already donated a generous share to our mutual fund."

At this, many of the men applauded and cheered.

"As you can see, he exhibits no lameness or disease. Is he as fit as he looks? I ask you, Menkhep. Pecunius rowed beside you yesterday, did he not?"

Menkhep emerged from the front of the crowd. He turned to address the others. "The Roman did his share of work. He's no slacker."

"And he may have even more useful skills, of which we haven't yet seen a demonstration," said Artemon. From the sidelong look he gave me, I knew he was referring to my alleged reputation as a killer. This prompted more nods and murmurs from the crowd.

"What does the soothsayer think?" someone shouted.

"Metrodora has already given her approval," said Artemon. Many in the crowd nodded thoughtfully. "All in all, I think Pecunius would make a worthy addition to our little band. But before we vote on the matter, let's make sure he wants to join us. What do you say, Pecunius? Do you wish to become a member of the Cuckoo's Gang? Do you wish to live among us and share an equal portion of whatever comes our way, whether it be good fortune or bad, plenty or poverty, life or death? Will you agree to honor the laws of the group, as determined by its members? Will you follow the orders of the man chosen to be our leader, whether that man is myself or another?"

When I hesitated, he looked at me shrewdly. "There is an alternative, of course. If you find our way of life repugnant, if you object to our laws, if you cannot obey the commands of whatever man leads us, then you needn't throw your lot with us. Not every man was meant to be part of the Cuckoo's Gang; we understand that. But you can't expect us to simply set you free. You'll be stripped of the coins and jewels you kept for yourself. You'll be put in chains, but you won't be harmed. If you can think of someone who might pay for your release, and if the prospect seems reasonably profitable, we'll hold you for ransom. If not, you'll be taken along the next time some of us venture to a town with a slave market. We'll put you on the auction block and see what you fetch. That way, we'll be rid of you and you'll be rid of us."

"And a slave!" I said.

Artemon shrugged. "It's not much of a choice, I'll admit. But there you have it."

My goal was to free Bethesda, and that would never happen if I myself were a captive. Still, I was repelled by the idea of becoming a member of the Cuckoo's Gang, especially since it appeared that a pledge of loyalty would be required from me. This was not a matter I took lightly, because a Roman's word is his honor. Just how binding was a vow made under duress, especially to a gang of brigands?

What would my father have done? What would my old tutor, Antipater, have advised? As far as I could see, I had no choice. I stared Artemon in the eye and did my best to feign enthusiasm.

"I wasn't born to be a slave," I said. "Neither was any man here, I'll wager. I choose to join you."

He smiled. "Don't tell me. Tell them."

I turned to the crowd. I looked from face to face. Some looked friendly, while some looked skeptical or aloof, but not one of them appeared to wish me harm. For the first time, I realized how diverse the group was. No single color predominated amid the wide array of flesh tones, from ebony to alabaster, with every shade between. Some had the tightly curled black hair and black skin of Nubians. A few had the flame-colored hair and ivory complexion of the northern races. Somehow, they had all found their way here, and so had I.

"I want to join you . . ." I began, and then realized, from the blank faces before me, that I was mumbling. I thought of Bethesda, swallowed hard, and raised my voice to a shout. "I want to join you—if you'll have me!"

"What do you say, men of the Cuckoo's Nest?" said Artemon. "Yes or no?"

"Yes!" shouted Menkhep. "Yes! Yes!" He pumped his arms in the air and encouraged the others to join him.

"Yes!" they yelled, at first in scattered shouts. But very quickly the shouts joined together and turned into a chant. Some of the men clapped and stamped their feet. Others raised their arms in the air. "Yes! Yes! Yes!"

At the front of the crowd, I saw Djet. Caught up in the excitement, he began to jump up and down and whirl about.

Looking out at a sea of faces and upraised arms, hearing the enthusiasm in their voices, I felt an unexpected stirring of excitement, and even a perverse sort of pride. Never before in my life had I been singled out to stand before such a large group and then been made to feel that I was somehow special—never mind that the men were all criminals and that I was playing a role. Was this how every new member was welcomed into the Cuckoo's Gang? I realized that each man there had experienced his own singular, exhilarating moment on the dais.

At last the shouting died down.

"Well, then, that's settled." Artemon clapped a hand on my shoulder. "Now you have only to take the pledge, and face the initiation."

I was not sure which I dreaded more, taking a false oath or enduring some unknown trial, but there could be no turning back.

"Is there a particular god by whom I need to swear?"

Artemon shook his head. "There are no gods here—or hadn't you noticed? 'By all the gods that are not'—that's how our oath begins." Many of the men laughed heartily at this. "You look at the men before you as you take the oath. It's to them that you make your pledge. It's they who'll make sure you keep it, and punish you if you don't."

I nodded to show that I understood.

"Very well then, Pecunius, place your hands upon your testicles."

"What?"

"Do it!"

I took a wider stance and clutched myself through my clothing, then flushed a bit at the good-natured laughter this evoked.

"Upon your honor as a man, and upon pain of losing those precious orbs between your legs—as well as your head—do you hereby swear that you shall be loyal to the men assembled before you, the brave, stalwart men of the Cuckoo's Gang?"

I cleared my throat. "I swear it!"

"Do you swear that you shall do nothing to betray us or bring harm to the group, and that you shall alert us at once to any threat that might harm us?"

"I swear it!"

"Do you swear that you shall obey the laws of the Cuckoo's Gang, as decided by its members and enforced by its leader?"

"I swear it!"

"Do you swear that even if you should become separated from us, or be captured by our enemies, or leave us of your own volition, you will continue to obey this oath, and do nothing that would bring harm to any member of the Cuckoo's Gang?"

"I swear it!"

"Very well then, by the gods that are not, I declare you to be a member of the Cuckoo's Gang. Now you may remove your hands from your testicles."

I did so, to uproarious cheering and laughter from the crowd.

"Now, Pecunius, you're truly one of us—if you survive your initiation."

XXVI

As if on cue, from somewhere deep in the thicket beyond the clearing came the peculiar, chilling roar I had heard when I first arrived.

My heart skipped a beat. "What *is* that noise?" I said.

Artemon gave me a thin smile. "Shall we go and find out? Follow me, Pecunius."

He stepped from the dais and made his way to a trailhead almost hidden by vegetation at the edge of the clearing. The narrow path headed in a direction new to me. The way was little used, to judge by the rank vegetation that turned the path into a tunnel of sun-dappled greenery. Looking over my shoulder, I saw that the rest of the men followed us in single file, headed by Djet and Menkhep.

After many a twist and turn, we emerged in another clearing, so similar in size and shape to the one we had just left that for a moment I thought we had doubled back. Then I saw the long, wide pit that ran from one side of the clearing to the other, so deep that I couldn't see the bottom of it. Artemon pulled me aside, allowing the others to file past us into the clearing. They encircled the long pit and crowded along its edges.

Ismene appeared, standing only a few feet away from me. She was

dressed in a voluminous midnight-colored robe spangled with yellow
stars. The garment was too big for her and looked like something filched
from a Babylonian astrologer. She wore no makeup, but her fingers were
encrusted with gaudy rings, and around her neck was a chain strung
with gleaming lumps of amber. Seeing her by the bright light of day in
such an outlandish costume, with her wild, uncombed hair forming a
ragged halo around her head, I couldn't decide whether she looked ridiculous or frightening.

The men crowded around the pit took notice of her. From the awestruck, almost reverent expressions on their faces, it was clear that they
saw nothing absurd about the woman they called Metrodora.

Menkhep stepped toward her, then dropped to one knee and bowed
his head. "Thank you, soothsayer! The mission you sent us on yesterday was a fruitful one, and all—almost all of us—came back safely.
Your foresight was true once again."

The others followed Menkhep's example, dropping onto one knee,
bowing their heads in her direction, and muttering words of thanks.
Even Artemon did so. I saw no choice but to follow their example.
After bowing my head, I looked up to see that Ismene was watching
me with a look of faint amusement.

Any amusement I might have felt was stopped short by a sudden
roar. It was louder than ever before, and much closer. In fact, it seemed
to come from the nearby pit.

My blood turned cold in my veins. I rose to my feet. So did the others. They took their eyes from Ismene. Some stared down into the pit.
Some looked at me, with grave expressions. A few flashed what I took
to be malicious grins, which took me aback, for until that moment I
thought that no one in the Cuckoo's Gang wished me ill.

Artemon led me to one end of the long pit. The men crowded along
the edge stepped back to make room for us. I saw what lay before me,
and sucked in my breath.

The pit was at least ten feet deep, with sheer earth walls on all sides.
I judged it to be twenty feet wide and at least twice that long. A slender wooden wall the height of the pit ran all the way down the middle,

beginning directly in front of me, dividing it into two enclosures, one to my left and the other to my right. The wall appeared to be a rather makeshift affair, thrown together from pieces of scrap wood.

Palm leaves and other bits of dried vegetation had been strewn across the bottom of both enclosures. Amid the leafy debris I saw human skulls and other bones. At first it seemed that the enclosure to the right was unoccupied; then a sudden movement caught my eye, as a crocodile, half-hidden by a palm leaf, gave a start and scurried with unnerving swiftness from one end of the pit to the other, scattering bones along the way, furiously swinging its tail and snapping its jaws.

Nothing could have been more terrifying than the crocodile, I thought, until my gaze fell upon the creature that occupied the other half of the pit.

Growing up in Rome, I had seen many exotic animals in gladiator games and other spectacles put on by the magistrates. In my travels, I had seen even stranger beasts, some in the flesh and some in paintings or mosaics. But I had never encountered or even imagined a monster such as this.

In basic form it resembled a lion, with four legs, a tail, and a mane, but there the resemblance ended. Lions are tawny gold, but this creature was multicolored—the legs were bright orange, the back was purple, and the mane was a fiery red with black spots. The mane didn't fall back from the creature's brow as that of a lion does, but radiated outward, as if a burst of flame surrounded the creature's face—a face that terminated not in a leonine snout, but in a strange sort of tusk, like that of a rhinoceros. Its tail was more like that of a scorpion than a lion, a horrible, segmented thing that made a clacking noise as it swished this way and that. The tail terminated in a hideously swollen, barbed stinger.

The creature stood at the far end of the pit. While I watched, it threw back its head and roared. There was a keening, howling quality to the sound that set my teeth on edge.

Just as the jerky, reptilian movements of the crocodile sent a thrill of revulsion through me, so the appearance of this creature revolted me. There was something unnatural about it, as if multiple animals had been chopped up and sewn together. What sort of monster was this, and where had it come from? I realized that Ismene was close beside me, and gave a start. Had sorcery created this abomination?

Ismene drew closer. She whispered into my ear. "Choose left, not right. Don't flee, but fight."

What doggerel was this? I was about to ask her to repeat herself when Artemon placed one hand squarely between my shoulder blades and gave me a hard shove. With a howl of protest I staggered forward and abruptly found myself atop the wall that bisected the pit. The wall was topped by a series of slender palm trunks laid end to end, like a rail. These trunks were as wide as my foot, but rounded, so that securing a steady purchase was difficult. As I struggled to find my balance, I heard a creaking noise and felt the whole wall jerk and sway beneath me. When I instinctively stepped backward, something sharp poked the small of my back.

"No turning back, Pecunius. You can only go forward."

I looked over my shoulder and saw that Artemon was holding a long spear, with the point pressed firmly against my back. I turned to look ahead, straining at every moment to keep my balance. From the men lining the edges of the pit I heard a roar of laughter. Did they mean for me to walk the whole length of the rickety wall, from one end of the pit to the other?

"Impossible!" I hissed, though clenched teeth. "This is madness!"

No one heard me. They were laughing too hard.

I had thought that the men of the Cuckoo's Gang were my friends, or at least not my enemies. They had welcomed me to their ranks; they wanted me to become one of them. Now the applause and cheers I had received only moments earlier seemed a cruel joke. No man could possibly walk the whole length of such a narrow, rickety wall without falling to one side or the other. And if I fell . . .

In my right ear I heard the snapping of the crocodile's jaws, and a clattering of bones as it swept the ground with its powerful tail. In my left ear I heard the bloodcurdling yowl of the monster.

"Best get on with it, Pecunius," said Artemon. He chortled and gave me a poke with the spear.

Standing there, trapped atop the wall with no way back, surrounded by laughing onlookers, gripped by the realization that my life might come to a horrible end in a matter of seconds, I experienced one of those supremely strange moments that come to a man only a few times in his life. My senses had never been so acute; every sight and sound seemed at once hugely magnified and yet distilled to its essence. Smells, too, registered with unprecedented intensity. Each of the creatures in the pit below me exuded its own particular stench. The monster emitted a sour, putrid smell, like that of a festering wound. The crocodile had a rank, moldering odor, like seaweed rotting under the hot sun.

And yet, in that moment, I felt no fear. Indeed, I seemed to feel nothing at all, as if I were a mere observer of a scene that was peculiar and mildly interesting but had nothing to do with me.

I looked at the faces of the onlookers, and wondered at their expressions. Yes, they were laughing, but in a good-natured way, not jeering or shouting insults. They seemed to be richly amused at my plight, yet exhibited no signs of malice, as if they were responding to a joke, not delighting at the prospect of a man about to be torn to shreds. What sort of men were these? Or more to the point, in what sort of situation did I find myself? That was my first inkling that all was not as it appeared to be.

Among them, poised at the very edge of the pit above the enclosure with the monster, I saw Djet. He alone seemed not to understand the joke. His eyes were huge and his face was pale. He swayed unsteadily, as if he might faint, but I had no fear that he would fall, for I could see that Menkhep was holding him firmly by the shoulders.

From somewhere I found the necessary motivation—I can hardly call it courage, since fear had deserted me—to raise my right foot and bring it down in front of my left.

"That's the way to do it!" shouted Artemon.

"That's the way!" said Menkhep. "Go for it! Go!"

The men began to clap and chant. "Go! Go! Go!"

Now they seemed to be encouraging me, not to fall but to get on with crossing the wall, as if such a feat might actually be possible. A thought occurred to me: if this was truly the gang's standard initiation ritual, and not some wicked trick, then many or most or perhaps all of the men present had gone through the very same ordeal and come out alive. If they could do it, then so could I.

I took another step.

"Go! Go! Go!" they shouted.

I glanced at Djet. His eyes were still huge, but he slowly raised his hands and began to clap in time with the others.

I took another step, and another. Then more steps. My balance was flawless. I took a deep breath, and felt at peace. After all, traversing the top of the wall was no more difficult than walking a straight line on solid ground.

Then, on my next step, the wall pitched ever so slightly to one side, then to the other, then seemed to sway madly back and forth.

The laughter and clapping abruptly stopped. I was surrounded by a chorus of gasps. I swung my arms and kept my eyes straight ahead to see that Artemon and Ismene had circled around to the far end, as if to meet me, if I should get that far.

By some process beyond rational thought, my body righted itself. Slowly the wall stopped its motion and became steady again. The swaying had been only a tiny thing, I realized, a matter of a finger's width, but it had felt enormous.

I took another step. I was now more than halfway across. Above the pounding of my heart I heard the men begin to laugh and chant and clap again.

In my abstracted, tightly concentrated frame of mind, I had almost forgotten the creatures in the two enclosures below. Had they been moving about and making noise the whole time? If so, I had not been aware of it, but suddenly I heard the snapping of the crocodile's jaws to my right and the roar of the monster to my left, both very close, as if each was right below me. The stench from both creatures combined to create a supremely foul odor that made my head spin. My heart pounded even louder in my ears, and I felt a quiver of fear.

"Begone!" I said aloud, not to the two beasts, but to the fear. For a moment, at least, the spell seemed to work, for I managed to take a few more steps.

Then I came to the gap in the wall.

Somehow, I had not seen it before. From the vantage of my starting point, the top of the wall had appeared to run continuously from one end to the other, without interruption. This illusion had persisted as I took one step after another. Yet now, looking down, I saw that the wall suddenly dropped several feet, then after a considerable gap returned to its previous height.

How was I to continue? At first I thought I would have to climb down to the lower level of the wall, take a few steps, and then somehow climb back up to the higher level to finish the journey. Then I saw that the lower level of the wall was not topped with a palm trunk, or any other sort of rail. It was made of a series of sharpened stakes, impossible to walk upon.

Now I saw another thing I had not perceived when I set out. Directly below me, tied to the wall, were two lengths of rope. One went off at a diagonal to my right, the other to my left. In essence, these were tightropes, one pulled taut above the pit with the crocodile, the other strung above the pit with the monster.

The onlookers saw that I had finally realized my situation, and roared with laughter.

"What now, Pecunius?" From a distance that was still considerable, Artemon gazed at me with his arms crossed and a sardonic expression on his face. I had thought he circled around to the far side to welcome me, but now it seemed he had done so just to see the look on my face at this moment. Next to him stood Ismene. Her face was unreadable, but when our eyes met, she slowly nodded and moved her lips, as if to remind me of the words she had whispered in my ear. *Choose left, not right. Don't flee, but fight.*

Neither fleeing nor fighting seemed to be an option at the moment, but I did face a choice between stepping onto the tightrope to my right or to my left. Ismene had told me to choose the latter, but why? I didn't particularly care for my chances with the crocodile, but I cared even less for the prospect of falling into the pit with the unnatural monstrosity on the other side. My inclination was to take the risk of walking across the pit with the crocodile—especially now that I spied something that looked like a cudgel amid the palm leaves strewn on the floor of the beast's enclosure. It was probably only a piece of wood that had come undone from the wall, but it looked as if it might make a hefty weapon, useful for keeping the crocodile at bay. I could even imagine lodging it between the animal's jaws, forcing them open and rendering them harmless.

I quickly scanned the other enclosure, but saw no similar cudgel or anything else I might use as a weapon against the monster. Even the human bones that littered the creature's enclosure had been trampled or gnashed into useless shards.

Was I to follow my own instincts, and attempt to traverse the tightrope above the crocodile's pit? Or was I to obey Ismene's instructions, and walk above the monster's lair? As if to make the choice even harder, both creatures suddenly became active. The crocodile thrashed about. The monster paced back and forth below me, threw back its head and released another bloodcurdling roar. The hot, foul stench of its breath rose up to envelop me like a noxious cloud.

Did it really make any difference which route I chose? I was no tightrope-walker, and either beast was surely vicious enough to rip me to pieces.

The strange detachment that had so far insulated me from fear suddenly evaporated. I was afraid—very afraid. My legs trembled. My chest grew so tight that I could hardly draw a breath.

"You can't stop now!" yelled Artemon.

"Go on!" called Menkhep.

"Go! Go! Go!" The men chanted and clapped in unison.

Ismene stared at me and soundlessly moved her lips.

I placed one foot onto the rope to my left.

Almost imperceptibly, Ismene nodded.

The rope under my foot gave just a bit, but seemed secure enough to hold my weight. I judged the distance to the edge of the pit to be no more than ten or fifteen feet. How hard could it be to walk across a rope? It would best be done quickly, I told myself. I looked ahead and saw the men crowded along the edge of the pit draw back, so as to allow me space when I reached the other side. They clapped and chanted and stamped their feet to encourage me.

"Go! Go! Go!"

I glanced at Djet and saw a look of sheer terror on his face. He covered his eyes.

I did not walk across the rope. I ran. It was easier than I had anticipated. My balance was perfect.

Then, a few steps ahead of me, I saw a place where the rope was badly frayed. Even as I watched, the strands unraveled. It occurred to me that such a weak spot in the rope could hardly be there by accident. More likely, someone had deliberately cut the rope nearly through, so that it would give way if any fool tried to walk across it.

The rope snapped.

An instant later, I struck the ground. My ankles gave way and I landed hard on my backside. The stench of the monster filled my nostrils. The horrible roar rang in my ears. Above me, the men clapped and cheered and laughed harder than ever.

XXVII

I scrambled to my feet—no easy task, for the palm leaves were slippery underfoot and my legs had turned to jelly. The monster was so close I could have touched it. I frantically stepped back, slipped on more palm leaves, and fell on my backside again.

I braced myself, expecting the creature to leap atop me, but instead it bolted back. It seemed that monsters could be startled, too.

I took advantage of the creature's momentary consternation to roll onto all fours, turn about, and race to the far end of the pit. I stood and turned and braced my back against the earthen wall. The monster stood at the opposite end of the pit, swishing its scorpion-like tail and baring its fangs.

Directly above the monster, looming at the edge of the pit, were Artemon and Ismene. The men who had been crowded along the right side of the pit, above the crocodile's enclosure, now rushed to the other side, so as to have a better look. Some laughed so hard they were doubled over, barely able to stand. Artemon also laughed, but was more restrained and controlled than the rest. Ismene stood stiffly upright and expressionless, looking down her nose at me.

Above the raucous laughter, I heard the high, shrill voice of Djet.

I located his face amid the throng. He was frantically pointing at something very near me. I scanned the ground beneath my feet, then looked at the section of the ramshackle wooden wall directly to my right. I still couldn't make out what Djet was saying, but I saw what he must be pointing at. Cut into the wall was a small door mounted on crude hinges with a simple latch to keep it shut.

The door would take me out of the monster's enclosure—and into the adjoining enclosure with the crocodile.

I stared at the monster, which now faced me head-on so that I confronted the full splendor of its flaming red mane and the terrible threat of its fearsome tusk. Recovered from the surprise of my fall, the monster peered back at me with its catlike eyes. It snarled and took a deliberate step toward me, then another.

I put my hand on the door latch and crouched low, preparing to push it open and bolt through. Then I heard a rustling noise from the other side. Was the crocodile already waiting for me? Could I reach the cudgel in time to make use of it?

I remembered the second half of Ismene's advice: *Don't flee, but fight.*

I glanced up at her face. Again, I saw her move her lips, as if to remind me of her parting words.

I shook my head and clenched my teeth. I had just followed the witch's instructions, going left instead of right, and where had that gotten me? What was I to think, except that Ismene was deliberately trying to get me killed? And yet, if that was her intention, and if my sorry plight was giving her pleasure, she had a strange way of showing it. I saw no satisfaction on her face, only a keen, unflagging insistence that I do as she had told me to do. Again I heard her words in my ear, not as one hears the echo of words in memory, but as if she were actually beside me, speaking aloud: "Don't flee, but fight!" Was this an audible act of witchcraft, or was my mind playing tricks on me?

If I were not to flee, how was I to fight? With nothing more than my bare hands against a creature with claws and fangs, not to mention a tusk and a scorpion's tail? With so many ways to kill me, perhaps the monster would at least give me a quick death, whereas a fight against the crocodile might be long, bloody, and horribly painful. Was that the purpose of Ismene's advice, not to save me but to guide me to a more merciful end?

In that moment I made my choice. I would not seek to escape into the adjoining enclosure. I would stand my ground and confront the monster.

I stood upright. I drew back my shoulders. I clenched my fists.

The monster cocked its head, as if surprised at my arrogance, then took another step toward me. The swishing of its scorpion tail made a clacking noise that set my teeth on edge. When it opened its mouth to roar, the horrible odor that spilled forth was almost enough to bring me to my knees.

I decided there was no point in waiting for the monster to attack. As I had seen, the creature was capable of being startled. If I made the first move, perhaps I might at least have the advantage of surprise.

I rushed toward the monster. To my amazement, it took a step back.

The horn was my chief worry, and grabbing hold of it was my goal. A bite or a scratch I might survive, at least for a while; even the sting of its tail might be mild enough to allow me to keep fighting. But if the monster managed to gore my belly with that horn, all would be over for me.

Above me I heard a sudden uproar from the men. In the blink of an eye, cheering replaced laughter. I had never heard such cheering except in the gladiator games at Rome, when a fight reached its climax and the audience erupted with excitement.

Before the monster could react, I grabbed hold of its tusk with my right hand. At the same instant, because I realized it was just within reach, with my left hand I grabbed hold of its tail, near the stinger. If I had the strength to hold fast to these two deadly weapons, and the dexterity to avoid its claws, perhaps I could somehow swing myself atop the creature and ride or wrestle it to the ground.

That, in retrospect at least, was what I may have intended. Or perhaps I acted purely from instinct and impulse, with no plan whatsoever.

Whatever I may have hoped to accomplish, nothing of the sort transpired, for in the next moment I found myself tumbling head over heels past the monster and onto the palm-strewn ground, clutching in one hand the monster's horn and in the other its segmented tail. Both had come loose from the creature with hardly any resistance.

Above me, the roar of cheering changed back to a roar of laughter.

One voice carried above the others. It was Menkhep: "This is our best initiation yet!"

He was shouting across the pit to Artemon, who was now directly above me, peering down with a serene smile and a sage nod of his head. Next to him stood Ismene, whose countenance at last betrayed the faintest trace of emotion, a look at once smug and satisfied and ever so slightly sympathetic to the confusion that overwhelmed me. When she stepped back from the precipice and vanished, somehow I knew that she was leaving the gathering, as if the drama—or comedy—had come to its conclusion.

I turned to look at the monster, which in the blink of an eye seemed to have transformed itself into a simple lion.

The unnatural colors—orange limbs, purple trunk, red mane—were exactly that, unnatural. Someone had dyed the creature's fur, and had also trimmed and arranged its mane, stiffening it somehow so that it held its radiant shape. The segmented tail was nothing more than a prop fashioned from hollow gourds and attached to the lion's real tail. The horn seemed real enough, but it had been hollowed out so that it weighed very little; what manner of beast it came from I didn't know, but the lion certainly never grew it.

I was trapped in the pit not with some hideous creature of magic, but with a lion. That fact should have been terrifying in itself—but what sort of lion was this, that allowed itself to be dyed and coiffed and fitted with a false tail and horn?

As the laughter died down, Artemon addressed me from the edge of the pit. "I see you've made the acquaintance of Cheelba."

The painted lion sat back on his haunches and gazed back at me with an air of offended dignity. I kept my eyes on the beast, not yet ready to let down my guard. I threw the false tail aside but kept hold of the horn, which might yet serve as a weapon.

"The lion has a name?" I said.

"Most certainly. Cheelba has been with us for well over a year now. He was among the booty we took from the caravan of a Nubian merchant. The merchant intended to give the beast as a present to King Ptolemy. A lion as tame as Cheelba is rare indeed—a worthy gift for a king."

"But—the stench from its mouth!" I pinched my nose, for at that moment the lion gave a great yawn that sent a noxious breath in my direction.

Artemon sighed. "Cheelba seems to be suffering from a rotten tooth. It puts him in a cranky mood—thus that plaintive roar he utters from time to time, not at all like his usual roar. Tame Cheelba may be, but so far no man among us has displayed sufficient bravery—or foolishness—to reach into the lion's mouth to pull that rotten tooth."

The lion settled, retracting all four limbs. It continued to gaze at me with a quizzical expression.

"Those colors . . . that absurd mane . . . the false tail and the horn—"

Artemon laughed. "You're wondering about Cheelba's disguise? That idea came from one of our confederates, a man with considerable skill at creating such artifice, who works to a very high standard. Even under daylight, the illusion was quite convincing, wasn't it? The artificer is no longer among us—he's off in Alexandria—so be careful how you handle that horn. I fear you may already have damaged the scorpion tail, throwing it aside so carelessly." He saw my peeved reaction. "Don't feel foolish, Pecunius! Every man here who met Cheelba under the same circumstances was fooled by the lion's . . . costume, if I may call it that. And most of those initiates made bigger fools of themselves than you did, I daresay."

Looking up at the crowd, I noticed a few cracked smiles and red faces amid the general merriment.

The lion blinked. It gave another yawn, filling the air with stench, then rolled onto its side, rested its head on one paw, and shut its eyes. Only its tail moved, stirring the air and rustling the palm leaves.

I drew a breath, and realized it was the first full breath I had taken since the ordeal began. My shoulders slumped. I suddenly felt exhausted and as weak as a child. Even the hollow horn felt heavy in my hand. At last I turned my back on the lion so that I could look up at Artemon, craning my neck to do so.

"What about the other side of the pit? What if I had chosen to walk across the crocodile's enclosure?"

He cocked an eyebrow. "Others have done so before you."

"Is that tightrope also rigged to break?"

Artemon shook his head. "No, the rope above the crocodile is intact. If a man can manage to cross it, he's passed the initiation. But very few men have managed to do so."

"They fell into the crocodile pit?"

"Yes."

"Did any of those men survive?"

"How inquisitive you are, Pecunius! But since you ask, I can remember only one such candidate. He survived, yes, but he wasn't allowed to join us. We patched him up as best we could and sent him on his way. Ismene said he would bring bad luck. Of what use is a bandit who's lost his hands?"

I shuddered. "The crocodile isn't a pet, then?"

Artemon laughed. "Mangobbler is no one's pet, even though he's been with us longer than Cheelba. Mangobbler seems always to be in a bad mood."

As if to demonstrate the point, there was a sudden banging noise from the other enclosure as the crocodile furiously lashed its tail against the wall.

The racket set my teeth on edge, but had no effect on the lion, which seemed to be fast asleep. Even its tail had ceased to move.

One end of a slender rope abruptly fell at my feet. I looked up to see that Menkhep held the other end, which was coiled several times around his fist. "Time for you to climb out," he said.

I looked at the rope, then at the lion. The beast began to snore. It whimpered and twitched its paws, as if dreaming.

Bethesda loved cats. Not huge cats such as this one, but the much smaller variety that one encountered everywhere in Alexandria and in all the other cities of Egypt I had visited. To the people of the Nile, cats were sacred animals, protected by law and custom against all harm. They were allowed to come and go as they liked, living in temples and public arcades and even in people's houses, where families venerated them like little gods and goddesses. As a boy growing up in Rome, I had seen lions at a distance in gladiator shows but had never encountered an Egyptian housecat. I had never imagined that people could coexist and even cohabit with such creatures, but Bethesda had taught me that one could not only approach them safely, but could even handle them in such a way as to bring pleasure to human and feline alike.

An idea occurred to me. A mad idea, surely, and yet . . .

Perhaps I was giddy from the ordeal I had just experienced, drunk with relief, and like a drunk man, suffering from impaired judgment. Or perhaps the experience had cleared my head, and my mind was sharper than ever. Whatever my mental state, once the idea occurred to me, I felt an overwhelming impulse to carry it out.

With my fingers I frayed the end of the slender rope, so that it terminated in a number of strong but pliable strands. When I was satisfied with this work, I slowly approached the sleeping lion.

I squatted beside the beast and cautiously laid my hand on its side. The beast responded with a sigh. I felt the rise and fall of its rib cage as it breathed. Though its mouth was closed, the odor from its rotten tooth at such close proximity made me wince.

Above me, the men grew quiet. "What's he up to?" Menkhep muttered.

I slowly stroked the lion's chest, then its face, feeling a thrill of fear and excitement. The dyed fur was coarser than that of an Egyptian housecat.

"Cheelba—is that your name?" I whispered. "Beautiful Cheelba. Good Cheelba."

Moving very slowly, I touched the lion's jaw, then its dark lips. Its eyelids flickered, but still it dozed. I pressed my fingers between the lips and made contact with the teeth, which felt hard and huge and very sharp beneath my fingertips.

I swallowed hard and took a quick, deep breath. I set the end of the rope beside me and used both hands to pry the lion's jaws apart. To my amazement, the beast let me do as I wished, though it snorted quietly and its eyelids flickered.

I spotted a sharp fang with a gaping black hole. It was this cavity that emitted the terrible stench. I took hold of the tooth and felt it move in its socket, as if it were nearly ready to come loose from the gums.

Holding the jaws apart with only a forefinger and thumb, I reached for the rope. At this point I could have used a third hand, but nonetheless I managed to slowly, carefully tie several of the stringlike ends of the rope around the damaged tooth.

Above me, I heard the men whisper and gasp, but no one laughed or raised his voice.

When I was done, the rope was firmly attached to the tooth.

I slowly rose and stepped back from the dozing lion.

"Menkhep," I said, keeping my eyes on the lion and my voice low, "can you give me enough slack so that I can climb up without disturbing Cheelba?"

He lowered more of the rope, then the men to either side of him joined him in holding fast to the other end. I took hold of the rope and walked up the earthen wall of the pit, using the last measure of my strength to put one foot ahead of the other. At last I reached the top, where helping hands lifted me up and over the rim.

Without a word, Menkhep and the others relinquished their grip on the rope and stepped back, so that I alone still held the rope.

I looked down at Cheelba, who still dozed, and then across the pit, at Artemon. He no longer smiled; his expression was hard to read. Was he impressed, or displeased by my initiative? It occurred to me that I might give the rope to him, so that he could execute the next step, but when I raised it slightly, as if to make the offer, he seemed at once to understand the gesture and rejected it with a small shake of his head and a very slight wave of his hand.

Menkhep patted me on the back. "Let's see you do it, then," he said. A murmur ran through the crowd like an echo.

"Yes, do it!" said Djet, who now stood close beside me, gazing upward. His eyes were bigger than ever.

I looked at Artemon. He slowly nodded.

I coiled the excess length around my forearm, slowly pulled the rope taut, and gave it a gentle tug. The knots I had tied around the tooth held firm. Cheelba wrinkled his nose and squeezed his eyes shut and reached up with one paw, as if the movement of the rope tickled his lips.

"Best done is quickly done," I whispered, quoting the old Etruscan proverb. "Stand back, everyone." For the span of several heartbeats I held the rope taut, then gave it a hard yank.

The tooth did not come free.

Instead, in an instant, Cheelba was on his feet, roaring loudly and swiping at the rope with his forepaws. The rope was coiled fast around my forearm; it wouldn't come free. Cheelba backed away, pulling hard on the rope. My only choice was to pull back, but I quickly learned that a lion is stronger than a man. I tottered at the edge of the pit, about to fall in.

Menkhep grabbed one of my arms. Djet grabbed both of my legs. Others moved in to grab hold of me, and then, in the next instant, we were all tumbling backward.

Djet scampered out of the way—a good thing, or else I would have crushed him. I landed hard on my backside.

Like a snapped whip, the far end of the rope came hurtling out of the pit. The lion's tooth, still attached, shot toward me like a missile. I saw it coming, and thought it must be headed straight between my eyes, but it struck a bit higher than that.

The pain was so sharp I gave a scream and reached up to clutch my forehead. The fang was only slightly embedded in the flesh. It came loose at my touch. I held it before me and wrinkled my nose at the smell. There was blood on my fingers, whether from myself or the lion or both, I couldn't tell.

The concerned faces of Menkhep and Djet hovered over me, then both withdrew as Artemon took their place. His smile had returned. He pointed at my forehead.

"That's going to leave a scar, I'm afraid. Ha! You can say a lion bit you, and you'll hardly be lying."

He grabbed one of my hands and pulled me to my feet. I swayed unsteadily.

"And that tooth should make a fine trophy, after it's been cleaned up a bit. Here, Pecunius, let me take it. I'll have it mounted for you and hung from a chain. You can wear it around your neck as a souvenir."

From the pit I heard Cheelba roar—a very different sound, more robust and less plaintive, now that his tooth had been pulled.

The roar of the lion was drowned out by that of the men, who lifted me up and carried me on their shoulders all the way back to the Cuckoo's Nest.

XXVIII

The rest of my initiation day was marked by the consumption of a great deal of wine and beer. My memories are hazy. Ismene was nowhere to be seen. Nor, of course, was Bethesda, the person I most longed to see and to touch after experiencing such a close brush with death. Even in a drunken stupor I managed to restrain my urge to go to her and I said nothing that would give me away.

I was taught a number of secret greetings that were used by the Cuckoo's Gang. Some were snatches of doggerel—I was to say the first half of a certain nonsensical phrase, and if a stranger also happened to be a member of the gang he would say the rest of the phrase back to me. Other greetings involved secret hand signals, some rather broad but others quite subtle. These were useful, so I was told, if I were to meet another member in a crowded place, or if I needed to signal across a room.

The more I drank, the sillier it all seemed, especially a hand signal that involved poking my little finger into my ear, first on one side, then the other. The proper response was to tap one's thumb to one's chin three times. After performing this signal back and forth several times, Menkhep and I were reduced to tears of laughter.

At some point, Cheelba entered the clearing. It seemed that he was just as tame as Artemon had indicated, for not one of the men drew back. Several of them dared to pet and stroke the beast, as one might an Egyptian housecat. Cheelba paused obligingly to submit to these caresses, but steadily made his way toward me. Had I been sober I might have bolted, but in my inebriated state I merely marveled at the lion's stately progress through the crowd. When he reached me, he stared into my eyes for a long moment, then nuzzled my hand. I felt his hot breath on my palm, and then the roughness of his tongue as he licked my fingers.

Djet looked on in wonder. The others gave a cheer. Even Artemon applauded. Cheelba raised his head and released a mighty roar.

Thus ended the day I became a member of the Cuckoo's Gang.

In the days that followed, I fell into the routine of the Cuckoo's Nest, insofar as a lair of outlaws and vagabonds can be said to have a routine. I confess that I took part in some petty acts of brigandage, but by the grace of Fortuna I was able to tread a precarious middle path: I neither caused injury to any innocent victim, nor did I break my oath of loyalty to my fellow bandits.

With Menkhep and a few of the others, I let down my guard sufficiently to reveal bits and pieces of my true past, such as the fact that I had traveled to all of the Seven Wonders of the World. A man who has seen the Wonders never lacks for an audience, even among criminals.

For the most part, those were miserable days for me, as I pretended to be something I was not and all the while watched and waited, in vain, for an opportunity to rescue Bethesda and escape. Had I been willing to attack and overcome the guard posted outside Bethesda's hut, I might have liberated her and fled the Cuckoo's Nest at almost any time, but we wouldn't have gotten far. Artemon's interest in Bethesda was too great, and his reach was too vast.

During this watchful period, I noticed that visitors arrived in the Cuckoo's Nest almost every day. From their hurried and secretive manner, I presumed these men were messengers, and some of them were, but others, as I was later to realize, would better be described as co-conspirators. On some days, two or three such visitors arrived. These men were escorted straight to Artemon, with whom they conferred in private. These visitors usually stayed no more than a night. Often they left only hours after they arrived, rushing off as if Artemon had charged them with some urgent mission.

I asked Menkhep if all this coming and going and secretive communication was customary. He shook his head. "Artemon's always been a planner and a schemer, always thinking ahead, but this is different. There's something big afoot. Just what it is, I don't know. The biggest raid ever, some of the men say—a raid so big, it'll change everything."

"What could it be?"

"Only Artemon knows. When he's ready, he'll tell us."

I felt a prickle of dread. Would I be coerced to take part in some terrible ambush or slaughter? Or would this scheme of Artemon's so disrupt the regular order of the Cuckoo's Nest that I might yet have a chance to escape with Bethesda?

One afternoon I caught a glimpse of one of Artemon's visitors just as the man was boarding a boat at the pier, preparing to leave. I saw only the back of his head, but that was sufficient for me to recognize him. How many men have a white stripe running down the middle of their hair?

The appearance of Lykos the artificer—the member of the Alexandrian mime troupe who took credit for making Melmak look as fat as the king, and for transforming beautiful Axiothea into an old crone—so surprised me that I thought I must be mistaken. I stepped toward the pier, hoping to get a look at his face. But when he turned about in the boat, I skittered back and hid myself. Somehow I realized that if Lykos were to see me the consequence would be disastrous—not for him, but for me.

Menkhep happened to walk by, and saw me skulking. "Playing hide-and-seek with the boy?" he asked.

"Something like that. Did you see that fellow who just sailed off?"

He nodded.

"Another of Artemon's visitors?"

"Arrived early this morning, before daybreak. He's been in Artemon's hut all day. The two of them must have had plenty to talk about! Now he's off in a rush. Heading back to Alexandria, I suppose."

"Alexandria?"

" 'My eyes and ears in the capital,' Artemon calls him. But he might better call the fellow his hands—hands that make such clever things!"

"What's his name?"

"He's called the Jackal."

"Are you sure?"

"Of course I am. Why do you ask?"

"I thought perhaps I'd seen him before, in Alexandria. But the man I'm thinking of had a different name."

Menkhep laughed. "You should know by now that the men of the Cuckoo's Gang go by many names, especially when they're out in the regular world. Too bad you didn't get a chance to meet the Jackal while he was here. You could have congratulated him."

"On what?"

"On doing such a good job with Cheelba's costume! It fooled you, didn't it? It was the Jackal who came up with that idea. He concocted the dyes and fabricated the false stinger and the tusk and all the rest. Very clever at making one thing look like another, that fellow. He specializes in forgeries and disguises."

"Does he indeed? What about kidnappings?"

Menkhep gave me a shrewd look. "You always seem to know more than you let on, Roman. How could you possibly know that the Jackal was behind the kidnapping of that pretty girl in Metrodora's hut?"

"Is that why he was here to talk to Artemon, about the ransom we're still waiting to receive?"

He laughed. "Eager for your share, eh? Yes, that's one of the things they talked about, I'm sure."

"Was it the Jackal who brought her here?"

Menkhep shook his head. "No, that was done by other agents of the gang, taking their orders from the Jackal. He himself could never be seen by the girl, because the two of them know each other."

"I see! So if this girl—Axiothea, she's called?—were ever to see the Jackal, and realize he was behind her kidnapping, that would compromise his secret identity in Alexandria. Therefore, since the time she was kidnapped, she has never laid eyes on the Jackal—and he has never laid eyes on her."

"Exactly. I do believe you're beginning to get the hang of this bandit business, Pecunius. Though sometimes I think you might be too curious for your own good."

I left him and went into my hut, needing to be alone and think.

The last time I had seen Lykos was the day I came upon Melmak in the tavern in Alexandria. Lykos had joined us toward the end of our conversation. "What news of Axiothea?" he had asked Melmak, sounding utterly innocent. The man scoffed at actors, but he himself was quite a performer. He had fooled not just me, but Melmak, as well.

What if Lykos had seen me during his brief visit to the Cuckoo's Nest, and had recognized me? Just as his presence there was no coincidence, so he surely would have realized that my presence was no coincidence, either.

I recalled our last, brief exchange in the tavern in Alexandria. Lykos had said, "You have that lovely slave girl—what's her name?"

And I had whispered, "Bethesda."

And Melmak had said, "Only she's gone missing, too."

I could imagine Lykos understanding the situation in a flash, realizing that the wrong girl had been kidnapped—a suspicion he could easily confirm by taking a look at the false Axiothea. Lykos would have told Artemon, and my purpose in coming would have been exposed. I would have been dead before nightfall.

XXIX

From that day on, I lived in fear that Lykos might come back. But soon enough, other events swept aside that worry, for at last came the day of Artemon's announcement.

Everyone was called to the clearing. An air of excitement hung over the assembly. This was the day everyone had been waiting for. When Artemon mounted the dais and raised his hands, we all stopped talking and fell silent.

"Men of the Cuckoo's Nest, a great change is coming. We can do nothing to stop it. But we do have a choice to make. We can either be destroyed by this change—or find a way to profit from it."

Artemon let this sink in for a moment, then raised his voice above the excited murmurs set off by his comments.

"You know that the Cuckoo's Gang has eyes all over Egypt. That includes our confederates on the easternmost branch of the Nile, in Pelusium. Those agents report alarming news. An army is about to march across the Delta. When I say an army, I don't mean an exploratory party or a small detachment, such as we've seen and dealt with before. I mean a true army—a disciplined, well-armed force of thousands of war-hardened soldiers who are determined to destroy or conquer every-thing in their path—including the Cuckoo's Nest."

"Whose army is this?" a man shouted. "Why are they coming here?"

"The men of this army serve Soter, the brother of King Ptolemy, who until now has been in exile. The purpose of this army is to sweep across Egypt, throw the king off his throne, and install Soter in his place. On their way to Alexandria, they will eradicate all resistance and deal with any other problems they encounter. Banditry is one of those problems. The new king wants to boast that he put an end to lawlessness in the Delta. That means the eradication of the Cuckoo's Nest and the execution of every man here."

"What can we do?" someone shouted.

"We can fight them!" said another. There were scattered cheers.

"Or perhaps . . . perhaps we can join them?" said another, a bit tim-idly. Jeers and catcalls followed.

Artemon raised his hands. "We are hopelessly outnumbered. To fight means certain death—death by the sword if you're lucky, death by crucifixion or hanging if you're not. Fighting is not the answer. Nor could we join this army, even if we wished to do so. Soter has vowed to take no outlaws into his ranks. He doesn't want his claim on the throne to be sullied by enlisting the likes of us."

"Soter was already king once. Egypt deserves a new king!" someone shouted. Many others grunted agreement and nodded. Were they thinking of Artemon?

"What are we to do?" said one of the men. "Are we to flee, and aban-don the Cuckoo's Nest?"

"That's exactly what we must do," said Artemon.

"But where can we go? How are we to get there?"

"I have a plan—not a hurried, makeshift scheme, but a plan that's been a long time in the making. Months ago, I saw this invasion coming—"

"Metrodora foresaw it, you mean!" said one of the men.

Artemon cracked a smile. "Perhaps. The important thing isn't who foresaw the danger or how, but that it was foreseen, and that preparations have been made for all of us to survive. We're not alone, we lucky few who live here as free men in the Cuckoo's Nest. We're not without resources. We're not without friends. The Cuckoo's Gang is more than the Cuckoo's Nest. The Cuckoo's Gang is a net thrown across the whole of Egypt, and beyond—a net large enough and strong enough to catch every man here and hold him safe. Never have we faced a greater threat, but if you agree to follow me, to carry out my orders, to obey without question, then every man here has a good chance to survive— and not merely survive, but to come out of this predicament richer than ever! We shall turn disaster to our advantage. We shall laugh in the face of misfortune. But for that to happen, you must trust me. Every one of you must put your trust in me, completely and without reservation."

"Of course we trust you!" shouted Menkhep. "There's never been a leader to match you. We'll do whatever you tell us to do, Artemon. Won't we? What do you say, men?" Menkhep turned about and pumped his hands in the air to rally the others. There was a flurry of foot stamping, clapping, and cheering.

I cleared my throat. For better or worse, I was now a member of the gang and had as much right to speak as the others. "What happens next, Artemon?" I shouted, but my words were lost in the din. As the commotion subsided, I shouted the question again, louder, so that my voice rang in the air.

Artemon searched the crowd to see who was asking. He saw me and gave me a nod. "Today we make preparations to abandon the Cuckoo's Nest, forever. Tomorrow, we'll depart in the long boats, and never look back."

As the others absorbed this in silence, I thought of Bethesda. What were Artemon's plans for her? "What happens after that?" I shouted. "We leave in the long boats, and then what? Where do we go? What happens when we get there?"

Artemon smiled. "It seems that our newest member is also the most eager to press me with questions. I've asked you all to trust me, but Pecunius can't stifle his Roman curiosity."

The men around me laughed. I could see they were caught up in a rush of excitement. Everything in their world was about to change. With Artemon to lead them, they were ready to take a desperate leap into the future.

"Call me nosy, but I'd still like to know where we're going," I said. "Why can't you tell us more, Artemon?"

From his place atop the dais, he looked down at me. "Why must I be secretive? Because among us there may yet be spies, men who would betray us to our enemies. You Romans are such famed strategists, Pecunius, surely you understand the need for secrecy, especially at such a juncture."

This statement prompted grunts and nods of agreement.

"For now, I can tell you this much," said Artemon. "We'll travel downriver to the inlet where we scavenged the shipwreck. A ship will meet us there—a large ship, big enough to accommodate every man here and all the treasure we can bring. There'll be a crew of sailors and rowers already on board, men who've taken the same pledge that all of you have taken."

"We're sailing away on the open sea?" I said. "Leaving Egypt?" Where would such a journey take me? What did it mean for Bethesda?

"Too many questions, Pecunius!" said Artemon. "That's all I can tell you for now. What do you say, men of the Cuckoo's Gang? Are you with me? Will you follow me? If any man here opposes the idea, now is the time to—"

Whatever else he might have said was drowned out by a roar of acclamations. The rootless, restless men around me were ready to follow Artemon anywhere.

For the rest of the day, the men of the Cuckoo's Gang were consumed with the work of dismantling their stronghold and sorting through their valuables, deciding what to take and what to leave behind. As much booty as possible was stowed in sacks and trunks and loaded onto the long boats. The excess was stored in crates and buried underground, to be retrieved at some future date. Artemon himself oversaw much of this work. The men were constantly pressing him for guidance.

At the first opportunity, I stole away and headed for the hut of Ismene and Bethesda. I took Djet with me, thinking he might serve as a lookout.

A vague plan had begun to form in my mind. The next day, the entire Cuckoo's Gang would head north, toward the coast. What if Bethesda and I headed in the opposite direction, upriver? With a ship ready to depart and an invading army on its way, surely no one from Artemon's gang would bother to pursue us. It seemed that our chance to escape had arrived at last.

But when I caught my first glimpse of the hut through a break in the foliage, I stifled a groan. Artemon had set not one man to guard it, but several. Watching from the bushes, I counted at least four. Amid the sudden uproar and excitement generated by his announcement, it seemed that Artemon was taking no chances that some harm might befall his beloved.

Almost certainly this meant that he planned to take Bethesda with him, and also that the hut would be guarded every moment until it was time to depart. My heart sank.

"You despair, Roman," said a low voice. I peered into the tangle of vines and leaves and suddenly perceived Ismene, standing only a few feet away. Djet gasped in surprise. The witch had approached without a sound. Or had she been there all along?

"What will become of us, Ismene?" I whispered.

"Us? If you mean the men of the Cuckoo's Gang—"

"You know what I mean!" I strained to keep my voice low. "Bethesda and me. Where is Artemon taking us? What will he do with her?"

"For now, she's as safe as she ever was. She's like a jewel that Artemon keeps in a box. No harm will come to her."

"But Artemon . . ."

"Even he doesn't dare to take the jewel from the box. Not yet."

"But tomorrow we head for the coast. What then?"

Ismene made no answer.

"Does Bethesda know what's happening? Does she know I'm still here?"

"She knows."

"They say you can see the future, Ismene. What do you foresee for Bethesda and me? Will she ever be mine again?"

"I'm not sure that she was ever yours, never mind the fact that you own her."

"You speak in riddles! Why do you torment me?"

I spoke too loudly. The nearest guard, seated on a stump in front of Bethesda's hut, turned his head in our direction and furrowed his brow. He reached for his spear and rose to his feet, all the while staring in our direction.

Ismene gave me a sour look, then loudly rustled the foliage and stepped into the clearing.

The guard looked at her, then peered beyond her, into the bushes. "Who were you talking to? Is someone there?"

"You dare to question me, little man?" Ismene's back was to me, but I could imagine her stern expression. The guard bowed his head and stepped back.

"Forgive me, Metrodora!"

Without looking back, Ismene disappeared inside the hut.

As silently as we could, Djet and I made our way back to the Cuckoo's Nest.

The long day drew to a close. The men had done all they could to get ready. They were weary but elated. Not one of them showed the least anxiety or regret at the prospect of abandoning the Cuckoo's Nest. Beer and wine were brought out, and the twilight hour took on a festive air.

I sat on the pier beside Djet, staring at the water and the boats crowded along the shore, riding low with their heavy cargoes. A lone ibis flew overhead; when I looked up, I saw the first star in the darkening sky. From the clearing behind us I heard echoes of laughter and singing. The merriment of the others made my own mood seem even darker.

I heard steps at the foot of the pier, and looked over my shoulder to see Menkhep. He held a wooden cup in one hand, and had a stupid smile on his face.

"You look cheerful," I said.

"And you don't. Why aren't you drinking, Pecunius?"

I shrugged. "Will you leave with the others tomorrow, Menkhep?"

"Of course."

"What about your trading post?"

"My brother will stay behind, for now."

"I should think he'll have a lot of customers at the trading post, with an army marching through."

Menkhep's expression turned sour. "They'll probably ransack the place and burn it down. Soldiers are swine." He took a swig from his cup. His smile returned. "But if all goes well, soon every man here will have more riches than he ever dreamed of. I'll be able to buy every trading post in the Delta, if I wish."

I looked at him intently. "You know more than you've told me, don't you? You know where we're going."

"Perhaps."

"Lucky man. Artemon trusts you."

"He's had to share his plans with a few of us; he can't do everything himself. But even I don't know the half of it. I'd tell you all I do know, except . . ."

"I understand."

"Maybe Artemon himself intends to tell you."

I cocked my head.

"That's why I came looking for you. Artemon wants to see you."

"Now?"

Menkhep nodded. "He's alone in his hut, looking at maps and scrolls. He wants you to come. Leave the boy with me. I'll look after him."

I rose to my feet. My legs were unsteady. With a feeling of dread, I walked toward Artemon's hut.

XXX

Alone in his hut, Artemon sat surrounded by lamps hung from metal stands. Every surface was covered with open scrolls, charts, and maps. I quickly looked from document to document, trying to read the scrolls upside down and make out the maps, hoping for some clue to our destination, but seeing none.

Artemon saw me looking at the scrolls. "A pity that I'll have to leave so many of these behind. I can take only the most important ones. I'll be up half the night sorting through them."

I took in the sheer volume of so many documents crammed into all the pigeonholes and leather boxes. "When Soter's army comes marching through, what will they make of such a library, here in the middle of nowhere?"

"The invaders will find no trace of all this. There'll be no trace of anything to do with the Cuckoo's Nest, except ashes. Everything will be burned. There'll be nothing left to link us to this place."

"And nothing to come back to—except all these crates of buried treasure."

Artemon snorted. "The things we buried today are hardly worth coming back for—mere baubles and trinkets. Let the invaders dig it up, if they wish. The important thing is that no trace of any man's identity remains in this place—no keepsake or letter or anything else that might have a name on it. It must be as if the Cuckoo's Nest, and the Cuckoo's Gang, never existed."

I thought of my old tutor, Antipater, who had faked his own death in Rome and put great effort into covering his tracks before we set out on our journey to the Seven Wonders. Did any man ever do such a thing unless he had some mischievous motive? Artemon's determination to remove all trace of our habitation made me uneasy.

"What will become of us all?" I whispered.

Artemon gave me a quizzical look. He shook his head. "Why can't you be like the others, Pecunius? I've never seen them so happy and carefree. They're tired of this place. What is the Cuckoo's Nest, after all, but a bunch of leaky huts in the middle of nowhere, surrounded by crocodiles and mud? The men are thrilled to leave this place behind and set out on a great adventure. They don't care where we're going, as long as it's far from here. But not you, Pecunius. You always seem to have something on your mind."

I shrugged. "Menkhep said you wanted to see me."

"Yes. I have something for you." He opened a small wooden box, drew out a silver necklace, and handed it to me. Attached to the chain was the fang I had pulled from Cheelba. The rot had been scraped away and the cavity filled with silver. The tooth had been cleaned and polished and mounted in a silver bracket. The design was simple but the workmanship was superb.

"We have among us a rather talented silversmith. I think he did a good job with this, don't you?"

I nodded.

"Aren't you going to put it on?"

I clasped the chain around my neck. I touched the lion's tooth, which lay just above my breastbone.

"It suits you, Pecunius. Perhaps it will bring you good fortune."

"If not, at least I'll have a reminder of the most terrifying day of my life."

He laughed.

"Thank you, Artemon. It's a fine gift. If that's all, I realize how busy you must be—"

"No, Pecunius, don't go. Stay. I thought you might share a drink with me, on the eve of our departure. I have here the last of the best of the wine that we salvaged from that shipwreck. According to a stamp on the amphora, it comes all the way from Mount Falernus. That's in Italy, isn't it? I'm afraid the silver cups are all packed away."

He poured from a simple clay pitcher into two clay cups. He made a show of smelling the wine before he drank, and I followed his example. As little as I knew about such matters, even I could tell that the wine was exquisite. I gladly drank it down, and felt its warmth spread through me.

Artemon refilled the cups. "This may be our last quiet moment for quite some time. Beginning tomorrow, everything will be a mad rush. Great events shall unfold, one after another."

"How much wine have you drunk already, Artemon?"

"Ha! You think my words are grandiose, don't you? I suppose, to a fellow who's seen as much of the world as you have, the Cuckoo's Nest is such a tawdry place that you can't imagine anything grand or noble could ever come from it."

"I meant no offense—"

"Perhaps we should rename this place the Nest of the Phoenix. The phoenix is native to the Nile. Did you know that? I've never seen one, but if such a magical bird exists anywhere, it's here in Egypt. The phoenix ends its life by bursting into flames—a shocking death. But then it stirs and rises from the ashes, reborn, more beautiful and resplendent than before." He gazed dreamily into space.

What a strange mood he was in. Like the others, Artemon seemed to be invigorated by the prospect of a grand adventure ahead. Their elation was open and raucous. His was quiet and concentrated, yet burned just as hotly. His face was flushed and his eyes seemed slightly unfocused, as if he had a fever.

"That was a thing to see!" he said, pointing at my necklace and abruptly changing the subject.

"What?"

"When you pulled Cheelba's tooth! The men were thunderstruck. So was I. No one else would have dared to do such a thing. You weren't just clever and resourceful. You were fearless."

I shook my head. "Just because you saw no fear, that doesn't mean I wasn't feeling it."

He laughed. "Oh, Pecunius, you have no idea how different your initiation was from that of most of the men. The ritual usually ends in the initiate's complete humiliation. The man in the pit pisses himself, tries to claw his way out, screams and begs and cries like a child. And the men watching laugh so hard they piss themselves as well. It's a comedy, a farce. Then all is revealed, the man is pulled from the pit, and everyone laughs some more, and no one laughs harder than the initiate in his piss-soaked loincloth. But you, Pecunius—you treated us to a very different sort of spectacle."

He looked at me thoughtfully. "Something sets you apart from the others. Even the best of them, like Menkhep, can't think more than few days ahead. They move about in a sort of stupor, ruled by the most basic emotions and appetites—fear, hunger, lust, vengeance. They need a man like me to guide them. But you, Pecunius—you seem to be ruled by some higher power, some greater purpose. Is it because you're a Roman? Are Romans truly different? Or is it something else? You're a puzzle, Pecunius."

I shrugged.

"I'll tell you one thing: no one benefited more from your quick thinking and bravery than Cheelba. That lion loves you, Pecunius. You've made a friend for life."

"Cheelba!" I laughed, remembering the lion's absurd disguise. I, too, was beginning to feel the effects of the wine. "What will become of him? Surely you won't leave him to the mercy of the soldiers?"

"Of course not. Cheelba's coming with us."

"A lion on a boat! Ridiculous."

"Ridiculous, indeed. All the more reason to take him along."

"What about the crocodile? You don't intend to bring that stinking creature with us, too?"

"Certainly not! Tomorrow, just before we set out, I shall lower a plank into Mangobbler's pit. If he has any sense, the beast will scamper out and take shelter in the lagoon. Hopefully, when the soldiers come, he'll bite off the foot of any man who dares to go digging for buried treasure."

We shared a laugh and drank more wine.

"Do you know, Pecunius, I've never gotten drunk with a Roman before."

"Nor I with a bandit king."

Instead of laughing, he suddenly looked thoughtful. "Is it true that in Rome, by law, every father wields the power of life and death over his children?"

"It is."

"What is that like?"

"For the father, or the child? I think you already know what it's like to have the power of life and death over others, Artemon." I remembered the wretched end of Hairy Shoulders.

"What about your father, Pecunius?"

"My father?"

"Is he still alive?"

"Yes," I said quietly. "He's back in Rome. At least I hope he's still alive. . . ."

"Are you close to him? Is there love between you?"

I sighed and held out my cup. "Yes."

Artemon poured more wine for us both. "I never knew my father. When I was growing up, I knew who he was, but the man wanted nothing to do with me. He disclaimed all knowledge of me. He rejected me. Disowned me."

I blinked. The wine had begun to blur the edges of things, so that even the ground beneath me felt uncertain. "I don't know what to say, Artemon."

"Thank the gods that you have a father, and that he loves you."

I nodded.

"I've never told any of the other men what I've just told you, Pecunius."

"Why me?"

He shrugged. "Why not? You're the man who pulled a lion's tooth."

We both smiled.

Under the spell of the wine, the cares that held me like bands of iron seemed to loosen a bit. I was glad for the respite, no matter how temporary. But what about Artemon? What cares gripped him? Who was he, and where did he come from? What dreams inspired him? What nightmares gnawed at his sleep? That night, sitting in a hut that would soon be ashes, he felt a need to unburden himself. I made a show of sympathy, and listened carefully. Even in my wine-dulled state, I knew that the more I knew about Bethesda's captor, the better would be our chances to survive and escape.

"I'll tell you something else that no one knows," he said. "I'm a twin."

"Is that a fact?"

"It is. You Romans are descended from twins, aren't you?"

"Romulus and Remus were the founders of the city. I'm not sure Remus had any children, before Romulus killed him."

"A twin killing a twin—imagine that! What a strange beginning for a race that wants to rule the world."

"I will ignore that slur against my people," I said. "So, Artemon and Romulus are each a twin. Is there any famous leader you don't resemble?"

"What do you mean?"

"The men compare you to Alexander."

"Do they?"

"And to Moses. I myself compared you to Scipio Africanus when I was talking to Menkhep the other day. Now I find that you're more like Romulus than I could have imagined."

"Unlike Romulus, I did not murder my twin," said Artemon quietly.

"Did the two of you grow up together?"

"Yes."

"Did your father also reject . . . ?"

The question was indelicate. Artemon lowered his eyes and did not answer.

I took advantage of the awkward silence to change the subject. "You say you plan to bring Cheelba with us, but not Mangobbler. What about . . . Metrodora?"

He smiled faintly. "What are the men of the Cuckoo's Gang without their soothsayer? Of course she's coming with us . . . at least for part of the journey."

"What about . . . the other woman?" I said, with a quaver in my voice.

Artemon raised an eyebrow.

"The captive, I mean; the one who's hidden in the hut with Metrodora."

He frowned. "Did Metrodora tell you about her?"

I shrugged. "All the men know she's there, even if most of them have never seen her. I've begun to think she's a legend, or a phantom conjured up by Metrodora."

"The girl is quite real, I assure you," he said, with a pinch at the corner of his mouth.

"Is she as beautiful as they say?"

"Why are you so curious, Pecunius?"

"What man wouldn't be? Except for the witch, I haven't set eyes on a woman since—"

"If you happen to see Axiothea during our departure tomorrow, I suggest you avert your eyes. Her face will be covered by a veil, anyway."

"Is it dangerous to look at her? Is she a witch, like Metrodora?"

"She has no need to cast spells," he muttered. "Her power is greater than that."

"You make her sound like a queen," I said.

His eyes lit up. His speech was slurred. "A queen? No. Not yet. But I could make her one. And I will! If only she'd let me. . . ."

He reached for the pitcher. Only a few drops remained. He poured them into his cup, then threw the pitcher aside. It struck something hard and broke into pieces.

I flinched. Artemon stared at me over the rim of his cup, suddenly wary. "If you're missing female companionship, Pecunius, have patience. When this is all over, you shall have the means to indulge in whatever pleasures you desire. You do trust me, don't you?"

"Of course I do, Artemon."

He nodded. "That was the last of the wine. I must get back to work. Sleep well, Pecunius."

I left him in his hut, poring over his scrolls and maps.

XXXI

The next morning dawned bright and clear, with a dazzling yellow sun in a pale blue sky. The men ate a final meal in the clearing, then Artemon gave the order to set fire to the huts.

Menkhep lit torches and passed them out to the men. At first they went about their work slowly, almost reluctantly. But as one structure after another was lit, the act of incineration took on a festive air, and soon the men were running about in a frenzy of destruction. Even Djet was allowed to wield a torch. When he set fire to our hut, I watched the flames dance in his wide-open eyes.

The huts became bonfires, at first burning brightly and bristling with flames, then collapsing on themselves and belching great clouds of smoke. Black pillars rose into the air, then spread and mingled, until the whole sky was filled with smoke. No patch of blue or golden sunbeam pierced the murk. The sky became a vast, mottled bruise of dark purple and brown, amid which the sun was a smeared crimson bloodstain.

When there was nothing left to burn, the men assembled along the shore. Coughing and rubbing their watering eyes, they took their places in the treasure-laden boats. Curtains of mingled mist and smoke hovered on the lagoon, obscuring the boats from one another. Beyond the distance of a stone's throw, all was veiled by a sullen haze.

From where I sat in Menkhep's boat, still tied to the shore, I dimly perceived the tall figure of Artemon striding down the pier toward the boat that would lead us. He was followed by a hooded form I took to be Ismene. After the witch came a veiled figure so completely covered from head to foot that I would never have taken it for a woman had I not known that it must be Bethesda. I longed to call out, if only to see her head turn in my direction, but I bit my tongue.

I heard a lion's roar. Sitting beside me, Djet stiffened and clutched my arm; he had never been entirely convinced of the lion's tameness. Cheelba trotted down the pier. The lion's disguise had all but vanished; the dyes had faded and his mane was restored to its natural glory. As the lion passed her, Bethesda appeared to startle back in alarm. Metrodora turned toward her, as if to give reassurance. Cheelba reached Artemon, who held out his hand and allowed the beast to lick it.

For a brief moment, poised to step into their boat, Artemon and the others became motionless; even the lion's tail was still. The mist turned them into figures from a shadow play. Then a curtain of smoke rolled across the pier and engulfed them, hiding them completely. By the time the smoke cleared, Artemon and the rest had vanished, along with the boat.

One by one, the other boats followed. As we cast off from the shore and headed out, I turned back to look at what remained of the Cuckoo's Nest. The huts had collapsed into smoldering heaps, but the fire had spread to the surrounding vegetation. Many of the slender trees were crowned with flame, and in patches here and there the low brush was aflame as well. The spreading conflagration gave birth to a wind that spewed cinders and ashes and whipped the trees.

With no one to stop it, the fire would spread unchecked. By nightfall, the whole island would be consumed, a vast smoldering heap of ash amid the waters of the Delta. The men of the Cuckoo's Gang would leave nothing behind them.

So rapid was the spread of the fire that as our boat headed toward the mouth of the lagoon, beyond which lay open water, flames approached from both sides, as if to converge and head us off. As long as we steered a middle course, keeping as far as possible from the shore on either side, the water would protect us. The illusion that fiery jaws were closing on us was still unnerving.

Djet screamed. Thinking the fire had frightened him, I held him tight, but he wriggled free and frantically pointed at the water.

Nearby, two bulbous eyes appeared, just above the water. Beyond the eyes, a powerful, undulating tail propelled Mangobbler the crocodile quickly toward us.

Djet screamed again. So did several of the men, who raised their oars and in a frenzy struck the water, trying to fend off the creature. Mangobbler only quickened his pace, so that a collision of boat and crocodile became inevitable. The creature's eyes glittered with firelight.

Mangobbler reached the boat and tried to scramble aboard.

Terrified, some of the men drew back. Others awkwardly swung their oars, desperately trying to hit the crocodile. Instead, oar struck oar, and Mangobbler was unscathed. With the beast determined to board us, and the men frantically jostling each other, the heavy-laden boat swayed so violently from side to side that I was sure we would capsize.

At that moment, with all in chaos, we passed through the gates of fire. All around us spread the choppy, brightly flickering water, as if we floated on a sea of flames.

Suddenly Mangobbler lost his footing. With his short legs flailing and his jaws snapping, he tumbled back into the water. The boat rocked violently in the opposite direction. We came within a hairsbreadth of tipping over.

"Down, down!" Menkhep shouted. The men hunkered low. I clutched Djet and held my breath. The boat steadied.

Some distance away, against a backdrop of red water, swirling mist, and sheets of flame, I saw the powerful tail of Mangobbler thrash the water as the crocodile retreated.

The men in the boat behind us, braking with their oars but unable to come to a full stop, struck us with a jolt. Djet let out a scream. Even Menkhep whinnied like a horse.

The men in the other boat, who had witnessed everything before giving us a final scare, roared with laughter as they dipped their oars and passed us. Was there no fright so terrible that it did not amuse these men, as long as it happened to someone else?

An hour later, we found ourselves again in a world of blue sky and golden sunshine. The smoke of the Cuckoo's Nest lay behind us, heaped like a thundercloud on the southern horizon. The smell of smoke clung to us like a perfume.

The men were more talkative than usual, sharing stories of the past and dreams of the future. They remembered lost homes and abandoned wives. They complained of indignities inflicted by greedy moneylenders, bullying soldiers, merciless tax collectors, and harsh overseers.

Their dreams of the future were simple. In some distant future, after having their fill of whores and drink and gambling, most of the men imagined for themselves not a life of luxury in a palace, pampered by slaves, but only a bit of peace and quiet in a simple house back in the city or village they had come from. A chance to grow old was itself a fantasy for these men, who were still alive against all odds.

As the hot sun beat down on us, my mind wandered. I studied the monotonous, watery expanse of the Delta. I thought about my father back in Rome. I wondered what had become of my old tutor, Antipater. But when the talk turned to "the girl," my ears pricked up.

"Her name is Axiothea," said Menkhep.

"How do you know?" said one of the men. His name was Ujeb. He had a reputation for timidity—he had shown complete panic when the crocodile appeared—but he was the type who could talk himself out of any corner.

"I know quite a bit about the young lady," said Menkhep, proud to show off his privileged knowledge as one of Artemon's more trusted men. "She comes from Alexandria, and she's an actress."

"No!" said Ujeb. "I heard she was a princess."

"No, just an actress."

"An actress, held for ransom?" Ujeb scoffed. "You can find that sort of woman on any street corner in Alexandria!"

"She's the favorite of a very rich merchant."

"Oh, I see. I'll bet she's lovely! I thought we might get a look at her this morning, but all I saw was a bundle of rags in the mist."

"Rags?" Menkhep laughed. "The garments she was wearing cost more than you'll steal in your whole lifetime."

Ujeb shrugged. "Like I said, I could barely see her. She could have been naked, for all I knew."

"I'd like to see that!" said one of the men.

This led to a series of lewd comments, each more vulgar than the last. I wriggled nervously, and was relieved when Menkhep spoke up.

"That's enough of that! The girl is under Artemon's protection, so there's no call for such filthy talk."

"Under Artemon's protection? Does that mean he's having her?" said Ujeb.

"Of course not, you buffoon! What a pity Mangobbler didn't pluck you off the boat and eat you for breakfast."

Ujeb turned pale. "I meant no offense."

"Then shut your mouth! No one has touched the girl since the day she arrived, and that includes Artemon. He follows the rules just like the rest of us."

"She's been captive a long time, but I've heard nothing about a ransom showing up," said Ujeb.

"These things take time," said Menkhep, "especially with all of Egypt in such a jumble."

"Well, if someone shows up at the Cuckoo's Nest to ransom her now, there'll be only Mangobbler to take the payment!" said Ujeb. The others laughed.

"Ujeb has a point," I said quietly. "Maybe Artemon's given up on the ransom. What will happen to the girl then?"

Menkhep frowned. "Maybe he intends to release her. It all depends on our destination, I suppose."

"I think we're headed for Crete," said one of the men. "Ever since war broke out between Rome and Mithridates, they say there's no one at all in charge of the island. I've heard it's a pirate's paradise."

"It could be Crete," said another, "but I'm betting on Cyrene."

"The Romans are in charge of Cyrene," said Ujeb.

The others glanced in my direction. I kept my mouth shut.

"The loss of Cyrene is the shame of Egypt," said Ujeb. "The bastard Apion gave it to the Roman bankers without a fight, while King Ptolemy was too busy stuffing his face to notice."

"Yes, we might be headed for Cyrene," said Menkhep. "If that happens, a native Latin speaker like our friend Pecunius might be useful to have around. He knows how Romans think."

Ujeb looked at Menkhep shrewdly. "You always seem to know more than the rest of us. Is it true, what some of the men say about Artemon—that he's the bastard son of Apion? If that's so, then why shouldn't we head for Cyrene, and claim his birthright?"

When Menkhep hesitated, I felt compelled to speak. "Do you really imagine the Cuckoo's Gang could take on a Roman army?"

"As I understand it," said Ujeb, "you Romans have your hands full fighting Mithridates, not to mention making war against your own allies in Italy. For all we know, the Romans have pulled out of Cyrene. It's likely to be easy pickings!"

"It can't be that simple," I said. If Ujeb was right, and Artemon was taking us on a mad expedition to claim a kingdom, what would happen to Bethesda and me? A bizarre notion occurred to me: if Artemon dreamed of becoming a king, it followed that he might make Bethesda his queen—which would make me her subject! At that point, the world would truly have turned upside down. But before such a thing could happen, it seemed far more likely that the men of the Cuckoo's Gang would all be killed in some foolhardy, ill-conceived raid, and me along with them.

Ujeb continued to elaborate on his fantasy of a regal Artemon. "If Artemon were a king, that would make him the equal of Mithridates. Think about it! The two of them could join forces against the Romans.

And we men of the Cuckoo's Gang, we'd be like the followers of Alexander, there at the birth of something big, much bigger than ourselves, and likely to see quite a nice profit from it. Just imagine. . . ."

He droned on, and the others listened, enthralled. I shook my head. They had departed for the realm the Greek playwrights call Cloud Cuckoo Land, and there was no point in calling them back to earth. I looked at the boats ahead of us and behind, and wondered in how many of those vessels similar conversations were taking place, as the men speculated about the adventure ahead of them.

If Ujeb's fantasies were absurd, what *were* Artemon's intentions?

I gazed at the watery landscape of the Delta, thinking what a long way I had come from my cozy bedroom in Alexandria. Had I lost my bearings along the way? What if Ujeb and the others were right, and I was the one wearing blinders?

After all, what did I know about how kingdoms were made, or where kings came from? Hadn't Romulus and Remus been petty bandits before they founded the city? What was Alexander but the leader of a very large and bloodthirsty gang who happened to have the love of the gods, at least for a while? Perhaps my best course was to follow the example of the men around me—to put my trust completely in Artemon and thank Fortuna that my destiny was tied to such a man.

Perhaps. Yet all my instincts told me that something quite terrible lay in store for us.

XXXII

The ship was waiting for us at the inlet, just as Artemon had said it would be. The sun was sinking as we drew alongside, lighting everything with a garish orange glow that cast long shadows.

It was by far the largest vessel I had ever boarded. In my journeys to the Seven Wonders, I had traveled mostly on small trading ships that sailed from port to port, closely hugging the coastline. Those boats, lightly manned and crammed with cargo, barely had room for passengers. The *Medusa*—the ship took its name from a brightly painted wooden statue at the prow—was a veritable floating island.

The ship was already manned when we boarded, with a crew of at least twenty sailors and perhaps sixty rowers, yet the deck was so vast that every man aboard was able to assemble below the towering mast. With Cheelba following him, Artemon ascended a short flight of steps to the roof of the cabin at the stern. He stood at the rail, where everyone could see him.

Where were Bethesda and Ismene? I hadn't seen them on board, but I assumed they must be inside the structure upon which Artemon stood, since it afforded the only secure and secluded quarters on the ship.

While Artemon talked, the lion sat next to him on its haunches and swished its tail.

"Welcome aboard the *Medusa*," he said. "Isn't she a beauty? This will be our home for a brief while. The men already aboard are our comrades, as much a part of the Cuckoo's Gang as any man here, no matter that most of them come from far away. Once we're under way, every man will be expected to take turns at the oars. If you've never done such work, you'll find it's not so different from rowing the long boats, except that you'll get blisters in new places."

He introduced the captain, a dark man with leathery skin and a bristling black beard. One of his eyes was missing, and in its place was a mass of scars. His smile showed a mouth full of crooked yellow teeth, with gaps where several were missing. His name was Mavrogenis and he was the very image of a pirate—so much so that he would have been at home in Melmak's mime troupe, frightening children and making their parents laugh. When the captain gave us all a leering smile, Djet clutched my leg and cowered behind me.

By the last light of day, the men made quick work of loading the cargo from the long boats onto the *Medusa*. When that was done, the boats were tied together and set aflame. As the fiery chain of boats drifted away from us, the watery mirror created the illusion that the sea itself was afire. Hissing clouds of steam wreathed the spectacle as the flames died down and flickered out. After that, the night seemed very dark.

Djet found a blanket. I located an empty spot on the deck large enough for the two of us to lie down. From the far end of the ship I heard a low rumble—Cheelba, quietly roaring in his dreams. The slight rocking of the ship quickly lulled me to sleep.

The next morning, the *Medusa* made a slow circuit of the inlet while Captain Mavrogenis acquainted the newcomers with the essential details of the ship's workings. His manner was brusque, but he seemed less threatening by the light of day.

It became apparent that some of the men had never been aboard a sailing ship—a few looked quietly terrified—but the great majority seemed elated that we were on the verge of embarking, and gave a cheer when the *Medusa* at last sailed out of the mouth of the inlet and onto the open sea.

We proceeded in a westerly direction, keeping just within sight of the coast to our left. An unfavorable wind slowed our progress and gave the rowers steady work. I took a couple of turns at the oars. As Artemon had promised, at day's end I had a fresh blister on each thumb.

We cast anchor within swimming distance of shore, not far from a treacherous reef that ran along the coast. Other ships, whose captains would know of the reef, could be counted on to keep their distance. As the light faded, I saw a bright point of light to the southwest. The light was too low on the horizon to be a star. It had to be the beacon of the Pharos Lighthouse.

Alexandria! The city was so near that a Titan could have reached out and touched it. Only a few miles of water and sand separated me from the place I most wanted to be, if I could be there with Bethesda. I ached at the nearness of both—the city within sight, and Bethesda almost within reach, separated from me by the walls of the cabin and the will of Artemon.

The evening was balmy and clear. The men made themselves comfortable wherever they could on the crowded deck. Food and drink were passed among us. When Artemon mounted the top of the cabin at the stern, with Cheelba beside him, the men fell silent and gave him their undivided attention.

Speaking clearly in a matter-of-fact voice, Artemon informed us that on the next day we would sail into the harbor of Alexandria. There, after the *Medusa* pulled alongside one of the deep-water loading docks, most of us would disembark. Provided that preparations in the city had been carried out to Artemon's satisfaction—and he had no reason to think they had not—a raiding party would proceed to the Tomb of Alexander. There we would steal the golden sarcophagus of Alexander, transport it to the harbor, load it onto the *Medusa*, and set sail before nightfall.

The announcement was so astonishing that no one said a word. Wide-eyed and gaping, the men looked at each other, wondering if they had heard correctly.

I stood. Artemon nodded, inviting me to speak.

"Will we have time to do a bit of shopping while we're in the city?" I said.

After a pause, the silence was broken by peals of laughter so loud I feared they might hear us in Alexandria.

As the men gradually quieted down, Artemon gave me a wry look and shook his head. He acknowledged my joke and threw it back at me.

"We shall be making a rather hasty exit from the harbor, Pecunius. I'm afraid you won't have time to haggle with the local merchants."

My facetious question emboldened the others to speak. Ujeb stood up. "Surely we're to be armed. What will we do for weapons?"

"There's a cache of weapons here aboard the *Medusa*," said Artemon. "Every man who goes on the raiding party will be properly outfitted."

"We're to fight King Ptolemy's soldiers?" said another. "I thought we left the Cuckoo's Nest to avoid such a battle."

"Ah, but the situation in Alexandria is not what you might expect," said Artemon. "Our spies have been keeping a close watch on the city; you've seen the messengers arriving with reports. So many of the king's soldiers have deserted him that the army can no longer maintain order. People loot shops and riot in the streets, and there's no one to stop them. Most of the soldiers who remain have withdrawn to the palace, where they've put up barricades. The royal tombs have been locked up tight and closed to visitors, but they're only lightly guarded. All those tombs contain fabulous treasures, but none is greater than the golden sarcophagus of Alexander. By weight and volume, it's the largest mass of gold in all of Alexandria. And it's ours for the taking."

"But how are we to break into the tomb?" a man asked. "And how are we to carry such a heavy thing all the way to the ship?"

"We will arrive at the tomb with a battering ram. We will also have hoists to lift and move the sarcophagus, especially suited for the purpose, and a wagon strong enough and large enough for the load."

"Maybe there won't be enough soldiers to stop us," I said, "but what if the common citizens get wind of what we're up to? The sarcophagus of Alexander is their greatest treasure. A couple of angry shopkeepers shaking their fists won't stop us, but a bloodthirsty mob might."

"You make a good point, Pecunius. We need a distraction. And we shall have one. Shortly after the *Medusa* arrives in the harbor, some of our confederates will instigate a riot at the far corner of the city, near the Temple of Serapis. A child will pretend to be maimed and blame the king's soldiers, and our men will whip up the crowd until there's a full-scale riot. That should attract all the more violent types—the arsonists and looters and head-bashers. It should also occupy any soldiers brave enough or foolish enough to be out on the streets trying to keep order."

"But surely people will notice if we go carting a golden sarcophagus through the streets," I said.

"The sarcophagus will be placed in a wooden crate with its lid nailed shut. No one who happens to see us will know what's inside."

Artemon gave me a steady look, as if challenging me to think of some other objection. He took a deep breath. "Every detail has been thought through. Every preparation has been made. You'll understand now why I couldn't breathe a word about this raid before today, and why all the planning had to be done in secret. I couldn't take the chance that some traitor among us might warn King Ptolemy, or that some drunken braggart might give us away. Every messenger and every one of our confederates in Alexandria was told only what he needed to be told. Even the men who're to meet us with the battering ram and the hoists don't know what they're to be used for. Now all that remains is for us to carry out the task. And tomorrow, after it's done, and we sail out of the harbor with the golden sarcophagus, we shall not merely be rich men. We shall be the stuff of legend."

I looked at the men around me. Their eyes glittered at the ideas Artemon had put in their heads.

I cleared my throat. "Even if everything goes according to plan, surely some blood will be shed."

"Their blood, not ours!" shouted Ujeb. He made a show of hooting and pumping his arms, and many of the others joined him.

Artemon quieted them. "Pecunius is right. It's possible that some of us may be wounded. Some of us may even be killed, or captured by the king's men, from whom we can expect no mercy. It is my belief that we will encounter almost no opposition, and be able to carry out the raid with very little bloodshed. Still, there's always a chance that something may go wrong. We may have to fight our way to the tomb, and then fight our way back to the ship."

"No man here is afraid of a little fight!" shouted Ujeb.

"Except you, Ujeb!" quipped Menkhep, to hoots of laughter.

Artemon waited for the men to quiet down. "If any man thinks the odds against us are too great, he's free to leave us. If that is your choice, come tomorrow, when the ship arrives in port, gather up whatever you can carry of your possessions. You'll have to wait on board until the raiding party returns—we can't have anyone running to the palace or stirring up trouble. But once the men have boarded and the sarcophagus is loaded, you'll be free to get off the ship and go your own way, while the rest of us sail off. You'll no longer be a member of the Cuckoo's Gang, and you'll have given up your share of the world's greatest treasure, but no man here will hold a grudge against you. I'll call you a fool, but I won't call you a coward."

"Abandon the Cuckoo's Gang?" said Ujeb. "On the day of our greatest adventure? That would be like walking out of a mime show just before the dancing girls come on! Ha!"

In the sea of faces around me, I saw a few men who looked as if they might be pondering Artemon's offer to leave the gang, but the vast majority shared Ujeb's enthusiasm.

"And then what, Artemon?" I shouted. "Where do we go after Alexandria?"

"I can't reveal that now, Pecunius, for obvious reasons. What if some among us choose to leave? What if one of us is captured? No man here would willingly betray his comrades, but we can't take the chance. Until the raid is over, our destination must remain a secret."

I nodded. "Fair enough. But won't the king's ships follow us? And what makes you think they'll allow a ship full of bandits to enter the harbor in the first place?"

"Like the rest of Alexandria, the harbor is virtually unmanned. It's all the king can do to keep the Pharos Lighthouse operating. We'll be given permission to enter and to dock. Arrangements have been made."

"Bribes have been paid, you mean!" Ujeb laughed.

Artemon smiled. "And further arrangements have been made to ensure that no one pursues us when we leave."

"More bribes!" said Ujeb.

"What if some reckless captain of the royal fleet decides to pursue us anyway?" I said.

Artemon crossed his arms. "If that happens, we'll simply have to outrun them, all the way to—"

He drew a sharp breath and bit his tongue, but he was only pretending to make a near-slip, teasing us with the mystery of our destination. For now, the men could let their imaginations run wild.

That night, I tossed and turned on the deck, unable to sleep. Many of the others were also wakeful. I overheard their whispers all around me. No one spoke of all that might go wrong. Instead they talked about what would happen after the raid, when we sailed out of Alexandria and into legend.

This was one version of a possible future: with a fortune in gold and a company of loyal men, Artemon would make himself king of lawless Crete, then sail with an army of pirates and outlaws to Cyrene, drive out the Romans, and put himself on the throne that should rightfully have been his. And then, master of Crete and Cyrene, the Cuckoo's Child would take Egypt as well, and then ally himself with that other audacious leader, King Mithridates of Pontus, and the two of them together would drive the Romans back to Italy and split the world between them.

Hearing such ideas spoken aloud, I bit my tongue and kept silent, thinking there is no notion so outrageous that men will not embrace it.

I found myself staring at the cabin at the stern. Was Bethesda inside, and with her Ismene? Was she asleep or awake? Did she know I was near? Had she been able to hear Artemon's speech? Did she know we would be in Alexandria tomorrow?

I saw a shadow approach the door of the cabin. By the shape and size, I knew it must be Artemon.

For a long time he stood at the door with his hand on the latch. Why did he hesitate? I couldn't see his face, which was hidden in darkness. At last he pulled the door open and stepped inside.

My heart pounded. My mind raced. What was happening inside that room? I rose to my feet and was about to make my way across the crowded deck when the cabin door quietly opened and Artemon stepped out, closing it behind him.

He saw me standing amid the sea of blanket-covered men, and gave me a vague wave of acknowledgment. I settled back onto the deck beside Djet.

What if I decided to take no part in the raid the next day, and stayed on the ship instead? Artemon had offered that choice. Might I find a way to rescue Bethesda, and escape with her? It seemed unlikely. Men would be left on board to guard the vessel, and to guard Bethesda, as well. When the raiding party returned, I would be ejected from the ship, cast out of the Cuckoo's Gang. Off they would sail to an unknown destination, taking Bethesda with them.

The possibility that I might come full circle, all the way back to Alexandria, only to lose Bethesda again, and forever, was intolerable.

What would happen if I did take part in the raid? Presuming I survived and returned to the ship, what opportunity would I have to rescue Bethesda? I envisioned a mad scenario: just as the *Medusa* sailed out of the harbor, past the Pharos Lighthouse, I would rush to the cabin, seize Bethesda, and pull her onto the deck. Holding her tight, I would leap into the water. While Artemon shook his fist and the *Medusa* sailed away, Bethesda and I would head for shore.

There was one problem: I could not swim. Would Bethesda be able to get the two of us to the Pharos Island alive? I imagined us dragging ourselves ashore, gasping and bedraggled but free at last.

And if that far-fetched scenario proved impossible, what then? Bethesda and I would sail off with the others, more completely in the power of Artemon than ever. That prospect, too, was intolerable.

It seemed to me that my only hope was Ismene. She had shown sympathy for my plight. She had helped me to survive the initiation. What plans did she have for herself? What plans, if any, did she have for Bethesda, and for me?

I stared at the starry sky above, and uttered a prayer to Fortuna that a witch might save me.

XXXIII

Just before sunrise, I was awakened by a woman's scream.

I thought of Bethesda and was on my feet in a heartbeat.

But the scream did not come from Bethesda. It came from Ismene. By the faint predawn light, I saw her atop the cabin at the stern, in the place where Artemon had stood to address us. Her eyes were closed. She held her hands above her head, palms pressed together and pointed skyward, like those of a diver, and then she began to whirl around, faster and faster. The loose cloth and tassels of her cloak whipped through the air.

Those who were awake roused those who slept, and soon we were all staring at Ismene as she whirled. It hardly seemed possible that a mortal could move in such a manner of her own volition. Some outside force seemed to control her, spinning her as a child might spin a doll.

As she whirled faster and faster, Ismene produced weird ululations that raised hackles on my neck.

"Some demon's taken hold of her," said Djet. He clutched the blanket to his face and peered above it.

"Stupid boy!" snapped Ujeb. "This is what happens when a prophecy grips her. When she comes to her senses, she'll tell us what the dark powers have shown her."

The ululations ceased. The whirling slowed and finally stopped. Ismene staggered but did not fall. She opened her eyes.

"Ananke has lifted the veil! Moira has blown away the mists! Egyptian Ufer of the Mighty Name has shown me the book of what is to be!"

The men cried out. "Tell us what you saw, Metrodora!"

"Metrodora, what will happen today?"

"Metrodora—"

"All of you, be silent!" she wailed.

Some of the men lurched back, as if she had struck them.

"There must be a sacrifice! For all to go well, a blood-red sacrifice is demanded!"

The men glanced at each other anxiously. Some of them looked at Djet in a way that made me uneasy. I pulled him close beside me.

Artemon appeared on the steps leading to the cabin's roof, but he stopped short of joining Ismene. He looked vexed and bewildered. "What are you saying, Metrodora?" he asked. "What do the dark forces want from us?"

"Blood-red sacrifice!"

Artemon turned pale. "Someone must die?" he whispered.

Next to me, Ujeb began to blubber. "This has never happened before! There's never been human sacrifice among us! Why now? Why now?"

"The curse!" Ismene cried. "All curses must be cast away! All must be purified!"

Artemon shook his head. "What curse, Metrodora? What are you talking about?"

"The curse of the ruby!" She thrust her fist in the air, then opened it to reveal the ruby I had given her, removed from its setting in the Nabataean's necklace. At that instant the first ray of sunlight shot across the horizon and struck the jewel. It seemed that Ismene held a little ball of fire.

"What curse do you speak of?" Ujeb's voice cracked. "Where did this ruby come from?"

"Stupid man!" shouted Ismene. "Your questions are pointless. All that matters is that the curse be cast away. Unless that's done, this ship will never reach Alexandria."

Men jabbered and dropped to their knees. Artemon looked taken aback. This, clearly, had not been a part of his plans.

"Who must die, Metrodora?" wailed Ujeb. "Is it me? Oh, please, gods, let it not be me!"

"Be quiet, you fool!" Ismene gave him a withering look. "No one has to die. But every man here must touch the ruby. The ruby already holds a curse. The ruby can take upon itself more curses—all the curses among us, large and small. For all to go well, the whole ship and everyone on it must be purified. All must hold the ruby!"

She approached Artemon, stared at him until he held out his hand, then pressed the ruby into his palm.

"Every man aboard the ship must touch it!" she cried.

Artemon descended to the deck. He passed the ruby to the first man he came to, Menkhep. Menkhep held the stone at arm's length, then passed it to the next man.

From man to man the ruby was passed. Some gazed at it in awe. Some averted their eyes in fear. Some fondled it with a kind of lust before handing it over. Others trembled and squealed when they touched it, as if it burned their fingers.

When it came my turn to hold it, I took a good look at the jewel that had once been mine. Was it truly cursed? Its previous owner, the Nabataean, had certainly come to a bad end, as had Harkhebi and the others who chased after it. But my possession of the ruby had bought the respect of Artemon, and by giving it to Ismene I had gained the chance to see Bethesda.

"The boy, too, must hold it," said Ismene, who had slowly made her way through the crowd until she stood before me.

I passed the ruby to Djet. He stared at it cross-eyed for a moment before he passed it on.

Ismene stepped closer. The others drew back. As all eyes followed the ruby, she stepped so close that when she whispered, only I could hear.

"There is another who touched the ruby, before I woke you."

"Bethesda!" I breathed the name, barely moving my lips.

Ismene nodded.

"Let me see her!" I whispered.

"That is not possible," whispered Ismene.

"But when—?"

"Follow Artemon today. Go on the raid. But do not return to the ship. Stay in Alexandria. Whatever happens, do not reboard the *Medusa*."

"And Bethesda? How will she—?"

Ismene abruptly turned and walked away.

From hand to hand the ruby passed, until every man aboard had touched it. The last to hold it was Captain Mavrogenis, who peered at it with his good eye, turning it this way and that. At Ismene's approach, he stiffened and handed it to her.

Ismene held up the ruby. It glittered in the light of the rising sun.

"Accursed thing!" she cried. "Thing of beauty that now holds within it every curse and particle of ill fortune from every mortal aboard this ship! Be off with you! Let Poseidon swallow you! Only all the waters of the sea can wash you clean!"

She drew back her arm and threw with all her might. A crimson streak hurtled through the air and disappeared amid the waves with a tiny splash.

Artemon looked aghast. Then, slowly, a smile lit his face. I think he anticipated the reaction of the men. For a moment they all stood dumbstruck, as shocked as Artemon, then some began to shiver and gasp, and some to weep. All their unspoken anxiety seemed to pour out of them in that moment. All night they had suppressed their fears, shunning words of ill omen, speaking only of success and glory. From what dark dreams had Ismene's scream awoken them? Still half-asleep and befuddled, they had been drawn by her into a ritual that none expected, yet all longed for.

We had been cleansed—not by water or by prayer, but by magic. Gone was the detritus of every man's offenses against gods and mortals. Gone was doubt.

We were ready for the day ahead.

• • •

As the anchor was hoisted and the *Medusa* set sail, Artemon announced who among us would go ashore and who would stay behind to guard the ship. I was in the first group.

Every man was issued a weapon. Those going on the raid were given shields and armor. Some of these items we had brought with us from the Cuckoo's Nest, but the best pieces came from a cache on the ship. The style and craftsmanship of these objects resembled the armaments used by King Ptolemy's soldiers. Where had so much equipment, of such high quality, come from? I wondered if Artemon's confederates had raided a royal armory.

Artemon unrolled a large and highly detailed map of the city of Alexandria—one of the treasures he had chosen to bring with him from his library. Upon it was marked the wharf where the *Medusa* would dock, and the route we were to take to the Tomb of Alexander and back. All the men were encouraged to study the map and acquaint themselves with the landmarks. Thanks to the rigid grid laid out by Alexander for his city, even the dullest among us were able to grasp the layout of the map. When it came my turn to look, the names and markings evoked a flood of memories and a rush of excitement. In a matter of hours, I would be in Alexandria again.

Artemon explained his plan for the raid. Some of the men asked questions, which he answered at length. He seemed to have thought of every detail and anticipated every eventuality. Even the most hesitant were won over.

The men of the Cuckoo's Gang sailed toward Alexandria in a buoyant mood. The weather was mild, the spume from the prow gave the air a salty tang, and the seagulls overhead seemed to beckon us onward.

Even by day, the beacon atop the Pharos Lighthouse shone brightly, thanks to huge mirrors that collected and cast back the sunlight. As we neared the city, the beacon grew larger and brighter.

The first time I had sailed into the harbor of Alexandria, some years before, I had been awed at the splendor of the city. I was awed anew. What visitor, no matter how familiar with the sight, could fail to be amazed at the world's tallest building, the lighthouse, rising from the waves? Beyond the lighthouse lay the islands of the harbor, glittering with temples and palaces. Along the waterfront stretched the bustling port and the splendid balconies of the royal palace.

As we passed the lighthouse, I gazed ahead at the distant waterfront and saw the very spot where Bethesda and I had eaten with Melmak and the mime troupe on my birthday, where I had fallen asleep and then had awakened alone, with Bethesda gone. That fateful day seemed a lifetime ago.

Every ship that enters the harbor must first be given permission, and we were no exception. With the Pharos Lighthouse looming to our right, a small boat came out to meet us. It was rowed by slaves and carried a single official, who looked slightly absurd in his elaborate costume, which included a helmet too large for him and a great many leather straps and brass buckles that appeared to serve no practical purpose.

Had the official been bribed ahead of time? Were the documents shown to him by Captain Mavrogenis genuine, or a convincing forgery? I was not close enough to observe their conversation, but a few moments later the small boat rowed away and the *Medusa* proceeded toward the largest of the wharfs that projected into the water.

I had never seen the harbor so empty. Mavrogenis had plenty of room to maneuver, but still showed impressive skill as he brought the big vessel to rest with our port side parallel to the wharf.

Before the *Medusa* entered the harbor, the men had hidden their armaments under the sleeping blankets. Now, very quickly, we threw the blankets aside and strapped on whatever armor we had been issued, took up our weapons, and assembled on the deck. Menkhep moved among us, making sure every man was properly outfitted.

I felt an insistent poking against my thigh and looked down to see Djet.

"What about me?" he said. "Where is my armor and sword?"

I was glad for the laugh he gave me, a distraction from the butterflies in my stomach. Menkhep, who happened to be passing by, also laughed.

"Don't be ridiculous, boy," he said. "You're to stay on the ship until we get back."

Djet looked dejected, then smiled. "I could climb up to the top of the mast and keep watch!"

"We already have a lookout posted up there," said Menkhep. He gave Djet an affectionate rap on the head and moved on. I peered down at the boy, realizing I had given no thought as to what would become of him. I squatted beside him and spoke in a low voice.

"You'll stay here on the boat when we leave, Djet. But if you see a chance—if it's safe to do so, if no one is watching you—get off the ship. You're good at that sort of thing. Good at hiding, too. Get off the wharf if you can, but otherwise, find some nook or cranny in that customs house over there and conceal yourself until the *Medusa* sets sail."

"And wait there for you?"

"No. Maybe. I mean . . ." I shook my head. "If you see me come back with the rest, don't reveal yourself. Don't call out or come to me, even if I get on the ship—especially if I get on the ship. Stay hidden. Then, as soon as you're able, make your way to the Street of the Seven Baboons." I managed a rueful smile. "Tell Tafhapy that you've finally returned from the very long errand on which he sent you."

"What about you? What shall I tell the master about you?"

I sighed, and again felt butterflies in my stomach.

"Tell him that you served me well, Djet, and I was very pleased. Tell him I gave you this, as a sign of my gratitude." From the coin purse tied around my waist—for I had decided to take with me all the wealth I had accumulated since leaving Alexandria, leaving none of it on the ship—I pulled a silver shekel from Tyre, a beautiful thing with an image of Hercules on one side and an eagle clutching a palm leaf on the other, and pressed it into his hand. I felt an impulse to hug him, and did so, so hard that I squeezed the breath out of him.

"Now isn't that touching?" said Ujeb. I looked up to see a smirk on

his face. "The Roman is saying a heartfelt farewell to his pretty Gany-
mede!"

Before I could answer Ujeb, Artemon appeared atop the cabin. He
wore a silver-plated cuirass that caught the sunlight, and carried a beautifully crafted sword. When he placed an equally magnificent helmet
on his head, an antique thing of Greek design with an ornate nose
guard and flaring cheek plates, he looked like an image of Achilles.

The helmet also served to hide his face. There were no helmets for the
rest of us, who had to make do with the traditional disguise of bandits.
Along with the others, observing the ritual that marked the commencement of any raid, I tied my scarf across the lower half of my face.

Like a general before a battle, Artemon stood before us and delivered a short speech. At first, my mind was so agitated and my heart
pounded so loudly I could hardly hear a word he said. Presumably he
was trying to rally our courage, or arouse our greed, or both. But as I
grew calmer, I heard him clearly, and realized that the speech was not
at all what I expected.

"What sort of man is this King Ptolemy? Why should we fear him?
A fat buffoon, some call him. The shame of Egypt. Now the people are
ready to get rid of him, and their only choice to replace him is his
brother, a man who already had his turn at ruling and was driven into
exile. That's what comes of letting blood determine who should be
king. Men are born to the throne instead of earning it, and there's no
good way to be rid of them.

"Far better to be a king of bandits than the king of Egypt, I say!
Their sort of king begins life on a bed of purple pillows, playing with
golden rattles, surrounded by fawning slaves. They possess everything
from birth, and know the value of nothing. Better to begin as the bastard son of a whore, I say, and become a brigand in the wild along with
twenty or thirty sworn companions, men who are absolutely trustworthy and full of spirit and afraid of nothing. Let that company grow to
a hundred free men, then two hundred, then thousands, spread all
across Egypt. Someday their number will be in the tens of thousands!
And the man who is honored to lead them will be the greatest king of

all, because he will be their chosen leader, a man who earned his crown not by inheriting a thing that was earned by his ancestors, but by his own hard work and merit.

"I told you last night that what we do today will make us legends. But the Cuckoo's Gang is already the stuff of legend. There is a not a man in Egypt who does not know of us, and envy us—our freedom, our boldness, our fearlessness! But time moves on, and so do we. Yesterday we closed the scroll of the past. Today we unroll the scroll of the future—and that future will be a story etched in golden letters and spangled with jewels, filled to bursting with glory!

"Last night I said that any man who wished to do so might stay behind, and leave the ship when we return, to take his chances as a free man in Alexandria. Does any man choose to leave us? If so, lay down your arms and step aside now."

No one moved. For once, Ujeb had no ready quip. Instead, his chin quivered and a tear ran down his cheek. I looked at Menkhep. He did not weep, but his eyes glistened.

Even I was spellbound by Artemon's words. I cared nothing for the bandit gang and all their false glory, yet I stood rooted to the spot.

I looked at the cabin. The door was shut. Was Bethesda inside? Would she be there when I came back—*if* I came back?

Artemon looked from face to face and nodded, as if to acknowledge and record the choice of every man present.

He turned and descended the steps to the deck, and then, to my amazement, took hold of a long leash, at the end of which was Cheelba. Artemon intended to lead us through the streets of Alexandria with a lion at his side—and why not? Cheelba's roar would send even the bravest opponents scattering in terror.

Outfitted, armed, and ready, with Artemon and Cheelba leading us, we filed down the broad gangplank and proceeded at a quick pace up the wharf.

XXXIV

I had never looked closely at the layout of such wharves, or the paraphernalia with which they were equipped. Now everything I saw seemed to be in stark relief, including the empty wagons and idle hoists scattered here and there. On a normal day, in normal times, these implements of transport and loading would all have been in use, but on this day, all was quiet.

Midway between the docking area and the shore, we came to the customs house. The building occupied the entire width of the wharf, so that we had no choice but to pass through it. The broad doors were unlocked and opened at a push.

The interior of the structure was divided into offices, checkpoints, and storage rooms. Every item leaving or arriving in the port of Alexandria was subject to examination, appraisal, and taxation, so it was not surprising to discover that the customs house was constructed a bit like a maze, full of baffles and dead ends. We had to turn this way and that, and pass through several sets of doors. Fortunately, Artemon seemed to know the way. We did not encounter a single armed guard, only a few idle clerks who fled before us in panic.

It struck me that when it came time to transport our stolen treasure through the customs house, the various baffles and detours would surely slow our progress. One of the passageways was so long and narrow that it would almost certainly pose a problem for any wagon large enough to carry a sarcophagus. But surely Artemon had taken all such factors into account, I told myself.

Once through the customs house we proceeded at a fast pace up the rest of the wharf to the shoreline. Above the rooftops of the city, far away to the southwest, I saw a pillar of black smoke. The riot near the Temple of Serapis was under way.

Following Artemon's plan, we took the quickest and most direct route to the precinct of the royal tombs. Some of the men of the Cuckoo's Gang had never been in Alexandria, and though scarves hid their faces, I could see by their eyes that they were agog at the magnificent buildings, statues, obelisks, and fountains.

We met no resistance. As the people we met scattered before us, I began to experience the particular exhilaration that comes from being part of a group of armed men before whom all others cower and flee. I saw the city in a whole new way, through the eyes of a conquering warrior. Whenever Cheelba roared, the rest of us mimicked the sound, making it into a sort of battle cry.

I have described already, at the outset of my story, how we approached the massive building that housed the tomb, dwarfed by the towering figure of Alexander on the frieze along one wall. There we were met by a small company of men pulling a wagon. In the wagon was the lidded wooden crate in which we would place the sarcophagus.

The wagon also contained winches, pulleys, rope, and other hoisting equipment, as well as a battering ram made from a single massive tree trunk. When Artemon called for volunteers to man the battering ram, I gladly sheathed my sword and grabbed one of the handles. Better to take part in the sacrilege of breaking open the tomb than to shed innocent blood, I thought.

Because all the royal tombs were closed to visitors due to the king's shortage of soldiers, there were few citizens about, and even fewer tourists. Only a handful of people observed us, and no one dared to oppose us, as we battered down the gate and rushed into the tomb.

Gray-headed guards offered the only resistance. Artemon and his men ruthlessly cut them down. By the time I entered the inner chamber, the last remaining guard, stabbed by Artemon himself, crumpled lifeless to the floor.

The wagon was wheeled into place. A hoisting mechanism was deployed to remove the lid of the sarcophagus. Before the mummified body was removed and set aside, Artemon invited me onto the dais to gaze upon the face of Alexander.

So it came to pass that I, Gordianus of Rome, at the age of twenty-two, in the city of Alexandria and in the company of cutthroats and bandits, found myself face to face with the most famous mortal who ever lived.

But only briefly—because a moment later, a small mob of outraged citizens broke into the chamber. The bandits drove them back, but one of them managed to hurl a rock at me. Artemon pulled me to one side, but the rock struck my temple. I fell from the dais onto the wagon, striking my head against one corner of the wooden crate.

Groggily, I drew back and saw blood—my blood—on the wood.

Then everything went black.

Dreams of darkness and confusion, of being tossed this way and that, of men shouting, wheels creaking, swords clanging, the smell of blood, the odor of the sea, the cry of gulls . . .

Gradually, in fits and starts, I came to my senses. I opened my eyes and saw wooden rafters high above me.

I was lying on my back, wedged in a narrow space between the crate and one side of the wagon. The wagon had been moving, but had come to a halt.

"It's not going to fit!" someone shouted.

"It has to!" said another.

Then I heard the voice of Ujeb: "I think the Roman's awake. His eyes are open."

"Good. I was beginning to think . . ." The face of Artemon suddenly appeared above me. "Welcome back to the living, Pecunius. Can you stand? The rest of us are tired of pulling your weight."

Before I could answer, he pulled me by my hands into a sitting position and then forward, out of the wagon and onto my feet. We were inside a building—the customs house, I realized. That meant we had come all the way back to the wharf.

My head ached. I touched my temple and felt dried blood.

"A superficial wound," said Artemon briskly. "Many of the men suffered far worse."

I looked around me. The boisterous, invincible company that had set out from the *Medusa* had been transformed into a bloodied, knocked-about group of desperate-looking men. Many were missing.

Artemon saw my confusion. "Coming out of the tomb, we met more resistance than I expected. Accursed Alexandrians! Always so unpredictable."

On the contrary, I thought, it was entirely predictable that an Alexandrian mob would take up arms—or rocks, sticks, and cudgels—against a group of brigands attempting to carry off their most sacred treasure.

"Menkhep?" I said, for I didn't see him.

"They tore him to pieces!" Ujeb blurted. "He was the first to fall. They took away his sword and then fell on him in a frenzy, especially the women. It was horrible! But we took revenge on them, didn't we? Not a one of that rabble was still alive when we left. We showed them what the men of the Cuckoo's Gang are made of! No one will ever call Ujeb a coward again." He raised his sword. It was covered with blood.

I thought of Menkhep, who had saved my life by guiding me safely to the Cuckoo's Nest, and then had looked after me in large ways and small. Having kept so much hidden from him, I could hardly call myself his friend, but the thought that he had died a horrible death made my blood run cold.

I looked around and realized that another member of the raiding party was missing. "Where is Cheelba?"

"Somewhere here in the customs house," said Artemon. "He bolted and ran a few moments ago. There's no time to look for him. Right now, our problem is how to get this damned wagon through this narrow passage." He sounded perplexed but determined.

"It's so heavy!" complained Ujeb.

"That makes no difference," said Artemon. "There are still enough of us to move the wagon. If we position it just so, it *will* fit in the doorway. We'll push it into the passageway, until the back end is flush with the doorway. Then we'll leave it where it is and circle around—that hallway over there will lead us to the far side." He pointed to a doorway twenty feet to our right; it opened onto a hallway that ran parallel to the passageway through which the wagon needed to pass. "From the far side, we'll be able to pull the wagon the rest of the way through. Yes, I'm sure that will work."

"Some of us should stay here and keep pushing," Ujeb suggested.

"No, pushing is useless. If the wagon goes even a little off-course, it'll get stuck. If we pull, instead, we can correct the course as we go, and get the wagon all the way through in one go. To do that, we'll need every man here. From the other side, we'll tie ropes to the yoke of the wagon."

"But wouldn't it be better to—"

"Shut up, Ujeb! No more arguing! You must do as I say. Now let's get to work."

I moved to join in the effort. Then I saw the smear of blood—my blood—on the corner of the crate, and almost fainted. The sight of Ujeb's bloody sword had hardly affected me, yet the sight of my own blood made me ill.

Artemon pushed me aside. "Go on ahead, Pecunius. You'll only get in the way. Return to the ship." He grunted as he put his shoulder to the wagon. "Tell Mavrogenis we're on our way, and to have everything ready."

My head pounded. The wharf seemed to sway beneath my feet. I made my way to the doorway he had indicated and walked down the long hall. How was it that Artemon, so boastful of planning ahead for every contingency, had failed to foresee the obvious complication of a passageway almost too narrow for the wagon?

I shook my head, thinking that Artemon was not half as smart as he wanted the others to think.

I reached the end of the long hallway and saw, to my left, the end of the passageway through which the wagon needed to go. Artemon was probably right that it would be easier to pull rather than push the wagon, using ropes tied to the yokes.

I was about to hurry on when I heard something—a rustling noise, then the clanking of metal, then a sound like muffled voices. Where did the sounds come from? With its high, raftered ceiling, the acoustics of the customs house deadened some sounds and caused others to echo. I looked above me, and thought I saw a movement amid the rafters.

Was some frightened clerk hiding up there? Or did the sounds come from some chamber hidden in the walls around me? The blows to my head made everything uncertain.

I hurried on—not running, because running caused a painful pounding inside my skull—but moving as quickly as I could.

Away from the others, finally on my own, I suddenly realized that Artemon had just given me my best chance to escape from him. I had only to find a hiding place and stay there until the *Medusa* sailed.

But where was Bethesda? Ismene had told me that under no circumstances should I reboard the *Medusa*. Did that mean that Bethesda, too, would have left the ship while the raid was taking place? Or had Ismene given me a serpent's advice, acting on Artemon's behalf and scheming to separate me from Bethesda forever? The throbbing in my head made it impossible to think clearly.

I decided to return to the ship. Without knowing Bethesda's whereabouts, I had no other choice. If I hurried, and if she was in the cabin, perhaps I might somehow be able to see her before Artemon and the others arrived. Despite the pounding in my skull, I ran all the way.

Captain Mavrogenis saw me approaching and lowered the gangplank. He scowled at the sight of my bloody face.

"What news, Roman?"

"They're on their way. They'll be here any moment."

"All went well?"

"They have what we came for, but a lot of men died."

He raised an eyebrow. "I don't see blood on your sword."

"I missed the battle. I was struck on the head—"

"But Artemon is well, yes?"

"Artemon is unharmed." I stepped past Mavrogenis. He called to his men, telling some to ready the cargo hoist and others to prepare the sail.

Djet was nowhere to be seen. I crossed the deck and stared over the water at the Pharos Lighthouse and the harbor entrance. In a matter of moments, Artemon and the others would arrive, the treasure would be loaded, and the *Medusa* would be on her way.

I turned my gaze to the cabin at the stern. All the men were busy. No one was guarding the door. I quickly walked toward it, my heart pounding. I put my hand on the latch. The door was unlocked. I pushed it open.

The cabin was dimly illuminated by light that leaked from small, shuttered windows set high in the walls. The room was more comfortably furnished than I had imagined. There were hanging lamps, cabinets, rugs, and sleeping couches. But there was no one inside.

I stepped out of the cabin. Mavrogenis was standing nearby, his hands on his hips, overseeing the hoisting of the sail. I grabbed him by the shoulders of his tunic, taking him by surprise. He was a big man, but I lifted him clear off the deck. His face went pale and his eye grew wide. The power of the Furies possessed me.

"The girl!" I shouted. "Where is she?"

"What girl?" he sputtered.

I shook him violently. "You know who I mean. The girl who was in the cabin with Metrodora. Where is she?"

He pointed toward the customs house.

I let go of Mavrogenis, ran to the gangplank, and hurried down, just in time to meet Artemon and the others arriving with the wagon.

XXXV

A rope for pulling the wagon was slung over Artemon's shoulder, and he was soaked with sweat. He had led the others at a furious pace. They dropped the ropes and staggered away from the wagon, gasping for breath. Ujeb looked ready to collapse.

Men from the ship hurried down the gangplank and pushed past me. They readied the hoist that would lift the crate from the wagon onto the ship.

The madness that had possessed me began to fade. My head throbbed with pain. The wharf seemed to sway. If I ran toward the customs house, would anyone bother to pursue me? Artemon had said that any man could leave the ship if he wanted.

For a moment, I was too dizzy to move. I could barely stand upright. I found myself staring at the crate in the wagon. I noticed something very odd about the crate.

"This is not the same crate," I said, so quietly that only those nearest heard me.

Among them was Ujeb, who cocked his head. "What did you say, Roman?"

"This is not the crate that we took into the Tomb of Alexander. This is not the crate that was in the wagon when I came to my senses."

"What? That's impossible!" Ujeb made a rude noise with his lips. "I'm the one who makes stupid jokes here, Roman, not you."

"It's not a joke." Others had overheard and were paying attention to me now, including Artemon, who had a very strange look on his face.

I stepped closer to the wagon. "When the stone struck my head, I fell into the wagon. I struck the corner of the crate, here." I touched the place with my fingers. "There was blood on the wood, and plenty of it. My blood. The sight of it made me queasy. Yet now . . . there's no blood at all."

Artemon shook his head. "You've mixed up the corners, Pecunius."

"There's no blood on any of the corners. See for yourself."

Ujeb frantically circled the wagon. "He's right! The Roman is right! What does it mean?"

"It means nothing," said Artemon. "This is the wagon and this is the crate that we took from the tomb."

I shook my head. "No, it can't be. Something strange has happened. Look inside the crate."

"The lid is nailed shut," said Artemon. "We don't have time for this. Soldiers may come at any moment. We'll open the crate after we sail."

"No, we must open it now!" cried Ujeb.

"He's right," said Captain Mavrogenis, watching us from the rail of the ship. "Open the crate, Artemon. Quickly!" He tossed an iron crowbar to Artemon, who deftly caught it but shot a furious look at the captain. They locked gazes for a moment. Then, his jaw rigid, Artemon jumped into the wagon and set about prying off one of the planks of the lid. I winced at the cracking of wood and the shrieking of iron nails.

Artemon tossed aside the plank. The very bottom of the sarcophagus was revealed, the part that was molded to show the outline of feet within. By the light of the late-afternoon sun, I saw the shimmer of gold and a cluster of emeralds that sparkled with green fire.

"There, do you all see?" said Artemon. "Now hurry up and get this thing aboard!"

Mavrogenis shot me a withering look, certain now that I was completely mad. The others got back to work. But I was not convinced.

I climbed into the wagon. I stared at the gold and the emeralds that were revealed through the break in the lid. Something was not right.

"Get him out of there!" shouted Artemon.

Before anyone could stop me, I drew my sword. I pried loose one of the emeralds and threw it against the wooden floor of the wharf. It shattered into pieces.

"Glass," I said. "Nothing but green glass. And this . . ."

With the point of the blade, I scraped the golden surface. The thin foil ripped and wrinkled, revealing something gray and soft beneath.

"Lead," I said. "The thing in this crate is nothing but lead, covered with gold leaf and pieces of glass."

Everyone looked at Artemon. His face showed no emotion. He stared at the crate in the wagon with the absorbed, abstracted look of a man performing multiple calculations in his head.

"Someone has betrayed us," he finally said.

"No, never!" said Ujeb. "We took an oath. We all took it. Every man of the Cuckoo's Gang took the oath, from Artemon down. No man would betray the oath!"

"How were we betrayed, and when?" I said, ignoring Ujeb. "The sarcophagus I saw in the tomb was most certainly genuine. It can't have been a fake. We all saw it. We touched it."

"Yes, the sarcophagus we loaded into the wagon was most certainly genuine," said Artemon. "Which can only mean that somehow, somewhere along the way, this crate was substituted for the other."

"Not just the crate, but the whole wagon," said Ujeb. "Look, there's not a drop of blood anywhere on it. Pecunius remembered seeing his own blood on the crate, but there must have been some blood on the wagon, as well. There had to be, after the battle we fought outside the tomb. This wagon has no blood at all on it."

"This is all a fake?" said Mavrogenis. "The wagon, the crate, the sarcophagus? How is that possible? Were you not with the wagon at every instant?"

"No," whispered Ujeb. "We left it for a just a moment, after we pushed it into the narrow passageway and circled around. It must have happened then. But how?"

We all looked at Artemon again. He closed his eyes for a long moment. When he opened them again it seemed to me that a profound transformation had taken place, that he had almost become a different man. I could not have explained what was so changed about him, yet I hardly recognized him. There was a cold, flinty determination in his eyes.

"The same trusted confederates who supplied us with the crate and the wagon must have planned for this deception all along," said Artemon. "How they did such a thing, I don't know. We'll figure it out later. But if the substitution took place in the customs house, then the genuine sarcophagus will still be inside. We must go and get it." He looked up at the armed men who had been left to guard the ship and now stood crowded along the rail. "All of you, come on!"

The men on the ship jostled one another as they streamed down the gangplank.

Mavrogenis stamped his foot. "Hurry, you fools! Go back and get the thing! Otherwise we'll leave here with nothing. Quickly!"

Artemon, his sword drawn, was already halfway back to the customs house. The others followed as quickly as they could. Even Ujeb took a deep breath and ran after them.

I stood where I was and watched them disappear into the customs house.

Mavrogenis glared down at me. "What do you think you're doing, standing there? Go help them!"

I shook my head. "Something isn't right."

"Of course it's not right! We've been betrayed. Why am I not surprised? Over and over I told Artemon, 'Your men in Alexandria must be absolutely trustworthy, or else—'"

"What makes you think they weren't?"

"What do you mean?"

"What makes you think they weren't trustworthy? What makes you think Artemon's accomplices didn't do exactly what Artemon told them to do?"

Mavrogenis shook his head and scowled. "Cowardly Roman!"

A few moments later, from the customs house, we heard the sound of shouts and the clash of weapons. The battle continued for quite some time.

Then the men of the Cuckoo's Gang appeared, pulling the exact twin of the wagon beside me. Some limped and staggered, but others seemed invigorated by the thrill of battle. When the wagon reached the end of the wharf, even as Mavrogenis's sailors prepared to load the crate, the captain himself descended from the ship, leaped into the wagon, and with a crowbar set about prying off the lid. Quickly he ripped off one plank after another, until the whole lid lay in splinters on the wharf.

Slanting sunlight reflected from the gold of the sarcophagus onto the captain's face. His eyes flickered with the green fire of many emeralds.

I leaped onto the wagon beside him. Before me I saw the solid gold sarcophagus of Alexander. Of its authenticity there could be no doubt. The beauty of the thing, seen in daylight, was breathtaking.

Then the crate was hoisted into the air, and Mavrogenis's men set about loading it into the *Medusa's* hold.

Mavrogenis looked about. "Artemon's not here. Where is he?"

I looked toward the customs house. A moment later, Artemon appeared. He was not alone. In one hand he held his bloody sword, and with the other he gripped Bethesda by the wrist, dragging her after him. She wore the green gown I had given her on my birthday, and her arms were outstretched in opposite directions, for clinging to Bethesda's other wrist, trying to hold her back, was Ismene. Artemon was stronger than both women combined. He pulled Bethesda steadily onward, toward the ship.

As if this sight were not startling enough, trotting up beside the trio, oblivious of their tug-of-war, was Cheelba the lion, with his head aloft and his leash trailing behind him.

Ismene suddenly released her grip on Bethesda. She turned back and disappeared inside the customs house. Bethesda's resistance was no match for Artemon's strength and determination. He began to run, dragging her behind him.

Even as they arrived at the ship, the sarcophagus was lowered into the hold. The *Medusa*'s sail snapped in the breeze. Mavrogenis ran up and down the deck, shouting orders at the rowers and sailors.

Eager to cast off, some of the men began to withdraw the gangplank, but Artemon yelled at them to leave it in place, and bounded toward it, pulling Bethesda helplessly behind him as if she were a doll. I attempted to tackle him from the side, but his momentum was too great. He knocked me aside, so that I almost tumbled into the gap between the ship and the wharf.

By the time I righted myself, Artemon and Bethesda were aboard the *Medusa*.

The men would almost certainly have pulled up the gangplank then and there, leaving me behind, except that Cheelba, who had been bounding after Artemon, suddenly balked at boarding the ship and drew back. The men along the rail called out to the lion, and left the ramp in place.

"Pull up the gangplank!" Artemon shouted. "Never mind the lion! Pull it up now!" There was an unaccustomed note of fear in his voice.

For a moment I thought he was frightened of me, and that he wanted the ramp to be pulled up at once so that I couldn't come after him. Then I heard a commotion from the direction of the customs house, and turned to see that soldiers had emerged from the building and were racing toward the ship, their helmets and weapons glinting blood red in the slanting sunlight.

Where had they come from, so quickly? It seemed impossible that so many men had emerged from the royal palace and run all the way across the shoreline and up the wharf without being seen by the lookout posted atop the mast of the *Medusa*. Had the soldiers come from inside the customs house? Had they been there all along? If that were so, how had we failed to see them, and why had they not opposed us at the outset?

Cheelba still refused to board. The men handling the gangplank finally gave up on the lion and moved to obey Artemon. But the ramp was heavier than they realized, and the task required more men, who came running to help. The gangplank began to lift off the wharf. At the same time, the *Medusa* pitched slightly and began to move slowly away from the wharf.

At the last possible moment, I leaped onto the gangplank. My weight wrenched it free of the men who were raising it, and the ramp slammed back onto the wharf, allowing me to scamper on board.

I ran headlong toward Artemon, taking him by surprise. He was bigger than I, but still I managed to knock him down, and the two of us went rolling across the deck. He must have been very weary, almost exhausted, for otherwise I could never have taken him down. As it was, we fought like men who were evenly matched, trading blow for blow and grappling at close quarters.

Some of the men around us began to hoot and cheer. Any fight, no matter what the circumstances, thrilled them.

But not everyone was amused. I heard Ujeb shout, "Stop them!"

"Why?" said one of the men. "It's the Roman's right to challenge the leader."

"Anyone want to bet on the outcome?" asked another, laughing.

"Where's Metrodora?" shouted another. "Why did she turn back?"

I felt the ship lurch beneath us. From the corner of my eye I saw a blur of green—Bethesda, who was watching the combat with wide-open eyes. The sight of her distracted me, and Artemon was able to land a blow against my head.

"Run!" I shouted to her. "Get off the ship!"

"No! Stop the girl!" yelled Artemon.

Before Bethesda could move, Captain Mavrogenis gripped her from behind. The sight of her struggling filled me with rage. I struck blindly at Artemon and the two of us went tumbling in the opposite direction. Somehow we ended up at the top of the gangplank, and then rolled downward, off the ship and onto the wharf.

Even as my stamina began to flag, Artemon seemed to find fresh strength. He rolled me onto my back, pinned my arms beneath his knees, drew a dagger, and raised it above me. Already smeared with blood, the blade glinted in the lowering sunlight.

My head pounded. Spots swam before my eyes. I had no strength left. Artemon had bested me. I had failed—failed utterly, for I had not even managed to rescue Bethesda. The bandits would sail off with her, and her last sight of me would be of my useless, bloody corpse lying on the wharf.

Then I heard a roar, saw a blur of movement, and felt a shuddering impact from one side. Artemon was no longer atop me. Instead, in the next moment, it was Artemon who lay pinned on his back on the wharf, with Cheelba atop him. His blade went clattering across the wharf and disappeared over the edge. Cheelba roared.

The soldiers converged on us. They were so close now that I could see the blood on their weapons and the fierce determination in their eyes—these were no weaklings such as we had encountered at the tomb—but the sudden, horrifying spectacle of a man fighting a lion with his bare hands stopped them in their tracks.

I looked at the *Medusa*, which continued to pull away. The gangplank was still extended, but a widening gulf had opened between the wharf and the ship. Amid the gaping bandits and sailors at the rail, I glimpsed Bethesda's face. Mavrogenis still held her fast.

I scrambled to my feet. I took a running leap toward the gangplank. For a moment, like Mercury, I seemed to have wings on my feet. Even so, I fell short. I plunged toward the water—then caught the edge of the gangplank with my fingertips. From somewhere I found the strength to pull myself up and over. I scurried up the ramp and onto the ship, then fell on my side, gasping for breath.

Above me, the sail fluttered and snapped taut, filled by the wind. The dark blue sky seemed to pitch and heave in counterpoint to the waves below. I closed my eyes for an instant, then felt strong hands grip my arms and pull me to my feet.

I looked toward the wharf, which was spinning to one side and rapidly growing more distant. Cheelba had vanished. The soldiers had seized Artemon and pulled him to his feet, so that he and I were mirror images, except that Artemon was covered with blood.

"We have to go back for him!" one of the men shouted.

"Impossible," I heard Mavrogenis say. "The king's men have Artemon now."

I looked at the captain. He relaxed his grip on Bethesda. She pulled free and ran toward me. The men holding me stepped back, allowing me to embrace her.

"But what will we do without Artemon?" wailed one of the men.

Mavrogenis thrust out his jaw. "For now, you'll take orders from me." He stared defiantly from face to face, and ended by glaring at me.

I pulled Bethesda close. She hid her face against my chest.

Mavrogenis cocked his head. "Artemon ordered the girl to be taken ashore during the raid, and locked in a room in the customs house. He meant to leave her behind—so why did he change his mind at the last moment and bring her back here? And how is it that the Roman knows her?" He scowled. "Until we know what these two are up to, lock them in the cabin!"

I held Bethesda tight. Men converged on us from all sides. In a matter of moments we would be overpowered, dragged across the deck, and locked away. Without Artemon or Ismene aboard to protect Bethesda, what would become of her? What would become of me?

"No, wait!" cried Ujeb. "No one lays a finger on Pecunius! Don't you fools understand? He's our leader now."

"What?" Mavrogenis glowered.

"Pecunius beat Artemon in a fair fight."

"Hardly!" said Mavrogenis. "The lion interceded."

"Maybe so, but Pecunius did what no man here had the courage to do—he took on Artemon. And now Artemon is stuck on that wharf, mauled by a lion and captured by the king's men, and Pecunius stands here among us, with hardly a scratch on him. I'd say that means Pecunius won. He at least deserves a vote. And until we get clear of this mess and can have a proper vote, I say Pecunius should be our leader. We can't be without a leader!"

Many of the men nodded their heads and grunted in agreement. The grunts turned into shouts.

"Pecunius bested Artemon!"

"The gods showed favor to the Roman!"

"Pecunius should lead us!"

"Madness!" I whispered under my breath. And yet . . .

Strange are the pathways laid down by the Fates. Unforeseen, and sometimes puzzling, are the gifts of Fortuna. Only moments before, I thought Bethesda lost and myself a dead man. Now I was reunited with Bethesda, holding her tight, and the men around me were shouting my praises.

The doors of the cargo hold were still open. With my arm around Bethesda, I walked toward the hold. Men stepped back to let us pass. Standing at the edge of the opening, I peered down at the golden sarcophagus. The sun was too low in the west to cast light directly into the hold. Even so, how brightly the gold shone! How dazzling were the emeralds and all the other precious stones!

Never, on that long-ago morning when I rose from bed, ready to mark my twenty-second birthday, could I have foreseen that the Fates would lead me to such a pass: to stand on the deck of a pirate ship and be proclaimed a king of bandits! Even more amazing, the golden sarcophagus of Alexander the Great was in my possession. That meant—for the moment, at least—that I must be one of the richest men in the world.

I thought of my upbringing in Rome and all the lessons my father had taught me. I thought of my journey to see the Seven Wonders. I thought of my aimless but amiable existence in the teeming city of Alexandria. Had all the strands of my life led inexorably to this moment, this juncture, this destiny?

I lifted my gaze and looked around us. The *Medusa* had reached the middle of the harbor and was fast approaching the Pharos Lighthouse. We were surrounded by water on all sides, far from the nearest land. It would have been better, if I had reached my decision earlier, when the shore was nearer, but there was nothing to be done about that now. I took a deep breath.

"Everyone, stand back!" I shouted.

To my amazement, the men obeyed me. I felt the thrill of command. No wonder Artemon has so loved his status as a king of the bandits, surrounded by minions to do his bidding. This was something I could get used to, I thought—and then shook my head at such foolishness.

I whispered in Bethesda's ear. She nodded to show that she understood.

I counted to three, and then, holding hands, we ran to the rail, leaped over, and plunged into the waves below.

XXXVI

"I thought you could swim. You call yourself a daughter of the Nile!"

Next to me, Bethesda sputtered and flailed her arms, desperate to keep her head above water. As terrible a swimmer as I might be, she was even worse.

Somehow I had managed to find the proper rhythm for treading water, kicking my legs and flapping my arms to stay afloat, but Bethesda was having a harder time. A measure of the peril she faced was her silence in response to my grousing. Normally she would have thrown my words back at me, but bantering was beyond her now. She was in dire straits.

I circled behind her and looped one arm around her. "Lie back against me. Relax and stop struggling! I can hold you up," I promised, though I was by no means certain that I could do so.

I peered around us. The waves were so high that at times I couldn't see the shoreline in any direction. The only point of orientation was the towering Pharos Lighthouse, which for all its immensity seemed very far away. The waves seemed to slap against each other at random, traveling in all directions at once. Were we being swept back toward the wharf, or out to sea? I had no idea, and lacked the skill to take us in any particular direction.

Worst of all, my stamina was rapidly dwindling. The excitement of the fight with Artemon had stirred the last of my strength, but that burst of energy was long spent. The water, colder than I had expected, was sapping whatever spark remained in me.

For the second time that day, I prepared to meet my ancestors. At least mine would not be a bloody, horrific death at the hands of another man. Neptune would take me, as he had taken so many men in the past. Fish would devour me, and no tomb would hold my remains except the vast sarcophagus of the sea.

Bethesda stopped her flailing and lay back against me, as I had told her to do. I had a goal now: to keep her head above water as long as I could. I struggled against the waves to maintain a steady rhythm, kicking with my legs and using my free arm as a rudder. So far, so good—but I could almost count the number of strokes left in me. I was cold, and exhausted, and ready for sleep.

Bethesda whispered something. I turned my ear toward her, but her words were not directed to me.

"I call upon you, Moira," she murmured. "I call upon you, Ananke. Egyptian Ufer of the Mighty Name, help us!"

Magic! The poor girl, in her extremity, was calling upon the same dark forces that Ismene had called upon. What incantations and bits of sorcery had Ismene taught Bethesda during their long, idle days together in that hut on the outskirts of the Cuckoo's Nest? What good was such witchery to two mortals who could not swim, yet who found themselves in the midst of a vast harbor? What a simple, foolish girl Bethesda was, and how I longed to kiss her and hold her at that moment, but it was all I could do to keep one arm around her as I desperately struggled to stay afloat. The end was very near.

"Bethesda," I whispered, for I lacked sufficient breath to speak more loudly. "Bethesda, leave off your incantations and listen to me." Before we both died, I wanted to speak to her openly and honestly, to express to her a certain emotion that no self-respecting Roman should ever feel for a slave, let alone utter aloud, but about which I could no longer be silent.

She seemed not to hear me, for she continued to murmur. "Moira . . . Ananke . . . Ufer of the Mighty Name . . ."

"Bethesda!" Could she hear me or not? "Bethesda, I love—"

"Use the hook, you fool!" someone shouted.

The boat seemed to materialize from nowhere. Suddenly it loomed behind me, so close I thought the hull would strike my head. Then something took hold of my tunic and lifted me upward. I held fast to Bethesda, then saw that a second hook had been slipped inside the neckline of her gown and was lifting her alongside me. Hands gripped us and pulled us upward and over the rail and onto the deck of the ship.

For a moment, lying on my back, I was completely disoriented, for it seemed we were not on a ship at all but had somehow been transported to another world—a world where all surfaces were of shimmering gold and silver or brightly colored paint or inlays of lapis and ivory, and every image was more beautiful and exquisite than the last . . . a world of gorgeous lotus blossoms and white-robed suppliants, of sparkling blue water and golden rushes, of iridescent peacocks and dazzling flamingos. Overhead, gauzy curtains wafted gently in the breeze and the first star of evening shone in the darkling sky.

"You're sure these two jumped off the pirate ship?" someone asked.

"Certain of it."

"But this can't be the Cuckoo's Child. He doesn't fit the description at all. And there was no mention of a girl."

"Even so, I saw them jump from the ship."

Suddenly an unfriendly face loomed above me, surmounted by an elaborate headdress such as a royal official might wear. "You, there! Who are you and why did you jump from the ship? And where is the Cuckoo's Child?"

I peered into the man's unblinking eyes. By the white robes he wore, and the elaborate jewelry at his neck and wrist, and the markings of kohl and other cosmetics on his long, dour face, I knew he must be some high-ranking chamberlain of the king's government.

"Where am I?" I said.

"Answer the question!"

I caught my breath. "If you mean Artemon—"

"Yes, yes, the Cuckoo's Child! We were to pick him out of the water."

I drew a sharp breath, startled by what he had just said. "We left Artemon back on the wharf. Cheelba the lion attacked him. Then the king's soldiers captured him—"

"What?" The chamberlain curled his lip. "That's not what was supposed to happen. Holy Isis, what sort of mess have you bandits made of things?"

I managed to sit up. Bethesda did likewise. I looked to see that she was all right, and then put my hand on hers.

"I am not a bandit," I said. "I am a Roman citizen named Gordianus."

"Is that so? You were seen jumping off that ship, which is full of bandits."

Yes, and I was their king! I wanted to say, but restrained myself. "It's true that I was on the ship, but only because I was captured by those bandits and forced to travel with them."

The chamberlain peered down his nose. "And the girl? Who is she?"

"Her name is Bethesda. She's my slave. She, too, was captured by the bandits."

Another voice, male but high-pitched and with an elegant accent, entered the conversation. "A lovely young couple captured by bandits! Oh, dear, it's like something out of one of those sordid mime shows! How delicious!"

The chamberlain turned about in alarm. "Your Majesty, you mustn't be seen on deck. Please return to the cabin—"

"Oh, do be quiet, Zenon! And get on with your interrogation of this attractive young couple. Even soaking wet, I find them quite beguiling. Especially soaking wet!"

The chamberlain rolled his eyes.

I blinked, and blinked again. Surely I was dead, or dreaming, or transported to another realm of existence. Any explanation seemed more likely than the impossible reality that I found myself aboard a royal barque in the presence of the king of Egypt.

Before me stood one of the fattest human beings I had ever seen. He was also by far the most elaborately dressed mortal I had ever laid eyes on. On his head, rising like a stem from a gourd, was a ridiculously tall atef crown. He had many chins, and each chin seemed to be festooned with its own fabulous necklace. His sheer bulk demanded many bolts of linen for its adornment, and these vast garments were so richly spangled with jewels and precious stones and golden accouterments, all lit by the lowering red sun, that I had to shield my eyes to look at him.

To rest my eyes from so much brilliance, I looked around me. The ship was a match for its owner, for never had I seen anything made by men that could rival it for sheer magnificence. Every surface was decorated with the costliest materials and the most exquisite craftsmanship. The result was so beautiful and so ornate that the vessel hardly seemed to be a ship at all, but rather a floating temple or palace. Thus would a god take to the water, if gods had need of ships.

Despite my weakness and light-headedness, I started to get to my feet, but the chamberlain indicated with a poke of his bejeweled staff that I should stay where I was.

"The Cuckoo's Child is on the wharf, you say?"

"Yes. And I think that's not the only part of your scheme that's taken an unexpected turn," I added. As befuddled as I was, I was beginning to sniff the truth.

"What do you mean?"

"The fake sarcophagus is on the wharf. The *real* sarcophagus is on the pirate ship."

Zenon turned stark white, as if every drop of blood had been drained from him in an instant—and been infused into King Ptolemy, whose round, fleshy face turned ruby red. The king's lips began to blubber. A variety of sounds issued forth, but none that resembled speech.

The chamberlain also spewed and stuttered before finding his voice. "Your Majesty, we know nothing about this man. Why should we believe him?"

"Why should you not?" I said quietly. "I have no reason to lie to the king of Egypt."

"Head for the wharf!" the king shouted. "Immediately and at full speed. We'll see if what the Roman says is true."

The ship gave a lurch and swung about, propelled at astounding speed by unseen rowers. Behind us I saw the Pharos Lighthouse and the sail of the *Medusa,* not yet clear of the harbor. Ahead of us, the wharf loomed closer and closer. King Ptolemy stepped behind a screen of gauzy curtains, as if to shield himself from the gaze of unworthy mortals. I heard a chomping sound, and realized that the king was noisily eating something.

On the wharf, Artemon was lying on his back. Several soldiers knelt over him, as if treating his wounds. There was no sign of Cheelba. The wagon with the fake sarcophagus was nearby, where Artemon's men had left it. As the royal barque came within earshot, the commanding officer on the wharf stepped forward and came to attention. He looked grim.

"Report!" shouted Zenon.

"The sarcophagus was taken," said the officer. "We did our best to hold it, but the bandits outnumbered us—"

"Outfought you, you mean!" snapped Zenon. "There was never to be a battle at all. How did such a thing happen? Bring forth the artificer!"

From among the soldiers a figure stepped forward. I gave a start. By the stripe of white that split his beard and the hair on his head, I recognized the man known to some as Lykos, to others as the Jackal.

The chamberlain pointed his staff at the artificer. "This is your fault, I'll wager. Your fakery failed to fool them!"

Lykos gestured to the wagon and the crate that held the forgery made of lead and gold foil. "My copy was perfectly adequate. You yourself saw and approved it, as did His Majesty. No, it was the Cuckoo's Child who betrayed us. The substitution took place in the customs house, just as we planned. None of the bandits suspected a thing. They were about to load the fake, when suddenly Artemon changed his mind. He led his men back to the customs house. They fell on us,

slaughtered the soldiers, and seized the wagon. By the time more soldiers arrived, the bandits had loaded the sarcophagus onto the ship
and set sail. Somehow Artemon was left behind. The lion attacked
him, then ran off. He fainted from his wounds before we could question him. Otherwise, I'd be able to tell you—"

"Never mind!" shouted Zenon. "Why and when and how don't
matter now. We must stop what's about to happen, and we have very
little time."

Zenon yelled orders at the captain of the barque. As the boat turned
about, Lykos spotted me sitting on the deck, and Bethesda next to me.
I saw a flicker of recognition in his eyes, followed by a frown of puzzlement. I couldn't resist giving him one of the secret signals of the
Cuckoo's Gang, poking my little finger into my ears, first on one side,
then the other. Reflexively he reached up to give the response—
three taps of his thumb to his chin—then stopped himself.

The royal barque quickly reversed course and went plunging through
the waves. The wharf receded behind us. Before us, the towering lighthouse loomed larger and larger. At first I thought we were pursuing the
Medusa, and indeed, as the pirates' distant sail began to grow, I saw
that the speed of the royal barque was more than a match for the bandit ship. Then I realized that our destination was not the open sea, but
the Pharos Island.

We drew alongside a small but ornately decorated pier that was
clearly reserved for royal use. The king, who had remained behind the
gauzy curtains during our transit, reappeared on the deck, smacking
his lips and holding in one hand the greasy remains of a roasted
chicken.

"There is no need for Your Majesty to go ashore," said Zenon. "I
myself will—"

"You yourself have made a mess of things so far!" snapped the king.
"Of course I'm going. Bring up the royal wagon!"

A few moments later, with a loud clattering of hooves, a magnificent vehicle drawn by gaily caparisoned horses arrived on the pier.
Assisted by attendants on either side, the king waddled down the

gangplank onto the pier, and then up a wide ramp and onto the plushly appointed wagon. The attendants had to get behind him and push the king up the last few steps. The awkward process was painful to watch, especially since the king kept barking at his attendants to hurry.

Beside me, I heard Bethesda suppress a giggle. Impulsively I covered her mouth with a kiss to silence her.

The king, who had just fallen back onto a mass of cushions, observed us. "Bring the young lovers, as well."

"But Your Majesty, there's no need—"

"How do you know? This Roman may know something you don't. That seems quite likely, since there's plenty you've failed to anticipate in this sorry affair! And bring along some food, as well. You know how hungry I get when I'm nervous. Now hurry, as quickly as you can! To the lighthouse!"

With a clattering of hooves, the king's wagon sped off, heading toward the long ramp that led up to the lighthouse entrance. A moment later, a second wagon appeared, this one not quite as magnificent as the first. Several retainers quickly stepped on board, including one who carried a large silver vessel crammed with delicacies.

The chamberlain grabbed my arm, pulled me to my feet, and hurried toward the wagon. I held Bethesda's hand and pulled her along behind me. As soon as we were in the wagon, the vehicle sped after the king.

Up the long ramp we flew, with the horses racing at a frenzied pace. In a matter of moments we arrived at the entrance.

I had visited the lighthouse once before, but that had been long ago. Even amid all the confusion and clamor, I gazed up in awe. No other building on earth is even nearly as tall. The tower rises in three distinct segments, each stepped back from the one below. At the top is a chamber where flames and mirrors produce the brightest light on earth, and atop that, a statue of Zeus welcomes all the world to Alexandria.

I had no time to gawk, for the wagon did not pause at the entrance. The huge doors stood wide open. The wagon sped inside.

The lower half of the lighthouse is four-sided, and hollow in the middle. A continuous ramp built against each of the four interior walls ascends from one story up to the next, and then to the next above that. Up this broad spiral ramp the king's vehicle raced, with our wagon hurrying to catch up. As we went round and round, ascending from one level to another, terrified workers scattered before us. Mule carts bearing fuel for the beacon were overturned. The smells of naphtha and dung filled my nostrils.

Up and up we raced, past tall windows facing each of the four directions, affording a view of the sea, then the setting sun, then the city, and then the harbor, in that order, and then the same sequence again— sea, sun, city, harbor—over and over, higher and higher, until at last we reached a level more than midway up the tower, and the wagon came to a halt. The king was already going about the awkward business of alighting from his wagon, assisted by anxious attendants who appeared to fear in equal measure that they might drop the king or else be crushed by him.

With King Ptolemy leading the way, we stepped through a doorway onto a parapet that circled the outer walls. I drew in a lungful of fresh sea air. Before and below us, as far as the eye could see, sparkled a broad expanse of open water.

Amid the glitter of waves at sunset, the sea was hard to read. Only after searching for a while did I make out the sail of the *Medusa,* now well past the harbor entrance and headed north. At such a distance, the ship was the size of a toy on the palm of my hand.

Then I discerned, to the west of the *Medusa,* another, larger ship, and then another to her east. They were warships. Their bronze ramming beaks caught the sunlight. They appeared to be converging on the *Medusa.*

"Use the mirrors!" screamed the king, even as he reached into a silver bowl of delicacies held forth by an attendant and stuffed a fistful of dates into his mouth. What he said next was an indecipherable mumble.

Zenon spoke for the king. "Signal the ships that there's a change of orders. They are *not* to ram the pirate ship! They are to capture the ship instead and bring it back to harbor, but by no means must they allow it to sink! Do you understand?"

He spoke to the captain of the crew that manned the huge signal mirror mounted against the wall, midway between the corners of the parapet. There were four such mirrors, one on each side of the tower. The captain looked fretful.

"Go ahead, you fool!" barked Zenon. "What are you waiting for? Is the message too complicated?"

"No, no, Your Excellency, we can give those signals readily enough. But the sunlight—"

"I can see the sun right there!" Zenon pointed to the half-circle of red that glowed above the western horizon.

"Yes, Your Excellency, but I fear the light's not strong enough. And the angle—"

"Do what you can! Now! At once!!"

The crew manning the mirror flew into action, tilting the huge lens of polished metal this way and that, attempting to capture the rays of the sun and send them toward the nearest of the warships. Indeed, I could see a spot of red light flickering on the sail of the ship, which meant that the men aboard must have been able to see the mirror flashing.

The ship, which had been speeding toward the *Medusa,* suddenly relented. I could see the row of tiny oars reverse direction in unison and push against the waves.

"You've done it. You've done it!" screamed the king, spitting out a mouthful of masticated dates. "Now the other. Now the other!" He pointed at the second warship coming from the east, which continued to race toward the *Medusa*.

The crew swung the mirror about, but the position of the sinking sun made it impossible to capture and reflect a sunbeam.

"It can't be done!" wailed the captain. He quaked before the fearsome gaze of the king, who was madly chomping a fresh mouthful of dates. "It simply can't be done!"

Helpless to intercede, we watched as the warship drove relentlessly toward the *Medusa*. I felt a stab of empathy, imagining the panic that must have broken out amid the bandits. Captain Mavrogenis would be barking orders at his crew, but to no avail, for the *Medusa* was no match for an Egyptian warship. Did Ujeb quiver with terror, or was he facing his end with unexpected bravery? Poor Ujeb, who had saved me! Had Ujeb not proclaimed me the new leader, Bethesda and I would still be aboard the *Medusa*, locked inside the cabin and facing certain death.

And what of the sarcophagus? I realized why the king and his chamberlain were so desperate to stop the sinking of the pirate ship. Against their expectations, contrary to their plan, the sarcophagus—and not its worthless replica—had been loaded onto the *Medusa*. If the *Medusa* sank, the golden sarcophagus of Alexander would be lost forever.

So it came to pass. As we watched in horror, the ramming beak of the warship struck the *Medusa*. A heartbeat later I heard the tremendous crack. The pirate ship broke in two. The sail collapsed. The mast crashed into the water. With stunning swiftness, the two halves of the ship reeled and pitched in the waves and then vanished.

I gasped. Bethesda covered her face. The chamberlain bowed his head. The captain in charge of the mirror swayed as if he might fall. The king choked on the dates and began to hack like an Egyptian housecat with a hairball.

Attendants rushed to pound their fists against the king's back, until at last a great wad of chewed dates shot from his mouth, flew beyond the parapet, and plummeted down to the blood-red sea.

XXXVII

As dawn broke the next morning, once again I found myself separated from Bethesda.

And, through no choice of my own, I was reunited with Artemon.

With manacles on our wrists and ankles and chained to opposite walls, the two of us sat across from each other on the straw-covered floor of a bare stone room. High above our heads a little window covered by iron bars admitted the only light. I had been delivered to this dank cell with a sack over my head, but I had some idea of its location, because from time to time, from the little window, I heard animal noises—a monkey's screech, an elephant's trumpet—which meant that we must be near the zoological gardens within the royal palace.

For several hours after the manacles were clamped onto me, I had been alone in the cell. Night came, and with it, complete darkness. Then the door had opened, and soldiers had delivered another prisoner. As they chained him to the opposite wall, by the light of their torches I could see it was Artemon.

The soldiers left, and the room was totally dark again. I spoke a few words to Artemon, but he made no answer. He was so quiet I couldn't even hear him breathing.

Overwhelmed by exhaustion, I slept like a dead man. When I woke at the first feeble light of dawn from the barred window, I saw that Artemon, too, was awake. He looked haggard and drawn, as if he hadn't slept all night. The bloody bandages around one of his shoulders I took to be the result of Cheelba's attack, along with a wound down one side of his face that would leave a large and ugly scar.

"Do you think we're the only ones left alive?" I said.

Artemon sat unmoving with his back against the wall and his eyes closed.

"Of all the men who were aboard the *Medusa,* I mean. Do you think all the others are dead?"

Artemon opened his eyes, but didn't look at me. He stared into space.

I coughed and cleared my throat, longing for a drink of water. "I ask, because it may have some bearing on how long the king lets me live. My little life can't have much value to him, except that I might yet provide a few clues as to what went wrong with his plans for the golden sarcophagus. I only hope that dour chamberlain doesn't insist on torturing me to get some answers, since I'd gladly tell him all I know. But I don't suppose I'll have a choice about that—"

"They're all dead," said Artemon, finally breaking his silence. He still wouldn't look at me. His voice was so lifeless and cold that it raised hackles on my neck. "The captains of the two warships had orders to kill any survivors."

"What about the men who fell during the raid? It's possible that some were only wounded—"

"Any man we left behind in the city, who somehow survived, was also to be killed." Artemon's lips twisted into a grim semblance of a smile. "I was the one who insisted on that stipulation, but Ptolemy readily agreed. There were to be no survivors, no witnesses . . . no one who might figure out what had happened and come looking for me later, seeking revenge . . . and no one who knew where all that treasure was buried, back at the site of the Cuckoo's Nest."

"You told me there was nothing in those buried crates worth digging up."

"I lied."

He spoke without emotion. His lack of any remorse in the aftermath of so much deceit and death was appalling, but I tried to hide my reaction. The important thing was to keep him talking, so as to learn as much as I could from him.

"What about Metrodora?" I said. "The last I saw of her, she was alive, on the wharf, holding onto the kidnapped girl. Then she seemed to vanish."

"Why not? She *is* a witch." Again, staring into space, he flashed that grim smile. "Metrodora alone was meant to survive. She . . . and the girl. On my orders, Captain Mavrogenis took them ashore while the raid was taking place. He locked the girl in a room in the customs house, and gave the key to Metrodora."

"So you intended to come back for the girl later. After the fake sarcophagus was loaded and the ship set off, you were going to jump off the *Medusa* and swim to the royal barque, while the *Medusa* sailed to its destruction. Then you and Metrodora would collect your payment from the king and go your separate ways—with you taking the girl. Is that right?"

He nodded.

"Was Metrodora your partner all along?"

"Almost from the day we met. She helped me, and I helped her. You saw how the two of us ran the Cuckoo's Nest. I gave the orders, but it was Metrodora who knew how to use their fears and hopes to control them. She called it witchcraft. Maybe it was. Between the two of us, there seemed to be nothing we couldn't get those fools to believe, and nothing we couldn't trick them into doing."

Again I suppressed my revulsion. I had never met a man so calculating or so callous. "But at the very end, something went wrong between you and Metrodora. I saw her holding onto the girl, trying to keep you from taking her."

"At the last moment, when I told Metrodora there had been a change of plans—that I was going to board the ship after all, take the girl and the golden sarcophagus with me and make a run for it—she refused to come along. She thought I was mad. I suppose I was."

He finally looked me in the eye, with a gaze so full of hatred it made my blood run cold. I swallowed hard and studied the chains holding him, making sure there was no way he could reach me.

"*You're* the one who caused the trouble," he said. "You forced the change of plans when you spotted the substitution. No one else noticed, except you—and then you had to point it out to everyone. Then you attacked me when I boarded the ship. Who are you, Roman? You call yourself Pecunius, but Metrodora told me your name is Gordianus. Why did you come to the Cuckoo's Nest? And how is it that you're still alive?"

I realized why Artemon had decided to talk to me. Just as I wanted to resolve certain questions that only he could answer, so he wanted to understand the man who had ruined all his carefully laid plans.

"You ask who I am, Artemon, and I'll tell you. But first, let me see if I understand exactly what happened. Whose idea was this scheme to steal—or pretend to steal—the sarcophagus of Alexander? Did it originate with you, or with King Ptolemy?"

"It all started when the king's chamberlain, that stick insect, Zenon, first contacted me a few months ago, through intermediaries. The messages we exchanged were tentative at first, as we felt each other out. Then the plan seemed to hatch itself, and we were off and running. Some nights I could hardly sleep for the excitement. The fact that I had to keep the scheme a secret from everyone at the Cuckoo's Nest made it all the more thrilling. Even Metrodora knew only the bare outlines."

"What was in it for the king? What did he hope to gain from it?"

"Enough gold to pay his troops!" Artemon laughed harshly. "The king is desperate. His brother's forces far outnumber his own, and they'll be here any day now. His own men have been deserting him for months. It's because he's run out of money. Ah, but how to get some more? By melting down some fabulous treasure—but which one? For the king's needs, only the grandest treasure of all would suffice: the golden sarcophagus of Alexander."

"The people would never stand for such a sacrilege," I said.

"Exactly. But what if the sarcophagus were to be stolen? What if there was a daring raid, and pirates absconded with it? Or better yet, pirates led by some traitorous member of the king's own family, some wicked bastard cousin and pretender to the throne?"

"The people would still be furious."

"Yes, but in such a circumstance their fury could be directed away from the king. If he lacked enough soldiers to protect the sarcophagus, whose fault was that? He could say, 'I might have stopped those scoundrels, if the few soldiers I have left weren't busy quelling that riot over at the Temple of Serapis!' In the end it would be the fault of everyone *but* the king—his brother, for marching on the city and causing chaos, and his own troops, for deserting their posts, and the people themselves, for going on a rampage and distracting the few loyal soldiers left, who should have been defending the city's greatest treasure instead of putting out fires."

"But in fact, the sarcophagus was not to be carried off. It was to stay here in Alexandria. . . ."

"Where the king could strip the jewels and melt down the gold. As if by magic, the royal treasury would be full again. The king could buy back his army, and have so much gold left over he could pay off the invaders as well."

"But what if the plot had been discovered?" I said. "What if something went wrong—as it did?"

"It was a risky business, to be sure. But the king had little choice. A wild gamble was the only thing that could save him."

"And you, Artemon? What was in this scheme for you?"

For the first time, his features softened a bit. He stared into space and sighed. "The days of the Cuckoo's Gang were numbered. Whoever ends up on the throne in Alexandria, the destruction of the bandit gangs in the Delta will become his highest priority. For a while, I thought about fleeing to Crete and taking the gang with me. Crete is wide open, they say—but that means every bandit king and pirate captain in the world is headed there, thinking to make himself master of the island. That's too much competition." He shook his head. "For all its delights, banditry is a dangerous profession. I'd had enough. I wanted a way out, preferably with my head on my shoulders, a royal pardon, and enough gold to last me a lifetime.

"So, when Zenon contacted me and put forth his scheme, it seemed that my prayers had been answered. I responded cautiously at first, and then with more and more enthusiasm. It was fascinating work, planning all the details of the raid. It was I who suggested that the Jackal would be the perfect man to make the duplicate wagon and crate, and the fake sarcophagus to put inside it.

"And when it was all over, with a full pardon from the king and a very large payment for myself and for Metrodora, I could travel anywhere I wished. I could begin a new life with . . ."

"With Axiothea?"

He bowed his head. "Yes. But then *you* had to spoil everything. You and that stupid lion!"

He glared at me and lurched against his chains. I flinched and pressed myself against the wall, but the chains held him fast.

"The kidnapping of Axiothea," I said. "Whose idea was that? The Jackal's?"

Puzzlement was added to the hatred on his face. "How did you know the Jackal was involved in that?"

"Answer my questions first, Artemon, and then I'll answer yours. Why did you kidnap that girl?"

"For money, of course. Her lover is very rich. And . . . for revenge."

"Revenge against whom?"

"Her rich lover, of course! His name is Tafhapy. I didn't just want his money. I wanted to make him as miserable as I could, by taking the person dearest to him."

"But why? What grudge do you have against this Tafhapy?"

"That's none of your business, Roman!"

"But the kidnapping was a failure. Tafhapy never replied to your demands."

Artemon frowned. "That was a disappointment. The Jackal assured me that Axiothea was precious to him. Why did he never respond?"

Because the henchmen of the Jackal took the wrong girl, I could have told him. But I saw no point in saying more about Bethesda than I had to. "Why did you change your mind at the very end?" I asked. "Why did you put the girl on the *Medusa,* and try to board the ship yourself, when you knew the king's warships would sink her?"

"Because *you* exposed the fake sarcophagus! What was I to do after that, with all the men watching me and hanging on my every word? If they realized I'd tricked them, even those fools would have turned on me. I decided to do what King Ptolemy had done—take a wild chance. I decided to steal the sarcophagus, after all. Then I'd set out across the sea and do what the men were expecting me to do—make myself king of Crete, with Axiothea as my queen!"

His eyes glimmered at the sweetness of that impossible dream. In my last moments aboard the *Medusa,* I, too, if only for an instant, had glimpsed such a dream.

"What about the warships? You knew they were out there, beyond the harbor, waiting to ram the *Medusa.*"

"We'd have outrun them! They came at Mavrogenis with the advantage of surprise, but I'd have known they were there, and we'd have slipped past them. It wouldn't have been easy, but we could have done it—I'm sure of it! And if that had happened, I'd be thanking you now instead of cursing you, Roman, for guiding me to the destiny that should have been mine all along. Instead . . . I'll end with nothing, not even my own head."

I felt a stab of pity for him. I suppressed it. Because of him, Menkhep and Ujeb and Captain Mavrogenis and scores of others had died horrible deaths. He had been willing to sacrifice all of them for a few bags of gold and a fresh start.

"Why Crete?" I said. "Why not Cyrene? Why not go there and claim your birthright as the son of Apion?"

Artemon stared at me for a moment, speechless, then threw back his head and laughed. "Oh, Pecunius, when will you cease to surprise me? I thought you'd seen through all my deceptions, yet you still believe me to be the king's cousin!"

"Then you're *not* the bastard son of Apion?"

"Of course not!"

"But Menkhep told me . . . and all the men seemed to think . . ."

"They believed what Metrodora and I wanted them to believe. And so did you, it seems."

"Who are you, then, Artemon? Where did you come from?"

"I'm exactly what I told you and the others in that little speech I gave before the raid. 'The bastard son of a whore' I called myself, and so I am."

"But not the son of Apion?"

"Give it up, Pecunius!" He shook his head. "I was born in Alexandria, the son of a whore and a freeborn Egyptian who never cared to claim me. I grew up poor but free alongside my twin sister."

"So it's true that you had a twin?"

His face softened. "Artemisia was her name. She was beautiful and clever—far cleverer than I—and always kind to me. Then our mother died. Artemisia went her way, and I went mine. A visiting merchant from Syria took a fancy to me, and took me back to Damascus with him. I'd taught myself to read and write, and he thought to train me as a scribe. How I loved all those books in his library! But while he fiddled with me, I fiddled with his accounts. When he discovered how many shekels I'd stolen from him, he was furious. He would have tortured and killed me, I have no doubt. Instead, I killed him. The Syrian was the first man I ever killed, but not the last. By the time I arrived in the Delta, I was quite experienced in the ways of crime. I fell in with that gang of fools, who desperately needed a leader, and it all worked out beautifully. The rest, you know."

He narrowed his eyes. "Now it's your turn to talk, Pecunius. Who are you, and why did you come to the Cuckoo's Nest? How is it that you know the Jackal? Why did you attack me after I boarded the *Medusa,* and how did you manage to get off? And Axiothea—was she still aboard . . . when the *Medusa* sank?"

I had intended to answer his questions, as he had answered mine, but now, I hesitated. Though Artemon was in chains, I still feared him. He had revealed himself to be a vengeful and remorseless killer. He already hated me for having ruined his plans. How would he react if he knew I had deceived him from the start and had come to the Delta to take back the girl he knew as Axiothea?

"Go ahead, Pecunius. Speak! What do you have to lose? In a short while, we'll both be dead."

His words sent a chill through me. Artemon had betrayed the king and was responsible for the loss of the sarcophagus, but what was my crime? Repeatedly I had told Zenon that Bethesda and I were prisoners of the bandits, but why should he believe me? Artemon was right. My fate was to be questioned under torture, and then disposed of. What had Artemon said? *There were to be no survivors, no witnesses.* Like everyone else who had taken part in the raid, willingly or not, I was to die.

And what of Bethesda? Surely her fate would be the same as mine. In trying to rescue her, I had brought about her destruction.

"Speak, Pecunius!" shouted Artemon.

I clenched my teeth. I shut my eyes. I wanted no more to do with him.

From somewhere nearby, distorted by echoes amid the stone passageways, I heard the sound of boyish laughter. Did I imagine it, or was there a child in the king's dungeon? I heard the sound again, closer than before. Unless I had gone completely mad, I recognized that laughter. It was Djet!

I heard the laughter again, just outside the door to the cell. A moment later, I heard clanking sounds as the door was unlocked and unbarred. The door swung open on creaking hinges.

Djet appeared in the doorway. Smiling and laughing, he ran to me and threw his arms around me.

"Djet, what happened to you?"

He spoke so quickly I could hardly make out the words. "I got off the ship as soon as I could, just as you told me to do, and then I hid in the rafters of the customs house, then I climbed on the roof and watched the *Medusa* sail off, and then I saw the king's boat—and you were on it! I ran to the master and I told him you must still be alive. And I was right!"

"But Djet, what are you doing here?"

"She insisted that the master come look for you, and plead for your release."

"She?"

"You know! Who else can make the master do whatever she says?"

Djet looked over his shoulder and pointed at Axiothea—the real Axiothea—who stood in the doorway. In such sordid surroundings, her beauty was all the more exquisite. Looking a bit wary, she stepped into the dimly lit cell, followed a moment later by Tafhapy.

Their gazes were drawn first to Djet, and then to me. Both nodded to acknowledge that Djet had been right: here I was, back from my journey but under royal arrest. Then, as they took in the rest of the cell, their eyes settled on Artemon, who stared back at them with a look of utter astonishment.

Axiothea gasped. Tafhapy stiffened and staggered back.

"Brother!" cried Axiothea.

"Son!" whispered Tafhapy.

Bewildered, I looked from face to face. Djet appeared to be as puzzled as I was.

A moment later, Zenon entered the cell, followed by King Ptolemy, who could barely fit through the doorway. My consternation was complete.

XXXVIII

Axiothea ran to Artemon and fell to her knees amid the filthy straw. She threw her slender arms around him and burst into tears.

"My dear, sweet brother, how long it's been! How I've missed you! I thought I would never see you again."

"Better that you hadn't," muttered Artemon, his voice choked with emotion. He tried to return her embrace, but the chains prevented him. "Beloved Artemisia! Why are you here? And why are you with *him*?" He glared at Tafhapy, who kept his distance, averting his eyes and wringing his hands.

"This woman . . ." I whispered. "This woman is Artemisia, your twin sister? And Tafhapy is the father of you both?"

The chamberlain struck his staff against the stone floor, demanding attention. "Get back from the prisoner, young woman! For your own safety—"

"Don't be ridiculous." Axiothea gave Zenon a withering glance. "My brother would never harm me."

From the sour look on his face, I could see that the chamberlain was as confused as I was. He was not a man who liked surprises. "Whatever relationship you may have with the Cuckoo's Child, young woman, it is not the king's reason for coming here. We will deal first with the business at hand. Tafhapy, you came to the king this morning to urgently plead for the release of this other prisoner, the Roman who calls himself Gordianus. Is this in fact the man you were referring to?" He pointed with his staff. I jerked back to stop him from poking my nose.

Looking dazed, Tafhapy glanced at me and nodded.

"You say this Gordianus came to you some time ago seeking information about his stolen slave—the girl with whom he was retrieved from the harbor." At this bit of information, I saw Artemon's eyes light up. "You say you put him on the trail of the Cuckoo's Gang, and for a traveling companion you sent this slave boy with him. Is that correct?"

Tafhapy nodded.

"So when Gordianus tells us that his sole purpose in approaching the Cuckoo's Gang was the retrieval of his property, he speaks the truth?"

"As far as I know," whispered Tafhapy.

"However, there is a complicating factor," said Zenon. "I thought the name 'Gordianus' sounded familiar, and sure enough, among the documents in my office there is a warrant for this man's arrest issued by the city fathers of Canopus, accusing him of murder and theft. A ruby is said to be involved—"

"That's a lie!" said Djet. "The Roman never killed or robbed anyone."

"You speak out of turn, slave!" Zenon glared at Djet, who calmly looked up at him. The distraught Tafhapy seemed incapable of interceding, and for a long moment everyone in the cell witnessed the peculiar spectacle of a slave boy and a chamberlain of the king of Egypt engaged in a staring contest.

It was Zenon who finally blinked. "You traveled alongside this Roman? Speak, boy!"

"Day and night," said Djet. "He's the bravest man I ever met. He saved us from the Hungry Crocodile, then from the Friendly Hippopotamus! He got the best of Mangobbler, and made a friend of Cheelba the lion—"

"We are not interested in whatever menagerie you may have

encountered in your travels. Did this man kill a Nabataean merchant in Canopus? Did he join the Cuckoo's Gang? Did he take part in criminal acts?"

I held my breath. A moment before, it had seemed that Djet was my savior, having brought Tafhapy to plead on my behalf. Now, with a careless word, Djet might bring about my execution.

Djet squared his shoulders, stiffened his jaw, and put his hands on his hips. He spoke not to the chamberlain, but directly to the king, looking him in the eye. "It was the owner of the inn at Canopus who murdered the Nabataean, not the Roman. Yes, he pretended to join the Cuckoo's Gang—that much is true. But he did so only to save his life and mine. His only purpose was to get back the girl who had been taken from him. He's no more an outlaw and a bandit than I am!"

Zenon grunted. "So you say. But a character reference from a child, and a slave at that, is hardly—"

"Oh, stop this nonsense!" The king stepped forward. His sheer bulk obliged the chamberlain to move aside. "It's obvious that the Roman is exactly what he says he is. You saw him with that slave girl yesterday, after we plucked them from the waves. Did they look like dangerous criminals? I think not, unless love is a crime."

The chamberlain rolled his eyes. "Has Your Majesty considered that this Gordianus may be a spy, sent here by Rome?"

"Oh, I hardly think so, Zenon. And what if he is? The Romans are our friends, are they not? They keep offering to help me keep my throne, with only one catch—I must bequeath Egypt to the Roman Senate in my will, as Apion did with Cyrene! They have nerve, I'll grant them that. No, no, when I look at this fellow I do not see a murderer *or* a spy."

"Even if the Roman is no more or less than he appears to be, Your Majesty, in such a delicate matter, there are other considerations—"

"You will rescind the warrant for the Roman's arrest, then release him and his slave girl at once, Zenon. Do you understand?"

The chamberlain sighed and bowed his head. "It shall be as Your Majesty decrees. Guard! Bring the key and remove the manacles from this prisoner. Then free the girl in the adjacent cell."

He could only mean Bethesda. All night, she had been only a few feet away from me!

In a matter of moments, I was freed from my chains and able to stand, if a bit unsteadily. I rubbed my wrists where the manacles had chafed them. A moment later, Bethesda appeared at the doorway, then ran to my side.

"Bethesda, did they harm you?"

"No, Master. And you? Your wrists are all red and raw."

"It doesn't matter, now that you're back—"

"Oh, do be quiet, the two of you, before I change my mind," said the king. "Now, Tafhapy—if only for my amusement, you will explain your relationship to these other lovely young people. The girl there, clinging to the Cuckoo's Child. Is her name Axiothea or is it Artemisia?"

Tafhapy's jaw quivered. "Both. Her mother named her Artemisia, but years ago, when she first began to act, she took the stage name Axiothea. That's how everyone knows her now."

"And this young man, the notorious Cuckoo's Child—is he her brother?"

"Her twin," whispered Tafhapy.

"I see. Artemon and Artemisia, twin siblings. Yes, they do look a great deal alike. And *you* are their father?"

"I am."

"By blood, perhaps," growled Artemon, "but in no other way is that man my kin. I never had a father!"

The king pursed his lips. "What does he mean, Tafhapy? How did you come to father these children, and what is your relationship with them now? I command you to explain!"

Tafhapy drew his bristling eyebrows together. At first he spoke with difficulty, but then the words came out in a rush. "My son speaks the truth. How did I father these children, you ask? When I was young, my father grew anxious at my lack of interest in the opposite sex. He took me to the most expensive brothel in Alexandria, and so that I should not be put off by the jaded nature or the overripe allure of the woman I was paired with, he insisted that I be given a virgin—a girl even younger than myself, as it turned out. Somehow or other I managed to consummate the act, which pleased my father greatly but only confirmed to me that such a thing would never happen again.

"But that was not the end of the matter. A few months later, the girl came to see me. She told me that I had made her pregnant. You may wonder how a girl in her position could be so certain that I was the father. In fact, she was no mere slave, and not strictly speaking a whore. She was the daughter of a freed man who was in terrible straits, and her one and only experience at the brothel had occurred on the night of my visit. By various means I ascertained that her story was not only credible, but almost certainly true. Her manner was so humble and sincere that I had no cause to doubt her.

"I told my father what had happened and I suggested that I should marry the girl. To me it seemed a readymade solution to my father's insistence that I must marry and beget grandchildren for him. But my father told me not to be absurd, that to marry a girl in such sordid circumstances was out of the question.

"A few months later, unmarried and destitute, the girl gave birth not to one child, but two. She contrived to visit me and brought the twins with her. When I saw them, any doubts about my paternity vanished. Look at my eyes, and then look at theirs. You'll see the resemblance.

"I approached my father again, and again he made his feelings clear. I was to have nothing to do with the girl or with her children. Yet, over the years, I felt obliged to give her a bit of money now and then. From time to time I saw the children as they grew up on the streets of Alexandria, wild and untamed—"

"We did the best we could," snapped Artemon, gritting his teeth, "and so did our mother." Axiothea tightened her embrace and hid her face against her brother's chest.

"Be that as it may," said Tafhapy, "with every year that passed, it became less and less possible that I could ever proclaim my paternity of such children. I lived in one world, they in another. Yet I knew who they were, and I think they knew who I was, for I had seen their mother pointing me out to them when my litter passed in the street."

"Oh, yes, we knew who you were," said Artemon. "The father who begot and then abandoned us. Tafhapy the Terrible, your business rivals call you. The words had a different meaning when our mother spoke them. How we hated and despised you, and everything you stood for."

"Alas, and who could blame you?" said Tafhapy, unable to look Artemon in the eye. "At some point, I no longer saw your mother on the corner where she used to beg—"

"Because she died!" snapped Artemon. "Sick and miserable, her life destroyed by you!"

"So I presumed. In fact, I thought that all three of you must have died, for I no longer saw you or your sister. All three of you seemed to vanish. I put away my memories of you. In time, I thought no more about you. Until . . ."

Tafhapy sobbed and caught his breath. "Until that day a year ago when I chanced to see a mime troupe performing in the street, and called my litter bearers to a halt so that I might watch. Among the players I noticed a beautiful young girl. There was something terribly familiar about her. Then I realized who she was. My daughter! 'Flee! Get away from her!' cried a voice in my head, and I almost called on the bearers to take me away. Then I realized that the voice I heard was that of my father—my father, who is now dead and no longer controls my life. 'You fool!' I said to myself. 'You'll never have another child. Forget what your own father wanted, and lay claim to your children!'"

Tafhapy gazed fondly at Axiothea. "I made myself known to her. She rebuffed me at first, but I persisted. Little by little I've sought to gain her trust. I seek to do so still."

"People thought she must be your lover," I said.

"Let them think what they will. Artemisia prizes her freedom and independence and the life she's made for herself, but as soon as she agrees, I intend to legally claim her as my daughter and make her my heir. I longed to do the same for Artemon, but when I asked her where her brother might be, she told me he'd vanished from Alexandria years ago. She had no idea what had become of him or where he'd gone." Tafhapy shook his head. "I had no idea . . . I never imagined . . . that the man they call the Cuckoo's Child, the king of the Delta bandits . . . is my son!"

I looked from father to son, from brother to sister, from daughter to father. I shook my head. "So it came to pass that Artemon, without knowing it, attempted to kidnap his own sister and demand ransom from his own father!"

All eyes turned to Artemon, who stared back at us defiantly. "The idea for the kidnapping began with the Jackal—"

"The man your sister knows as Lykos," I said.

Axiothea raised her eyebrows. "Lykos the artificer?"

The king frowned and looked at Zenon, who explained in a whisper, "The man with a white stripe in his hair."

The king nodded. "Ah yes, that fellow."

"Very well, I'll call him Lykos, if you prefer," said Artemon. "On a visit to the Cuckoo's Nest, he told me there was a beautiful girl in his Alexandrian mime troupe, called Axiothea—a name that meant nothing to me. Lykos said this girl had made herself the lover of a famously wealthy merchant called Tafhapy—a name I knew all too well, and despised. When Lykos suggested that we kidnap this actress and demand a ransom from her rich lover—never guessing that Tafhapy was secretly my father—I readily agreed. The money meant nothing to me, but the chance to subject the man I hated most in the world to a bit of misery—that was irresistible. Lykos arranged the kidnapping and hired the henchmen—who obviously took the wrong girl!" Artemon stared at Bethesda, who pressed herself close to me. "Now I understand why Tafhapy never responded to the ransom notes, and why you, Roman, came secretly looking for the girl." He sighed and shut his eyes. "If only the kidnappers had taken the girl they were supposed to take—if only they had brought Artemisia to the Cuckoo's Nest—I would have been reunited with my long-lost sister, and who knows what might have happened then?"

Tafhapy abruptly dropped to his knees. Humbly he approached King Ptolemy, shuffling forward across the stone floor. He clasped his hands beseechingly and gazed up at the king.

"Your Majesty! I came here today to save the life of a man who means nothing to me—this Roman called Gordianus. In your great wisdom and mercy, Your Majesty has seen fit to free him, and for that I thank you. But now I beg for the life of another, who until this hour I did not even know to be alive—my only son! I know he's a notorious criminal, but whatever he may have done, I beg you, for my sake, spare his life!"

The king peered over his enormous belly at Tafhapy, who proceeded to fall onto all fours and abase himself amid the filthy straw. "Really, Tafhapy, you have no idea of the magnitude of your son's betrayal, or the enormity of his crimes. He's not just a thief and a murderer, but a traitor of the worst sort. His treachery has brought untold disaster upon me. There is no possibility of a pardon for his crimes, no possibility whatsoever!"

Zenon loudly cleared his throat.

The king wrinkled his brow. "What is it, Zenon?"

The chamberlain shrugged and made a succession of gestures, each more fawning than the last. "Your Majesty always knows best, and as you say, there can be no possible pardon for such a scoundrel—unless, of course . . ."

"Unless what?"

"Unless the party seeking such a pardon could offer a substantial amount of gold—not an amount equal to that which has been irretrievably lost as a result of Artemon's treachery, for that would be impossible—but enough to pay for the king's . . . shall we say . . . upcoming travel expenses."

"You mean the cost of all the bribes, bodyguards, and baggage-carriers to get me out of Alexandria before Brother Soter arrives?"

"To put it bluntly, Your Majesty, yes, that is precisely what I mean."

The king sighed. "And what would you estimate that amount to be?"

"Roughly speaking . . ." The chamberlain named a sum so staggering that every person in the room drew a sharp breath.

The king gazed at the groveling figure at his feet. "Well, Tafhapy,
what do you say? Can you cough up that much money in the next couple of days? And is the life of your long-lost bastard worth such a sum?"

All eyes turned to Tafhapy. He remained on all fours but raised his
head. He chewed his lower lip. His bristling eyebrows moved this way
and that, expressing a succession of conflicting emotions.

"Well, father?" said Axiothea. She stared at Tafhapy and crossed
her arms. "What do you say?"

Artemon also moved to cross his arms, but the chains prevented
him. He had to be content with duplicating his sister's cold stare.
"Yes . . . father. Am I worth such a ransom?"

Tafhapy swallowed hard. "Give me until sundown tomorrow, Your
Majesty. I think I can raise it by then."

Axiothea burst into tears. Artemon shivered like a man with a fever; his hard features softened and he looked at his father with an expression I could not hope to fathom. Tafhapy, too, began to weep, and
so did Djet. Caught up in the flood of emotions, Bethesda and I held
each other tightly. Even the dour chamberlain looked pleased with
himself.

The king clapped his hands and called to an unseen attendant in
the hallway. "Bring me something to eat, at once! Happy outcomes
make me hungry."

A short while later, the king and his chamberlain left the cell and rejoined the royal retinue in the hallway outside. The rest of us followed.
Only Artemon was left behind, pending delivery of the ransom.

On the way out, we passed through the royal zoological gardens.
Whoever laid out this part of the palace had decided that caged men
and caged animals belonged in close proximity, though the animals
had better living arrangements, with cleaner quarters and blue sky
above them.

As we passed the various cages, pits, aviaries, and open-air enclosures, I gawked at a dazzling array of animals, birds, and reptiles such as I had never seen before. My nostrils were filled with unfamiliar smells and my ears with strange cries, squawks, and hissing noises.

Then I heard a familiar roar. From the far side of a large cage, the lion Cheelba came bounding toward me.

I cried out his name. I thrust my arm between the bars. Cheelba opened his mouth in a yawn, rubbed his face against my hand, and licked my fingers.

The king watched in wonder. "So it's true, what I was told, that this lion is tame."

"Mostly true, and mostly tame," I said, thinking of Cheelba's attack on Artemon. Through my tunic, I pressed my fingers to the tooth that hung from a chain around my neck. "Cheelba will defend a friend, if necessary."

"What a splendid addition to the menagerie!" said the king. "Nothing adds zest to a royal procession like an exotic animal or a savage beast. In the next such parade, this lion can lead the way. He shall amaze the populace and bring credit to the House of Ptolemy! When might we use this lion next, Zenon? Perhaps for . . ."

The king caught himself and fell silent. Very likely, I thought, the next royal procession in Alexandria would be the one celebrating his brother's accession to the throne.

The king swallowed hard. "Whoever may benefit from this beast, let it be recorded that it was I who added it to the royal menagerie. Write it down!"

One of the scribes in the retinue busily scraped a stylus against a wax tablet.

As we proceeded through the gardens, Djet fell back to walk beside Bethesda and me. He saw me frown, and asked what I was thinking.

"Just a small detail that nags at me. Something I meant to ask Artemon."

"Tell me."

I spoke more to myself than to Djet, since I had no reason to think he would know what I was talking about. "How was the wagon with the false sarcophagus substituted for the other? Artemon duped every-one into leaving the wagon unattended for a moment—I understand that part—but where did the other wagon come from? It can't have been in that narrow passageway already, it can't have come in from the side, and it was too big and heavy to come from above or below. . . ."

Djet laughed. "I can tell you!"

"You can?"

"Of course. I saw everything."

"How?"

"I was hiding up in the rafters."

"Ah, yes, I see. Go on, then."

"It's the oldest conjuring trick there is. As soon as you and Artemon and the others were out of sight, soldiers came out of a room that you had passed on your way in, pulling the second wagon. Very quickly they pulled the first wagon backward, out of the narrow passageway, and brought up the other wagon to take its place. Then they took the first wagon back to the room where they had been hiding. That seemed to be the end of it. But a while later, Artemon and his men came running back, and Artemon knew exactly where to look for the first wagon. Then there was a terrible fight, and all those soldiers were killed, and off Arte-mon and his men went with the first wagon. That's when I climbed up on the roof. I saw the fight you had with Artemon, and then Cheelba saved you, and then more soldiers appeared, and then the *Medusa* sailed off, and *then* the king's boat sailed up to the wharf—and you were on it! When I made my way home, I told the master you must be the king's prisoner, and Axiothea said we must come look for you."

I nodded. "By coming here today, you saved my life, Djet. In fact, you saved all of us in one way or another, even the king."

"Yes, I know," he said, as if it were quite a small thing. Then he ran ahead to walk beside Axiothea and his master.

XXXIX

"The rioters are burning something—again!" Berynus unfolded his long legs, stood up, and walked to the parapet. He shielded his eyes against the late-morning sunlight and squinted in the direction of Alexandria. "Look at that huge plume of smoke."

I was on the rooftop terrace of the eunuchs' new home in a tiny fishing village a few miles west of the capital. Kettel's massive bulk was seated next to me on a long couch piled with pillows. Nearby, Bethesda sat cross-legged on a rug on the floor.

"When will the chaos stop?" I asked.

"Not until King Ptolemy makes his exit, preferably by ship, and Soter's men arrive and start banging a few heads," said Kettel. "In the interim, the lawlessness in the city is likely to get worse, not better. You made a wise choice, Gordianus, coming to stay here for a while. Are your quarters comfortable?"

The guest room I had been given was larger and far more elegantly furnished than my shabby apartment in the city—too elegant for my taste, actually, with all sorts of bric-a-brac strewn about—but the surroundings were irrelevant. Bethesda was back with me, and that was what mattered. We could have been sleeping in a tent or on the beach under a starry sky for all that I cared, as long as she was next to me.

"The room is very comfortable," I said. "Still, I can hardly believe that the two of you gave up your splendid apartment in Alexandria."

Kettel made a face that caused wrinkles to form on every side. "At our age, we've had quite enough of the aggravations of city life. This latest round of rioting was the straw that broke the camel's back, as the Nabataeans say. While you were off traipsing about the Delta, the two of us packed up and left the city. Berynus had been plotting our move to this lovely village for quite some time, actually. We have so much more room here, and the beach is right outside our door. Here on the roof terrace, under this lovely striped awning, we can while away the hours, reading, writing our memoirs, and breathing in the fresh sea breeze. And Alexandria is only a day's journey away, should we ever be foolish enough to crave a visit."

I looked toward the city. The Pharos Lighthouse rose from the horizon no taller than my thumbnail. The plume of smoke rose twice as high.

Berynus wrinkled his craggy brow. "You don't think they've set the Library on fire, do you? So much smoke . . ."

"More likely it's coming from one of the warehouses on the southern harbor," suggested Kettel. "Bolts of linen could produce a dark smoke like that, and burn for hours."

I had spent only a few days in Alexandria before coming to the village, accepting an invitation that had been waiting for me at my apartment in the form of a letter left by the eunuchs with my landlord. To simply be alone with Bethesda in my old room, with no immediate danger hanging over us, lying for hours in our bed, venturing out only to find food when we needed it, was bliss—at first. Then I had begun to feel uneasy. The frequent smell of smoke and the sounds of violence from the street reminded me that the city was growing more and more dangerous. It also occurred to me that until King Ptolemy was well and truly gone, he might at any moment change his mind about my release and drag me back to his dungeons. The more I thought about the eunuchs' invitation to retreat for a while to a sleepy fishing village, the more I liked the idea. So here we were, relatively safe but at loose ends, waiting, like the rest of Egypt, to see what would happen next.

"Master . . ."

I turned to Bethesda. In the presence of our hosts, we followed the decorum of master and slave, sitting apart from one another and with Bethesda showing deference. What we did in the privacy of my room was another matter.

"Yes, Bethesda?"

"Master, you said that we might take a walk along the beach before your midday meal."

"Ah, yes, so I did. A nice walk will strengthen my appetite." A walk had been Bethesda's idea, but I was happy to indulge her.

"Don't be too long. Kettel has made his special octopus and hearts of palm salad," Berynus called after us, as we descended the stairway that led us directly to the beach.

As we walked along the shore, I took Bethesda's hand. The waves lapped gently on the sand. Gulls wheeled and squawked above us. Low dunes hid the fishing village to one side and the distant city skyline to the other. In such a secluded spot, we might pretend that no one else existed.

"What will happen to Artemon?" said Bethesda.

I felt a slight prickle of jealousy, that another man should occupy her thoughts at such a moment. "I believe it was the king's intention that he should be banished from Egypt. How the king will enforce such a decree, if the king himself goes into exile, I don't know. Artemon is very, very lucky to be alive."

"Do you think he'll reconcile with his father, as Axiothea has done?"

I shrugged. "Who can say? Tafhapy paid a steep price for his son's freedom, but I'm not sure that Artemon knows how to be grateful. He certainly has no sense of loyalty, or even common decency." How flagrantly Artemon had broken the bandit oath, bringing destruction on all to whom he swore allegiance, while I, who cared nothing for the bandits, never brought them harm through word or deed.

I looked at her sidelong. "Did he ever . . ."

She smiled, very faintly. "You've asked me before, Master. No, he never touched me—except for that single kiss, to which you yourself were witness. I think that the pity he felt for his mother, and the love he feels for his sister, have made him a man who respects women, no matter that he seems to have no respect for other men."

For a while, as we walked along the beach, I thought about the puzzle of Artemon, for I was still disentangling lies from truth. Despite my skepticism, at some point I had accepted the idea that Artemon was a great leader, able to control the destinies of others and to orchestrate events far away, and that the Cuckoo's Gang was a veritable shadow state. How much of Artemon's power had been real and how much illusory, no more genuine than the disguises conjured by Lykos? Artemon's reach had never been as great as I had been led to think. Yes, the Cuckoo's Gang had men in Alexandria and elsewhere; Lykos was one such agent. But the vast network of spies and confederates necessary to pull off the raid—without the king's collusion—had never existed. Even the weapons and armor aboard the *Medusa* must have come from King Ptolemy.

"What will become of Axiothea?" I asked, to change the subject. "Now that she's to be acknowledged by Tafhapy, will she ever return to the mime troupe? It seems unlikely that Tafhapy would allow his daughter to run though the streets naked, or to marry a man like Melmak."

Bethesda smiled. "I think Axiothea will do whatever she wants to do, and it won't matter what Tafhapy thinks."

"You're probably right. And Melmak and his troupe? What will become of them?"

Bethesda shrugged. "If King Ptolemy loses the throne to his brother, Melmak will no longer have to wear that cumbersome fat suit, for they say Soter is a slender man. The troupe will still have plenty of material. One king is as easy to ridicule as another. Are they not all ridiculous?"

I nodded. "Your brain is always working, isn't it, Bethesda?"

"As is yours, Master."

"You must have been terribly bored in your hut at the Cuckoo's Nest, day after day, with all that time on your hands."

"You have no idea! But not all my hours were idle. Ismene and I had our chores and routines. And I learned many things from her."

I frowned. "What sort of things?"

Bethesda shrugged and made no reply, but I knew she must mean magic. I felt a bit uneasy at the idea that my slave had been schooled by a witch of Ismene's caliber. A man likes to think that his decisions and actions spring from his own will, rather than being caused by some potion he's drunk or by words scrawled on a lead tablet.

"Bethesda, these things that Ismene taught you . . . you would never use such knowledge to cause me, your master, to—"

"Ah, look! There she is. She said she would meet me here an hour before noon, and here she is!"

Bethesda pulled her hand from mine and ran to the far end of the nearest dune, where Ismene stood leaning on a cane as if she were a much older woman, dressed not in the elegant clothes she had worn as Metrodora but in the drab garments of a fishwife.

The two women embraced. I walked across the sand to join them.

"Ismene, what are you doing here?"

She gave me a long, appraising look. "I shall be leaving Egypt soon. Before I go, I wanted to say farewell to the two of you."

"The last time I saw you was on the wharf in Alexandria. You were there one moment and gone the next. I realize you must have run back into the customs house, but by then it was swarming with the king's soldiers. How did you get away?"

"By making myself invisible, of course."

"Seriously, Ismene—"

"If you don't want the answer, don't pose the question!" she snapped.

In fact, there were a great many other questions I wanted to ask her, but Ismene turned her attention to Bethesda. The two of them fell to chatting as they walked down the beach with their arms around each other. I followed behind.

Suddenly Ismene gave a stifled cry and pointed toward the surf. "There! Did you see that?"

"What?" I saw only foam and bits of seaweed.

"There, that glint of red!" She disengaged herself from Bethesda and strode a few steps into the water, then bent down and appeared to pick up something.

"What is it?" said Bethesda.

"See for yourself." Ismene extended her arm toward us. Resting on her open palm was a dazzling ruby.

I looked from the stone to Ismene and back again. "This can't be the same ruby that—"

"It's come back to me!" she declared. "I cast it into the sea, gave it up to Poseidon—but now it comes back to me, washed clean of all its curses."

For a moment I was astounded at such a coincidence. Then it occurred to me that Ismene might have only pretended to throw the ruby from the *Medusa,* and had now pretended to find it.

She saw the doubt on my face and tucked the jewel away. "Do you know the Hebrew proverb about rubies, Gordianus? You must know it, Bethesda. No?" Ismene affectionately touched Bethesda's face, then looked straight at me as she quoted the verse. " 'Who can find a virtuous wife? For her worth is above rubies.' Wise words for *you,* Gordianus."

I cleared my throat. "As I think you know, Ismene, I have no wife."

The witch smiled. "Not yet, Gordianus. Not yet."

CHRONOLOGY

B.C. 331 The city of Alexandria is founded in Egypt by Alexander the Great.

c. 280 The Pharos Lighthouse is built.

143/42 Ptolemy IX (Soter) is born.

c. 140/39 Ptolemy X (King Ptolemy) is born.

110 23 March (Martius): Gordianus is born at Rome.

c. 106 Bethesda is born at Alexandria.

101 After the banishment of his brother, Soter, King Ptolemy X orders the murder of his mother, Cleopatra III, and makes himself sole ruler of Egypt.

96 Ptolemy Apion dies and bequeaths Cyrenaica to Rome.

93 23 March (Martius): Gordianus turns seventeen and puts on his manly toga; he and his tutor, Antipater of Sidon, depart on a journey to see the Seven Wonders of the World (as recounted in the novel *The Seven Wonders*). On their travels, Gordianus encounters the witch Ismene in the ruins of Corinth.

91 Outbreak of the Social War, as the Italians revolt against Rome.

June: Gordianus and Antipater reach Egypt and journey up the Nile to visit Memphis and the Great Pyramid; they then travel to Alexandria.

Much of Upper Egypt, including Thebes, revolts against King Ptolemy.

90   Gordianus acquires Bethesda; the events of "The Alexandrian Cat" (included in the collection *The House of the Vestals*) take place.

89   War begins between Rome and King Mithridates of Pontus (First Mithridatic War, 89–85). In 89 and 88, Mithridates has massive successes all over Asia Minor and in the Aegean.

88   Mithridates takes the island of Cos, seizing the Egyptian treasury there and taking the son of King Ptolemy hostage.

23 March (Martius): Gordianus turns twenty-two. The events of *Raiders of the Nile* commence.

AUTHOR'S NOTE

(This note reveals elements of the plot.)

In a Q&A session during the book tour for my previous novel, *The Seven Wonders,* a reader noted a change in tone from previous volumes of the *Roma Sub Rosa* series. He asked if this might be attributed to the influence of the ancient Greek authors I'd been reading for my research (as opposed to the Roman sources I usually consult).

As sometimes happens when I talk to readers, this unexpected question, coming out of the blue, gave me a flash of insight. As much as I love the Romans, one can grow weary of all those murder trials, gruesome histories, and self-aggrandizing memoirs. For *The Seven Wonders,* I found myself immersed in the work of Greek authors whose books were all about travel and exploration, love and sensual pleasure, religious exaltation and athletic glory. It made a nice vacation from the endless litigation of Cicero and the relentless warfare of Caesar.

So, looking to follow *The Seven Wonders* with the further adventures of young Gordianus in Egypt, for inspiration I turned directly to the ancient Greek novels. Yes, the ancients had novels, too. Only a handful of these works have survived since they were written some two thousand years ago, but their delightful, romantic, melodramatic motifs—separated lovers, mistaken and concealed identity, far-flung travel, capture by pirates, love tested and redeemed—inspired many later writers. Shakespeare used such motifs in his comedies, and in at least one play, *Pericles, Prince of Tyre,* he drew directly from one of the ancient novels. The easiest way to read these works in English is to open the massive one-volume *Collected Ancient Greek Novels* edited by B. P. Reardon.

A few years ago (thanks to an invitation from Professor Marília P. Futre Pinheiro), I was privileged to speak at a gathering of scholars who specialize in the ancient novel; this was in Lisbon in 2008 at the International Conference on the Ancient Novel (ICAN). The paper I delivered can be read at my Web site (look for the link at the home page). The gist of my talk: as a modern novelist, I feel a greater kinship with the ancient historians, who used novelistic techniques, than with the ancient novelists, whose devices now seem hopelessly antique. My own reading of the ancient novels was essentially for research, not inspiration, as I gleaned curious details and pondered the mind-set of the original audience for those novels.

And yet, as I've continued to read and reread the ancient novels, they've seeped into my imagination, seducing me with their sheer delight in storytelling. Perhaps the best is *An Ethiopian Story* by Heliodorus, which begins with a tale of bandits in the Nile Delta. Among the exotic details, Heliodorus tells of the flamingos and the phoenix to be found in that region, and the fabulous emerald mines farther south.

With *Raiders of the Nile,* I decided to pay homage to those ancient Greek novels and to the exuberant, episodic storytelling those first novelists invented. Even as I was pondering how I might do so, into my hands dropped a book called *Invisible Romans* by Robert Knapp. As Chair of the Classics Department at the University of California at Berkeley, it was Professor Knapp who invited me to deliver the commencement address to the Class of 2002. (That speech, too, can be read at my Web site.) Knapp's book exceeded my high expectations, as my much-highlighted and dog-eared copy can attest. Using sources often overlooked by historians (such as epitaphs on grave-stones, magical spells, books of dream interpretation, and, not least, the ancient novels), Knapp gives us a better understanding of the ordinary people of the ancient world. Of particular interest to me was his chapter titled "Beyond the Law: Bandits and Pirates." With great insight, Knapp quotes the speech of Samippus in Lucian's story "The Ship," an echo of which can be heard in the pre-raid speech of Artemon in this novel.

Was King Ptolemy as grotesquely fat as described here? This detail comes from a passage by Posidonius of Rhodes (fragment 77, quoted by Athenaeus, 12.550A–B). Gordianus previously met Posidonius in *The Seven Wonders,* and may meet the great scholar again. In fact, I am thinking it may have been Gordianus who told Posidonius about the king's obesity.

What do we know about the ancient mime shows? We can still read a few of these ribald skits by an author known as Herodas or Heron-das. The Loeb translation of his mimes is by I. C. Cunningham; another translation is by Guy Davenport.

As the rest of the Mediterranean world was swept up in the war be-tween Rome and Mithridates, what was going on in Egypt? Our sources are sketchy at best, but an intriguing picture emerges from Samuel Sharpe's *The History of Egypt Under the Ptolemies* (see pages 167–76 in the 1838 edition), and from Chapter XI of E. R. Bevan's *The House of Ptolemy.* The latter can be read at http://penelope.uchicago.edu /Thayer/E/Gazetteer/Places/Africa/Egypt/_Texts/BEVHOP/11*.html. (This link goes to Bill Thayer's LacusCurtius site, one of the Web's most essential resources for lovers of the Ancient World.)

Was the original sarcophagus of Alexander the Great really made of gold, and was it later melted down? If so, who did this, and when, and why? Our only source for this remarkable event is Strabo's *Geography,* 17.1.8. Strabo informed readers of the first century A.D. that the pre-served body of Alexander might still be seen in Alexandria, but "not, however, in the same sarcophagus as before, for the present one is made of glass [or alabaster], whereas the one wherein Ptolemy I laid the body was made of gold. The latter was plundered by the Ptolemy nicknamed *Kokkes* and *Pareisaktos,* who came over from Syria but was immediately expelled, so that his plunder proved unprofitable to him." (This passage is adapted from the translation of Horace Leonard Jones, now in public domain.)

Strabo's account is murky at best; the geographer gives no dates, and the details may have reached him in a hopelessly garbled state. To begin, which Ptolemy is he talking about? The nickname *Pareisaktos* may have meant "usurper" or "pretender to the throne." But what about the more obscure *Kokkes*?

An insightful consideration of the evidence can be found at the Web site by Christopher Bennett charting the genealogy of the Ptolemaic Dynasty. At his page for Ptolemy IX (called Soter in this novel), which can be found at http://www.tyndalehouse.com/egypt/ptolemies/ptolemy_x _fr.htm, Bennett examines the epithet *Kokkes*. Scholars disagree as to its meaning. Bennett notes one possible interpretation: "J. E. G. White-horne, *Aegyptus* 75 (1995) 55, thinks that the phrase was modeled on a phrase 'Kyke's child' which occurs in a poem by Anacreon attacking an enemy of his who unexpectedly enjoyed a sudden and undeserved change of fortune, and proposes that possibly both these phrases may be translated as the 'cuckoo's child'. . . ." (My own free translation of Anacreon's poem serves as the epigraph for this novel.)

Bennett delivers a sober summation of the evidence: a Ptolemy called *Pareisaktos* and *Kokkes* "came from Syria, melted down the golden coffin of Alexander, and was immediately expelled by the Alexandrians. Strabo says he did not profit by this action. The identity of this Ptolemy is, of course, unclear, since this is all we know about him under these names. It is almost universally assumed to refer to Ptolemy X, but the facts are arguably consistent with Ptolemy IX, Ptolemy X or Ptolemy XII."

Then comes Bennett's startling conclusion: "It is also possible that the prince involved is otherwise unknown; indeed Strabo's description might even be consistent with Ptolemy 'o Kokkes' being a Syrian pirate who seized the gold in a daring *razzia* on the city."

A statement that daring is a veritable provocation to write a novel.